The
MONKEY'S
WOUND
& other stories

The MONKEY'S WOUND

& other stories

HAJRA MASROOR

Translated by TAHIRA NAQVI

PENGUIN BOOKS

An imprint of Penguin Random House

PENGUIN BOOKS

USA | Canada | UK | Ireland | Australia
New Zealand | India | South Africa | China

Penguin Books is part of the Penguin Random House group of companies
whose addresses can be found at global.penguinrandomhouse.com

Published by Penguin Random House India Pvt. Ltd
4th Floor, Capital Tower 1, MG Road,
Gurugram 122 002, Haryana, India

First published in Penguin Books by Penguin Random House India 2022

10 9 8 7 6 5 4 3 2 1

ISBN 9780670096114

Typeset in Adobe Caslon Pro by Manipal Technologies Limited, Manipal
Printed at Replika Press Pvt. Ltd, India

www.penguin.co.in

Contents

Introduction

I

Hajra Masroor was born on 17 January 1929, in old Lucknow in an undivided India. Her father, who worked with the British-Indian government, died when she was eight. Saddled with financial burdens, her widowed mother took her son and six daughters and moved back to Lucknow to live with her father.

Masroor belonged to a family of writers and poets. Her elder sister Khadija Mastoor, her younger brother, Khalid Ahmad, and her mother Begum Anwar Jahan were all writers. The sisters are often referred to as the Brontë sisters of Urdu fiction which is why mention of one necessitates reference to the other. In her essay titled 'Mukhtasar Haalaat' (Brief Accounts), Hajra mentions how they both worked together to create stories, their writing developing as the two shared ideas and themes.

. . . In our house children were allowed to reach out for the books on bookshelves and for this reason when they had finished reading

children's magazines they read whatever they could lay their hands on. Our parents subscribed to nearly all the important literary, religious and some of the women's magazines that were being published in those days. I read everything regardless of whether I understood it all or not. The same was true of newspapers.

. . . This is about the time when the flames of WWII had reached the borders of Hindustan and political unrest had slowly begun to turn into public disturbances. One day I thought I should write something and I wrote a few sentences in a romantic vein. My first piece of prose was about the blue sky, pigeons flying high and colorful kites and it ended with the question: Do planes dropping bombs have the right to pass through these blue, peaceful skies? Signing with a friend's name, I sent this narrative to a newspaper and it was published more prominently than needed on the first page of the newspaper. I showed this to [my sister] Khadija and she was so happy one would think we had both stumbled upon a hidden treasure. Our elders, however, never came to know of this bold step I had taken.

. . . And then, after a few days, on a hot afternoon, I started writing at Khadija's command and when the pen halted I realized that I had written my first afsaana *[short story]. It was about a beggar who lived and died on the streets. Khadija had written an essay and soon, both my story and her essay were published . . . we began to write regularly and published our work freely, something that our elders deemed to be unwarranted boldness. We should have solicited their advice about topics for our stories, and our elders, surprised by our initiative, complained. The reason was that we had been writing profusely and had been publishing our work as well, and the subject of many of our stories centered around 'stirrings of love'. We were told that readers would draw the conclusion that we were the heroines of our own stories, we*

would be dishonored, our future would be bleak. In short tensions arose and sides were taken . . . Ahmed Nadeem Qasmi, the editor of the literary journal Adab-e-Latif, *suggested seriously that I change the last paragraph of one of the stories I had sent him. 'Try to abstain from explicitness in your writing', he advised. My sister and I took his advice seriously and continued as time wore on, to ask for his help in literary matters. Our friendship developed and he became like an older brother, someone we now called 'Nadeem Bhai'.*[1]

The renowned poet, fiction writer and journalist, Ahmed Nadeem Qasmi, an old family friend who became a father figure to Hajra and her siblings and later assumed the role of guardian for the girls after their move to Pakistan, said in a tribute: 'I had always seen [the two sisters] them in each other's company, and when I asked Hajra why she had such few friends she replied that Khadija's companionship had filled the need for girl friends'.[2]

Although the sisters were close and began writing about the same time, they were distinct in their writing styles and choice of subject matter. While Khadija wrote two novels along with short stories, Hajra, except for a play, stayed loyal to short fiction.

The Progressive Writers' Movement was created in 1935. It drew nearly all the well-known writers of Urdu fiction into its fold, some as actual participants, others as intellectuals deeply invested in its philosophy and embrace of modernism. At the time that Hajra started writing in the early forties, the literary

[1] Masroor, Hajra, *Majlis-e-Farogh-e-Urdu Adab*, Doha, Qatar.
[2] Qasmi, Ahmed Nadeem, *Majlis-e-Forogh-e-Urdu Adab*, Doha, Qatar.

world of Urdu fiction was dominated by towering names such as Ismat Chughtai, Saadat Hasan Manto, and Krishan Chander. Influenced by the new realism in the West, these three along with other writers (especially those who were in the forefront of the Progressive Writers' Movement) began experimenting with form, content and technique. Unwilling to exercise restraint in terms of their critique of existing social traditions, religious obscurantism and the hegemony of British colonial rule, they created a new wave of writing in Urdu. Some, especially Ismat Chughtai and Manto, defied all barriers—literary and stylistic—that were imposed by earlier reformist writers like Rashid-ul Khairi and Deputy Nazir Ahmed, and forged ahead with fiction and prose that did not hesitate to shock or disturb.

This was the world in which Hajra found herself when she began writing and it is to her credit that she was able to stand on her own as a writer of short stories that dealt boldly and effectively with the complexities of social and political upheavals faced by ordinary people. In 1944 she published *Charke* (Wounds), her first collection of short stories followed by two other collections, *Hai Allah* (Oh God), and *Chori Chhupe* (In Secret). It wasn't long before she joined the group of writers like Premchand, Chander, Manto and Chughtai, who had imbued Urdu fiction with new perspectives in terms of scope, language and subject matter.

Patras Bokhari, a well-known humorist, essayist, broadcaster and diplomat, wrote in his preface to her third collection, *Chori Chhupe*:

> *This new collection is like a breath of fresh air. She has maintained her femininity in her earlier collections as well, and here too she is continuing to engage her femininity. Her gaze is*

even more elevated and deep but she is also weaving the nets of
individual and interpersonal relationships here, unusual and
mysterious nets . . . Schopenhauer maintains that humans are
like those thorny bushes, which, when they are cold, edge towards
one another for warmth, but then they prick each other and move
away and begin to shiver again.[3]

He then goes on to analyse several stories and make observations
about Hajra's style and particularly her language. 'Her language
is a living language,' he says, 'that jumps toward meaning in a
straightforward manner, it does not turn its gaze upon itself
self-consciously and because of this spontaneity and simplicity
it easily expresses that which often gets stuck in the throat
of affected literary language or is rendered with exaggerated
reserve.' He ends with, 'We will not rest until her fourth
collection appears'.

II

When Partition came in 1947, Hajra and her family moved
to Bombay (now Mumbai), followed by Karachi in the newly
created state of Pakistan, and then finally to Lahore. Once
settled into their new lives, Hajra and Khadija, mentored and
guided by Ahmed Nadeem Qasmi,[4] quickly became part of the
literary scene in Punjab. Qasmi was the first general secretary of
the All Pakistan Progressive Writers' Association, which was a

---

[3] Masroor, Hajra, *Chori Chhupe*, https://www.rekhta.org/ebooks/chori-chhupe-hajra-masroor-ebooks.

[4] Ahmed Nadeem Qasmi, was an Urdu language Pakistani poet, journalist, literary critic, dramatist and short story author. He wrote fifty books on topics such as poetry, fiction, criticism, journalism and art, and was a major figure in contemporary Urdu literature.

continuation of the All India Progressive Writers' Association, and the sisters became members. In 1948, Hajra and Qasmi were appointed co-editors of *Nuqush* (Imprints), the foremost Progressive literary journal, where they proceeded to publish new works by established progressive writers, both from India and Pakistan. Hajra was active during this time, not just as an editor of *Nuqush* but also as a writer.

At this time the Progressives in Pakistan were facing a great deal of opposition from various quarters harbouring newfound ideologies that were a result of the social, literary and political changes created by Partition. The Progressive Writers' Association still had very strong ties with the Communist Party and its agenda and clashed with those who were clamouring for a return to 'the good old traditions of poetry and prose'. Kamran Asdar Ali has discussed these traditions and related issues in detail in his article.[5] There was also open condemnation of Marxist, secular, ideas which were seen as a threat to the cause of the new Muslim homeland. Muddled ideologies from the left and the right, the secular and non-secular, the classical literary traditions and the newer standards represented by the manifesto of the Progressive Writers' Association, all seemed to be seeking common ground, with little success.

By the late 1940s, the All Pakistan Progressive Writers' Association had started to purge from its ranks those who did not completely toe the new party line. This became more evident after the introduction of the new manifesto which targeted 'nonprogressive' writers during the first Association conference held in Lahore in November 1949. During this conference the 'nonprogressive' intellectuals were severely criticized for

---

[5]   http://journals.cambridge.org/abstract_S0026749X11000175

their perceived political failings, their alliance with the state machinery and lack of social consciousness. The manifesto clearly divided the Pakistani cultural scene into factions and spoke positively of those intellectuals who raised their voices against the ruling class and struggled against oppression and for independence, peace and socialism. Masroor writes in her 1949 editorial for the ninth edition of *Nuqush:*

> *How optimistic we were about Pakistan's second year when we presented* Nuqush's azaadi *(freedom) number at the end of August! But our government dealt us such a kick that all our hopes were dashed. Just as the azaadi number hit the bookstands, three of Pakistan's most important journals were given the order for closure . . . every Progressive writer's past and present and subsequently future imagined and illusory 'crimes' were displayed in notable newspapers as well as in third-rate magazines . . .*[6]

To make matters worse, when *Nuqush* published Manto's story 'Khol Do' (Open it), the government ordered its closure. Relaunched six months later, it was shut down again. But this time, Hajra and Qasmi had to relinquish their job as editors.

This was a difficult time for Hajra and for all who were staunch supporters of the principles espoused by the Progressives. Hajra and Qasmi also found themselves the target of disparagement and criticism for refusing to pander to the new trends that opposed progressive ideology. After the 1949 meeting of the All Pakistan Progressive Writers' Association, Hajra, her sister Khadija and Qasmi received a great deal of negative criticism. Hajra's daughter, Naveed Tahir told me that

---

[6]   Masroor, Hajra, *Tuluh* (The Dawn). *Nuqush*, 1949.

she remembered 'a cartoon which depicted both sisters dancing
and Nadeem Mamu (Qasmi), as the *tabalchi* (person playing
the Tabla)'. She said, 'it was . . . published in a right wing
paper . . . because they (the sisters and Qasmi), were (thought
to be) leftist or Progressives, or even allegedly Communists . . .
I don't remember the editor, perhaps Shorish Kashmiri . . . a
conservative'. [7] The publication Naveed Tahir mentioned was
Chattan, edited by Shorish Kashmiri.

This was a source of immense strain for Hajra but in time
she learnt to ignore the criticisms levelled against her and her
family. She continued to write, but there is little doubt that
the spontaneity and boldness with which she had once tackled
forbidden subjects were tempered by a certain degree of caution.
A story like 'til oT pahaaR' (The mountain in the shadow of the
sesame seed), included in her first collection *Hai Allah*, would
not have been possible. The writer Mumtaz Shireen observes
in her epilogue to Masroor's omnibus collection, *Sab Afsanay
Meray* (All My Stories), published in 1990, that Masroor's work
follows a particular trajectory, a linear development in terms of
her handling of subject matter and her choice of subjects. It is
true, as Mumtaz Shireen suggests, that Masroor's earlier stories
are brutal in their explication of life's bitter and harsh realities,
especially those dealing with women in South Asian Muslim
households, the style and commentary somewhat reminiscent
of Chughtai's fiction, but I don't agree with Shireen when she
says that Masroor's writing after 1947 became tempered and
reflective due to her maturity as a writer. She was a mature
writer earlier as well and as Qasmi says, 'already she had made

7   Personal conversation with Naveed Tahir, Hajra Masoor's daughter, 3 March
    2022.

a place for herself among those writers of Urdu fiction who had introduced Urdu fiction to a new scope and possibilities in terms of style, language and subject matter'.[8] I view the shift in her work as a response to the challenges of the new country where Islamic values and traditions would have prevented the kind of freedom writers had enjoyed in the diverse, multicultural and multireligious atmosphere of pre-Partition India. This was the same environment in which Manto was ceaselessly hounded by the courts for the brutal realism in his stories, especially those dealing with Partition.

Hajra may have tempered her approach somewhat but she didn't compromise her commitment to writing with honesty and candour, as can be observed in her later work. Mumtaz Shireen compares her story 'Teesri Manzil' (The Third Floor), from the collection of the same name, to Truman Capote's famous story 'Breakfast at Tiffany's':

> *I felt as if I had read Truman Capote's 'Breakfast at Tiffany's', a story that I think was the one of the best I had read in years. If there's another short story like it, it is 'teesri manzil' (third floor). There is no obvious similarity between these two stories because Truman Capote's story is a sophisticated comedy, but Dorothy[9] enters your heart clicking her castanets and twirling in a Spanish dance . . . this dancing, lively girl, like Manto's Mozel,[10] is a memorable character of Urdu fiction. For the first time the character of a Goan Christian girl has been presented in such a complete and successful manner . . . the life in Karachi's flats*

---

8 Qasmi, Ahmed Nadeem, 'Shakhsiyat Number', *Nuqush*, pp. 661–673, Lahore: Idarah-e-Farogh-e-Urdu, January 1956.
9 Dorothy is the female protagonist in Masroor's story.
10 The female protagonist of a story titled 'Mozel' by Saadat Hasan Manto.

and apartments has been drawn so effectively that one cannot
help commending her sharp observations. Astute analysis, skillful
exposition, unflinching candor, openness, and courage – these are
the special hallmarks of Hajra Masroor's fiction.[11]

III

In the early 1950's Hajra Masroor married Ahmed Ali Khan,
then the assistant editor of *Pakistan Times*, who later went on
to become the editor of the newspaper *Dawn*. They had two
daughters, Naveed Ahmed Tahir and Nosheen Ahmed.

In all Hajra produced six collections of short stories, three
published before the Partition in India, and the remaining three
after she migrated to Pakistan. She also wrote a book of one-act
plays. She mentioned in 'Mukhtasar Haalaat' that she intended
to write a novel, a long play, and an autobiography, but her
husband's death in 2007 affected her so deeply that she became
a recluse and stopped writing.

In 1962 the Majlis-e-Taraqi-e-Adab (Board for
Advancement of Literature in Punjab, Pakistan), conferred
upon her the Writer of the Year Award for her collection of
one-act plays, *Woh Log* (those people), for which Faiz Ahmed
Faiz and the well-known playwright and writer Imtiaz Ali Taj
wrote the preface and introduction respectively. In 1965 she
also won the Nigar Award for Best Story and Script of *Akhri
Station* (The Last Station), a film made in (what was then)
East Pakistan, based on Masroor's short story 'Pagli' (The
Crazy Girl). Directed and produced by the noted poet and

[11] *Sab Afsanay Meray* #867, https://www.rekhta.org/ebooks/sab-afsane-mere-hajra-masroor-ebooks.

film lyricist Suroor Barabankvi, it was regarded by the famous actress Shabnam as the film that inspired her to render the finest performance of her film career. In 1995 Masroor received the Pride of Performance Award for Best Writer, and in 2005 the Anjuman-e-Forogh-e-Urdu Adab, Doha, Qatar, honoured her with their special Aalmi Urdu Adab (International Urdu Literature) Award for the promotion of the Urdu language.

Hajra Masroor died after a protracted illness in Karachi on 15 September 2012 at the age of eighty-two.

1

In The Darkness

'Zehra, make some paans for me quickly', Shaukat told his sister in an agitated tone.

Putting down her stitching, Zehra pulled the paandaan over.

'Why so slow? Hurry up, my friends are waiting', he said again, his brow creased in a frown.

'Oh God, Bhaijaan, you want everything to happen in a second', Zehra said calmly as she cut up a chunk of *chalia* (betel nut), into tiny pieces. 'I'm preparing them.'

Shaukat left after instructing her to knock on the door when the paans were ready.

Zehra swiftly rolled up the paan leaves, set them on a tray and walking up to the adjoining room, knocked on the door. Shaukat came out, took the tray from her quickly and went back inside.

She wondered who this friend was and yielded to an impulse to take a peek. She squinted through a crack in the door. Sitting on a chair in front of her was a handsome young man. She was about to move away when she heard him speak.

'Shaukat sahib, I can't agree with your statement that a woman's activities should be restricted within the four walls of the home.'

Zehra had never heard anyone talk like this. Her whole life had been spent in an environment where a woman's status was not much higher than that of a slave. Moved by a longing in her heart, she again placed her eye next to the opening in the door. This time, she gazed closely at the young man.

Shaukat said, 'Does that mean that you want the Hindustani woman to be free like the Western woman and create unpleasantness in her life?'

Shaukat's response was as bitter as quinine for Zehra. But what could she do?

A mocking smile appeared on the young man's lips and he said, 'Now that you are set on making a comparison between family life in the West and the East, may I ask how many households there are in Hindustan where family life could be considered pleasant?'

This reminded Zehra of her parents' relationship. The two fought constantly. After a quarrel, Abba calmly left the house to be with his friends, while Amma, her dupatta covering her face, made herself sick with crying. Similar events happened with Zehra's friend Rabiya's mother next door.

'Oh!' Shaukat said. 'But divorces don't take place every day here.'

'And indeed, how can divorces take place when men control religion and women? The unfortunate creature is reduced to being a domestic animal. You may hit her, scold her, reject her, and she'll still roll over at your feet for the leftovers from your table. But if, on the other hand, she didn't want for sustenance, she would scratch your face when you scolded her and . . .'

Shaukat interrupted him. 'But why do you present the Hindustani woman as someone so helpless?'

'Because in reality she is helpless. Forget everything else. Here's an example: The Hindustani wife knows why her husband returns home so late, yet she calmly opens the door for him and, exhibiting the utmost fortitude, serves him dinner, presses his feet, and doesn't utter a word of reproach. As opposed to her, the Western wife deals harshly with her husband if he treats her badly.'

Shaukat laughed loudly and said, 'Nicely put! In other words, the purpose of the Western woman's freedom is unrestrained licentiousness and this is how she reforms her husband.'

'But what I want to know is this: *when* has the Hindustani woman won her husband over by her passivity and her fortitude?'

Hearing footsteps approach, Zehra hastily removed herself from the vicinity of the door. If Amma saw her there, she would make a terrible fuss and snap at her, saying it was appalling that she, an unwed girl, was sneaking glances at strange men. She quickly turned to the sheet on the settee and began straightening out the wrinkles.

Amma came in and began scolding her in a low voice.

'What are you doing here? You've forgotten you still have to do the cooking.'

Sorry that she was unable to hear the rest of the conversation, Zehra came to the kitchen. She was still thinking about what the young man had said.

How sympathetic he was towards caged birds! Who knows what else he was going to say. Bhaijaan's arguments were falling flat before him. She thought, 'I didn't want to move from there, but that wasn't possible. Amma is always grumbling and fretting.'

She leaned against the wall next to the stove. The odorous smoke rising from the soggy firewood was stifling. Today, sitting here, she felt extremely unhappy. For the first time, she felt that the house was a prison and the kitchen, sooty with smoke, was a black hole, and her father and brothers were like cruel sentinels who inflicted bloody wounds on her tiny heart with the lashes of their tongues. And her mother! She too was a poor woman who, like a domesticated dog, led a life of suffocation for the sake of a few rotis.

After she was done with the cooking, she came out of the kitchen and saw Shaukat reclining on a charpoy in the courtyard. She tiptoed up to him and sat down at the foot of the bed. She was hoping that when he started talking about his friends as usual, he would probably also say something about that young man who had, in a flash, jolted and awakened her slumbering emotions. But Shaukat was lost in his own thoughts, and with his gaze pinned on the sky, he seemed to be searching the stars. Zehra felt like initiating a conversation about the visitor herself, posing the question in a teasing sort of way, but she immediately realized that if he asked her why she wanted to know, she would not have an answer for him. Just then, her father walked into the house with a heavy, crunching step and Zehra quickly got up to heat his supper. At the same time, she was tickled by a strange thought—what if she had taken in food for the young man? This nebulous idea brought a smile to her lips and in the dim light of the lantern, her teeth suddenly gleamed.

That night she had no appetite and after finishing all her work quickly, she went to bed. Away from everyone, she wanted to luxuriate in her thoughts of the young man. She wanted to think about him even though she knew nothing about him except that he harboured sympathetic thoughts about women in his heart, and that perhaps he was her brother's class-fellow. But this was not important. She saw him in another light altogether. When a Hindustani girl thinks about a strange man, she only envisions him as a husband. Again and again she wondered what it would be like if she were married to him. How expansive the 'if' was. Lying in bed, she was filling her head with thoughts about her future life. How much a man who understood his wife's pain would love her, how happy their life would be. Then she would not have to spend all her time handling the stove and pots and pans in the dark, stifling atmosphere of the kitchen. She would study a lot, have nice conversations with him, and together they would travel extensively. First she would go to Delhi, where an aunt of hers lived. She was very well educated, and Zehra had heard that she now addressed meetings. How surprised she would be to see her! 'Why, is this the same Zehra?' she'll ask', 'The one who couldn't even express herself properly? How articulate she is today', she'll say.

Toying with her fantasy, she drifted into a world of dreams. Flowers, the colour of red-hot coals, colourful butterflies, intoxicating fragrances all around—and the gilded clouds rained down a golden powder. Zehra saw all this and was dumbfounded. And then, within minutes, the flowers faded and died, the colourful wings of the butterflies were singed, the golden clouds donned a black mantle and began to rain down stones, and, dazed and bewildered, she drifted into the darkness.

Then she saw something else.

She is in the midst of a huge crowd and she and her companion are standing next to each other. Before them, on a well-arrayed stage, a mullah with a long beard is shouting himself hoarse.

Brothers in faith! How shameful that in direct violation of the commandments of God and the Prophet, you have given women unlimited freedom. There is time still for you to drive them back into the home. End their defiance by severely punishing them for it and . . .

Zehra felt sparks coursing through her veins as she heard this. With her companion at her side, she pushed and jostled through the throng like a wounded lioness and went up to the stage. She was about to push the speaker away and say something, when she suddenly realized that her companion was missing. And now, she was alone. It was as if she also lost the power of speech along with her companion. The crowd was advancing towards her with a dreadful roar. Zehra awoke with a start and found herself in bed under a star-studded sky, her body drenched in sweat.

'It was nothing', she muttered, 'just a dream', and she tried to return to sleep. She moved the image of the young man back into her mind's eye and shut her eyes.

Then she started dreaming again. She saw a beautiful, radiant dream in which the young man was the hero.

Finally, she slept calmly.

She awoke at daybreak, as usual, but this morning, she kept her eyes shut so she could enjoy the lingering effect of her enchanting dream.

'Zehra!' Her father's harsh voice fell upon her ears like a hammer, startling her.

'You're still asleep?' her father said. 'Will I have to go to the office without eating today?'

Zehra felt her dreams scatter and she was back in the same world where the purpose of her life was to wake up in the morning, cook, clean the dirty dishes, and then darn frayed garments in the afternoon, back in the world of torment and monotony. She was now getting tired of the torment that life's monotony could be.

'Get up quickly!' her father scolded her when he observed her lethargic demeanour. And she quietly left her bed. But there was a storm brewing in her heart when she saw that Shaukat was sleeping peacefully and no one had bothered to wake him up; he could sleep as late he wished to. He didn't do any work around the house. If he was ever asked to buy paans from the market, he acted as if it was beneath him to do that. Except for going to college, all day he lazed around on his bed or roamed here and there for fun. Once, when Abba said, 'You have failed two years in a row and don't study at all, and I don't have the strength left now to continue working hard and feeding the fire of your bellies', Shaukat was so enraged that he threatened to leave the house. Amma wept and wept so he wouldn't go. Zehra thought, 'If I had been in Amma's place I would not have tolerated his insolence for a minute. But he's a man and so he's pampered and he doesn't even have to pick up a stick. As for me, even when I pick up everyone's shoes, all I get are harsh words. Well, these people know that I have nothing with which to justify my haughtiness. If I had a college education like Maryam Apa and been a well-placed teacher in a school, today I would receive the same kind of respect she does.'

This was the first time such rebellious thoughts were finding a place in Zehra's heart. That day, she lost her patience repeatedly when Shaukat ordered her about, and instead of lowering her head and breaking into tears at her father's uncalled-for chiding and rebuke, she viewed him with bitterness in her heart. Then, suddenly, this rebellious courage that had taken root in her, lifted her spirits.

When her friend Rabiya came over to borrow some salt, Zehra, deliberately flattening the rotis into crooked shapes in her presence, asked, 'Rabbo, why was your father bellowing today?'

'I accidentally put too much salt in the food today', Rabbo replied, scratching her dirty, matted hair with her fingers.

'So what? A human being can make a mistake.'

'Yes, a human being can make a mistake, but not a *girl*', Rabbo said and remembering her father's anger, burst into tears.

'Stop, you silly girl. Aren't girls human beings?' Zehra laughed sheepishly when she saw Rabiya's tears. 'We girls are always behaving like wet cats', she then remarked. Throwing a burnt roti into the bin of coarsely ground grain, she cast a glance at Rabiya's pale and melancholy face.

'I say sister, that's enough. As long as we were children, we suffered beatings at the hands of our brothers and fathers; when we reached puberty, we had to take over the chores in the kitchen, and do the stitching and mending, and when we become adults . . . ' Unable to continue, she began drawing a pattern on the wall with her fingers.

'And when we become adults, we are given into the service of a man as if we were slaves. If we work hard we get enough to eat. Bear a dozen or so children and then die one day, and make an exit.' Zehra spoke boldly.

A blistering sigh escaped Rabiya's lips and she said longingly, 'It's because we're girls.'

'*Unh!* What do you know? Do you know what the Western woman is like?' Zehra hastily began recounting the young man's conversation. But Rabiya grabbed some salt from the spice box and dashed off because she had left meat cooking on the stove.

'Could you please prepare a paan for me?', Shaukat said gently that night; he had been observing his older sister's bad humour all day.

'In a minute', Zehra said. Something was making her feel elated. Shaukat left the room and she quickly pulled the paandan over and started making paans for him. She applied the *katha* and *chuna* with great care, deposited thinly diced chalia next and then, placing two cardamom seeds daintily over everything, rolled the paans artfully. Finally, arranging the two rolled paans nicely in a tray, she slowly walked over to the room adjoining the men's quarters as if she were a Hindu goddess on her way to the temple to worship Krishan Murari. It was dark in the room, but the shaft of light falling through the crack in the door guided her. She peeped. The same young man sat before her. His face was beaming, he seemed to be excited and happy.

Shaukat was saying: 'Will your decision be acceptable to your parents as well?'

Zehra was startled.

'Yes', the young man said, 'they will have to give in to my decision.'

'But, but . . . ' Shaukat began to say something, but was interrupted.

The young man shrugged his shoulders, laughed and said, 'Now, we'll be married.'

To Zehra, it felt like the crack in the door was spewing out a dreadful darkness. The paan-tray fell with a loud clunk to the floor and she extended her hands and tried to find something to hold onto in the dark. Her mother entered with a lantern and Shaukat rushed in as well.

'What happened?' Shaukat asked when he noticed Zehra flattened against the wall.

'It was dark, I stumbled and fell.' The words escaped from Zehra's trembling lips.

Her mother looked at the tears in her eyes and said, 'If you walk in the dark without a light what else will you do but stumble?'

Zehra's gaze was pinned to the rolled up paans crushed under Shaukat's feet and she was saying to herself, 'I had held onto the light coming from the cracks, but how was I to know that these very cracks would start spewing darkness?'

'Make more paans', Shaukat said as he went out.

And like a dutiful sister, Zehra wearily returned to her room to prepare fresh paans.

2

The Monkey's Wound

She cowered on the loose-roped cot on the veranda, like a new bride. It was an afternoon of torrid heat and unrelenting fever, making her miserable. All the members of the household were shut inside the room, comfortably chatting and talking. There were moments when she too felt like seeking refuge from the sun's insufferable heat, by getting up and going to the room, but she was afraid that if she did, she would have to face a torrent of vitriolic advice. That was why, despite the heat and her fever, she valued the little privacy she had. She felt as if the marrow in her bones had melted and every fibre of her being was being fried in it, and that her ribs, arching like a bow, were being crushed by a strong hand as if they were just straws in a *jharu*. This odd sensation caused her to cough. The same cough—as if someone were beating a rhythm on a hollow, crumbling wooden box! Something came up in her throat as she was coughing and, pulling aside a few loose ropes in the cot, she bent down and spat it out. A tiny gob of blood landed on the floor with a *chup* sound. Before the sight of blood could generate any thoughts in her head, she heard the *khun-khun* sound of the monkeys and froze. She was terrified of monkeys. Without turning her neck, she rolled her eyes and looked in the direction of the noise. 'Oh my God . . . ' The words escaped from her dry, chapped lips, the burning sensation increasing. *Uffoh!* So many monkeys there were, leaping about in all directions from the tree in the backyard to the roof. She was suddenly seized with the urge to run into the room, but fear made her immobile. She was afraid all these monkeys would attack her if she made the slightest movement.

Sitting on the parapet, blackened with mildew, was a sickly, whimpering monkey surrounded by several fat monkeys busy scratching a black, ghastly wound on his back with their sharp nails. She began to feel sick at the sight of the monkey's loathsome wound. The monkeys were thoroughly absorbed in their activity. No sooner had one started puttering around in the wound than the other bared his teeth, slapped his eyelids, and followed suit. It was a case of a single, wounded individual surrounded by a thousand surgeons. And all that the sickly, feeble monkey did was fling his head down in pain. He looked like he was close to death, and she thought, 'Why doesn't the fool run away from here? What's to be gained from losing his life by having his wound examined?' But he was an animal lacking in reason. Still, the unfortunate monkey's helplessness aroused great pity in her. She wanted to save him from the pack of monkeys who, pretending to be helpful, were merely spectators. But . . . but suddenly, someone placed strong hands over her ribs and pressed her down. Coughs accompanied by a tickling sensation ranging from her chest to her throat. Her chest filled as if she had soaked up the juice of several paans at once. She hastily coughed up spit. *Hee . . . eeee*. Bright red, living blood.

Her limbs felt watery and she started rubbing her head against the splinter-ridden cot. The monkeys were making noises and the people in the room were complaining about her habit of isolating herself. She wearily stretched her legs and placed her hands on her chest. The sounds of her family grumbling and the *khun-khun* of the monkeys seemed to descend into her ears like red-hot rods. 'How similar the monkeys and my family are', she thought. And she began to feel the veins in her body throbbing. Suddenly, it seemed as if someone had said to her, 'You too are like that sickly monkey, deliberately courting deadly diseases.' And, as if to offer proof, images of the past emerged on the surface of her feverish brain.

'A mature twenty-three or twenty-four-year old, like a second-storey room—it's difficult not to worry now', Amma would mutter anxiously and she suddenly became overly conscious of the heavy burden of her daughter still being single. In her own family, girls her age, or even younger, had been married for years. Several already had four or five children each, and some, deemed old and worn-out merchandise by their husbands, were back in their parents' homes attempting to repair their tattered youth with the help of amulets and the prayers of holy men. But as for her, God knows what kind of a fate she had come into the world with, because no one had bothered to throw a stone at this unique berry tree. She was not at all bad looking. She was well mannered and well bred. Yet, her marriage could not be arranged. It is true, though, that except for her and her mother, no one was as worried about her. As far as the father was concerned, all he could do was gurgle on the hookah all day long, or proudly add to his progeny every other year. The older brother was absorbed in his own affairs. Today, he's in love with the washerwoman and tomorrow it's the sweeper woman who has his heart. And he wasn't doing any of this surreptitiously either; everything was undertaken openly. He didn't show the slightest hesitation in sighing, passing lewd remarks, or scratching himself both in proper and improper places in front of his youthful sister.

So, this was the environment in which she was spending her life. Her mother tried very hard to keep the vigour of her youth pressed down under the slab of household chores, but God help us! There comes a time when the winnowing basket loses its balance. You must have seen dal cooking on the stove, and you must have also observed that when the dal comes to a boil, the person watching its progress immediately removes the lid of the pot. This way, the bubbling is tempered, is it not? And if the lid is not removed, the dal boils over, thereby creating its own release. Her life was like this now. Her eyes, lowered by the weight of modesty all this time, began to look up here and there, as if in search of something. The house next door had been vacant for a long time, but it was said a student was to be renting it soon. Well, that was that. The lava churning in the earth's belly found a split in a layer on the earth's surface from which to erupt. While she would be working, her gaze would be drawn to the wall behind which someone was sure to be pacing. Her mother would be scolding her for her lack of concentration, but she didn't hear her; her eardrums would be vibrating, hoping instead to imbue a strange, masculine voice. Her parents would be quarreling about something, while she would be jumping the wall in her imagination to be held in an embrace. It was lava, wasn't it? It was bubbling inside.

'Why are you going on the roof?' Her older brother was a veritable psychologist.

She squeezed the wet, dyed dupatta tightly between her hands. 'I'm going up to dry my dupatta.' She frowned. Will a hungry person not be angry if a plate of food is pushed away from him?

'Isn't there enough sun here that you feel the need to go upstairs?' He glared at her like an honourable brother, and then lit a cheap cigarette.

Muttering, she threw the dupatta on the cot and sat down. The brother, satisfied, began humming,

Holding your gaze in mine,
O beloved with the fanciful eyes.

Fuming, she silently cursed him.

Today, she looked all around. No one was there to stand in the way of her desire. *Uffoh!* How many days she had yearned to peep through this hole! Taking this to be her opportunity, she placed her eye on the hole. It wasn't long before a fair-complexioned face appeared before her and then, *chap*! was gone. Just one glimpse, just one! Her longing swelled. If only he would come before her one more time. She stayed with her eye pinned to the hole. The location of the wretched hole was such that one could neither sit nor stand. She bent as if in a posture of genuflection. Both hands on her knees, eyes on the hole, and her ears directed to the doors of the room. Her back began to ache from the awkward position she was in, her hands became numb, and once or twice, the rubbing of her eyelashes against the hole caused specks of dirt from the area around it to fall into her eye. But she remained glued to the hole, while all kinds of strange longings stayed glued to her.

Days passed: one, two, three. Then months. Her body longed to travel through the hole the way her glance did, but finally, exhausted from the effort, she realized that was an impossible task.

'Amma!' Her younger brother was racing down the stairs noisily. 'The wretch cut my kite off.'

'*Arrey* son, who?' Amma was flabbergasted. She had given him four paisas only yesterday to buy a kite, and today the kite was gone.

'That same person who's living next door. He was saying, don't fly kites on the roof, you'll fall down.' He angrily stamped his foot.

'So, that wasn't so wrong, was it?' she said, pausing in her kneading.

'Come on, you be quiet', Amma scolded her. 'Who is he to give advice? If the boy doesn't fly the kite on the roof, will he fly it on his mother's chest? So son, why did he cut off your kite?'

'I said, who are you to stop me? I'll fly kites as much as I want, you don't own this place. And that's when he took a cable and cut off my cord.' The boy then proceeded to spit out three or four heavy curses.

She was enraged, and felt like leaving the dough she was kneading to go up and give him a few hard slaps. And Amma? She didn't stop him. A little fellow like him using such profanity! She was so much older, but once, when she was angry and had used a harmless curse commonly heard in the house, Amma had threatened her with a pipe, but . . .

'He's nothing, that self-appointed guardian . . . my son, you should fly kites on the roof when he's not around. One should stay away from low-class people like that and you know, your father is a very strict person—if he gets wind of this no one will be safe.' 'Well, we'll see about that!' she muttered again.

Had she been punishing herself all this time for this? That someone should curse him?

Her brother shouted, 'What do you mean when he's not around? He's there as soon as it's evening and he also has his bed there. Maybe he also sleeps on the roof. May he die, may I see his funeral . . . ', her brother cursed.

But she was smiling to herself. As if she didn't hear the curses at all. As a matter of fact, she was thinking of something altogether different at this moment. What a delectable thought it was! The bird in the cage was getting ready to fly.

That night, Amma untied the bunch of keys from her waistband and giving it to her, said, 'Here, take these, put the lock on the storage room door and lock the door to the stairs. Today, he's gone after the child's kite, tomorrow he'll clean out the house, the wretch!' And then, baring her rotund, shiny stomach, she calmly stretched out her legs on the charpoy. As far as she was concerned, she had made the necessary arrangements to protect her house.

But something else was going on in her mind. She was thinking, as she unbolted the lock on the storage room door, 'The two roofs are adjacent to each other. Why shouldn't I say today, everything that has been brewing in my heart all this time?'

And she bolted the lock on the door to the stairs. But the key to that lock disappeared from the bunch and was stowed under her pillow.

The police station's tower clock struck two. Everyone in the house was sound asleep. She slipped the key out from under her pillow, got up and began walking in her bare feet. A moist whiff of breeze gently fondled her emotions. Someone moved a foot, and she tiptoed to the water trestle. For a few moments, she stared at all the faces in the light of the stars and then, making certain that everyone was asleep, she calmly unfastened the padlock. Now, she was faced with the opening of the door. But the door opened easily without any creaking noises, pliant like a hungry beggar woman who turns into a corpse for the sake of a few pennies.

How fast her heart was beating! As if it would smash her ribs. Dancing in front of her eyes, in the darkness of the stairs, were all the stars she had been counting since evening fell. The veins in her temples throbbed with the force of her emotions. And on top of this, the buzzing of the mosquitoes.

She laboriously climbed the stairs. She was halfway up. Her body felt like a mountainous weight. Anticipation, fear, darkness, and her stilled breath made her head swim, and then a wave of kaleidoscopic colours radiated before her eyes.

Gadda-gad! Rolling like a ball down the stairs, falling, bouncing, she hit the leg of her father's charpoy.

'Hoho, hai, thief! Allah!'

The radiating colours in her vision suddenly recoiled when she heard the screams. The wick in the lantern was quickly raised.

'Hai, hai, it's her.' The mother beat her own shaking bosom. '*Arrey*, I knew this strumpet would be up to no good. Hai, why didn't you die!' The poor mother was about to faint. Her father shouted,

'I'll slaughter her, don't anyone stop me, I say—she's just been upstairs, the wretch.' But how admirable that although he was out of control, he was keeping his voice down—*arrey*, what if someone in the neighbourhood heard about his dishonour?

The older brother probably awoke from a dream about his newest paramour. His condition was simply indescribable. Also, he had often in the past tried to explain indirectly to his sister, 'Look, this is a well, no sister should fall into it.'

But she had not heeded his advice, so there—he grabbed her plait and began to swing her about. The father's integrity was suffering from inner turmoil, and when he saw such an easy way out, he too joined in. Because the mother was in her twelfth pregnancy, she avoided the exertion, but she proceeded to churn out all the singular expletives she could remember at this time.

But despite the pain she was in, she couldn't scream. A failure of resolve makes you a coward and it is the coward who is afraid of the world. She didn't have enough courage to open her mouth to protest against these criminal arbitrators.

Many months passed. She thought that just as her older brother's waywardness was always excused with, 'This is the age for such things', her great sin would also be eventually forgotten. But you fool! Did you forget about women's honour?

A woman is a puppet whose strings are held in society's mangled hands. And when these mangled hands feel an itch, the strings make the puppet dance. But if this puppet comes to life, and she begins to act according to her own volition, then what will society's inert, decaying body have left to play with? She thought that just as members of her family had lent a deaf ear to the demands of her youth, they would, similarly, forget this incident and accept their mistake. But this was her conviction. In the eyes of her virtuous protectors, however, the sinful scar that marred her life could never heal.

'Tramp', her brother would say at the slightest provocation.

'*Arrey* . . . ' Her mother would take one look at her downtrodden expression and spout hefty curses in one breath. An ordinary abrasion was scratched by poisonous nails until the scratch turned into a big wound. A wound that would putrefy on the inside and become toxic. Whose poison then engulfed her life with the agony of death? But these horrifying nails still had no rest.

'Why are you stretched out here?' It was her mother. 'The wretch has a fever all the time, and this scorching heat on top of that and the sunlight. But I know, why sit with the others, everyone will talk and the dear girl's mind will wander.' The mother continued grumbling, and taking the lota, disappeared into the lavatory.

Feeling worn, she curled her legs. On the kitchen roof, the villainous monkeys continued with what they thought was the treatment of the wounded monkey.

Her chest contorted in pain, and a stinging susurration travelled from her chest to her throat, melting her bones, burning and frying her insides.

'Allah!' she called out ardently, and then raised her pleading eyes towards the blue sky that rested on the world like a vast lid. For a long time, her glance attempted to cross over to the other side of the lid—where she thought a world of justice and compassion existed. But her pleading eyes failed. Wearied, she finally realized that Allah Mian had become content after placing a lid upon His world, just as she once put some leftover dal in a bowl and was satisfied that she had saved it. But when she remembered the dal after a whole blistering afternoon had gone by, and went to look at it, she saw that the dal had putrefied and gone bad.

3

Oh God!

Poor Daadi! She didn't interfere in anyone's business. All day long she sat on her wooden settee in a small, box-like chamber, and rattled away a black *tasbih* (rosary) with large beads. Rattling the tasbih had become a habit now. Whether she was talking to someone, giving someone advice, expressing an opinion on the matter of a marriage or receiving news about a sad occurrence or someone's illness, her tasbih continued its rotation; and all this time, she also coughed constantly, scattering white blobs of phlegm all around the room.

There were two things Daadi adored most in the world—her tasbih and Nanhi, her orphaned granddaughter. It was true her other son also had three children, but because they were being nurtured in the shadow of their parents' care, they were not as deserving of her love. For a while now, Daadi had two worries that consumed her daily, and those were death and Nanhi.

While reciting her prayers, she would suddenly roll her dim, sunken eyes to seek out Nanhi and if she didn't spot her, she would open her hollow, toothless mouth and shout:

'Oh God! Where is the wretch!'

No sooner had this cry emanated from her throat, than a lively girl of ten or eleven would emerge from some part of the house. A small, twisted braid hung down her back, just like the tail of a mouse, and a dupatta hugged her neck like a hangman's noose. Dragging her worn-out slippers she would appear and quickly jump onto Daadi's settee.

'You silly girl!' Daadi would say, pressing her toothless jaws together to the accompaniment of the rattling of the tasbih and, cowering, Nanhi would put on a frightened expression.

'You're a big girl now, but you don't understand anything.' Daadi would fix her beclouded gaze upon the girl's robust physique, and the poor girl would lower her eyes and squirm self-consciously.

'Is this a dupatta, you witch?' Daadi's failing vision travelled up and down her entire body and, lowering her thick lashes, the girl quickly adjusted the dupatta. Just like Amina Apa and Bari Amma. But then she felt anger at Daadi, who didn't wear a dupatta herself but was quick to admonish others.

'Come and sit here. I'll break your legs if you get up from here, you wretch.'

After delivering this threat, Daadi would happily return to her tasbih. Muttering under her breath, Nanhi would crouch in a corner of the wooden settee and glare at Dadi with blazing eyes. Again and again she would be tormented by the thought of some unfinished game, or a story she hadn't heard in its entirety, and she would start praying silently for Daadi to fall asleep so she could quickly dash off to be with Amina Apa. But God help us! Was it possible that Daadi should doze off during the day? She would sit there reciting her prayers, her eyelids fluttering forcefully with each word, spit spraying out from the corners of her mouth as she worked hard with her recitation. And Nanhi's heart burned with despair. With her seated nearby, Daàdi, in the meantime, calmly rolled off beads on her tasbih; the sound of the beads was like someone's teeth angrily clattering.

It was a moonlit summer night. Supper out of the way, everyone was resting and Daadi was saying her night prayers. Tired of lying in bed, Nanhi got up and went to Amina Apa.

Amina Apa was older and vivacious. Although she was sixteen or seventeen years old, she loved to romp about and play like a little girl. And she laughed very easily, breaking into giggles at every little thing. Perhaps these were the special qualities that endeared her to children.

'Amina Apa, I'm feeling very restless', Nanhi said coyly, pulling Amina Apa's hand.

'Let's play then', Amina Apa said, as if waiting for her cue. Rolling up the legs of her shalwar, she immediately got up.

'Yes, yes, we'll play *chupi chapol* (hide and seek).' Nanhi was elated. 'Ask Sallu Bhaiyya and Riazu too.'

What objection could Sallu Bhaiyya and Riazu have to joining them in a game of hide-and-seek? All four of them stood in a circle and Sallu Bhaiyya began reciting '*AkaR bakaR*'.

'*AkaR bakaR bumbe* . . . ' he started saying, thumping each person's chest with his forefinger as he went around the circle. But the minute his finger moved towards Nanhi, she felt Daadi's penetrating gaze piercing through her chest, and she involuntarily pulled down the dupatta hanging around her neck to cover her bosom. Sallu Bhaiyya's raised finger remained suspended in the air; he was nonplussed by this little girl's adult reaction.

The game started. Nanhi was the thief. The sleeping cots in the courtyard were designated as the boundary. Nanhi ran to catch the others. A commotion ensued. One person dodged, another gave Nanhi a whirl. There! Someone ran really fast and landed right next to her. Just as Nanhi was about to make a grab for him, someone pulled her braid. She turned around to see Daadi towering above her. The poor girl broke out in a cold sweat.

'Oh God! What will I do with this wretched, unruly creature.' Daadi's hand flew across her cheek in a noisy slap. Nanhi reeled and sat down. A light seemed to flicker for a moment before her eyes and then darkness prevailed.

'*Arrey*, what's the matter Daadi?' Sallu Bhaiyya ran to ward off Dadi's hand.

'Let me be, why so concerned?' Daadi's filmy eyes looked frightening in the moonlight.

'Come away Sallu, Nanhi is hers alone, she's no relation to us.' Bari Ammi got a chance to confront Daadi. She didn't like her anyway.

'What? But how can anyone just get up and hit her like this?' Sallu Bhaiyya was bewildered by Daadi's strange behaviour, and Nanhi's melancholy heart blossomed when she heard those sympathetic words in her defense. There was someone here who could come to her aid if she was in trouble. But Sallu Bhaiyya's words fueled Daadi's anger.

'Who are you to ask me this? Wait until your father is home, we'll decide once and for all. Why, what's this? Should I no longer have any rights over Nanhi? Such a big girl and jumping about like this and if I stop her then the mother's cherished one is ready to climb all over me. Everyone is conspiring to ruin my child.'

Bari Amma was already annoyed and when she was accused of being responsible for corrupting Nanhi, she became livid.

The situation worsened until Daadi not only beat Nanhi up but she also pounded her own chest.

Nanhi lay with her face down on her cot and sobbed late into the night, wondering all the while why Daadi was jealous of her alone. Wasn't she the same Nanhi whom Daadi forced to play if she saw her sitting quietly for even a short period of time? And now if Daadi didn't find Nanhi sitting with her back touching hers, she felt out of sorts. Why did Daadi hate her now?

When she woke up in the morning, Nanhi saw an expression of extreme displeasure hovering over Daadi's face. Daadi turned her face away from the breakfast tray and when her son offered salutations, she turned her back on him instead of touching his face and reciting words to ward off the evil eye, and she didn't once look at Nanhi. Her attention was directed only to her takht and her tasbih.

It seemed as though Daadi hated everyone now, but Nanhi was determined to get into Daadi's good books again. She didn't remove herself from her presence for even a minute. Finally, around late afternoon Daadi's anger diminished. She motioned to Nanhi to come closer. Nanhi happily obliged.

'Look Nanhi, if you don't do as I say I'll never set my eyes on your face again.'

'But Daadi, I do everything you say.'

'All right, then don't spend so much time with Sallau and don't talk to him either.'

'Why?' Nanhi was startled by this new injunction because Sallu Bhaiyya was the only one in the house who really sympathized with her.

'Grown up girls stay away from boys', Daadi said, as if divulging an important secret.

'So I'm grown up now?' Nanhi seriously wanted to know what was in store for her.

'Hush!' Daadi was afraid to clarify the point further because she was afraid the stupid girl could ask her what it meant to be grown up. She immediately remembered her own childhood, when a mere sign from her mother was enough for her to understand everything. Not only that, at age seven, she wore her dupatta with such perfect decorum that the women who visited the house began to worry about arranging marriage proposals for her. And on the other hand, here was Nanhi . . .

Daadi's silence prodded a question in Nanhi's mind, which she was sure would defeat Dadi once and for all.

'Then why does Amina Apa play with Sallu Bhaiyya? Why don't you stop her? Why are you always after me?' Nanhi's eyes filled with tears as she spoke in an impassioned tone.

'You witch!' Daadi said lovingly, patting Nanhi's head. 'She can play with him, she's his real sister.'

'And I?'

'You're his cousin, his uncle's daughter.'

'Then we're both his sisters.' Nanhi failed to see too much difference between sisters and cousins.

'What are you, the daughter of a lawyer? You're so quick with explanations, aren't you? Enough now, I've told you what to do. Amina can do what she wants, but you shouldn't. No one will say anything to her but everyone will spit on you.'

'But dear Daadi, why will everyone spit on me?' Nanhi's sense of curiousity was fully aroused.

'Stop now, you witch!' Vexed by her cumbersome questions Daadi boxed her ears, but instead of breaking into tears, Nanhi draped her arms around her grandmother's neck.

'All right, I won't sit with Sallu Bhaiyya now, but promise you won't be angry with me again.'

At that moment, her disappointment at not being able to talk to or be with Sallu Bhaiyya was overshadowed by her joy at having grown up. A strange kind of joy, but at the same time her mind was burdened by an unusual weight, under which a thousand questions squirmed like worms in a piece of rotting fruit.

For two or three days, the exhilaration of having grown up made her forgetful of everything else, but soon the bitterness of solitude diminished this thrill Every time she saw Sallu Bhaiyya, her heart restlessly demanded that she talk to him and also say, 'Dear Sallu Bhaiyya, Daadi has told me I'm grown up now and so I shouldn't talk to you, and if it weren't for her I would like so much to talk to you.'

But Sallu Bhaiyya was somewhat piqued with her; he would walk past her arrogantly without glancing in her direction, as if he no longer cared about her. Nanhi's heart burned to see him behave like this, but what about her promise to Daadi!

One day, Nanhi woke up very early in the morning. Daadi was saying her prayers in her room and everyone else was fast asleep. Suddenly she thought this was a good time to wake Sallu Bhaiyya up and tell him everything, so he would know she wasn't to blame. She looked around her, then left her bed, tip-toed to his bed and slowly removed the blanket from his face. As she gazed at him surreptitiously, she realized how nice he looked; dishevelled hair, a silken down covering his upper lip and on it, tiny beads of perspiration.

She was always perturbed by perspiration, whether it was hers or someone else's. She immediately started wiping off his perspiration with a corner of her dirty dupatta. He woke up, and was bewildered to find Nanhi standing near him so early in the morning. He looked about in alarm, roughly pushed her hand away and then, covering his face with the blanket again, he turned on his side.

Nanhi looked towards Daadi's room. On the prayer rug, Daadi was turning her face to the left and the right as she performed salaams. Nanhi understood immediately why Sallu Bhaiyya had hidden his face. She rushed back to her bed and lay down. Her heart beat violently at the stealth of her act. Oh God! Wasn't this the same Sallu Bhaiyya with whom she had spent hours alone, listening to him read stories from books, the same Sallu Bhaiyya who carried her on his shoulders as they roamed in the bazaars? Now Daadi's 'Hai hai' had turned her innocent actions into something serious.

'Hai Allah!' Daadi would groan to the accompaniment of the *khataa-khat* of her tasbih. 'All day long she's lazing about, the strumpet! Don't you have anything to do?'

A new hardship had been imposed upon her. Daadi could not bear to see her lying down or quietly sitting and doing nothing.

'What should I do then?' Daadi's change of hue every day, like a chameleon, made Nanhi look pale and melancholy.

'Ari . . . repair the tears in my kurtas, at least.'

Once she had burdened Nanhi with the weight of pubescence, Daadi now thought that if she sat around with nothing to do she would be visited by the devil; it was wise, Daadi surmised, to place more and more weight upon her so her attention would not wander. But poor Daadi didn't know that too much beating numbs the body and soon loses its effectiveness. And this is what happened with Nanhi—she became accustomed to hearing 'Hai, hai' all the time.

At first, in keeping with her promise, she avoided looking directly at Sallu Bhaiyya and only glanced at him from the corners of her eyes. But Daadi's increasing lack of confidence in her made her stubborn and, sitting next to Daadi, their backs touching, she began staring openly at Sallu Bhaiyya and Riazu. Using excuses related to food or expenses, she bickered with Daadi for hours. She silently cursed her and repeated in her heart the very expletives that fell from Daadi's mouth. She began to hate Daadi and felt extremely hostile towards her. And Amina Apa's free and easy behaviour in the company of her brothers made her feel like she was on live embers.

To make matters worse, Daadi forbade her to speak to Amina Apa. One day, just to irk Daadi, Amina Apa swept up her sari, tucked it up at her waist like a lungi and slapped her fat thighs, just like a wrestler. Bari Amma saw this and merely smiled, but Daadi was shaken to the depths of her soul. She thought Amina Apa was beyond redemption, and Nanhi could no longer be kept in her company. And so, Nanhi was left only with Daadi's shrivelled-up fellowship.

Even now, Nanhi hadn't grasped why she was 'grown up'. Girls her age were in school with boys. If she hadn't lost interest in studying, she herself would still be attending school. But what this innocent girl didn't know was that Daadi was one of those people who, taking every sick person to be at death's door, groan and moan, but when that person actually loses hope and dies, their eyes dry up like a desert.

A hot summer afternoon and a desolate silence everywhere. It was just mere chance that Daadi was asleep along with her tasbih and Nanhi was lying on her cot, perspiring heavily, with who knows what kind of thoughts racing through her head. Daadi's constant restrictions had made her inquisitive. She had so many questions that she wanted answers to: Why had she been forbidden to speak to Sallu Bhaiyya? All her feelings spun around this one question.

She turned to look at Daadi who was still asleep.

'Let's go and ask Sallu Bhaiyya, he's very nice . . . he won't laugh at me . . . it's Amina Apa who is always laughing, she'll start giggling right away.' With these thoughts occupying her mind, she rose from her bed and strayed out onto the courtyard in her bare feet. Coming out of the darkness of the room into the bright sunshine momentarily blinded her vision, and the soles of her feet burned from contact with the hot bricks. Slowly, tip-toeing, she made her way towards Sallu Bhaiyya's room. Gently pushing the door ajar, she entered.

Sallu Bhaiyya was asleep. The same dishevelled hair, the same silken, downy moustache wet with perspiration. Her heart beating violently, she leaned against the side of his bed. She felt strange coming stealthily to his bed after all this time. She recalled all his acts of kindness, and then remembered Daadi's prohibitive command. Her heart filled with heaviness, she placed her head on his chest. She wanted Sallu Bhaiyya to feel sympathy for her.

Sallu Bhaiyya woke up. When he saw Nanhi bending over his chest, after all the restrictions that had been imposed upon her, he forgot Nanhi was Nanhi and saw her as a woman—a woman who is bashful when she sees someone's finger moving towards her bosom, who peers at someone from the corners of her eyes, who is not afraid to wipe off someone's beads of sweat when she's alone with him, and who, overwhelmed by her emotions in the silence of the afternoon, tries to listen to someone's heartbeat.

Daadi's premature fears flung a veil over Sallu Bhaiyya's reason.

'Hai Allah!' Daadi entered Sallu Bhaiyya's room with faltering steps and the moment she adjusted her dimmed vision to the moist darkness of the room, a loud cry of 'Hai Allah!' fluttered and was trapped in the toothless hollowness of her mouth.

At a great distance from the earth, and soaring high in the sky, an eagle screeched and reminded Daadi to recite the kalima (the prayer) for warding off evil.

4

Making a Mountain Out of a Mole-Hill

She and I were in the same hotel, in adjoining rooms, but we didn't know each other at all. She was often seen standing in the doorway of her room. Skinny and gaunt, she had pale white skin and straight, dry, golden hair that was cut short and left open down her back. She was around ten or eleven years old. There was nothing innocent about her. Her face was dull and colourless. When I saw her, she reminded me of the taste of white, salty turnips. That was all I had seen of her at a quick glance, because it was difficult to look squarely at the wretch. A midget of a girl, but the way she pinned her gaze on me made me feel as if she was intent on finding fault with how I looked, dressed or carried myself. She made me feel as though there were hundreds of ants crawling all over my body. I wanted to box her ears and slap her a few times, so she wouldn't look at me like this the next time I was leaving my room. But there was something formidable about her presence. I was frustrated because I was not be able to say anything. So let her look, what difference does it make, it's her own eyes that will have to endure the torture, I would say, in an effort to console myself.

But this girl is a mystery—if she likes me then why doesn't she befriend me instead of staring at me the way she does? Children her age usually snatch what they like from others. But she? Well, whatever. I have no concern with this mystery. The doctor's orders are that I should rest in bed and avoid too much thinking. In other words, despite being above the level of the earth, bury everything worth thinking about in the depths of the brain. Yes, if you are not always well, you should be worrying about that instead. And after all this effort, I would finally be able to stop thinking about that girl.

Since I wasn't used to the mountain air, and also because I was quite careless about my treatment and diet, I was bound to be punished. I caught a chill, my cough worsened, and the pain in my chest was aroused. When Mumani Jaan and Bhaijaan were ready to go to the movies as planned, they gave me a questioning look. I was still in bed.

'Why don't you go, I don't think I'll come with you.'

'Why?' both asked, irately.

I was afraid to tell the truth, as that would have resulted in a fresh tirade about my careless attitude towards diet and treatment. And the situation would be further aggravated when the two would proceed with a threat to complain to Amma, and this would be followed in time by a letter from Amma: 'You're a very bad girl, you are not taking care of yourself at all.' I decided to lie.

'Look, today I'd like to finish this really nice book I'm reading and I'm in good spirits at this time and I'll hum and sing a little—and there's something else too—staying shut up at the cinema for two-and-a-half hours, well, that won't be good for my health. And secondly, my eyes . . . my glasses are also broken.'

Clutching the pillow as the pain became unbearable, I created a pile of lies.

'Oh, what a good girl you are.' Bhaijaan was the first one to be duped.

'All right then, lock the door behind us.' Mumani Jaan was also deceived.

Once I was alone, I began to mourn my illness. A moment ago I couldn't even utter a word out of fear and now this.

Oh God, ahhh . . . I burst into tears from the severity of the pain. This pain, this cough— what's wrong with me? Every doctor I go to taps my chest and my back, and says, 'It's nothing, take four bottles of this medicine, eat well, stop worrying and you'll be fine.' For God's sake! I've consumed pills from dozens of bottles, obtained from dozens of doctors, and these idiots, when they say it's nothing, then they must have some other name for the cough and the pain. What do they care? Fine, I'll die one day.

Feeling suffocated, I squeezed my face between my pillows, but then the coughing began and I felt as if I was about to faint. Suddenly, I felt the touch of someone's hand on my back and through a blurry haze I saw it was the same girl leaning over me, a few strands of her golden hair falling on my face.

This girl, the puzzle, so bland, so dull, so rude—no, no, she isn't, she's just very serious and is wise beyond her years—she's never talked to me, but now I'm in her debt. Is this not astuteness?

I made an effort to get up.

'Don't get up, otherwise you'll start coughing again', she said in a very casual manner, and then proceeded to lovingly rearrange my tousled tresses.

Her informal mode of address irritated me. Well . . .

'What's your illness?' she asked in a worried tone.

'It's nothing.'

'What?' she said, surprised.

'This is what doctors call my illness', I explained. Her surprise turned to amusement and, rolling her large but dull eyes, she began telling me stories about the incompetence of doctors. My pain was diminishing so I was able to turn my attention to other things.

'What's your name and who are you with?' I asked.

'Zarina, and I'm with my father.'

'Your father must love you very much.' I frequently ask children this question. I don't know why.

'Unh!' Her lower lip protruding, she stared into space. 'He likes women with red lips like you just to make me jealous. Anyway, when I'm as old as you then I'll see if he likes me or not.'

I felt like a fool.

'Where's your mother?' I asked her when I saw she had fallen silent.

'She's dead', she said in a tone that implied she was angry with her mother for dying. This distressed me. I had made the poor girl sad for no reason. Now I had to amuse her.

'You're a very nice girl. Are you here for the first time?'

'No, we come here every summer.' She started playing with my fingers.

'Your fingers are very pretty, small, like that of a child's.' She squeezed my hand between hers and laughed. I looked at my fingers and thought they were, indeed, pretty. I smiled.

'And your face is very pretty too.' Suddenly, she pinned her gaze on me and I was flustered. She's lying, the wretch. I had just looked into the mirror a while back and had found myself looking really awful. It's also because I'm sick.

'Believe me, you look so pretty to me.' She held my face between her hands and slowly pressed it with her palms. Her demeanour was solemn, and the old hardened look floated on her face again. I was irked by it.

'You should laugh all the time', I said nervously, 'I can't stand serious children.'

'Really?' She caught her lower lip between her teeth, and smiled.

'Zarri, Zarina'. Her father was calling her in a strange sort of way.

'You're all right now? Is it all right for me to leave?' She lovingly leaned over me.

'Yes, yes, you can go, you're a very sweet girl', I said.

Suddenly, there were noises coming from the adjoining room. Every night it was like this. That was why Bhaijaan had decided to take rooms in some other hotel.

'Why does your father make such a commotion?' I asked. Might as well get the answer while I could.

'You know those grown-up girls who come every night? They give him a lot of sherbet with soda, and Abba just loves this drink and gulps it down all by himself. And when he's full with the drink, then he does fun things. One day he took the girl's sari . . . '

'Zarri, you wretch Zarri!' The shout was accompanied by a silvery laugh and she ran out without finishing her sentence.

The next day, she arrived in my room early in the morning, but finding me asleep, she left. This information was passed on to me with harshness by Mumani Jaan, who expressed a great deal of astonishment. That was when I narrated to her the story of our friendship.

'Oh, I see', Mumani Jaan said with a sigh of relief.

A little later, I called Zarina through the open door as she was walking past my room. She talked to me for a long time. After this, to use her words, we became very good friends. She would stay with me nearly all day, and would chatter incessantly. Sometimes, she would say things that shocked me. It was usual for her to speak and ponder over things that were far too serious for her age. But I couldn't reprimand her for her insensitivity because when I did, she instantly became sad. Also, she showed such affection that I couldn't bring myself to chide her. She would run errands for me and do my chores with so much enthusiasm; even a loyal servant wouldn't be so conscientious. She always stared at me as if afraid of seeing signs of displeasure appear on my face. But when we went out for a walk she would turn into her old hardened self, and I would tell myself I wasn't going to be her friend any more.

'Don't look here and there', she would say.

'Why?' I would get really upset.

'People stare at you.'

' . . . '

'No, but you won't know that people are staring at you,' she would reply. And I would feel as if someone had dumped hot ash over me. I would wish then that I could slap her until she was red in the face, but once again something intimidating about her presence stopped me. All the time, I cursed myself for being intimidated by her like this, and think that the fun we were supposed to be having would be ruined.

'Let's go back now', I would say wearily, and like a security guard, she kept an eye on my glances or the glances of people who looked at me, and followed me like a shadow. But when we arrived at our destination, her roughness, her harshness was transformed once again to a sweet gentleness, and I would not be able to announce the end of our friendship as planned.

I had been feeling depressed since morning. Mumani Jaan had left for her mountain-climbing traning with an old friend who was fat like her and, of course, Bhaijaan was left here to roam around on his own as usual. Now it was just me and my tangled-up thoughts. Suddenly, she arrived.

'Why are you lying in bed so quietly?'

'No reason'. I was displeased with her presence at this moment.

'Why didn't you comb your hair? It's full of tangles.'

She entangled her fingers in my hair.

'Didn't feel like it.'

'All right, so let me comb it.' She quickly got the comb from the dressing table.

'No, look, let me be, I don't feel well.' It was true, I was feeling very weak.

'You don't have to get up. I'll comb your hair while you're lying down', she said cheerily and began to loosen my braids.

'Oh no!' I shuddered and pulled back.

'What?' She cocked her thin, pale neck to one side and smiling, she pursed her pasty lips and swallowed. Then she began untying my braids carefully.

I felt embarrased about my 'Oh no'.

She ran the comb gently through my hair and I was overcome by a deep sense of fatigue, and shut my eyes. This is a bad habit I have; no sooner does someone touch my hair than I begin to feel drowsy. At this moment, she stopped combing my hair and I felt her hand stroking my face and before I knew it, I felt her burning breath on my face and her burning lips upon my lips. Sparks writhed in the veins all over my body and frightened, I quickly opened my eyes.

'I like you very much.' She squeezed my face with her burning palms. I felt as though I had achieved something special.

'How long will you stay here Zari?' I didn't ever want to be separated from her.

'As long as you'll stay. I'll be lonely without you.' She chewed her lip.

'A lot of girls come here. You can be friends with them. You won't feel lonely then.' I spoke impulsively.

'Oh no, they're all very snobbish. All they want to do is to spend time with Abba.' The look of innocence disappeared from her face.

'Come on, let's talk about something else', I hastily changed the topic, feeling good, like one does after trying to scare a child with talk of a jinn. After this, she started chatting about the friends she loved very much. I felt disturbed by the strange expression on her face and the look in her eyes.

'Here, give me the comb, I'll fix my hair, you're distracted', I side-tracked, and forgetting her girlfriends, she became tangled up in my hair again.

After this, it became her custom to spend hours fixing my hair. She would try a hairdo, look at it from every angle, then re-do it and one day, she just went too far. She took the scissors and cut a lock and then, arranging the short bangs on my forehead like a *jhumar* (a piece of jewelry worn on the side of the head), she examined her handiwork and was delighted. When I said I didn't like it, she clung to me and kissed me and kissed me, until I began to feel suffocated.

'Get away from me', I said wearily, trying to push her away.

'No, no, no . . . ' She clung even more tightly. Irritated, I caught her by the shoulders and pushed her away with force and, being so thin and slight, she hit the wall in a second and for a moment, my heart stopped at the thought that she might be hurt.

'Oh no, oh no . . . ' I bit my lips remorsefully. Now she'll be angry with me, I thought, what a horrible person I am to repay her love in this manner.

I looked up cautiously and saw her pinned against the wall, eyeing me in a very strange sort of way—how can I describe that look—her chin was resting on her bosom and her dry golden hair cascaded from her shoulders to her chest, and her face looked harsh and wild like that of a young man's—I felt I could not move.

'Listen', she said authoritatively as she advanced towards me. 'Don't ever do this again, or else . . . ', and then she put both her hands around my waist and pulled my head down to her bosom. Feeling angry, I remained motionless. I wanted to dash her head against the wall again. Who was she to speak to me like this? But suddenly, I felt something warm and moist seeping onto my bosom. *Arrey*! She was sobbing . . . Oh! I patted her head lovingly. I thought, How stupid I am, what rubbish do I keep imagining.

Her sobbing ceased but she continued to hold on to me closely, just like a frightened little girl.

The door opened suddenly and she jumped up to move away from me. 'Oh? What is this?' I was shocked. The person to come into the room was Mumani Jaan, drying her hair with a towel as she walked in.

'That was a quick bath, wasn't it?' She glared at Mumani Jaan, reminding me of a dog to whom I threw a piece of meat once and then playfully picked it up before he could grab it. I felt distressed by the expression on her face.

'Why are you standing over there?'

She came and stood next to me again. And I felt nauseated; I felt a strange kind of discomfort, as if a repelling itch had spread over every fibre of my being.

'Please go, don't talk to me right now', I said angrily. For a few minutes, she stared at me and then quietly left the room. I felt as though a burden I was carrying had been lifted.

She didn't come to see me all day. I went past her room several times but couldn't see anything as the door was shut.

'She's just a child', I tried to console myself, but some hidden fear lifted its head from some corner of my heart and mocked me and I started thinking, I don't want to ever meet a girl like her again. But what kind of a girl is she? What answer did I have to that question? Except that the whole day it oozed like a boil in my brain from all my worrying, and I developed a very high fever at night. 'Allah! If Zari had been here she would have massaged my head, if she comes she'll untangle my hair, I feel my head getting heavy, if Zari will come then . . . '

I felt Zari's absence deeply, but she didn't show up. Late into the night, I pretended to cough in the hope that she would hear me and come. By daybreak, the fever abated and my anger escalated.

'It doesn't matter if the wretch doesn't come—am I a nobody? And in any case, what's so special about her? She's so ill-mannered, does she think I'm some toy?'

I passed the second day in turmoil as well. In the evening, she arrived as did the fever. She was wearing a beautiful frock and had neatly tied back her dry, golden hair with a red ribbon. In the white light of the lamp her thin, small face looked alluring. She sat down on a chair and began casually swinging her legs.

I was right. Doesn't she know I'm sick? I felt emotional and my eyes smarted.

'You've come after two days Zari. Why?' Mumani Jaan asked, her hands busy with knitting, a smile so wide appearing on her face that it seemed to make her skin crack.

'I was angry with you.' Zari parted her pale lips elegantly.

'Oh? Why?' Mumaani Jaan muttered.

'Well, you don't know how to take a bath', she said and, in an instant, the cloud over my heart was blown away by this innocent breeze.

How superstitious I am, staring at a straw because I'm afraid it might turn into a mountain. Why, how can a straw become a mountain? Amma is right in saying that my thoughts will turn me into a fool, and that all I could do was worry where the feet would go if not one in front of another when one walks. I broke into a smile.

'All right, all right, you can take out your anger on me later, but first worry about your Shadaan. Her sadness at being without you has brought on the fever again.' Mumaani Jaan's crackling laughter echoed, and my heart began to beat really fast in anticipation of her response.

Laughing, she came and sat on my bed.

'So you were really sad without me?' She twisted my fingers hard and lifted her eyebrows arrogantly.

'Un hunh', I shook my head. At that moment I wanted to tease her because she had bothered me so much. Her shimmering skin seemed to collapse and, turning away from me, she faced Mumaani Jaan who, with her back towards us, was taking something out of the cupboard. I twisted her fingers hoping that she would feel better, but it seemed she was intent on holding on to her anger. This silly action of mine made her love bloom again. Before Mumani Jaan could face us again, she started to squeeze my face with her own burning one. But the moment Mumani Jaan turned, she straightened.

What? The same again? My heart lurched and struck my ribs. I glared at her angrily. There was perspiration shining on her upper lip and her hand continued to pump mine. It was as if . . .

What kind of a girl is she? I felt a hammering striking my brain. My eyes closed of their own accord and when I heard Mumani Jaan's low, anxiety-filled scream, I was filled with a strange kind of fear.

A severe-looking, thin, boyish face, the expression on it undescribable, dull, parched lips and clenched fists—I was trembling. Oh no, that severe-looking face was transformed into many faces, all deadpan, dull faces.

They seem to be jammed into the walls all around me. What should I do now? The glances emerging from lifeless eyes are staring at me from every side. My entire body is becoming riddled with them—where should I go? Uff, these clenched paws, how the perspiration is pouring from them and why are they advancing towards me? And these pallid lips? There's no place left. Now these hands will grab me, now these lips will move towards me and become glued to my body—I shuddered with fear. I woke up.

Tick, tick, tick—the clock's pendulum swung with a regular beat. *Uffoh!* It's one o clock at night, I thought. Mumani Jaan and Bhaijaan are asleep, so why is the light still on? How quiet it is, and what a chilly night and I'm not feeling well—I wonder what happened in the evening? I kneaded my pounding head on the pillow. I felt so weak I couldn't move.

'*Sii, sii . . .* '

Startled, I turned to the side of my bed and saw her sitting on her haunches on a chair, covered in my shawl, shivering. Her lips had turned blue from the cold.

'You here at this time?'

'Yes.' She got up and bent over me.

And I felt as though a shot had been fired.

5

Ashes

'Shadaan, look at this.' Ruqaiya thrust the packet of cigarettes at my face.

'*Arri*, where did you get this?' I was thrilled. Cigarettes, and that too when four or five like-minded girls are in each other's company. Smoking can be a lot of fun, especially when one does it surreptitiously. Shut the door and puff away without any care.

'I've stolen them', she said casually like a seasoned thief. 'Your older brother was sleeping in the room outside, I happened to pass that way and, with no one watching, I quietly swiped them. Any objections?'

'All right, but let me check carefully to make sure you didn't steal anything else from my Bhaijaan.' I mischievously grabbed her tiny hands in a strong grip.

'His heart, for example . . . ' Suraiya teased from afar and, freeing her hands from my grip, Ruqaiya delivered a wallop on Suraiya's back. Then she lowered her face and, raising her eyebrows, said with the utmost seriousness:

'You wretches! If someone confesses to the theft then it's obvious that the person is not familiar with your character at all. If you start smoking in front of everyone, do you know what will happen? Even though nearly everyone knows that our degenerate little band smokes?'

'Well, what will happen?'

'You'll all remain unmarried forever. All those women who have sent proposals to your parents for their brothers and sons will curse you and immediately withdraw their proposals. You can test this yourself if you don't believe me, my dear girls. Actually we're all thieves, our characters permit us to be deceitful. I'll give my own example. Every night, I write a letter to Aziz Sahib. Ammi knows, but every day she asks me what I'm writing. Do you know what I tell her?' Ruqaiya's sombre expression took on a more serious aspect.

'What do you tell her?' all of us pressed eagerly.

She bit her lower lip between her teeth and then said with a poisonous smile, 'I say that I'm preparing notes on religious studies.' She continued, 'There's more. My reply satisfies Ammi completely, even though the next morning she sees the envelope with Aziz Sahib's address on it lying next to my pillow. But Ammi awakens me lovingly and when I'm awake, I pretend I'm avoiding her gaze and I stealthily slip the envelope under my pillow.'

'You're such a rascal', I said lovingly.

'You see, I have to hear curses just because I tell the Aziz Sahib story', Ruqaiya said wryly, and we all broke into rambunctious laughter. Completely hollow, vacuous laughter. Because the topic of conversation had turned somewhat sombre, we all felt a little gloomy and the desire to smoke vanished. However, in the next instant, Ruqaiya planted a kiss on the packet of cigarettes and made us feel lively again. We now debated whether to smoke in secret or not, since the house was filled with guests present for a family celebration. If someone saw us smoking, a commotion would ensue. In any case, members of my family were always looking to pin something on me so they could have an opportunity to spice up the story of my transgression, and present it for public consumption. I don't know why I had been singled out to be the thorn in everyone's eye. My only sin was that whatever I heard, saw and understood, I shaped into poems, or that I smoked in secret.

We began peeping into every room. Everywhere, there were colourful dupattas flying about. I was terrified by the lightness of these airy diaphanous dupattas.

'Look, here's an empty room!' I shouted excitedly.

'Are you blind? There's someone buried in the sofa', Ruqaiya pushed me into the room, and I advanced slowly on tiptoe.

'Unh! Come on, slowly. It's only Bari Apa sleeping all by herself.'

The girls walked in after me and sat down on the chairs, all of them resembling colourful bouquets.

'Now, light a cigarette', Suraiya blew her hot breath into my ear.

'Why, do your own work, my dear. I'm only going to light my own cigarette.'

I took a cigarette and ran off with the intent of lighting it up and smoking by myself.

'Arri, learn to share, you wretch!' Shamsa whispered fiercely after me.

I entered the kitchen. All the unwashed dishes stacked in front of him, Kallu was busy licking and savouring different tastes.

'*Arrey* Kallu, can you give me the matches?' I wanted a cigarette badly.

'They're over there on the shelf, *bitiya* (term implying daughter)', he said, pushing away a plate he had just licked clean. 'Why waste food', he added, pulling another before him. 'I thought I should make use of it.'

I was amused at his argument, but when I sought out the matches on the shelf, I lost my temper.

'So this empty box of matches is just for display?' I felt like slapping him on his bald head. 'Is there any fire left in the stove?'

'No bitiya, I doused the embers after I finished cooking.'

'*Arrey*, why don't you check?' I insisted stubbornly.

Muttering, he got to his feet.

'It's all ash, nothing but ash, there's no fire here. Look.' Without warning he stuck his black, ladle-like hand into the ashes and then jumped back with a loud yelp, forcing me against the wall as he fell back.

'You fool! Idiot!' I started calling him names angrily.

'My hand is burned, bitiya.' He plunged his ash-covered hand into the water as he continued to groan.

'Come on, say it again, you fool—it's all ash, nothing but ash, there's no fire in here. And now when your hand is burnt you're crying.' I was laughing loudly.

A tiny ember in the bosom of the ashes caught my attention as it lay dying slowly, and I placed the top of the cigarette on it. And then, I saw that the soul of the dying ember had been transferred to my cigarette. Hiding the lit cigarette under my dupatta I returned to the room where the others waited.

'Close the door first', Shamsa ordered without getting up.

'I'm not doing anything more, I've just accomplished a really big job.' I fell on a sofa, and sank into its depths.

'Well, let's see what arrow our poetess, our dove of Hind, has brought back hidden in her heart', Suraiya said, after she had lit her cigarette with mine.

'I have just discovered after some experimentation that ashes are not always cold. As a matter of fact, what Ruqaiya was saying earlier about character—well, that thing about concealment . . .' I was out of breath, and drawing on the cigarette had also made me lightheaded. I didn't know what I was saying.

'Well, well, what a discovery!' Ruqaiya widened her eyes and a wave of laughter followed as applause. All of a sudden I panicked. Apa had woken up with a start.

'Oh, it's you people. I see, you have all turned into a railway engine.' She spoke in her usual bland manner and then, hastily adjusting the dupatta over her bosom, she glared at the dupattas hanging around our necks or falling off our shoulders. This was to bring notice to our shamelessness. Unh! How long can one bother with dupattas—we're all girls after all. But Apa was determined to create unpleasantness.

'What is this mannish habit you've taken on.' This was meant to be a criticism of our smoking. I felt exasperated.

'So Apa, are there some specific feminine habits that you know of? Hunh?' How long could I control myself? 'The paan Amma chews constantly, the fistfuls of tobacco Khala Jaan consumes every day, and the cupsful of tea you drink all day— you think men don't do any of this because it's a blow to their masculinity and so it's all right for you? Hmm?'

She made a wry face and said, 'Well at least we don't smoke.'

Suraiya burst out laughing at this inane remark. Apa couldn't take any more so she left the room in a huff. Our faces fell and the smoke of the cigarettes became as bitter as a leaf from a neem tree. What is this? We can't be happy in the house for even a short while. She had criticized my cigarette smoking a thousand times, but would it be asking for too much to remain silent in front of my friends? What world does she inhabit, I don't know. Everyone's laughter is like poison to her, poison!

'Mentally your Apa is an old woman', Ruqaiya said, flicking ash expertly from her cigarette.

'She was born an old woman.' Everyone burst out laughing and I thought of Shamsa and Suraiya's older sisters, who were such fun you never got tired of spending time in their presence. And then there was my older sister, Apa. A corpse shrouded in a dupatta. If she behaved like an elderly woman at twenty-two, what would she be like when she actually became an elderly woman?

I was overcome by a feeling of sadness. I felt like launching into a furious confrontation with Apa today.

'It's a beautiful poem', I thought, after I had completing writing my poem. I was pleased with myself and felt like reciting it to someone. Amma was in bed on the other side of the room, reading a book. Perhaps I should recite it to her, I thought. No, no! I suddenly remembered the fate of another poem I had read to her. She heard it and said, 'I say girl, who told you this filthy stuff?' And that day, I realized with a great deal of anguish that I had been born in the wrong family. The thing was that Amma believed in experience. She firmly believed that a person couldn't achieve real understanding without real experience. According to this theory, intellect and imagination, poor things, were meant only to be scoffed at. There, this has reminded me of a story.

It is said that once there was a raja who lived in Hindustan. He was wise and learned, the best of poets. He had a daughter. The raja wanted his daughter to be wise and learned like him and for this reason, he appointed a highly-accomplished pandit to tutor her. Well, the princess was very intelligent and in a few years, she was able to vanquish some of the most erudite of scholars. She had a poetic temperament, and the education she received polished her talents further. Soon she was writing poems that were eloquent and profound. By sheer accident, one of her poems fell into the raja's hands. A poem rich with the emotions of romance, in which the pleasurable feelings of the embrace of love had also been described. The raja's blood boiled when he read the poem (perhaps it was Khatri blood). *Uffoh!* What kind of an education did the pandit give my unmarried daughter, which now makes her so knowledgeable in such matters, he thought. That was it. Thus accused, the poor pandit was ordered into exile. But the pandit said, 'O Raja, I want to hear you recite one of your poems in court before I leave.' The raja was a patron of learning and because he was also a poet, he was susceptible to praise, a weakness often found in poets. He agreed. The next day, he began reciting a poem in which he had drawn the picture of a poor man's cottage, presenting descriptions that were rich with imagery. For example, he said that a spider had stretched a web over the stove and the holes in the floor resembled the holes in a sieve. The poem was not quite finished when the pandit screamed, 'People this is not a raja, this is a shudra, (untouchable) a shudra! Get him out of here.' His words astonished everyone in the court, but the raja controlled his rage, reddened in the face like a beetroot and said, 'What proof do you have?' The pandit replied, 'Well, you claim to be a raja belonging to a long line of rajas and your life has been spent in palaces. So how do you know that when the stove remains unlit, a spider can spin a web over it? Have you ever seen this happen in your kitchen? And have you ever bothered to go and see your kitchen? If not, then you must have been a shudra before you became a king.'

The raja replied in a commanding voice, 'You stupid pandit, is there such a thing as intelligence or not?'

Then the pandit tied a knot in his braid and said, 'You think that intelligence is only yours to have and your daughter can't have it?'

Thus, the raja's face, which had been as red as a beetroot, changed to the colour of a brackish turnip.

Arrey, just look where this story started and where it has taken me. All this contemplation leaves little room for anything else. All I wanted to do was to recite my poem and instead, I was forced to narrate a tale.

'Then who should I recite it to?' I wondered again. 'Bhaijaan is interested in hunting and there's no mention of hunting anywhere—what interest can he have in the poem? Khala is asleep, and Apa—well, she'll have to do at this time.'

'Apa', I called, and she turned her face with its disinterested look towards me, making my heartbeats, which were fluttering excitedly, become sluggish. 'I wish that this accursed dolefulness would depart from this world', I prayed with an anguished heart.

'What is it?' Her lips separated only to create a tiny hole and then stuck to each other again.

'I've written a poem', I said enthusiastically.

'All right.'

What an apathetic 'all right' that was. I felt myself burning with disappointment.

'You must have written it for Akhtar?' she asked, making me livid. God have mercy on us! How stupid that when you write a poem, it should be for someone special. Really, Apa's education has been a total waste. But the truth of the matter is that she

just wants to upset me all the time. And that Akhtar! Hunh!
What a silly man. You can look at him instead of bothering to
go to watch a Charlie Chaplin film. Only recently he had come
to Abba with a proposal for me. Thank God Abba is a serious
man and he didn't encourage that comic affliction, or else my
life would have been ruined. I would have killed myself. By
God, I'm revolted by his mustache. But what does Apa really
think of me? Does she really believe I would be in love with
the likes of Akhtar? I wanted to confront her violently on this
issue. Whenever we're together, she talks like this. But we have
to talk to each other if we're living in the same house. If I had a
choice, I would have abandoned her along with her venomous
seriousness a long time ago.

'Rearrange your dupatta', I said and walked away in a huff.
She grasped my sarcasm and giggled apathetically.
'Won't you read your poem?' Her voice trailed after me.
'When I write something along the lines of *Tauba-tun-
Nasooh* then we'll see.' I rejected her words with disdain.

That day, I kept thinking about Apa for a long time
afterwards. What will happen to her? I don't understand how
she lives when she has no interest in anything at all. Except
perhaps in offering ridiculous advice. She's weary of the movies,
she feels out of place at get-togethers, and she has only two
friends who arrive once after many months, to engage in long
discussions on strange topics like the lightness of the dupattas
worn by girls these days and the stubborn leering of men. These
subjects are discussed with such displeasure that you would
think Apa and her friends had just swallowed quinine. And
as for men, they're the worst of God's creations as far as she's
concerned. I've never heard her say anything nice even about
the best of men. The fear of 'public opinion' had taken such

hold on her head that there was no room left for anything else, except the proclamations of God.

Zia . . . Zia! Zia everywhere! I forgot all my old ways. I liked him the very first time I met him. Whenever I saw him, I couldn't tear my gaze away from his person and sometimes, I wanted to hide my face in his arms and become oblivious to the world around me, oblivious to even myself. My heart was tormented by strange emotions. It was as if Zia had blinded me. He came to live in our neighbourhood and it was as if he had come to live within my soul. Zia, dear Zia . . . Everyone came to know. Amma and Abba no longer worried about my marriage. The women in the family gossiped excitedly. 'You'll see, the wretch will ensnare poor Zia.' And then followed such stories of my romance that I longed to make them real. My friends teased me. 'Hey you, what's this? You always said you would never fall in love—now, what's this strange behaviour?' In the meantime, Apa's glumness and her reprimands became somewhat more pronounced.

'Apa, my dearest!' I felt a tender sort of affection for her in those days because I realized that once I was married, her seriousness, unfortunate thing that it was, would be left without support. To whom would she offer advice then?

She was lying prone on her bed. I inhaled deeply, bent over her and blew a cloud of smoke over her face. She shivered.

'*Unhuh* . . . what's this . . .' Squirming, she waved away the smoke with her hands. 'You look just like a man.' She smiled and I saw embers afloat in her cheerless eyes.

Uffoh! So this corpse is also breathing at last, I thought, and so I said impulsively, 'I feel we should celebrate your wedding soon.'

'Shut up!' It seemed as if layers of gray ash had suddenly appeared under the clear surface of the skin on her face, and I felt that the embers afloat in her eyes had spewed ash and died. That was it. I knew with absolute certainty that Apa was not of this world.

'So get up then. Everyone is ready and waiting downstairs, we're going to the cinema.' I shook her arm.

'Look, you know I'm not interested in the movies one bit. The same old ludicrous tales of love and passion—*chii!*' Her face took on its usual pallid expression.

'Then I won't go either', I said, really upset this time.

'Please, you must go . . . and anyway, Aziza is coming to see me today.' Her cold, detached tone made me regret the concern I had felt. Feeling embarrassed, I quickly left the room to go to the cinema with the others.

But I wasn't able to have any fun. For one thing, I felt guilty for leaving her alone at home; after all, how long were we to be together now? What difference would it have made if I had stayed home today for her sake? And as for her indifference, well that was customary. Also, the film was very boring and during the interval, I realized I was subjecting myself to torture for nothing.

'Amma, I'm going home, Apa must be feeling depressed at being abandoned', I whispered in Amma's ear.

'My word! Feeling maternal towards Apa all of a sudden, hunh? Why, all the time you're fighting with her and . . . ' I rushed out of the cinema hall without listening to her lecture.

Apa will certainly be happy to see me. She won't say anything because she feels that expressing gratitude is the same as belittling oneself, but she will know that I love her, she will appreciate the fact that I gave up the film just to be with her. With these thoughts racing in my head, I entered the house.

And I'll also meet her Aziza, I told myself when I saw that the lights were on in her room.

Let me go in quietly and surprise them, the two philosophers. Since this was a rather complicated plan I decided to check the situation first. I raised myself on my toes and peeped through her bedroom window.

'Apa' I said, and paused to look at the scene in front of me. Apa had her long arms entwined around a man whose back was to me.

'How will I live without you, tell me . . . ', she was saying repeatedly, her eyes widened abnormally and filled with a strange expression—as if instead of dying, she was planning to devour her lover—at least, that's what her eyes seemed to be saying. My body trembled with surprise and I felt something like sand between my teeth—I couldn't keep my balance and the thin heels of my sandals struck against the hardness of the cement floor. Holding my breath, I sidled along the staircase and hid in the darkness—and feeling the tremor I had been seized with, I thought, Apa is not cold ashes, she's a stack of hot embers.

When the door of the room opened, a band of light travelled from the veranda to the courtyard like a brightly-lit street and, crouching near the staircase, I saw, with burning eyes, that Apa's beloved was my Zia . . .

Suddenly, it seemed that a violent dust storm had arisen and a stack of ashes decorated with glistening embers had fallen over me . . .

In the kitchen, Kallu cackled coarsely over something, and holding my head between my hands, I burst into sobs.

6

A Baby Girl

It has been raining since sundown and I'm feeling restless for no reason at all. For some years now, I have frequently been feeling this way. A stifling, subdued disenchantment and uneasiness— and on top of it, this light drizzle all evening—I don't know why I hate these sluggish, dull sensations. It's said that after a heavy rain, the water safely drains off from the roofs of houses like rivulets, but it is this slow drizzle that causes the newly-constructed houses to collapse as well. Despite a thousand attempts to heal myself, I'm becoming more and more restless. The longer one lives, the more predicaments to contend with. If you sit down with a needle threaded with a long strand, you end up with repeated knots. I'm also nearing thirty-five now, aren't I? Cold, freezing air travels silently through the window by my bedside, and still I feel as though there's a stove filled with hot coals blazing in my head.

It's not very late, but already I don't hear people on my street; the dogs too have fallen silent and at this time, I find the stillness more disturbing than usual. Living in this house, on this street, I sometimes feel like the storybook princess whose angry father shuts her up in a castle in a forest.

My mother and five sisters are huddled inside quilts on neatly arranged beds in the large bedroom; quiet, inert under the weight of their quilts, as if they too are overcome by a dilemma. All these beds in one room, positioned alongside each other in a row—as if we are all prisoners or patients in a general ward, or orphans in an orphanage.

Oh God! Oh God! My head is exploding and it seems as if someone inside me has begun to whine. Oh God! Everyone is asleep, everyone is buried under quilts—no one speaks. Are they now unable to speak because all of them overstuffed themselves with too much bread? Well, what can they do? Of course, they'll eat. After all, my income constitutes an ill-gotten gain, doesn't it? For Rs 150, I squander my brains on half-witted girls while the most these people can do is eat their fill and doze off. And Chacha Jaan isn't home either. This gentleman is not any less selfish than the others. The poor fellow is known as the protector of his brother's widow and daughters. Smooth-talking—the wretch—and lazy. And he'll be home at eleven. Who will open the door? As though everyone is his servant. The wretch. Certainly, he's embezzling our small inheritance—how else could he stay out this late? Who knows what bites he's taking at his age, nibbling here and there like a muskrat. He's been a widower since Chachi Jaan's death, three years ago. Says he 'adores' his deceased wife. Well, maybe he does adore his 'deceased' wife because while she was alive she was known to have constantly struggled to alter the direction of the reins of his love; she used dozens of amulets and recited hundreds of prayers, but to no avail. There wasn't a day when it seemed she was sitting on a throne she had purchased with her own money.

But, then, Hindustanis are well known for their worship of the dead. It isn't hard to conceive of Chacha Jaan's love for his deceased wife. No doubt, he spends his nights out of the house because he's mourning her death. And if I die, everyone will start loving me as well. Ahh, what a girl she was, never married and after her father's death, took care of her mother and sisters just like a man. Oh God! It's better to die than to live like this. But I still have to get up and open the door because that old Faizu is so lazy he pretends to be asleep when he hears the knocking. I pray for Chacha Jaan's demise . . .

And my agitation grows. The sense of daily monotony and a feeling of dullness begin to prick at every fibre of my being. My grown-up sisters and my old mother sleeping on beds alongside mine. I feel like pushing away their beds around, I feel like flinging my pillow at the lamp on the table, I feel like picking up the pet cat sitting under the table and hurling her out of the window onto the red-brick surface of the street, so that she would squeal loudly as she scampers off, shattering the silence of the street. And then my sisters, thinking I've gone mad, would begin screaming, and my mother, seeing her son-like daughter slip out of her hands, start beating her chest. But I soon realize that this would be all very silly because afterwards, I would still be in this house and everything else would be the same as before. Yes, just a little commotion, like the antics of the 1942 Independence movement, like election acrobatics, like plays enacted by actors, like . . .

'Oh God!' someone inside me stomps her feet and whines again. As I turn on my side wearily, I feel the newspaper scrunch under my head. I pull it out and throw it under the bed in disgust. I'm tired of reading the paper. 'Pakistan . . . undivided Hindustan . . . British India . . .' All at once, my anxiety propels me in another direction. I feel the urge to shout slogans so that all the people in my neighbourhood who hold disparate political views would be startled, and would start swearing at me. How nice that would be. They would all suffer the same injury at least once, they would feel the same pain, experience the same emotion! I would shout my slogan louder and louder, on the streets, on the roads, in the cities—until Gandhiji would see his undivided Hindustan and Mr Jinnah would see his Pakistan as a real and substantial entity. In other words, 'British India zindabaad!' But may God forgive me, can I really do this? Besides lying in bed and feeling uneasy late into the night, I will experience no other revolution in my life. Neither subjective nor objective. Teach young girls all day; suffer the bigotry of Hindu teachers (despite being totally unaware of the ABCs of politics, my headmistress is an undivided Hindustani); attend secret Pakistan meetings arranged by Muslim teachers in which hatred is expressed for the sins of the Hindus; the meetings that are dispersed congenially as soon as anyone—even the water woman—makes an appearance; then come home and listen to everyone's nonsense and talk to everyone. And at night, wander about in a maze—on the first of the month, a small sum of money in one's hand and while budgeting salt, chillies, flour and dal, postpone the longing for a new coat until next month—a curse upon all this.

Chacha Jaan will arrive at eleven. Because he stretches out on his bed all day long while he serves as our guardian, we should get up and open the door for him at night. In his own words, Chacha Jaan is afraid of God. For this reason he's our guardian, and because the government of Britain is afraid that the civilized nations of the world will censure it, it cannot abandon this half-savage Hindustan, which it fears may return to the Stone Age. The British have their eyes on the Congress and the Muslim League, and my sister Nazima and I are withering away for this worthless young man for no good reason. This stupid young man who doesn't know how to love and who is already engaged to the middle-aged daughter of my distant uncle, Khan Bahadur. Heartbroken, I have applied for the position of head teacher at a school in Bengal and, abandoning her decision to commit suicide, Nazima has consented to become a teacher at a local school. Even though she regards employment to be demeaning for a woman. What a strange joke this world is—I pray to God that atom bombs will rain from the sky—but listen, does anyone know if America and England have allowed even Allah Mian to be privy to the secret of the atom bomb?

My head starts throbbing. I don't know why this throbbing loves so much to roam—here one moment and then, somewhere else. My entire wretched body becomes one throbbing entity. I lift my head and fling it down on the pillows.

I'm tired of drawing water / O my sisters of yore.

Someone is singing merrily in the street. Euphoric and nonchalant. And suddenly, I realize that my arms are tired too, not from drawing water but from lying still on my chest, from lying carelessly by my side, from being folded in a halo around my head—*Uff!* May all these thoughts perish! So dear God, please let the school in Bengal approve my application. I promise that when I'm there, I'll fully exercise my reactions to the subordination I have experienced in my present position, I will eat a moderately rich diet composed of fish and rice, and in my free time I will only read books on spiritualism . . .

Dear God, let my application be approved.

Khat-khat. The chain on the door is rattling.

Rattle the chain on the door slowly / O beloved, come quietly. The pain in my heart spurts achingly again.

But that is Chacha Jaan knocking. The wretch! I wish some day our house is burglarized and tall, hulking dacoits forcibly carry off all the women.

Khat-khat . . .

That old Faizu's slumber is heavy with the torpor of a young man's sleep. And no one else is waking up. That's fine. I'm not getting up either. Even if he freezes in the cold, I don't care. Why is he coming home after midnight?

He's not ashamed to hold back half of what belongs to his unwed nieces.

'*Arrey*, where did you spend the night?'

Perhaps Faizu took pity on him. Chacha Jaan begins climbing the stairs and I begin to get furious.

'Are you awake Zahida?' he says, pausing by my bed. 'Well, it's not really that late.'

'Hmm', I mumble.

'Here, take this mithai.' He throws a small packet on my quilt and immediately a commotion results in all the quilts. 'Distribute the sweets among the girls, it's *tabbaruk* (food that's been blessed)', he says, taking off his coat.

Heads are lifted from the beds. As if indeed these are all girls, not women.

'Let's see it, what is it Hazrat Apa Jaani?'

I'm vexed by this exhibition of greed. I hurl the packet of sweets towards Amma's quilt.

'Have the vapours travelled to your brain, Apa Jaani?' Sajida says with her usual silly laugh.

'No, there's nothing wrong', I reply, suppressing my resentment.

Sometimes, I feel intimidated by all of them for no reason at all. The sweets are distributed and I cover my face with my quilt. My anxiety is enhanced by all this fuss and I decide that I will definitely go to Bengal. The question of Bengal's magic affecting me simply does not arise. And it is said that the men of Bengal are such cowards that they quietly tolerate the seizure of their product, namely 'the magic of Bengal' by non-Bengalis. Hunh! My braid is really short, so what do I have to fear. I will happily eat rice and fish—and—the famine in Bengal has ended anyway.

'Do you want a baby girl? Any one of you?' Chacha Jaan asks, dropping into a chair. And I sit up with a start on my bed and my sisters do the same. But Amma seems to have dozed off from the effects of the sweets she has just consumed.

'Yogurt, will you take some yogurt?' the fair-complexioned milk-woman asks us everyday as she does her rounds.

'Yes, yes!' we all speak in unison.

'The offspring of some starving Bengali?' Amma asks, irately.

'No, no Bhabi Jaan, what do we want with the offspring of these wretched people.' It's as if Chacha Jaan's honour has been threatened.

'My goodness! You think the Bengalis are inferior because they are suffering from a famine, the famine that has been brought about by the capitalists.' Zehra roars in imitation of Pandit Nehru's oratory.

'But my dear, to take advantage of the helplessness of those who are starving and steal their sons is an affront to humanity.' Fatima also speaks up angrily, she who has the special privilege of being a brainy high-school student.

'And to continue watching babies dying in the laps of starving mothers and fathers from want of a single drop of milk is definitely humane.' Sajida says with a graceless laugh. The poor thing is especially fond of the laughter that emits from her wide mouth.

All the girls burst out laughing as if someone has just cracked a joke.

'May God forgive us! All of you are always so busy showing off your own self-designed philosophy on every occasion.' Chacha Jaan's sombre voice silences everyone.

Then Sajida starts laughing. Nazima thinks it best to rest her chin on her knee and rock her body. And Fatima suddenly remembers to knot her hair in a bun. The others are content merely to smile. And I find myself thinking, A child, if I can have a child then . . . My femininity is invaded by maternal feelings.

'Oh my!' I blush. That idiot. He's happy to be Khan Bahadur's son-in-law. I'm far nobler than you, I can even take someone else's baby and make it mine. Anything to cover up my own inadequacy.

Outside, the drizzle is transformed into droplets of rain and it sounds as though someone is playing a melody on the roof.

'The baby girl is the offspring of a decent family, do you understand?' Chacha Jaan offers solid endorsement.

'She isn't a result of your decency, is she?' Amma asks with a playful laugh. All his nieces burst into giggles. And I feel as if a wave of salt water has leapt up in the ocean in my heart; what if she is, indeed, the fruit of Chacha Jaan's devotions? What a curse! I will strangle the baby if that's the case. Yes!

Visibly disconcerted, Chacha Jaan sits down on the bed.

'By God Baji, you're joking of course', he mumbles, bashfully lowering his gray-haired head. He looks so silly, I too feel embarrassed.

'Whose baby is she Chacha Jaan?' Nazima asks.

'A poor man's. His wife died day before yesterday. She left behind two daughters and a son. The baby girl is six months old. We can get her. There is no one to take care of the children and the poor father is in the merchant's employ. How will he look after the baby? The older daughter is five and the boy is three . . . '

'If I can get the boy . . . ' Amma's yearning takes the form of words. This is just too much—six daughters and no son.

'He won't part with the boy because he'll carry on his name', he replies in a business-like manner, and I wonder why is it that instead of spending their time grappling with the struggles of Pakistan and indivisible Hindustan, our leaders don't attempt to find out if it's a boy who carries on a name or a girl. Because Pakistan and indivisible Hindustan have direct, basic links to this puzzle.

'Well then, what good is a girl, and then a girl who's still nursing?' Amma's interest wanes.

'Will we get the older girl as well?' Nazima asks thoughtfully.

'No, he isn't going to part with a girl who is grown-up', Chacha Jaan replies. 'Soon he'll have someone to cook for him.'

'What's the use then? If we have the older girl, she'll clean the baby's soiled diapers and, after a few days, she can carry her around in her lap. Why, who wants just a piece of flesh and years of nuisance.' Nazima's farsightedness compels her to pull the quilt all the way to her neck.

'I'll take her.' How much sweeter than Nazima's is the sound of my own voice in my ears. Nazima raises her head and looks at me as if she can't believe that the same Zahida who could never bear to carry her own younger sisters when they were babies, is now willing to take on this baby girl.

'I can take her too. What's the cost?' Nazima speaks up just to challenge me. And I feel as if someone has struck at my heart. She's not my sister, she's my rival. If she hadn't come in the middle, Khan Bahadur Mamun would not have got such a young son-in-law. The wretch! Slothful. Snatches the glass of water from someone else's lips.

'How disgusting! The rich lady will pay for a human being.' I speak bitterly, as if covering up live coals with a griddle.

'Be quiet Nazima Baji. As far as Apa Jaani is concerned, human beings have no price.' Sniggering in her usual coarse manner, Sajida drops a firecracker in our midst and I feel as if I'm burning. I want to get up and slap both these girls. How rude that they are younger than me and . . .

My freethinking and all my progressive sentiments are suddenly deflated.

'So tell us Chacha Jaan, or else Baji and Apa Jaan will start auctioning the baby', Amina screams from inside her quilt.

'Just raise the child, that's all the price her father has asked for', Chacha Jaan says in a tearful voice, thus fulfilling his role as a broker.

'Oh God, our poor country! May God bring about a socialist revolution here soon.' Fatima's voice chokes. 'The poor children and their parents. Oh God.' She's always impelled by the belief that she knows all about humanity.

'And nothing'. Zehra's pessimism voices itself. 'Nothing will happen in Hindustan, nothing. Just keep drying up from inaction while fattening a useless communist inside yourself.'

'Show me the baby tomorrow', I announce decisively. 'I'll raise it. I've decided that I will go to Bengal. I'm nearing thirty-five, I'm not that attractive, won't marry, or let's say no one will want to marry me, so if I have this baby then I can always provide people with a grand reason for remaining unmarried all my life and I'll also have a reason to live.'

The rain outside is turning heavy.

'What are you going to do with a baby? Don't you have enough sisters to raise already?' Amma throws a stone in the path of my fast-moving train.

'Yes'. I'm on the verge of tears. 'My sisters, I nurture them, even if they treat me like dirt. I'm not complaining to anyone, but I do feel that I need someone all my own, someone I can have some control over. I want . . . I want . . . ' My voice catches on a sob, my eyes are burning and my temples begin to throb.

'The obsession for personal ownership will drive humanity into the cave of destruction', Fatima declares vehemently. 'You will raise this child just so you can have control over it? According to Karl Marx . . . '

'Be quiet, you daughter of Karl Marx', Zehra mutters. 'Apa Jaani gives us money so she can humiliate us like this.'

'Yes, that's our misfortune. Before we could be independent, Abba died. Well, please be assured that we won't remain a burden on you for long.' From her place in the quilt, Amina provides Zehra with reinforcements.

'Shut your beak, teacher sahiba of the future', Fatima says, irately.

'Oh God! I want to smash my head. No one has any idea how I feel. No one has any sympathy for me. I can't share my pain with anyone, and if I try to, everyone degrades me—this is my status . . . ' I want to weep without restraint.

Nazima makes clucking noises and turns on her side and I wish I could kill myself right there and then.

'The baby then, you must see it tomorrow Apa Jaani', Fatima returns to the original topic.

'Yes', Chacha Jaan says, 'I'll bring her over tomorrow. Zahida, if you take her and raise her you will receive heavenly rewards. She's suffering from diarrhoea, but once she's treated, she'll be well.'

'She'll be a pain, the wretch', Amma says, trying to shove a mountain down the path this time. 'Whoever takes her will have to be responsible for her. I can't deal with children any more, that's the truth. And I know that no one among you will be able to take care of her. Bringing up a child is a very strenuous job. You don't have the ability as yet.'

'Amma Jaan! Weren't you fourteen when Apa Jaan was born?' At times like this Fatima always uses her poison. Amma is silenced.

'If the baby girl is pretty then you must take her', Sajida exclaims amidst gales of laughter. 'It will be nice to have a baby running around. I'll stitch lots of pretty frocks for her.'

'Get her father to sign a statement saying he's given us the baby forever and he has no more rights over her', Fatima advises.

'All right, let's get her first', Zehra says. 'She's a girl, in a few years she'll be old enough to do some chores around the house, she'll massage Apa Jaani's feet.'

'Yes, she'll be a support for Apa Jaan's old age', Nazima adds, forgetting her own impending old age.

'A curse on you all!' Fatima screams. 'Sitting here and weaving a web of slavery for an innocent girl. It's better that she dies.'

'Keep your opinions to yourself, all of you.' I'm incensed now. 'You don't even know how to talk. Chacha Jaan, please do bring the baby girl tomorrow morning.' I announce my decision.

'All right, all right, now go to sleep, it's very late.' Chacha Jaan gets up to go to bed.

Outside the clamour of the rain is increasing.

'Meow! Meow!' The cat circles my bed as if in direct defiance of Chacha Jaan's order. I drop my head on the soft pillows. A cold air rips through my body.

A tiny, laughing, active, playful being overwhelms my thoughts. All the deprivations and misfortunes of life that always pricked me like thorns, are suddenly buried in my mind as if they were never there.

My cooking pot begins to bubble turbulently, and I begin to dance around it as if I'm starving.

I will take her with me to Bengal. Away from them all. I will pluck off all these sisters who are stuck to me like parasites. Away from the mother who loves my salary more than she loves me. I will leave her behind with her mouth gaping wide. And a curse upon the stupid Khan Bahadur's son-in-law. When I arrive in Bengal, I will hire a nanny who will take care of the child in school while I'm teaching. I will sit grandly on the chair reserved for head teacher and rule over all the teachers and the girls. And the baby, seated in the ayah's lap, will look at me and chuckle happily. When I come back from school I will be busy with the baby. I'll bathe her and dress her in beautifully-stitched clothes, I'll comb her hair and then prepare her milk bottle carefully and feed her myself. Dressed like Bengali women in a light dhoti, my hair unbraided, I will sit on the cool floor and rock her cradle:

The cradle of moonlight, the string of moonbeams.

Aha! The little daughter will be carried on a wave of music to the peaceful island of slumber, and observing the tiny innocent smile playing about her lips as she sleeps, I too will smile. A smile brimming with genuine maternal feelings. Ahh! At night, she will sleep beside me and I will sing her lullabies.

Come O slumber, come/ Put my little daughter to sleep.

She will cling to my breast, and batting her eyelashes, smiling, she will slowly fall asleep. When I suddenly wake up startled from a dream, on a Bengal night as dark as a woman's tresses, I will not be alone. She will be close to my bosom, breathing gently. Ah, my God! And then my little one will start talking in a short while, she will begin to slowly understand my words. When I laugh, she will giggle, when I fall into a pensive silence she will hold my face between her soft hands and gazing at me with a worried look, she will want to know the reason for my sadness, and then I will embrace her tightly. 'My little one, my child, it is nothing, nothing at all. Bring your book and I will teach you.' And my little one, my intelligent little girl, will read her lesson fluently. Allah!

Allah, let me get my little girl!

My heart begins to throb violently with joy.

'Listen everyone!' I lift my head and gleefully try to show everyone my lofty house. 'I'm only taking the child because I want to regard her as my child alone. Do you understand? Whether she is dark complexioned, whether her features are like the dirty pots and pans scattered in the kitchen, I will raise her as if I'm her real mother and I will take her with me to Bengal. My life is now devoted to her.' The parapets of my dream house are now reaching up to the heavens.

'*Hunh—hunh!*' My sisters are saying '*hunh, hunh*' as if I'm telling them a story.

'What do you think? Do you believe I can't even make a little sacrifice for the child?' I'm angry again.

'Hear, hear!' Sajida begins clapping.

'You insolent creature—you wretch!' Rage suddenly paralyzes my tongue.

'Zahida', Amma calls out.

'Yes, what is it?' I ask furiously.

'If you love the child, if you devote your life to raising her, what will the world say?' Amma's tone reeks of imperious severity.

'What will the world say? I don't care. Yes.' I look down my nose at the entire world.

'How can you not care when the world says that she's your illegitimate child?' she says. 'Educated girls already have a bad name.'

DhaRRaaam! My house collapses.

I've missed the train. I'm standing alone on the railway platform and my ears reverberate with the hissing of the engine.

I am silent. I'll regard the child as my own and call it my own. But if someone else says the same thing, or thinks the same, then I will drown in shame, my virginity will be tainted. It's possible someone awaits me in Bengal—it's possible—but who will have the guts to marry me once he sees me carrying the blot of an illegitimate child? The dormant desire to be married attacks with full force.

'Oh God, Oh God!' I'm feeling uneasy again.

Outside, a drizzle begins.

7

Whispers

'Oh!'

Look, Sita is sleeping on the floor on a black dhurrie, but you can't tell if she is actually sleeping.

It seems that she's closed her eyes in intense pain. She's been here since yesterday, taking care of you, but how lost she looks; she doesn't look anyone in the eye, she even avoids looking at you.

As if she's done something wrong.

She's still young, but whenever the feelings of your innocent-looking sister sparkle in her big eyes like fine pearls, it seems that she has understood the world more than you have. But you, Gita Rani, you've become an otherwordly creature after your arrival here.

What atrocities that shabby-looking lady doctor and other midwives perpetrated on your beautifully-shaped, supple body two nights ago, how they pounced upon it, but there were no tears of anger nor a look of contrition in your eyes. What a strange woman you are! Everyone agrees, but listen, being strange is nothing to be proud of! Now, see, you've been lying in bed since early evening, neither asleep nor awake. How strange your eyes look—yes, eyes that are vacant do look peculiar—no surprise, no fear, no bashfulness, no tears, no sleep—in which there's no hope, no despair, no stirring of thought, no stirring of any emotion. You know Gita, it seems that these are not your eyes, but two craters filled with water in a dark cave that have never been stirred by a gust of fresh air. And then, resting on your eyes these long, thick lashes, how still they are—why don't your lashes blink? Your lashes are like those vines that have climbed over grimy and desolate window casements and have been scorched by the harsh sun and dried up . . . *Uff*, these eyes? These lashes! The protectors of desolation and misfortunes—for God's sake Gita, move your eyelashes, let your eyes move, these lashes and your eyes are the focus of your feelings. What will happen if they remain lifeless like this? Minutes ago, you swallowed a mouthful of bitter medicine as if it were water. The bitterness did not produce any signs of life either in your eyes. If only a glimmer of weariness had appeared—a bit of disillusionment had peeped through—one can put out a fire, although the heat lingers for a while, but it seems that you have filled your eyes, these two windows of your feelings, with molten steel; that you have erected a wall of steel in the middle. What is it that you've decided, Gita? You're not going to become a stone goddess by lying here on the hospital bed. A lot of time has gone by and and many epochs have turned into a dream. The era preceding the Stone Age is over, the Stone Age is gone as well, and the age of stone goddessess is also departing—what's the point of sitting on a train and engaging with the scenes that are passing you by? Look at your supple body made of flesh and bones, which can bow at the feet of Bhagwan, dance with devotion and which can sway and tremble in the arms of Bhagwan Das—how insulting for your body if it turns into stone? Especially in this day and age, when stones are used not so much for worshipping by people as for cracking one another's head.

It seems that you've forgotten how your thin, skinny, nervous, broken-hearted brother's head was cracked with a stone that had the puja sindur on it—just think if you, the principal of the Theosophical College (and one who is an advocate of non-violence), would be lifted up and thrown at someone's head like this and you are bathed in someone's blood—*Uff!* You should shudder at such a thought. And it's also worth remembering that before deciding to become a goddess, you couldn't smash the head of the person who smashed your fate. For this reason, Gita Rani, jump out from the confines of this stone fortress, otherwise you will stifle and you will die, and then this body of yours will be placed upon a high pile of firewood and consumed by fire and rest assured that even after this your statue will not be created, you will not be worshipped, because, O principal of the Theosophical College, science has advanced and turned into an atom bomb and gods and goddesses are fighting for no reason in the heavens over the fact that in a world inhabited by innumerable human beings, even the ratio of one god to one worshipper is barely possible any more. It's obvious there's no need left there and Gita, the heavens actually don't need you as much as your family does. You were aware of this before, and you should still know this. You remember the experiment in which your lover felt he had less need of you than your needy family? Ah, that lover Shyam who practiced sacrifice as a profession—he was a student at the same university where you were and he was crazy about your beauty and your simplicity. At least, you thought he was crazy about you. When he placed his lips on your soft, burning lips; when he held your beautiful face between his hands; when he clasped your delicate hands in his, then you looked at his closed eyes and trembling lips and came to this conclusion. However, one night, while you were strolling with him on an isolated road along the banks of the Gomti river, you had mentioned marriage, and he had bestowed a lingering kiss on your lips and lovingly pleaded that he couldn't marry you because you're very precious to your family, as precious as a gold-embroidered sari hanging in the showcase of a shop in Hazrat Ganj would be for a female labourer. On the banks of the Gomti, on a moonlit night, under the half shadows of tall trees, how great was the sacrifice made by your lover? So yes, Gita, you who are as precious as an embroidered sari, you Gita, think about living and continue to be the curtain that conceals the nakedness of your family, because your sister Sita, despite her budding youth, has still not become a gold-embroidered sari; neither of your two brothers could recover from illness and become a clerk or an officer in the Indian Civil Service— no charitable remedies have affected your mother's asthma to this day nor has your father's lame leg been straightened, your widowed sister has not been able to achieve the joy of being married by dying, as she had avowed—do you understand? For this reason, blink your inert lashes, chew your lips with your white teeth and cry bitterly for this reality—but it seems you're not listening to anything!

Gita! O Gita Rani!!

Tell me, lying here like this, on what hazy speck outside the window have you fixed the pupils of your eyes? All specks don't have meanings, you dip the pen in ink and sit down to write and push down the nib hard, and so many meaningless dabs spread on the paper—for this reason, you shouldn't stare at specks. Look at something else, look at the sky on which you had pinned great hopes and expectations, look at the stars that blink like tearful eyes and which you counted at night to help you fall asleep—look at the moon whose light is whiter than your bedsheet, and mingled in its whiteness is the yellowness of autumn leaves and also the yellowness of the two-tola gold with which you wanted for so long to have a necklace made— and the hue of turmeric yellow on your face—there is much in this moonlight. Look here, how sad the poor moon looks behind the tree laden with mangoes. It seems that the moon is remembering the night of the full moon in Brindaban, when the light as white as cow's milk had enveloped Radha and the gopis, and the garments of passionate love that covered their naked souls were suddenly stolen, and now those crazy women were wandering on the banks of the river Jamuna—leaping in their ears is still the melody of the flute and it seemed the tangled breathing was wandering about, calling, 'Which way has Shyam gone?' *Uffoh!* How passionate is that call. Meera turned that cry into the soul of her songs, the same that you sang every night during puja. *Which way has Shyam gone, tell me someone, which way has Shyam gone.*

Raise your thin, delicate, black arches and think about the first nights drenched in the melody of these bhajans, the nights that gleam even now in the darkness of your being, as though hundreds of glow-worms have been strung into a necklace hanging in a dark chamber. It's possible that in these three days, those who know you have forgotten about the shimmer surrounding your existence, but you haven't forgotten, have you? The Theosophical College Hall, oh that dwelling of rainbows with a roof that was also like a big, long rainbow in which one could detect hues of gold and silver, with walls that had been painted with light colours in the shapes of delicate bows, in which the seats had been arranged in circular rows and that small, curved stage in the middle of which stood a statue of Krishan Bhagwan, his smile hidden behind the flute. A few minutes before the religious chanting started, dressed in an inexpensive, white Bengali sari, you would gracefully walk onto the stage and sit down cross-legged next to the statue, and you would become a magnet for people's eyes. There would be others on the stage as well, girls from the hostel and staff members, and Miss Thakur whose face was never bereft of makeup and who always looked very attractive; Mrs Shankar, who because of her heavy hips, thick lips and dark complexion seemed to be an image from the Ajanta carvings; Das who looked like a celluloid doll because of her red-and-white complexion and short height; and that Chetan Mama with the long neck and stooped back, who had always played a big part in the goings-on in college from the very beginning. Along with them, there was a college clerk who had a round, dark face and a defect in one eye that was successfully hidden behind golden-framed glasses. But despite being surrounded by all these people, you stood out as someone separate, just like a lily blooming on the surface of a pond. It is said that aged wine is more intoxicating than new wine. Perhaps so, but the truth is that among all the people on the stage, you were the only one who seemed like yourself at first glance; at second and third glance, your appearance seemed even lovelier, and finally your beauty appeared as a priceless gift from the heavens. Miss Thakur, who was reduced to helplessness when faced with you and who secretly begrudged you your grace and the high regard you were afforded, used to say that your deep spirituality had created a romantic melancholy in you and that this is really what makes you so attractive, since in reality you're a dark-skinned, insipid looking woman.

Once the statue had been garlanded, Chetan Mama would strike the harmonium keys, Bhagwan Das would begin to strum the guitar, Mrs Shankar would start thrumming her slender fingers and soft palms on the tabla, Miss Das would pick up the tiny, miniature cymbals with childlike excitement and start chiming them, and you would take the *khartals* in your hands and start clapping them together, and Miss Thakur would sit down in the middle, assuming a charming pose, as if the kirtan was in her honour.

Tiny waves crested in the river of music and song, and the audience in the hall would start rocking slowly. Then gradually, those tiny waves wove themselves around each other and became louder, then leapt, sprang up and advanced—people would start rocking with greater speed. On the floor of the hall and on the chair handles, the *dhap-dhap* of the beat and the *thap-thap* grew louder and swirled like a vortex; a vortex of raag and rhythm in which everyone and everything seemed to be spinning. Then, slowly, within this whirling, arose your voice, loud but soft as silk, like white mother-of-pearl, swirling and spiralling. *What path have you taken O Shyam?* Your favourite bhajan. The eddy was stilled. And your voice unfurled in the hall like the scent of burning incense. The other voices and instruments intertwined with your voice gently and gracefully, reminding one of some *Alif Laila* princess being carried by her maidservants on the wave of a meandering river. The souls of the listeners would begin to sway like dainty boats. The rainbow colours spread out in the hall would lose their intensity, and the brightness of gold and silver would be enhanced. Just a sparkling glimmer everywhere.

The white sari wrapped around your body would seem whiter than milk and the yellow and red petals of the rose buds in your hair would appear to be blossoming. How beautiful your face looked, lifted towards the statue as you sang. Your moistened, dreamy eyes, your thin nose, your soft, moist lips, and the bindi on your wide forehead. Everything fresh and bright. Your purity shone in your beauty, like the white foam of the ocean's waves striking the shore. The smile on Krishan Bhagwan's face would deepen, which you would feel. And Bhagwan Das' eyes behind his glasses would become radiant, which you couldn't see. Most of the ordinary people in the hall would suppress their turbulent emotions, and say that you look like a pure spirit in search of peace. Ahh, the peace that was nowhere to be found. Tsk, tsk! It's true, isn't it Gita? Answer me. True that you've always been a person of few words and you like this rule of confession, that to stay silent is part of the magnificence of the gods. But now you should be convinced that you're not anything like a god or a goddess. You're just Gita, the Gita about whom the doctor has said that if she remains silent like this for a few more hours, the veins in her brain will burst and what good will that do, Gita? People will say, that's okay, she has paid for her sin. How insulting that the world should shake off your funeral with such loathing from its folds, the way a spider is flung off. Isn't it insulting? But *uff!* You're like a raised inscription on stone, you seem to have wandered really far from the limits of the past, present and the future—you've lost everything!

Where are you, Gita? Have you really forgotten everything? Or do you want to forget? Well, tell me, have you forgotten that night as well? The same night when you were feeling very sad, so sad that even those who knew of your sadness and your pensiveness could see you were sad; unusually sorrowful—

yes, that very afternoon, a friend of yours had written to you informing you that Shyam had gotten married to a very unattractive Bengali girl who had brought with her loads of dowry, along with 10,000 rupees in cash. In other words, Shyam married a girl who was not valuable for her family, but her family was valuable for her.

How tired and weary you were at the kirtan that day. You didn't even tie up your long hair in a bun, nor did you adorn it with red and yellow rosebuds. The day-old bindi on your forehead looked muddy. It's true that Shyam was the one, who seven years ago had shaken off your hand and had brought you face-to-face with a reality that you had been inhaling, but with your eyes closed. He made you open your eyes. You would become conscious of that reality when the monthly 200 rupees of your salary would be used up in the house before the month was over. But even then, after hearing the news of his marriage, you behaved as though you were watching the dance of the flames on the funeral pyre of someone very dear to you. Perhaps, because love is a cobweb, which if it gets into every nook and cranny of your being, it gets stuck to the body and despite efforts to scratch it off, can't be removed. That day, you refused to start the kirtan. The other girls who were in awe of you began to chant their own favourite bhajans and you silently stared at the statue of Krishan Bhagwan. It seemed you were in a daze. But no, at that moment your soul was as agitated as a large stone hurtling down from the top of a mountain. At the back of Krishan Bhagwan's statue, you could see Shyam again and again, everything he had done and said; the way he kissed you; the way he boldly stared into your eyes; his smile, his singing—the songs by Rabindranath Tagore that he sang as he twirled your locks; the revolutionary poems of Kazi Nazrul

Islam that he recited to shred the old system; the ones he sent you in his letters when you were afraid to meet him openly; and then after all this, when he took you to the top of a mountain and pushed you down from there—you were remembering everything. And the girls continued to rock and sway as they sang:

Say Hari, Hari
Say Hari, Hari

The kirtan was over. The audience dispersed. The girls returned to the hostel. Miss Das and Miss Thakur got up whispering to each other, Mrs Shankar fixed her sari and followed Chetan Mama because she was afraid to walk alone to her quarter on cloudy, rainy nights. You didn't get up. No one had the courage to ask you anything or say anything to you. You just kept sitting in front of the statue, lost in your thoughts. The strings on Bhagwan Das' sitar were loose, so he was still sitting there engrossed in fixing them. When he finally picked up his sitar and left, you placed your cold cheek restlessly on the feet of the statue and washed it all at once with a torrent of tears. The statue was smiling, because it was made for smiling and you were weeping—a thousand complaints against Bhagwan were screaming inside you. Bhagwan, you didn't give anything except tears to your devotee—tears that boil secretly, tears that are washing your feet today—you made Shyam win, the Shyam who pushed your devoted *pujaran* from the top of the mountain! You kept crying, the statue kept smiling and Bhagwan Das' eyes behind his glasses were laughing gleefully. He had crept in quietly. When you lifted your head, he pretended to be busy picking up the cymbals and khartals, and annoyed, you got up and walked out of the hall.

The freezing atmosphere outside and the wet earth made you feel as though the weight lying on your chest had become heavier. You crossed the long veranda and courtyard and entered your quarter, and without eating anything, you came to your room and sat down on your bed—Sita was sound asleep on the bed next to yours. Her course books lay strewn about next to her pillow. You gazed at her innocent face. But your mind was dazed, tired, you couldn't think clearly. You were sitting, and you kept sitting on the edge of the bed. It didn't occur to you that you should arrange Sita's marriage as soon as you can because you love her so much, so that she doesn't have to become a gold-embroidered sari for her family, nor did you think about your two sick brothers whom you had wanted to see healthy and self-reliant, and you didn't think of your widowed sister who couldn't become a bride even in death. You didn't think of your mother and father who were stuck to you like a disease, and how strange that you didn't even see that dream again in which you suddenly become wealthy, your family's woes are over, and free from the burden of your responsibilties you have found, among your acquaintances, a husband who is a thousand times better than Shyam, and the unmarried Shyam is left in a state of torment and regret.

No thoughts. No dream. You're just sitting there quietly, your hands placed limply in your lap. Yes, but there's one thought that has taken shape: you have lost, you have been left far behind, you were a silly fool all this time, you have nothing.

The door and the two windows looking out on the lawn were open and remained open. Moths were dashing about around the light bulb, but you didn't even turn off the switch. Thunder rumbled distantly and dollops of rain started coming down. But you didn't pay any attention to it. Your mother coughed and wheezed and fell asleep finally, but you were not aware of that either, in the other room, your widowed sister finished her recitation of the Ramayana, and a hush fell over the entire quarter. There was silence in the other quarters as well, but you still didn't lie down.

Someone went past your door repeatedly, but it was as if you didn't notice that either. Who knows what had happened to the trustworthy dignity of the college principal, who kept everyone in awe of her. A man paces back and forth in front of her door, and that too while she's sitting on her bed? And you stayed in that position as if you were buried under a heavy weight. What kind of a weight was that? You didn't have the ability to analyze it.

Then, no one knows how and when Bhagwan Das came and stood in the doorway. His eyes behind the misty glasses looked as if they were fixed at someone bathing in a bathhouse. His dark complexion had turned darker, and his lips were quivering. In the damp air, his coarse cotton kurta and his dhoti flapped, his long, dry hair became awry. The moment you saw him, you stood up. You wanted to scold him, you wanted to fire him from his job, or . . . your clouded brain didn't show you a way. And then, no one knows how the light bulb was engulfed by darkness and both of you drew closer to each other. His arms pinioned you and your long hair was wrapped around his arms. The moths fluttering in the dark could not see this.

In the silence of the night, you were in the grip of a strange kind of drowsiness, you had dreams that skipped about in new ways, *channa-chan*, *channa-chan*, as if gopis were dancing on the shore of the Jamuna, dazed and mystified, while colourfully decorated water containers were floating down the Jamuna— the flute was being played, here, there, the ankle bells were tinkling and big, fat snakes were lazing around on the paths in Brindaban—and then suddenly, somewhere your Shyam with his ugly wife, buried under the weight of piles of dowry, was screaming—and dressed as a gopi, you're churning milk, *jhapa-jhap*, and making butter, white soft butter! You're laughing, singing, and fat cobras are dancing on your bangles . . . and then you saw that the rope you were churning milk with was also a black cobra—you were about to scream—what kind of frightening dreams were these . . . and what a strange night it was.

Rain fell steadily all night, interspersed with lightning and thunder and the next morning the sky had cleared. The morning light found you smiling drowsily on your bed. It was a smile that had appeared for the first time on your face, new, strange and arduous, as if holding chameli flowers in its grasp. Ahha! Smile now Gita, you must still remember that night . . . no, you won't smile? Well then, surely you remember how long that onerous smile stayed on your lips? About two months? And then your lips quivered all the time, the way the empty hand of a person suffering from body aches quivers after lifting something heavy. Perhaps the chameli flowers in your smile had dried up and had fluttered away in the breeze. Ahh Gita, what a bitter reality this is! And you remember those medicines that were more bitter than this reality, the medicines you swallowed surrepetitiously and which made your face turn so pale one would think you were sharpening a knife to cut out your own flesh. But you were doing this too, fearfully. Krishan Bhagwan loved Radha and made her rebel against her life, he celebrated their love and ardour and then he left her and went to Gokul, because he had another programme besides this bond with Radha. Bhagwan Das, despite your wish, refused to make you his because he was already the father of two sons and had an ailing wife. First, he put his palms together pleadingly, then he kissed your hair and said that he loved you and for this reason he would never marry you because he wanted you to marry someone important and rich, and live a life of luxury. But when you expressed your Sati-Savitri-like devotion, he explained that there had merely been an exchange between you and him. That was all! And it's not strange that someone buying a wheat harvest would get some some chaff with it. After this, you couldn't say anything to him, the woman couldn't say anything to the man, the college principal couldn't say anything to her office clerk, although you wanted to say that what he had given you was like handing someone a sword without a handle as a gift. You wanted something else. A companion, a friend.

You said nothing. With your ashen face you just started sharpening the knife to cut off your own flesh. Gita, you poor thing! To hide the purchase you had made surrepetitiously and stealthily you wanted to bury it in the cellar and ignite the chaff. Worrying about this was causing you to lose weight, and your complexion was turning sallow. Miss Thakur believed that a sexual hunger had awakened inside you because these days at the kirtan, you complained to Shyam instead of looking for him. 'I've turned a dark hue, my beloved.' Miss Das maintained that Miss Bose had fallen in love because the expression of yearning on your face now was characteristic of those who are madly in love. Mrs Shankar said that your sickly complexion was due to a liver dysfunction and Chetan Mama, after observing your appearance and behaviour came to the conclusion that you had developed arthritis, and your own family surmised that you were drained by the stress created by your responsibilities. Everyone had his or her own theory about your condition. But it was true that you were conscious of your responsibility, the responsibility whose foundation had been laid securely with cement and mortar, which you couldn't budge even though you were trying your best. It could neither be washed away by bitter medicines nor did the foundation shift after you lifted heavy, unwieldy trunks and beds behind closed doors, neither did the pitiful invocations to Bhagwan bring it down. The magnificent building continued to be raised in the darkness and in the meantime, like a poor old woman, you couldn't manage the few pots and pans in your cottage. Finally, you lost hope. Hope begets restlessness, and hopelessness brings about peace. You were finally at peace because, having lost, you had decided that you would take three months off and go away somewhere!

Git! O Gita!

But you didn't go anywhere. You're still in the Women's Hospital of the town where the Theosophical College is located. It was only day before yesterday that you were forced to come here after you suddenly developed pains. Just a few days ago, you had succeeded in having your leave approved. Your leave begins today. But you're still here, although as if you're nowhere. Sita has been asleep for a while on the black dhurrie, but her eyes are squeezed shut as though she's in terrible pain. And you're stretched out on the white bed sheets, still and unmoving, as if even the burning rays of the past couldn't melt you.

Stretch out on the bed Gita, move your arms and legs, gather your long hair and arrange it on your pillow and, feeling the tingling of milk in your breasts, sob, moan, weep, because the one who would have eased the natural ache in your breasts is not nestled in your arms. Instead, he is in a magnificent mansion far far away from the confines of the hospital, sucking at Begum Ghafar's withered breasts and she is certain that the fountain of maternal love will erupt from her bosom in the form of milk. *Uffoh!* Gita! And lying here on the hospital bed, your bosom is engorged, as if in a short while, bursting with milk, it will explode like the mouth of a volcano, there will be milk flowing everywhere on your bed, in the entire hospital, in that grand bungalow where an infant, born two months early and coming into the world crying, is sucking at a dried-up breast. There will be milk everywhere, until everything will sink in the milk, including the stones, that those belonging to two different religions hurled at each other just before sunset today, those knives as well which pierced the bellies and chests of human beings, the blood too that has congealed on the streets and also the fire that was ignited because a Hindu child had been placed in the lap of a Muslim, and the shame too that consumes your family. In essence, everything will sink in the flood of milk, will be cleansed and purified by motherhood, the milk that the spirit of motherhood creates, the spirit which you, Gita, expressed without first seeking permission from society. But all this will only happen if you so desire. You look as cold as the stove in a Bengali house ravaged by famine, the cold stove that you tried to warm up by collecting contributions in a place so far away from Bengal, including in the donations your favourite and only Banarasi sari that you sent to a relief committee in Calcutta, because you loved Bengal, its culture, its literature, its music and songs, its dance, its colour—in other words you loved everything about Bengal. So much so that people who knew you thought you were biased in its favour. But at this moment, it seems that except for the cold stove, you love nothing about Bengal. Are you exacting revenge from Bengal because it couldn't offer you a companion from its vast expanse?

Gita! Gita!!

There is widespread disturbance in the township. The husk attached to the wheat is flying about everywhere. Your name is on everyone's lips. The ones who are cheerful and contented are laughing at you, those who are disgruntled are calling you names. The college administration has decided to ask for your resignation. It's fine if a rotten egg is placed in front of you, but the moment it breaks, it makes the observer feel nauseated. And today, a group of conscientious townspeople have formed a delegation and, and jumping over and circumventing the blood in the streets, have appeared before the authorities to say that, Sir, the meaning of handing over the product of a Hindu's clandestine misdeed to a Muslim so that he may make it his own means that one more Muslim has been added to a population of ten crore Muslims. The Hindus can't tolerate this because the only relationship existing between the two groups that lived together for years is now merely that of a struggle between the minority and the majority. The hospital authorities ignored this increase and that is why so much trouble ensued. Otherwise, well, Sir!

Gita!! O Gita!!

Look how slowly this blighted night creeps, as if it is carrying on its shoulders the bier of the world's dead conscience. And the moon is hanging over the mango trees that are heavy with blossoms, a pale and sad moon. The light of the stars slowly dims and there is a muted tinkle in the breeze, as though there are witches dancing in the burial grounds, celebrating. *Uff!* How horrible this night has become. I'm standing at your bedside, whimpering, and you are immersed in your own self, like a disgruntled, oppressive husband. But Gita Rani, can anyone reject one's own life? It is cowardice to renounce life, it is desertion. Everyone is laughing at you, making fun of you.

Bhagwan Das is laughing, Shyam is snickering, righteousness and religion are tittering, politics and patriotism are cackling— and the statue placed in the hall of the Theosophical College has actually been made just for laughing. But you neither laugh nor cry. Laugh, break into loud laughter, and embracing me lovingly, come out laughing. That will silence everyone. All the dreadful wellsprings of laughter will dry up. Only your laughter will remain, filled with life and pure truth.

Gita! O Gita!!

Hold me close. Clasp me to your breast. Listen! Listen! What is this fluttering in the air, as if there's a heavy mantle flying about, what is this thumping of heavy boots, look, there's darkness all around, the shadow of death's black mantle, the yellowing moon is darkening, the stars are disappearing. Get up, Gita!

O Gita!

8

The Third Floor

Halima Bai, seated in a room on the fourth floor of the Halima Bai Building, suddenly lost her temper. She had been listening to the convoluted, detailed complaints presented by Dilliwallah, the leader of the delegation.

'But how can I believe what you say, just like that?' she said. 'Look, tell me, if someone comes to your house and says something, you will first investigate and then . . . '

Infuriated, Dilliwallah interrupted her.

'If you don't throw her out, we'll have to bring the police in. This is not proper at all, that too in a place where respectable people live . . . '

'O baba, why do you get so angry? She's not related to me, but let me investigate first.' Saying this, Halima Bai sent for the custodian steward and instructed him, in a severe voice, to make inquiries. After this, the delegation led by Dilliwallah made its exit.

Halima Bai banged the door shut and cast a glance through her window at the Rabiya Bai Building. This was her

90

grandmother's property. Seeing it, she remembered her old, sallow-skinned grandmother for whose death she had to wait a long time. The Rabiya Bai Building was dilapidated, its paint tarnished, windows blackened with broken panes, and it had squeaking wooden floors. She would say to her steward, 'When this building collapses, I will build an eight-storey apartment building in its place. It's no use renting out small rooms these days. If the rooms are big, the Americans will pay ten times the rent we get now.'

But for now, the building stayed. Miss Dorothy Pereira, the accomplished ballroom dancer, lived in one of the flats of that buidling. She was the person against whom a complaint had just been lodged by the people in that building. Halima Bai was disappointed because Miss Dorothy was not only the building's oldest tenant, she was also Halima Bai's best tenant. Whenever Halima Bai's workers casually mentioned that a rent hike was in order, Miss Dorothy agreed to pay without a word of protest. She also didn't ask for a reduction in the rent when she had the flat whitewashed once a year.

'She's alone, but there has never been any disturbance of any sort in her flat', Halima Bai thought. Her eyes sought out Miss Dorothy's rooms again and again. The shutters had been painted blue, and all the glass panes in the windows and doors were intact and clean.

But the issue was not related to keeping the place clean. If that were the issue, then one would be looking at the area in the corridor outside Dilliwallah's own room, which was the filthiest in the building. As a matter of fact, the entire building was a pile of filth. The discarded remnants of leather from the Fancy Shoemakers factory on the ground floor were always strewn about on the footpath outside. On the second storey, the

Bohri woman would remove the tails and whiskers of shrimp and throw them on the stairs. And whenever her neighbour, Mr Douglas, suffered a fit of coughing during a violin lesson, he would open the door and spit out the phlegm at the Bohri woman's door. If the question had been one of making a mess, then the naïve and simple Memon woman, Miss Zenab Bai, could also be faulted; she was a good neighbour, but she would wrap her baby's faeces in a piece of paper and dump it quietly in the trash can outside Dorothy's door.

'*Uffoh!* People are crazy, they can't mind their own business', Halima Bai exclaimed. She drew the curtain on the window overlooking the Rabiya Bai Building, and sat down to finish stitching the trim on her black dupatta.

Halima Bai was justified in wishing that people mind their own business. But except for Miss Dorothy, there was no other tenant in the Rabiya Bai Building who minded only his or her business. People living here had come from different parts of the country and, in an effort to forget the reality of their own lives, they spent their time probing into the lives of others. But Miss Dorothy Pereira was so absorbed in her own life that everyone found her extremely attractive. The men were in love with her and although the women in the building were jealous of her, all of them tried to imitate her mannerisms and the way she dressed.

She usually stayed inside her flat the whole day. Dressed in an old Japanese kimono with a large floral print, and doused in talcum powder, she walked on her wooden Japanese clogs like a skiff bobbing on the waves, its sails unfurled. Who knows whether her gait had something to do with the special shape of her Japanese clogs or if it was something else. Nevertheless, her gait was indeed unusual. Dilliwallah's rapidly maturing daughter gazed at her so attentively that her mother, Razia Begum, was forced to exclaim, 'Girl, why are you looking at her swaying about like that? It would be right to keep someone like her out of one's sight.'

But Miss Dorothy wasn't about to stay out of sight. Every morning, she roused her little servant boy sleeping in the corridor outside her door, and not only cleaned her own flat but also supervised the cleaning of the corridor. How could the sweeper woman engaged to clean the building be expected to clean the corridor when, being the lazy person she was, she didn't even wash the toilets properly? Razia Begum looked askance at all this cleaning because she was sure that Dorothy was merely making preparations to receive her lovers. However, Dorothy's other neighbour, the Memon woman Zenab Bai, often maintained that if the people coming to Miss Dorothy's house were her lovers, they would stay the night once at least.

'But that's because they come during the day', Razia Begum explained with vehemence. 'She's not some respectable woman who has to entertain her lovers at night, in secret, so her husband doesn't catch her.' Hearing this Zenab Bai became exasperated and kept her mouth shut.

But how could this remark be ignored? Everyone knew that whenever Miss Dorothy had guests, the door of her flat remained wide open. If the door was shut, one could be sure that she was alone. And when she was alone, her neighbours were certain that she was either taking a nap or she was practicing her dancing.

When Miss Dorothy first came to this building, she tried to conceal her involvement with dance from the other tenants. But when the Bohri woman living below her flat began complaining about the excessive *khat-khat* from upstairs, Miss

Dorothy came right out and proclaimed that dance was her life and she would dance no matter what. How would she stay alive if she didn't dance? When their quarrel worsened, the Bohri woman's neighbour, Mr Douglas, the violin-wallah, switched rooms with her. And for this reason now, when Miss Dorothy danced upstairs, Mr Douglas played his violin below in tune with Miss Dorothy's dance steps. The old man Douglas, who had a black funeral chit stitched to his white coat every second or third month, was frequently unemployed and looking for work. Miss Dorothy didn't have any contact with him either except for an occasional 'Hello'. But she did invite him over once a year at Christmas, for lunch. None of this discouraged the young Babu on the second floor from intercepting the small notes addressed to Mr Douglas, which contained such messages as, 'There's an opening for a violin player in such-and-such hotel, or film company—go immediately. Maybe you'll have some luck.'

Because of these notes, the Bihari Babu viewed Mr Douglas with suspicion and often kept his ear glued to his door in order to check Mr Douglas' quiet exit to the third floor. But when he would suddenly wake up the next morning after having fallen asleep during the time he was supposed to be on the lookout, he would discover, to his dismay, that the door to old Douglas' flat was shut. 'See, there! He's still asleep, he must have stayed up late, of course!' he would tell himself.

His distress continued and one day he arrived at Dorothy's door. His soft knock in the silence of the night resulted in Dorothy's sudden appearance at her door, and seeing him she began to speak in a very loud voice.

'I will hand you over to the police—who do you think I am?' Dorothy had Babu's tie in her hand. Dilliwallah and the

Memon shopkeeper freed him from Dorothy's grasp with much difficulty.

Following this event, Dilliwalla's wife, Razia Begum, was overheard making a claim with absolute confidence during a *milad* held in the building.

'Listen to me, that woman my husband was keeping in Bolton Market made a similar fuss one day and, convinced that she meant what she was saying, my husband had a nikah with her. Just wait and see, now this Miss Dorothy will also make a grab for somebody. She's a really crafty Bumbaiwalli.'

Zenab Bai, who was from Bombay, took offence at this. 'Miss Dorothy is not from Bumbai, she's from Goa.'

Miss Dorothy was from Goa. She had never tried to cover up this fact. So many times, standing in the corridor, she had admitted in the presence of Zenab Bai and Razia Begum that as a child she travelled with her mother from Goa to Bumbai. And she loved Bumbai, she loved Bumbai very much.

'I went to school there, and I was a governess to the children of a very rich seth.' She leaned against the wall and had a distant look in her eyes.

'Governor . . . your mother perhaps', Razia Begum said sourly.

'Governess', Dorothy tried to explain nicely. 'A person who takes care of children—that's what she is called in English.'

'An ayah then', Razia Begum said decisively.

Swaying, her Japanese clogs making a noise with every step, Dorothy walked away to her room. Zenab Bai followed her. She had been present as well because it was only after Dorothy had given the baby sweets, that she started talking about her childhood and her mother.

That day Dorothy talked about herself at length with Zenab Bai.

'So much I did in Bumbai. I learned ballroom dancing there. The owner of the dancing school, he paid me so much to dance as partner to the young men, but I didn't care about the money. I was fond of dancing. Everybody there would say, you're like Loretta Young, you should work in films. But the filmwallahs there didn't appreciate my beauty. Then people advised me to go to Hollywood, but I couldn't come up with enough money for the fare. There was a film director in Bumbai, the bastard swallowed money he had borrowed from people. He also gobbled up my money. When I asked for my money, he said, come with me to Pakistan, I will help you find work there, there's a demand there for directors and heroines. Then, I came to Karachi. But the filmwallah here didn't appreciate my beauty either. Have you seen Loretta Young in *The Garden of Allah*, Bai?' She paused in the course of her tale and posed the question to Zenab. But Zenab Bai had never seen an English film. Dorothy was disappointed. She had to face disappointment often.

'The men there hadn't seen Loretta Young either', she said with a sigh and then, taking out the pins from her golden hair, she shook it loose. Suddenly her golden hair surrounded her face like a waterfall shimmering in the sun.

But Mr Douglas, on the other hand, had seen Loretta Young's films and had also seen Dorothy Pereira in Bumbai. 'She was a number one popular dancer. Her mother took care of the seth's children while she attended school. Then one day, her mother yelled at the seth, accusing him of keeping her daughter in his room. I tried to calm her down, told her to stay quiet. And she did and afterwards, Dorothy began to soar in the skies. In those days, I was giving violin lessons to one of the seth's sons. A little, doll-like girl, she was, and now she doesn't even talk to Uncle, just writes notes.'

Surrounded by pictures of his dead relatives, Mr Douglas would look at Dorothy's handwritten notes and talk to himself in solitude. One of his daughters, married to a Sikh, was living in Lucknow.

'If I were in Lucknow, would this have happened?' Mr Douglas would ask Hanif, the owner of Fancy Shoemakers. 'One should marry within one's own faith.'

'Of course, of course', Hanif would offer vehement agreement. But there's no harm in falling in love with someone not of the same faith as yourself, Hanif would silently tell himself because he had fallen in love with Dorothy Pereira the day she got off a car and walked into his factory. Baffled by her presence, Hanif and all his workers immediately stood at attention. In the first place, it was Dorothy standing before them, and secondly, she had just got out of a car; furthermore, she was also speaking.

'Look, I want a pair of sandals just like these. I can't find them in the bazaar.' Dorothy retrieved a picture of a half-naked Marilyn Monroe from her purse and extended it towards the worker. The sandals in question encased Monroe's feet.

'I'm the proprietor', Hanif croaked. After this, a price was quickly agreed upon and, walking away with her usual melodic gait, Dorothy strode up the Rabiya Bai Building staircase. In the meantime, Hanif's soul, dragged out of his body, followed Dorothy.

Hanif had never set foot on the third floor, although Dilliwalle sahib had often invited him to come up. 'Look here young man', he had said, 'the Dilli and Lucknow quarrel has been laid to rest now and all that matters is Karachi. Come and visit us sometime, your aunt always praises you, she says he's a very decent young man, he never lets his eyes wander unnecessarily.'

But Hanif was always too busy working. Also, Razia Begum had come to him so often, accompanied by her young daughter with orders for shoes for her, that he was now afraid of her. He had told her repeatedly that he didn't accept private orders and if she wanted a pair of shoes made in his factory, she should go to a shoe store where they were being sold. Did she think he and his workers were cobblers?

But that day, he wanted to make the trip to Razia Begum's house. After all, she lived on the third floor, the same third floor on which Dorothy Pereira lived, Dorothy, whose flat was famous for its cleanliness and decoration, who travelled in cars, cars that were not hers. As a matter of fact, the story, according to Zenab Bai, was that these cars were the property of the film companies who employed her to give their heroines dance lessons. It was rumoured that she danced in films as well. What these films were, no one knew. Once Hanif happened to get a glimpse of Dorothy in a group dance sequence in a film and he turned to tell his friend who was with him, but in the very next instant, she had disappeared.

'You know, it's said she makes thousands', his friend, who had been duly impressed, said. 'But our friend Kallu was saying that she also dances in hotels with young men and probably gets a lot of money for that as well.' Someone else had also suggested that dancing was merely a cover for making money in other ways. Hanif's friend continued to provide further information about Dorothy. He had no idea that Hanif had been her admirer for a long time. If the episode in which Babu sahib of the second floor had been insulted on the third floor hadn't already taken place, Hanif would have declared his love to Miss Dorothy a long time ago.

'Listen, who knows what's true and what's not, sometimes people say one thing, sometimes another', Hanif would say in exasperation, when he heard his workers exchange all kinds of gossip about Dorothy. But when, contrary to his policy, he began working on the sandals for Miss Dorothy himself, the master craftsman, Bundu, giggled meaningfully.

'Are the sandals bait then?'

And indeed, the sandals did end up as bait.

It was mere coincidence that he worked on the sandals late one night and arrived later than usual at Kallu Lucknavi's shop. The food, except for a plate of chana dal and meat, was finished. He ate the dal and meat and when he returned, he spread out a bedding on the floor of his shoe factory and picked up the picture of Marilyn Monroe that Miss Dorothy had left with him; he wanted to imprint the design of the shoe on his mind.

And then, with the intent of memorizing the pattern, he gazed a long time at Dorothy's favourite sandal, and before long, Marilyn's leg metamorphosed into Dorothy's leg. In the ensuing confusion, he developed indigestion. Early in the morning, he made a dash for the common toilet on the ground floor. Finding the toilet occupied, he ran to the second floor, swearing as he made his way up the stairs. When Mr Douglas tried to engage him in conversation, he gestured his condition with his hand and sped towards the bathroom. But one of the toilets was broken and swimming in a sea of filth, and the other one was blocked. Under ordinary circumstances, he would never have considered going to the third floor, but since he wasn't really thinking, he found himself on the third floor. The moment he touched the door handle someone released the latch from the inside and he nearly hurtled into Miss Dorothy Pereira. Miss Dorothy's semi-smouldering cigarette fell from her mouth and slipping down her Japanese kimono, landed on the floor, and her aluminum mug crashed noisily against the door.

'Hello', Miss Dorothy said in a flustered tone. But he was already inside the bathroom with the door shut behind him.

A combination of bathroom odour and cigarette smoke. 'Sometimes, when things are mixed, they're strangely interesting', he told himself, the thought leaping like lightning through his mind.

When he had finally recovered from his predicament, he broke into a laugh. How strange he felt—surprised, disappointed and affectionate all at the same time.

Should he have met Dorothy here or not is another question. Anyway, Hanif had the sandals ready by evening, as he had promised. After that morning's debacle, he was unable to touch the sandals himself. God alone knows what these lovers do once they creep into your head, because once they're there, they only make you suffer. If Hanif hadn't gone to the third floor with the shoebox tucked under his arm, the matter would have not gone any further.

When Hanif arrived, he found the door to Dorothy's flat ajar.

Everything appeared soft and dreamy in the blue light. The pink tasselled curtains, the blue dhurrie, the red cotton carpet, cushioned chairs and paper flowers. And buried in the cushioned depths of the chair was a thickset man. Suddenly, Hanif remembered that he had seen a car parked downstairs and he felt as if the shoes on his feet were weighing him down.

In the very next instant, Dorothy was trying out the golden sandals to make sure they were comfortable. She was wearing a black kamdani sari at this time. Her short, golden hair tucked in with hairpins seemed strangely at odds with her dark complexion.

'Beautiful choice', the fat man said, gazing dreamily at her.
'What is the price?' He turned his attention to Hanif.

'Price of what?' Hanif asked in a sarcastic tone.

'Forty rupees dear', Dorothy said, opening her purse. And
the fat man extended five ten-rupee notes towards Hanif.

'Keep it all, it's a reward', the fat man said and Hanif felt as
if he had suddenly developed springs on the soles of his feet. He
leaped and clutched the fat man by his throat. Dorothy began
teetering on the heels of her new sandals.

'Who do you think we are, you pimp, your servants?'
Hanif screamed. And the dreamlike atmosphere underwent
a transformation. The fat man freed his neck and raised his
hands.

'I'm very sorry, mister, please, please . . . '

Dorothy came between them and placed a hand on Hanif's
hand. In the next instant, Hanif was running down from the
third floor, his entire being drowning in outrage. As he was
crossing over the scattered strips of leather on the footpath, he
saw the car in which Dorothy was about to leave with the fat
man. He hit the side of the car with his clenched fist and then
blew at the dust he had picked up from the car.

'The bastard thinks I'm a cobbler. I would have bashed him
so well, he wouldn't have forgotten the licking easily. If only she
hadn't come in the middle . . . '

On his way to the Irani's hotel, Hanif continued muttering
angrily to himself. 'I say Hanif, you're a fool. It was silly of
you to follow the example of Nawab Mirza Afghan and start
making shoes. All the time you said, "Well, a pearl will always
be a pearl, it doesn't matter", so now stitch those pearls on the
shoes! Who knows who you are in Karachi, or that your father
was from a good family? If you had finished school, then you

could have become an office superintendent. How difficult could it have been to pass tenth class after you had passed ninth?

But when Hanif returned to the bedroom in his factory, after spending a long time at the Irani's hotel, it was late at night and he had mollified himself. 'Hunh! All kinds of people from high-class families do all types of work these days. Doesn't our own Sayyed Sahib run an animal hide business?' Then he stepped out of his room and examined the sign on his shop. 'Fancy Shoemakers.' He was pleased with himself. 'Thank God there's a language in one's country that can transform the worst possible meaning into something attractive. How awful if the sign said in Urdu 'Shoemakers of Very Good Shoes.'

Then he moved his bedding roll with a kick and sat down on it with the air of someone sitting on a very fancy sofa.

'Proprietor, Fancy Shoemakers', he murmured under his breath and gazed at the wall as if Dorothy was standing before him. 'And you are?'

'Miss Dorothy Mug-walli.' The words jumped into his head and, bending to remove his shoes, he laughed triumphantly. He was feeling so sure of himself that if Dorothy had indeed been here in his presence, he would not have trembled fearfully.

But when Dorothy did come, Hanif was dreaming that his mother and his wife had arrived and he had found a room close to his factory for which he didn't have to provide a down payment. In reality, his mother and his wife had come with him from Lucknow, but were still living at his uncle's house in Rawalpindi, counting the days to their move to Karachi. He saw in his dream that his wife was sitting close to him and when he tried to kiss her, she shyly moved her face away from him—and pushed away his hand.

His eyes flew open. There was light in the room and
Dorothy was shaking his hand, trying to wake him.

'I was so upset at dinner time, I'm very sorry—you were
insulted, I was so angry. You left your forty rupees in my flat.
Here mister, take your money.' God knows what else Dorothy
was saying. Her golden hair, released from the bonds of the
pins, had come loose and betrayed their length, her lips were
dry and her eyes were drowsy and tinged with sympathy. Hanif
thought he was still dreaming.

'Now don't be angry, all right? I don't like to hurt people.
I've never gone to anyone's room, but I thought I will definitely
come here, don't tell anyone. I don't like anyone to be insulted
and that's why I came to say sorry. Here's your money . . . '

Somehow, Hanif's swimming head came to rest on his
knees. Once again, he was overwhelmed by the feelings of
shame that the incident had generated. There was something
else as well; he wanted to weep and within seconds, he broke
into tears. Distraught, Dorothy leapt to his side and bending
over, kissed his cheek. 'No, no, don't cry, no . . . ' Dorothy was
saying.

But Hanif felt as if a volcano had erupted inside him.
Because Dorothy was in his room, she wouldn't threaten to call
the police.

'I love you, Miss Dorothy . . . I love you.' During his
attempts to embrace the struggling Dorothy, this sentence in
English kept falling out of Hanif's mouth.

Finally, as though she was flashing the blade of a knife as a
self-protective measure, Dorothy said, 'Then you'll forego the
forty for the sandals and give me an additional ten.'

What does it matter that the residents of the Rabiya Bai
Building didn't get a whiff of the deal that took place that

night? Razia Begum was fully aware of all the details of the deals that followed. The new sandals appearing on Dorothy's feet didn't drop from the sky; it was obvious they came from downstairs. And the tray set elegantly with tea that Dorothy's servant took downstairs every morning, and the tray arrayed with qorma and chapati that he brought back upstairs, were not part of just a business deal.

Razia Begum thumped her chest with her fist and proclaimed, 'Such women make men prepare tea for them, but if they start making tea for the men instead, then it means the wretches are out to get them.'

No one was ready to accept Razia Begum's theory. True, Hanif had come to the third floor many times to visit Dorothy, but he always sat in the room with the door fully open. Her face half-veiled with a corner of her dupatta, Razia Begum had passed by that door several times on the pretext of visiting the toilet, taking a quick peek each time, but she was unable to catch a glimpse of a single objectionable occurrence. But she continued to bemoan that a good person like Hanif was about to be corrupted. As a matter of fact, others could also see that there was little hope for Hanif. Either he was in the factory all day, sewing strips of leather on the machine himself in the presence of his workers, or he could be seen knotting those strips together as he walked about. Ustad Bundu, his main worker, went around prophesying the ultimate collapse of Hanif's business to all the residents of Rabiya Bai Building. And indeed, Hanif had changed completely. Who knows what magic potion Dorothy mixed in with his tea? He was constantly making trips to the third floor, dressed in a suit, a necktie dangling from his hands. Dorothy showed him how to tie a necktie every day, but he promptly forgot and had to go to

Dorothy so she could knot it for him. Sometimes, the two went out on a rickshaw. But there were nights when Dorothy went alone to the film company. On the mornings following those nights, Hanif would return the tea Dorothy had sent down for him.

'I have to go to the film company, Hanif is making a mistake', Dorothy would complain to Zenab Bai after the tea was returned, speaking Urdu in the special Bombay lingo. 'You tell me Bai, I will die if I don't dance. You know Bai, I love to dance.' And then, shutting the door she would start her morning practice. Even Zenab Bai liked watching her dance with such abandon. Just then, Mr Douglas' violin from the second floor seemed to be crying out, 'Dorothy is dancing! Dorothy is dancing!' On hearing this, Hanif's grievances would disappear and Zenab Bai would see Hanif standing in his doorway, watching Dorothy as if he were mesmerized.

When Dorothy went out with Hanif, she would always be wearing sandals that matched the colour of her sari. When she climbed down the stairs with a musical *thak-thak* of her heels, the women from the third floor peered at her through the doors of their rooms. In Zenab Bai's presence one day, Razia Begum's daughter said very longingly, 'Ammi jaan, could you get me red sandals like the one Dorothy has—shall I go and ask Hanif Bhai?'

Razia Begum stopped to think. Then she said, 'Ah, now our girls will compete with her. And this Hanif, may he be cursed, he runs from respectable people as if they will bite him. He didn't make sandals for my daughter and every day he's with that wretch with a new box under his arm.'

This was the first time that Razia Begum didn't scream and shout. Instead, she donned her burka and went around warning all the residents of Rabiya Bai Building, who had children, of the danger that awaited them.

'Even a witch spares her own neighbourhood when she's looking for sustenance.' This was the important proof she had.

The next day, a delegation was formed and a complaint was lodged with Rabiya Bai Building's owner, Halima Bai. The custodian had to be dispatched to the third floor to investigate.

Dorothy's door, painted blue and sporting a shiny handle, was shut. Zenab Bai was pleased that Dorothy was alone at this time. She was standing quietly and expectantly in her doorway, and behind her husband, her face covered with her dupatta, but not her bosom, Razia Begum was thinking, 'Let's see, she'll say no to everything, but how will she deny the story about Hanif.'

The violin was playing on the second floor and in the room on the third floor the *khat-khat* of heels could be heard. Of late, Dorothy had developed a great fondness for Spanish gypsy dances.

Halima Bai's custodian kept beating his stick as he walked down the corridor. Behind him was a line consisting of most of the male tenants of the building. The playing of the violin ceased but the *khat-khat* continued. The custodian pushed the door open with the handle of his stick.

Zenab Bai's heart stopped. Dorothy was not alone behind the door today.

Her arms draped around Hanif's neck, she was still clicking her heels and twitching like a chicken that has been freshly slaughtered.

'You see, you see, the place has been turned into a brothel.' Wali Sahib was the first one to speak.

'Throw the whore out', Babu Sahib from the second floor, screamed.

Dorothy jumped away from Hanif. Then, dressed in her short skirt and a blouse that revealed her stomach, she came out defiantly.

'Why did you open my door, Ameen Bhai?' The tenants of the building had heard Dorothy speak in such a loud voice for the first time. She was addressing the custodian. 'You will shut my door yourself, do you understand, you will shut the door now!' Dorothy screamed.

'Yes, so that you can have fun here', Wali Sahib clenched his teeth and lunged at Dorothy.

'You can also have fun in your house Molbi Sahib', Dorothy shouted. 'This is my house, I pay rent.'

'Who do you think you are to talk to us like this? You wretch, you vile creature, harlot, you have no place in this respectable neighbourhood.' Razia Begum couldn't see her husband being insulted and jumped into the fray.

And then, what took place next should not have taken place. Dorothy ripped apart the respectable neighbourhood and she uttered as many insults as she knew both in English and Bambaiya. She accused Razia Begum of nursing plans to entrap Hanif for herself. A skirmish ensued among the women.

'Yes, I am crazy with love for Hanif, he is crazy for me, I will give my life for him', Dorothy was blabbering, as she hit Razia Begum and Razia Begum pummelled her.

Suddenly, Hanif's stony form came to life. He walked into the corridor and boldly took hold of Dorothy's hand.

'I'm warning you all, don't you dare touch my woman', Hanif said forcefully, glaring at everyone.

'She's not your woman', Babu Sahib said, moving back.

Just then, all of Hanif's workers arrived. Now Hanif became bolder.

'Oh, so she's not my woman. I see!!' Hanif's face turned red. Then he turned to his worker, Bundu Khan. 'Ai bhai, Bundu Khan, tell someone downstairs to run and fetch some laddus. Maulana Wali, the fight that started in Lucknow has been left behind there, we're in Karachi now. Please say the words of the marriage vow and Allah will ease your problems.'

After saying this, he gently pushed Dorothy back into her room and shut the door.

When the custodian returned to Halima Bai, he brought laddus with him. Halima Bai's interest in this matter was limited only to Dorothy's status as a permanent tenant.

But the interest of the tenants of Rabiya Bai Building remained intact.

Ustaad Bundu, Hanif's worker, worried too much about Hanif's future. He used to say, 'You wait and see, one day when you sit down and put the figures together, you'll realize how stupid you've been. Mian, one can only be successful in this business of making shoes if the employer keeps an eye on the workers. When I'm working, I also have to keep an eye on the workers.'

But dressed in pyjamas, his sandals flip-flopping, Hanif went up to the third floor and tried to explain the correct way of cooking qorma and kababs. Dorothy was very intelligent, but managing the spices in different recipes is not child's play. Something went wrong every day. Although, when she stood in front of the stove and turned out chapatis expertly, Hanif was reminded of the chapatis cooked by his wife. The wife who couldn't wait to come to Karachi and would make his mother write frequently to him. When these letters fell out of Hanif's pocket and landed on the bed with springs, Dorothy took them to Razia Begum. She would get tired of hearing the same thing in the letters, but Razia Begum didn't tire of expressing the same sympathy each time.

'Ah, the poor thing, how far away Hanif has kept her, and then what must this be like for you? If we knew beforehand that Hanif had a wife and children . . . '

'Oh, so what, it's all right', Dorothy would shrug her shoulders and say, and, reaching inside her kimono with her hand, she would rub down the talcum powder she had hastily sprinkled on her bosom earlier.

'He says he's been in love with me ever since he saw me. What can happen?' You know, it's not possible to get a room in Karachi with a down payment and in Bumbai too, it's the same. I put down 3,000 for a three-room flat', Dorothy's expression seemed to say, as if she had just returned from Bumbai and then she would turn on the heels of her Japanese sandals and disappear into her flat. When Razia Begum made a trip to the bathroom a little later in the hope that she might catch Dorothy complaining to Hanif about her rival, she would instead be extremely disappointed to see Dorothy brushing off Hanif's shoemarks from her rug.

'Who knows why, despite my instructions, Hanif forgets to clean his shoes first on the straw mat before he comes in', Dorothy had lovingly complained about him to Zenab Bai many times.

What to say about Hanif? Everyone could see that after becoming Dorothy's prisoner, he had lost all sense. Leaving the workers in the care of Ustad Bundu, he would calmly come to Dorothy's flat with a bunch of coloured and golden leather strips. He had already kept a sewing machine there. He would adjust the leather into the machine, sit on the floor with his legs crossed and call out:

'Darling please give me lunch quickly, I have a lot of work to do.'

In the other room, Dorothy would quickly take off her apron, sprinkle herself with talcum powder again and come in and shout in mock anger.

'If you sit on the floor like a Hindu, I'm not going to give you food.' She would make a face and taking his hand try to pull him up. How could he ignore the little table she had set up in the other room.

'Oh, I forgot Memsahib, I forgot', Hanif would say, trying to kiss her, and then he would attack the food. Afterwards, forgetting the 'lot of work' he would fall sleep on Dorothy's bed and would sleep so soundly that he didn't know when she got up from the bed, when she washed the dirty dishes, when she ironed his wrinkled suit and polished his shoes.

'How silly you are Hanif', she would mutter to herself as she picked up the dirty shoe. 'People will say that you are the proprietor of a shoe factory and wear such dirty shoes. You'll wear the same shoes when we go out to the pictures or to a hotel, won't you?'

Dorothy was always worried about the day when this would happen, but Hanif forgot to take her out.

'He forgets everything when he sees me. Silly. He should worry about his business.' Dorothy would see the leather strips lying next to the machine and her anger grew. Then she would sit at the machine and start sewing the leather strips.

Hearing the sound of the machine, Zenab Bai would often drop in. On such occasions, Dorothy opened up a bundle of complaints before her.

'You know, Hanif has given everything up after he got me. All day he stays with me, then he says the business is suffering. He doesn't even take care of his accounts. If I don't go and demand the payment for the supplies at the shop, the workers won't get paid in the evening. You tell me Bai, how long can it continue like this?' Bent over the machine, Dorothy talked endlessly and she forgot that Zenab Bai's baby was whimpering. Actually after having lived with Hanif for so long, she had also become quite forgetful. In the morning, when she left to buy vegetables and meat and walked down the corridor, clattering her heels, the wicker basket slung on her arm, she promised the little boy, 'I will bring you toffees', and when she returned she had forgotten her promise.

'Don't tell anyone, but I know that Hanif's business has failed', she had confided to Zenab Bai many times.

But what was strange was that the number of workers in the Fancy Shoemakers factory was on the rise, and Hanif had told his Makrani neighbour on several occasions that if he gave up his room he would be willing to give him a down payment of 2,500 rupees.

This was why Razia Begum had insinuated that Hanif also appropriated Dorothy's earnings. 'The nikah was just a coverup', she whispered conspiratorially.

'Bai, how can I believe this. Dorothy doesn't even go to the film company in the evenings any more.' Zenab Bai shook her head with a worried look.

'Oh, don't pay any attention to that. What do you think is going on when she goes out during the day, all dressed up?' Razia Begum knew how to offer justifications.

'O Bibi, I know—she goes to pick up Hanif's business bill, and she also has to buy vegetables and meat from the bazaar— he just let one of his workers go', Zenab Bai said.

'Hunh! All excuses my dear. If there was nothing going on, the *khat-khat* of her dance we hear every day would have stopped and the old man downstairs would not be doing *noon-noon* on the English sarangi to keep tune with the *khat-khat!* Razia Begum stomped off to her room and plopped a paan into her mouth. And once again, Zenab Bai wished she could tell her that Dorothy has told Hanif that dance is her life—she will die if she can't dance. And Hanif, in turn, is crazy about her Spanish dance—tiny castanets in her hand, and wearing a short, ruffled skirt and blouse—Zenab Bai had seen with her own eyes that Hanif sat dressed in a suit instead of pyjamas and shirt, and she danced before him.

'I don't like it when Hanif wears pyjamas, I insist he wear a suit', Dorothy would complain to Zenab Bai. And then she would say, 'Hanif's business is down, he works too hard, he gets so tired, and that's why I look after his business. When the business improves, we'll hire a manager and then Hanif and I will go out every evening—hotel, picture, Clifton . . . ' And as she said all this, Dorothy's eyes took on a dreamy look, which made the little shadows hidden by her cheekbones emerge and her wide mouth opened a tad, revealing a shiny gold-capped tooth.

The Makrani tenant handed over his room to Hanif. The number of workers increased. Dorothy's small dining table was brought down and occupied a corner of the room. Hanif sat here and read novels while keeping an eye on the work, and also took orders for supplies. And this was when Dorothy was rushing. The moment a car or motorcycle pulled up in front of the building, Dorothy would leave everything she was doing and dash off downstairs.

'There, you see, it's her old lovers', Razia Begum would taunt. And Zenab Bai would be compelled to respond. It was her misfortune that she was friendly with Dorothy, who shared everything with her.

'Dorothy will go downstairs and talk in English with the men who come for the goods, Hanif can't speak English. Dorothy says without English, people won't give any advance.' Zenab Bai informed Razia Begum and looking down from the window, Razia Begum and her daughter laughed and laughed until tears streamed down their cheeks.

The Bihari Babu from the second floor had sworn to his Bohri neighbour that Hanif had withdrawn 1,500 rupees for a down payment to the Makrani from the bank he owned and the account was in Dorothy's name.

'And look how he uses her, what a shameless fellow', Babu said.

But Mr Douglas always said, 'Do you see how the Christian wife helps her husband, do you see how Hanif has changed? And do you know how good she is at dancing the Spanish dance? She's always been crazy about dancing. When she was a little girl, she would watch the seth's women dancing and copied their moves in no time.'

And the old Bohri woman looked at MrDouglas as if he had gone mad. What was this but madness that when Dorothy was dancing he was always downstairs, but he still knew how well she danced.

Then one day Hanif's wife, mother and his two children arrived from Rawalpindi in response to the letter Razia Begum had written to Hanif's wife. Weeping, lamenting, they came up straight to the third floor and sat down in the corridor with the veils of their burkas lifted.

'Oh, what has he done, left us in a strange place and turned away from us, *arrey*, he has set up a nice life for himself in Karachi.' Hanif's wife beat her breast and lamented in such a way that Razia Begum, Zenab Bai and the other women of the building gathered around her and also began to weep. Hanif's face was red with fury. He couldn't treat his wife to two slaps across the face in front of so many people. He dragged his wife by the hands and put her in Dorothy's flat and then gently picked up his mother by the arms.

'Amma, what can I do? It's impossible to find a flat here, otherwise I would have sent for you.'

That was when Dorothy arrived on the third floor with her basket of meat and vegetables. The women were still congregated in the corridor.

'Hanif Bhai, Dorothy is here', Razia Begum announced in a loud voice with her dupatta on her face, as if a runaway child had just returned.

Dorothy came in. Everyone was waiting. Then they were all disappointed.

Dorothy emptied out one of her rooms. The door in the middle was shut.

'What can be done?' Dorothy said, speaking in Bambaiya. 'No rooms will be available without money down and Hanif's business is very slow right now, the workers demand a lot of money, then they want a break for lunch in the afternoon, then they're out for two hours and no work during this time. I told Ustad Bundu, this isn't right, he said well they want to have a lunch break, so I said okay, we'll make a canteen, I'll give them lunch, the money for the food will be taken out of pay. There are canteens in all big factories. Now there's one room here, I'll manage somehow, and then when Hanif's business is not in loss, I'll charge a profit on the down payment.' Dorothy pushed all the furniture in her drawing room into one corner, and behind the curtain she set up a stove on a metal table next to the bed with springs, and placing a large pot on it, she sauteed the meat and then began to blow the coals with a pipe.

'But this second wife, you tell her to take care of the work in the canteen', Zenab Bai teased her.

'*Uffoh!* Hanif never liked her. He says she's a very lazy woman, she never took care of Hanif', she said contentedly with a wave of her hand.

In the evening, Mr Douglas waited a long time to play his violin and finally, when he had donned his white coat and was about to leave for the tuition session at the seth's house, he heard a noisy thumping coming from Dorothy's room. He jumped up and standing near the window and began playing the violin. 'Wonderful, wonderful', he kept saying as he played.

In the meantime, worried by the thumping sound, Razia Begum hastened to Khanam's room and when she found out what this noise meant she started crying and lamenting.

'*Arrey* Hanif, what's this horrible thing you're doing?'

Hanif couldn't explain anything to his mother and instead had to talk to Dorothy.

'Mr Douglas I said, "But dancing is my life, I'll dance and you'll watch me, after this I'm ready to die." Then Hanif said, "You don't know my mother, and so you should dance at Mr Douglas' home."' Dorothy smiled lovingly at Mr Douglas. 'May I dance here?'

Dorothy went into a corner of the room and changed into a long skirt and blouse and sat down on a chair, waiting for Hanif. Then, dressed in a suit, his tie in his hand, Hanif arrived at Mr Douglas's flat and then Dorothy danced and danced wildly.

A manager was hired to take care of the management of the factory. He was Hanif's brother-in-law. Dorothy had no time left after her work at the canteen, the designing of new sandals, taking new orders and collecting bills. So a Pakistani Anglo-Indian girl was hired as part-time help.

Soon after this, Razia Begum's daughter's wedding was arranged with Hanif's brother-in-law. Hanif's mother suggested that Hanif's daughter, by God's grace was now fourteen, and since times were bad, she should also be married. Razia Begum helped with this and Hanif's daughter was also engaged.

When business is expanded, profits decrease and then the weddings came along. The matter of Hanif's daughter's dowry became an issue. One day, she arrived in Dorothy's room with a bundle tucked under her arm and after struggling for a while she remembered the English word with which she was supposed to address Dorothy. 'Fair Darling, Baby said, "Mummy, look, these are the clothes Daadi is giving me for the wedding." I saw the clothes and felt such shame. Can you do something, Darling?'

Dorothy brought the matter of the dowry to Hanif's attention that very night, but Hanif resisted.

'What can I do? You're the one expanding the business, I can't do anything.'

'Can I say something darling? You won't be angry will you? I'll give Baby all the four saris you gave me, and also the golden sandals.'

Hanif showed his displeasure and Dorothy kept kissing him. He extricated himself from her embrace and left because this was the time she went to Douglas' house to dance.

And then Dorothy strutted down the corridor to Douglas' flat, and there she danced until she was wiped out.

Both weddings took place. The canteen kept afloat. Hanif's wife became ill, she was vomiting and so food from the canteen travelled there as well.

And then, like a cat, a newborn baby was heard crying in Dorothy's other room.

That day, Halima Bai's steward came to Dorothy's door and asked if she could increase the rent a little. Dressed in her skirt and blouse, tinkling rings on her fingers, Dorothy was coming out of her room without a kimono.

Hearing the steward mention the words 'rent increase' Dorothy suddenly turned into the Dorothy of five years ago when he had come to her door with a complaint from Halima Bai about her undesirable behaviour.

'What did you say? Increase the rent? Yes, why don't you come and rip off my skin?' she said, moving towards him with her chest stuck out, both hands on her hips. The steward flinched.

'You say rent? I say return the money I spent for the whitewash and painting these last ten years. Get out of here and go and tell your Halima Bai to return my money. What are you staring at me for?' Dorothy made a face, and tinkled the rings vigorously in front of his face.

And the steward's tongue was loosened and he lashed out at her. What he was saying was not nice. Razia Begum, Zenab Bai and Hanif's mother observed the scene from their doorways.

And, cursing and swearing, Dorothy went down the stairs to fetch Hanif.

But the factory keys in his hand, Hanif's brother-in-law was coming up the stairs and he told her that Hanif had gone with Miss Nina to book new orders.

It was then that Dorothy entered Mr Douglas' room, cursing and swearing.

'You see, Mr Douglas?'

Mr Douglas listened silently to the entire story, buffing his violin with his handkerchief and shaking his head the whole time.

Then Mr Douglas moved the bow over the violin strings. Dorothy, who had been standing all this time, sat down. When the melody gained momentum, she spread out her legs, her head resting against the back of the chair.

Mr Douglas saw spots of turmeric and marks made by charcoal on the skin of her thin legs. The tempo of his bow gained speed.

Dorothy's eyes were half-shut and her hands fell on the arms of the chair. Mr Douglas observed bits of dried flour crusted under her nails, and then the tinkling rings fell to the floor with a loud jingle.

'I'm tired, I'm very tired', Dorothy muttered, shutting her eyes. Mr Douglas placed the violin in its case and throwing on the white coat with the black border he left for his tutoring session, but who knows why his head was shaking as if he had heard the news of a loved one's death.

Razia Begum was whispering to Hanif's mother. 'She was prowling restlessly in the corridor all night like a cat, the wretch. She told Zenab Bai she was going to take care of the baby, because what do women in burkas know about raising children, she said—you see, she's from the ayah caste, isn't she? Protect the baby from her, my dear, she's not to be trusted.'

That was when Halima Bai looked out at Rabiya Bai Building through the window of her room. It appeared to her like her grandmother, dilapidated, sallow, grimy and then, peering through half-shut eyes she tried to single out Dorothy's rooms. The blue paint had worn away, the glass on the windows was cracked and foggy!!!

'Oh, so this is what Dorothy said', she turned to look at her steward and said wearily, 'Aiman Bhai, we'll have to demolish this building now, there's not a single proper tenant left there any more. We'll build new and bigger flats, whatever the white men want, give them.'

9

Bhag Bhari

This goes back to the time when I had just started my medical practice. During my years at the medical college, I had never had the experience of money raining on me. What else could one think of when one saw the big, long cars belonging to our senior professors? But when I obtained my degree and came to this bazaar, I realized that here in this shabby room on this street, it was impossible to get back wealth; acquired by selling my widowed mother's jewellery, it had been spent on books and college fees. What I did later on is another story and it's not important to mention it at this point. Yes, so, at that time when I was asked to deliver a baby in a far off village, I was very pleased. I put on an act and made a face and mentioned the anxiety that my innumerable patients would go through, but when the simple fisherman who was the messenger, raised my fee considerably, I agreed immediately. Two hundred rupees a day is not an insignificant amount. I was surprised and wondered, at the same time, why I had been selected in the place of any one of the other experienced and well-known lady doctors in the city.

I quickly informed my mother but instead of being pleased, she looked worried.

'It's too far away, don't go, a young unmarried woman may be a doctor a thousand times over, but still . . . '

I too was a little concerned about the 'still' factor. Then, I thought of a scheme. I told my younger brother to apply for a six-day leave from college and, at the same time, I convinced our old female servant, Mai, to don a white shalwar and kurta and accompany me by posing as a nurse. When I returned to the shabby room that constituted my clinic, it was immediately agreed upon that the nurse would get ten rupees a day during our stay in the village.

Then I asked, 'What time will the train leave?'

'I've brought the car', came the reply.

And I was worried this time, because in travelling from the village to the city, the car may have seen so much wear and tear that we might have to face car trouble on our way. My fears were proven unfounded though, when I left my mother praying for our safety. On the road outside, a brand new Cadillac waited for us. I regretted not demanding a higher fee.

On the way, my younger brother probed and was able to find out that we were headed for the district of Sargodha, to the house of a landowner. His wife had been insistent that a lady doctor from Lahore be called in to deliver her baby. This was a much-awaited first baby.

At the door of a large sitting room, in an area lit by yellow sunshine, the evening rations were being distributed to a dozen hunting dogs, about ten or twelve men controlling the dogs in chains. The dogs were briefly startled by our arrival but then returned to the job at hand. In this yellow sunshine, seated on a cushioned chair, his legs crossed, was the master of my

200-rupees-a-day, Malak Gul Nawaz—white silk dhoti and blue silk shirt, a heavy turban on his head and a hawk perched on his wrist. Its feathers pulled back, the hawk was clawing at the meat of a freshly-dead pigeon in Malak's hand. This was also the time of the hawk's meal.

I could never have conjured up this image of the Cadillac owner in my mind, but I was still quite impressed with my surroundings.

'Doctorni Sahib, you've gone through a lot of discomfort, I will make you happy', Malak Sahib said in a heavy voice, and with a piercing look.

The minute I entered the women's quarters, I realized that Malak Sahib's appearance was reminiscent of a picture of a king in one of my school books. A rolled-up turban extended down to his forehead, he was sitting cross-legged on the chair, a hawk perched on his hand—the only thing left was to hear him say, 'Ask and you shall receive.'

The appearance and atmosphere of the women's quarters were about the same as that of any old-fashioned home owned by a wealthy family. Sitting on colourful peerhis (low chairs), were several women dressed in multi-coloured dhotis and draped in thick shawls, all with silk trims, all looking somewhat harried. On a bed covered with a cotton sheet, was an old woman, also looking anxious and snorting hemp. I surmised that she must be an elder of the family. In fact, I was sure that she was Malak's mother, the elder Malakni. I expected her to get up and welcome me but I she didn't. I paused hesitatingly next to her bed.

As she observed me closely, Bari Malakni pulled up her shawl from her neck to her nose so that only her eyes were visible, which were now pinned on me. I was so upset that I prayed that all these women would immediately go into labour.

'Where is the patient?' I asked in a faltering tone.

All the women raised their necks like wild does, and stared at me with surprised looks.

'Where's the patient?' This time Mai asked sharply.

'God forbid, there's no one sick here', one of the women wearing large shiny flat nose rings on both sides of her nose replied sternly. Everyone else's gaze was fixed on me to express approval for what she had said.

I thought I had arrived late and hence was the object of everyone's displeasure. Perhaps, the poor thing was dead. And wearing an expression of extreme sadness, I returned to the Malak living room, which was crowded with sofas.

'I'm sorry Malak Sahib that I couldn't see the patient.'

I saw that my brother's face turned white when he heard what I had said, as though he had been crushed. Obviously, someone like him would need money for his education. But a smile appeared on Malak Sahib's fleshy face.

'Oh Doctorni Sahib, I hadn't informed my mother that I've sent for lady doctor from Lahore.' Malak Sahib got up and motioned me to follow him.

'But Malak Sahib, what's the use of going in now?' I said, looking disconsolate.

'Doctorni Sahib, please don't mind, actually my mother doesn't want to go against any tradition or custom and for this reason, I didn't mention anything to her', he said with a touch of bashfulness. And not understanding a thing, I followed him.

But the moment we came inside, an argument ensued between Malak Sahib and Bari Malakni. She kept pointing to me, and making a face said repeatedly, 'Sick, sick . . . hunh', she said, 'sick . . . '

I utterly failed to grasp the situation. Later on, Malak Sahib looked at me intently and whispered, 'Bari Malakni is very upset because you referred to the first pregnancy as "sickness". You know, pregnancy is a blessed event.' etc., etc.

'She's over there—in the palace ahead.' Malak Sahib pointed to the door of a big room as if he was giving information about some important politician's whereabouts and instead of laughing, I ended up feeling uncomfortable.

On enterering the big, dark room that had just one door and where I was to see the pregnant woman, I looked around for windows and skylights and then, disappointed, I turned to the women who were present in this room. A shabby-looking crone sat on the bed, her hands clasped around the pregnant woman's stomach and several other women like her were pressing the woman's head, or massaging her hands and feet. Everyone glared at me in such a way that I quickly diverted my attention to the decorations in the room. There were all kinds of coloured cots in every corner of the room, draped with beautiful cotton coverings, a variety of pots, crockery and fans on ledges. So this is the palace, I thought.

The pregnant woman was around thirty or thirty-five and was wearing all the jewellery typical of her region. If she weren't in the throes of labour, she would look quite beautiful.

I immediately addressed Mai and said that the pregnant woman be transferred to some other place, away from this crowded and airless room.

Mai passed the suggestion on to the woman and a commotion ensued. Fingers were raised to lips and noses to express surprise and displeasure, and during this commotion, breathless and panting, Bari Malakni walked in.

My suggestion was rejected by the combined ruling of all those present, since this type of room in the women's quarters was known as the 'palace' and it was essential that the daughter-in-law of the family deliver her baby here.

'The women should vacate the room.' My second suggestion was also vetoed because allowing the baby to land in the hands of a strange woman was in their view a foolhardy act. I then asked Mai to lift the bed covering at the foot of the bed, so I could have some privacy while I examined the pregnant woman.

This was her first pregnancy. The patient said, 'After many prayers and offerings, I have finally succeeded in carrying the baby full term. Before this, I could never complete all nine months. A beggar woman said that only one life will survive, the mother's or the baby's. Memsahib, please save both. We'll give you a big reward, we'll make you happy.' The patient was ashen from pain and fear. I comforted her and said everything is all right. On hearing this, the patient's eyes filled with tears of gratitude. And her nose started running. I had great difficulty cleaning her nose after I had wiped her eyes, because her nostrils were covered up by large nose bobs.

I had reassured her, but after hearing this story I was worried. Childbirth in an older woman is generally fraught with difficulty and the woman was having strange kind of pains and the baby's heartbeat was also somewhat sluggish. I prayed silently, 'O Allah, let me not fail, or else not only no Cadillac, but nothing else either.'

Night fell and the women were still talking to each other and taking turns pressing the patient's body. Mai whispered that I should also place my hands on the patient's stomach, because the women had been heard to say that the Doctorni was going to charge for doing nothing.

When the patient started moaning loudly and bit her lips, I ordered the women to leave the room. But some of the women immediately got up and placed two bricks next to the bed, and all of them began lifting the patient from the bed so that she could sit on her haunches on the bricks, and started saying, 'Bismillah, may all be well by Allah's will', as they tried to move her.

The patient was making an effort to do their bidding, and seeing all this I screamed in terror.

'Leave her alone, all of you, get out of here, you will kill her.'

No sooner did they hear this than the women started to make a fuss again. Mai took hold of the patient's arms and helped her lie down. And without any privacy, the baby finally appeared and began to cry weakly.

Shouts of felicitations and blessings rose up and more women thronged into the room from outside and several were crammed in the doorway, trying to look in. I could see that the patient was not doing very well. I gave an injection intravenously in the crook of her elbow. Seeing the needle, many of the women cried as though in pain. The patient fainted.

Suddenly, I heard guns being fired outside and then I heard the sound of drums and trumpets. After this, a lengthy process of rituals and practices to ensure good omens began and my attention was diverted from the patient.

Naturally, all this was very intersting for me, but what was strange was that even now the attitude of the people in this household was not friendly towards me, even though I had followed the example of other women and presented money in many of the rituals. But because I had had to fight with them for the patient and the baby every step of the way, the women merely put on a show of civility.

The beating of drums continued late into the night. The patient should have slept because she had fever. But she showed so much interest in all this commotion, that I was forced to keep my mouth shut. When, at the invitation of Malak Sahib I went out to the living room, my brother told me that there had been fireworks all night, and thousands of Malak Sahib's tenants sang and danced and Malak Sahib was showered with offerings. I was astounded by this ritual involving gifts.

But the next day, my astonishment turned to extreme fear.

It was winter and to make matters worse, clouds began to appear as dawn approached. I wanted to take a bath because I felt as if I was covered in layers of dirt. I had decided that since I was not on friendly terms with anyone in this house, I would not ask for hot water to run my bath. When the patient, who had barely had any sleep the night before, and who was running a high fever, turned on her side to face me and her eyes shone like her diamond nose bobs, I asked, 'Can I have some hot water for a bath?'

'Of course, of course, ji', she said with a smile and addressing one of the women who sat around the baby, said, 'Tell Bhag Bhari to heat water for Memsahib.'

After giving her an injection, I told Mai to take out clothes for me from the suitcase.

'We will give you the clothes, Memsahib, as a reward', the patient said with a playful smile.

And I was incensed. Does this illiterate woman think I'm a nurse and is going to reward me because she has given birth to a son?

'I'm a doctor Malakni, I'll just accept my fees, no clothes please', I replied indignantly and she looked at me in surprise.

'Memsahib, you've done us a great service, we would also like to do something for you. Allah has finally made this day possible.'

'All right, give my Mai something, I actually . . . '

Suddenly a girl of ten or twelve darted in. Beautiful, healthy, clear complexion, fine braids pulled back to reveal a pointed hairline, silver rings in her ears—this was Bhag Bhari.

'We'll give your Mai a suit of clothes as well, we've had a son, you know.' The patient was intent on convincing me to accept her gift.

And Bhag Bhari looked at me shyly.

'Did you prepare the hot water, Bhag Bhari?' the patient said to her. 'Take Memsahib to the bathroom.'

And I went to take a bath. While bathing, I kept thinking in exasperation—what kind of people are these, they're not conscious of anyone's status. Hunh! She'll give me clothes indeed!

Afterwards, I wrapped my hair in a towel and came out in the courtyard to relax in the sun. Bhag Bhari saw me from some corner of the house and ran and got an earthen brazier and placed it next to me. I softened towards her.

There was a lot of hustle and bustle in the house. A constant stream of women continued to arrive. A musical programme was now being organized.

Suddenly, Malak Sahib appeared near the women's quarters, coughing and clearing his throat as he approached. He stared at me closely, then asked a few questions about the new mother and the baby, after which he walked away towards Bari Malakni. A few minutes later, he left.

'Bhag Bhari, Bhag Bhari, Malak ji will be taking a bath, take a towel to the bathroom outside', Bari Malakni ordered.

And Bhag Bhari darted off with her usual alacrity to the men's quarters.

I was getting bored with all the arrangements in progress for the music programme. I wanted to take a nap. In my opinion, the new mother also needed rest. But my efforts were of no use. At this moment, I remembered a saying by some Western writer, which said that the countryside consists of nurturing graves. But oh my God, how noisy these graves, how stubborn and inflexible these corpses, how similar to each other. I'm a city dweller, but I can vow that if you bring the city chickens or dogs here, they will fall into a meditative trance and die, I told myself bitterly, and couldn't stop thinking. I didn't even think of my 200-rupees-a-day salary, and then suddenly, it seemed I was lost in the meditative trance of death. Truth was, I was extremely sleepy.

All of a sudden, Bhag Bhari stumbled past me, weeping, her face was flushed. Suddenly, she staggered and fell on the floor. Her blue dhoti was red with blood stains. I ran to pick her up. A commotion ensued and without warning, a woman came running from the direction of the kitchen and began to lament and weep in a forceful, melodious voice. This was Bhag Bhari's mother.

Bhag Bhari immediately opened her eyes.

'Ma'e! Malak ji! Malak ji Ma'e!' Bhag Bhari said, stretching out her arms towards her mother and then shut her eyes. The mother began to lament again in a loud voice.

What had transpired was clear. As a virgin, I was trembling fearfully. All the women gathered around her. Mai saw me shaking and helped me back to the new mother's room. All at once, Bari Malakni's thunderous voice was heard creating pandemonium in the courtyard.

Mai went to check on what was going on. I sat still, in shock.

In a short while, the commotion subsided. The new mother, her eyes opened wide, had her ears pinned to the racket outside.

When Mai returned, she related the story briefly to me. Bari Malakni was trying to stop Bhag Bhari's mother from weeping and wailing, saying that it was bad luck to weep in a house with a newborn child. But when she continued to wail about her child's condition, Bari Malakni lost control. 'Your daughter is always too feisty', she said, 'why didn't she leave immediately after taking the towel to the bathroom? He's a man, what can he do?' She also said, 'You're in no position to weep and wail about your daughter's honour, have you forgotten the time when your husband would be in the fields and you'd be in Malak ji's *baithak* . . . '

When Bhag Bhari's mother weepingly complained to the other women there, Malakni became even more furious and said, 'Why, let's see who these Marium-like women are that you're calling out to.' After this, Bhag Bhari's mother gradually calmed down somewhat. But when she refused to be silent, Malakni threw her out of the house. The mother wanted to take Bhag Bhari with her when she was being driven out, but the response she received was, 'No, she won't go with you, there's too much to do at the haveli today, all the close relatives and family members are gathered here—Bhag Bhari isn't dying, is she?'

'Oh no', Mai said, 'the poor girl is soaked in blood, my God, how stupid are these people? They've further angered Bhag Bhari's mother, and she's left in such a huff that she's bound to come back with the police, you'll see.' She drew a long breath as if to say 'It's all over', and then became lost in thought.

I anxiously stole a look at the new mother. She was resting silently, with a serious look on her face. At her side, lay her first baby, tangled up in amulets and charms.

I thought, why does the devil walk alongside human beings? Finally, a child and the doors of the jail have been opened for the father. Anyway, no matter how sorry I feel for the new mother I will tell the truth, even if I don't get paid the 200-rupees-per-day amount.

After this, a drumbeat began outside in the courtyard and someone started singing.

I was frightened by the sound of the drum playing at this particular moment. The sorrowful new mother seemed to be revived by the words of the song, and slowly bending her thickly braided head over the infant, she kissed him and smiled faintly, a cautious smile, as if it was a spider's web and she was afraid that a filament might break with the slightest movement.

I drew a long sigh and said, 'Such a fate this baby brings with him.'

'He's blessed with good fortune, may my precious son live forever', the new mother responded in a startled tone.

I realized I shouldn't have said what I did about the baby. A mother's heart will not inflict the responsibility of the worst and most terrible thing on her child. Nevertheless, I spilled out all my legal knowledge to her.

She listened to me with surprise and fear, her eyes wide open as she stared at me, then sighed deeply and began to kiss the baby.

Her face was red with fever, or with the force of her thoughts. I stopped talking. The courtyard of the haveli rang with the sounds of beating drums and singing. A woman came inside, bent over the new mother and whispered something in her ear that was inaudible to me, and left.

I took her temperature. The fever had risen. The baby was also running a fever. I wanted to leave as quickly as possible. I could have given them medicines and left, but I felt as if there were chains on my feet.

It was clear what these chains were.

A little later, the same woman who had whispered in the new mother's ear, returned. This time, Bhag Bhari was with her. There wasn't the same shyness in Bhag Bhari's eyes I had seen earlier, when I had first seen her. Leaning against the door, she looked at me mutely.

'Memsahib, please treat her as well', the new mother said, looking at me pleadingly and I was dumbfounded to find myself face-to-face with the greatness of this rustic woman, the wealthy landowner's wife.

Whatever I could do for Bhag Bhari, I did. How weak and numb she was at this moment.

Another day passed. Because the new mother's breasts had become engorged, her fever worsened. She drifted in and out of a stupor. But I left that day. I may have stayed on another day in consideration of the condition the new mother was in, but Mai was insistent that I take off that very day.

Here's what happened. It was early morning and, sunk into one of the expensive sofas, I was having breakfast with my brother, while Malak Sahib, after inquiring about the well-being of the new mother and the baby, had settled outside in his favourite pose, taking in the sun. His hunting dogs were being fed. Somewhere nearby, a drum and trumpets were being played. And in that moment, I decided that I should stay on for a few more days. I was making money.

Just then, I observed Bhag Bhari's mother appear from behind one of the houses. Her black dhoti, long red kurta and bright yellow chaddar shone in the winter sun. On her head, was a large tray covered with a gold-trimmed red dupatta. There were several other women behind her, all carrying something or the other on their heads. There were men too. Some were dancing, and some playing drums and trumpets. Led by Bhag Bhari's mother, the procession approached the house. The dogs, fighting over food, began to bark loudly. The hawk perched on Malak Sahib's hand was startled by the sound of the drums and the trumpets, and the disturbance created by the dancing men, and flew off and then, moments later returned to his perch. Soon, tossing the reins of a strutting, prancing horse towards one of the men with him, the *thanedar* (chief police officer), walked towards Malak Sahib.

All the women in the haveli came out like a flood. Many dressed in silken attire joined in from the living room. My brother ran out anxiously and, while being jostled in the huge crowd of women, I saw Bhag Bhari's mother placing the large tray at the feet of Malak Sahib.

Shouts of 'They've brought the baby's clothes', reverberated in the house and outside. I quickly ran inside looking for Mai. The courtyard was empty. In the delivery room, the new mother was sitting up on her bed, Bhag Bhari's braids clutched in her grasp, her face darkened with the expression of someone in the throes of labour. She was startled to see me.

'The ill-bred girl spilled water on the bed', she addressed me.

Her face suddenly assumed a calm and peaceful expression, as if she had just delivered her baby. Rising on Bhag Bhari's face were white welts in the shape of fingers and there was no sign of water on the bed or anywhere in the room.

I quickly found Mai and whispered urgently in her ear. She agreed vehemently with what I had said and we immediately began to make plans for our departure. At that moment, I felt as if I was alone in a house, a house whose walls had collapsed.

When I arrived home, I placed the 600 rupees I had made in three days in front of my mother and began arguing heatedly with her. Right or wrong? In other words, was I a fool to leave immediately or not? My mother kept saying I was right, my brother insisted I had become unduly anxious and was foolish to run off.

Before any decision is made regarding this, let me tell you that the procession led by Bhag Bhari's mother and carrying garments for the infant—the hats and the kurtas—had come from Thanedar Sahib's house.

10

Death and Milk

The journey was long and the night was black. The breeze was still pleasant enough, but at a moment like this, even the softness of the breeze felt mysterious, deepening the darkness and the desolation.

They were both walking gingerly on a trail in the middle of the fields. A false step on this side or that, and they would feel a branch from the harvested crops crunch under their feet, making them overly cautious in making their way, as if it was a snake they had just stepped on. Only moments ago, Chaudhry had twisted his ankle when he stepped on a twig and for this reason, he now walked slowly and painfully with the help of a stick and as a result, Rahmat was also forced to slow down.

They were both returning from the market nearby after having exchanged their golden harvest for cash. They had quickly started off for their village before sunset. But the remains of the harvested crops along the way had ruined their return journey. The sun had set a while ago. The ghouls always came out in the dark, but if there was some money in your pocket, it was not uncommon at this time of scarcity, for the faces of looters and murderers to appear all around you in the dark as well.

Rahmat was a mild-mannered but talkative man, who was a master of conversation about gutsy actions although he had had very few opportunities to actually exhibit courage or bravery. His steps gained speed, but the thudding of Chaudhry's stick stalled his progress. The problem was that besides being scared of ghouls and thieves and the dark, he was also afraid of Chaudhry.

'Why are you suddenly so quiet, Rahmatay? Say something, brother', Chaudhry said softly with a groan, after they had walked some distance in silence.

'Aaw . . . aaaw . . .' Rahmat pretended to yawn and then, taking off his turban he unravelled it and then started wrapping it back around his head. 'I'm sleepy', he said wearily. He had talked a lot of nonsense all the way from the market and now, he just wanted to get home quickly.

Silence reigned once more. The rustling of the shoes on the dirt could be heard clearly, and the thudding of Chaudhry's stick rang like an exploding bomb in the quiet of the atmosphere. Rahmat wanted to continue walking in silence the remaining distance to their house, without hearing the sound of their footsteps echoing in the air, or having to listen to the sound of Chaudhry's rapid breathing.

A few lights could be seen twinkling like fireflies in the distance, and Chaudhry calculated that they were now about half a mile from Nurpur, the village where Chaudhry's cousin lived, the two of them sworn enemies, ready to kill if the opportunity presented itself. Chaudhry had just met him in the market, and as always they saw each other and clearing their throats, they spat on the ground simultaneously, a scene that frightened the merchants in the market, but luckily neither of them had a knife at that moment.

But was there a dearth of knives in Nurpur at this time? Chaudhry must have surely felt the hair rise on his body, but he wouldn't even admit this secretly to himself. How could he tolerate the insult of this age-old enmity nurtured by their elders, and also, he was no ordinary man. In his youth, he had taken on a dreadfful tiger all by himself, for which the tehsildar (tax collector) had arranged to have the government award him 200 rupees. Everyone in the village was intimidated by him. He had seen many ups and downs in life and had dealt courageously with all of them. So how could he turn into a coward in his old age?

Chaudhry paused for a minute and inhaled deeply, as if he had been holding his breath all this time. Rahmat saw that Chaudhry seemed to be grinding his teeth and his white beard was moving. Rahmat guessed without difficulty that the lights they were approaching belonged to Nurpur, the village where Chaudhry's uncle's son lived.

Rahmat told himself he wasn't worried. Was he Chaudhry's wife's brother that he should be afraid? It's fine, he thought, at least once they had crossed Nurpur they would pass through two other villages and their own village would then not be so far from there. But despite telling himself all this, Rahmat felt something crawling inside his blood. Fear!

It was still early so Nurpur was lit up with lights.

People will be on the streets still, the doors of the homes will still be unlocked—the inhabitants of Nurpur will know that I'm a poor refugee, Rahmat kept consoling himself, but the onslaught of fears would not cease. An enemy is always blind.

He wanted to walk fast so he could get ahead, but, Chaudhry! And then Chaudhry's son and his grandsons are also in the same village and he too has to live there, Rahmat thought.

'Chaudhry, say something interesting, recount a story, or an incident', this time it was Rahmat who begged.

'Rahmatay, all the interesting stories vanished with youth', Chaudhry said, sighing. And then he lifted his arm up and flexed his muscles.

'But brother, these hands still have enough strength to strangle the strongest young man', Chaudhry's voice suddenly seemed artificial to Rahmat, and he cowered and paused.

'Why are you stopping? All right Rahmatay, tell me, when you entered the train compartment and started to attack the rioters, didn't they retaliate?' Chaudhry began a conversation about bloodshed to warm his own blood.

'Oh I told you, I held my breath as I hid under the corpses and . . . ' Taken aback, Rahmat blurted out the truth and Chaudhry broke into such a loud laugh that Rahmat felt like breaking his bones. The wretch wanted to talk enthusiastically about bloodshed and corpses when there was a real chance of a blood bath ahead.

'My brave fellow, let me tell you something today', Chaudhry suddenly became serious. 'If I had been a king, for this act of . . . ' Chaudhry stopped mid-sentence, and began to clear his throat. He was walking relatively faster. They were both feeling apprehensive but they no longer feared for their lives, despite the fact that they were advancing towards danger at greater speed.

It is said that when Cleopatra suffered defeat, she sat on her throne before the asp bit her. Chaudhry was experiencing similar feelings. Before helplessly walking into the jaws of danger, he wanted to recall a single incident from his younger days illustrating his courage and superiority, one in which he had played a role.

Actually he was consumed by Nurpur and he was not ready to accept this reality.

Then, in order to stoke the embers in his enfeebled blood, he began this story:

'In these very fields that you refugees now plough, there were once many Hindus who farmed the area. There were also others who were traders, cloth merchants, owners of retail, jewellers, one or two pedlars, and some were government workers. There must have been thirty or forty Hindu families living there. I don't recall that there was ever a fight over a cow or musical instruments, but when our kalima was accepted both by Pakistan and the British then the period of rioting started, and when some of our young men began paying attention to rumours and also began to spread them, I called them all together and said, "Children I'm warning you, no one should dare make a move against anyone without consulting with me. I've fought with a tiger alone, anyone who refuses to accept what I'm saying should come before me now and test his strength."'

'Why did you do that Chaudhry?' Rahmat blurted out.

'The Hindus didn't bother us in any way. I thought if they created any trouble, then we would see', Chaudhry replied in a heavy voice. 'And then what happened is that the Hindus realized that Chaudhry is not in favour of clashes, those who were scared started coming out and believe it or not, they would say "parnam"(Hindi salutation) to me. The shops re-opened, their women started fetching water again, the children played together.'

'And then one day, I was sitting in my house smoking hookah after supper. The *mirasi* (belonging to singer caste), was pressing my body, and during this time I dozed off. Suddenly I heard a cry from below, "Chaudhry come quickly, we've been ruined." Still feeling a little drowsy, I came down and saw that the one-legged Samdu was there, arrogantly leading a group of young men. Ever since Samdu had taken a job in the army, he had been hungering for leadership, but who could stand up to Chaudhry? I held back an abusive retort with great difficulty because I realized that there was some trouble brewing in Diyaram's haveli. All of the homes belonging to the Hindus were plunged in darkness, but there were lights dancing in Diyaram's haveli all the way to the rooftop. I was startled and wondered if all the Hindus had assembled in front of the haveli and were making plans to attack us. If that were the case, then Chaudhry's face would be blackened for ever and if even a single kalima-reciting brother was even pricked by a needle it would mean death.'

'I was lost in thought and Samdu was jumping on his one leg and exclaiming, "Chaudhry, there's silence in all the homes of the Hindus, the kafirs have left with all their belongings, what will the other villagers say to us, that our kalima-reciting brothers are arriving from there having abandoned all their belongings while here . . . "'

'This business of "here and there" confused me. I accompanied the men who were slowly increasing in numbers. On the way, we passed the cloth merchant, Tara Kishan's house. I kicked the door with my leg but it was already open and I went right in. Everything was in its place, nothing had been removed or taken but there was not a soul within. All the houses along the way belonging to Hindus were the same.

People started to loot these homes and being in the state I was, I couldn't stop them. This surreptitious departure of the Hindus in such a sneaky way was like a slap on my face.'

'By the time I arrived at the haveli, only a few people remained with me. I snatched a sword from someone's hand and struck the main door with it. The glistening metal ring clanged. The door was locked from the inside.'

'Diyaram, open the door, what preparations are you making in there, you cheat, you kafir', I was screaming and inside the heaveli the whirpools of light kept increasing and decreasing. I could smell the odour of burning ghee.'

'We began to break the door down. The door hadn't quite splintered when suddenly, it opened and Diyaram came out, breathless and panting. He stood in front of me and pressed his hands together and said, "It's you Chaudhry Baba, we thought they had come."

'I screamed, "Tell me who are the wretches who would come, where is everyone and what preparations are underway inside?"

'Hearing this, Diyaram put his hand that was as soft as a kachori in mine and said, weeping, "Come and see for yourself Chaudhry, but come alone. You're like our father." After saying this, he pulled me in anxiously but I snatched my hand from his grasp. I was beginning to feel sorry for him.

"Chaudhry don't go in alone", several of the people who were with me, screamed.

"You're also scared of me, Chaudhry?" Diyaram looked me straight in the eyes and asked boldly.'

'Rahmat, you know I'm not afraid of anyone, I've tackled a fierce tiger by myself, and received a reward . . . '

Chaudhry could see that they were approaching Nurpur and were about to walk past the first house in the village. How bright the lights of Nurpur were, Chaudhry thought, having never noticed that before.

'Then what happened, Chaudhry?' Rahmat asked impatiently.

'I told everyone to wait outside while I went in with Diyaram.'

'What was going on inside?' Rahmat couldn't contain his curiosity.

'I'm telling you, it was very hot inside. I went inside and felt my senses reeling. In the middle of the courtyard, a huge pyre was burning, there were sticks everywhere that people were picking up to throw on it. All the Hindus were gathered there and their faces looked pale even in the glow of the flames. A lot of things were crackling in the fire, and I saw five women and some young children present as well. Some of the younger ones were asleep with their heads resting on ther father's shoulders, while a few of the older ones were sitting like statues next to Diyaram's old and frail mother. The women were dressed and made up as if they had come to attend a wedding. The moment all the people saw me they became as still as statues.'

'I couldn't understand what was going on. Suddenly Diyaram fell to the floor and grabbed my feet. He said, "Chaudhry you were protecting me but we know that the entire village of Nurpur is coming to attack us today. This is a fact. And Chaudhry ji, don't get tangled in a fight with your own brothers because of us. We're ready to die, but with honour. We have neither done you any harm nor are we doing anything that is going to help us in anyway." Saying this, Diyaram stared at me. The mention of the villagers of Nurpur made my blood boil. I realized that my uncle's sons were going to commit atrocities just to taunt me. But at that moment, I didn't know what to do. When Diyaram saw me hesitate and look confused, he gestured to the Pandit and said loudly, "Hurry up, finish this business," and in the next instant, the men leapt at the the women. One of the women ran out screaming, pulling her hair, another fell down and dashed her head on the ground, and some of the men lifted up two other women. I saw that the faces of these women looked horrible. These were women whom I must have seen coming and going in the streets a thousand times, but I didn't recognize any of them at that moment. And in the next instant, two women had been flung onto the burning pyre. Then the third woman, distraught and overwrought, was now in the grip of the men, and also the one who had dashed her head on the ground and who was now unconscious. The woman screaming wildly was thrown towards the pyre quickly, but she was thrown with such haste and with such aversion that her body landed on the other side of the pyre, on the ground and with a loud thud, while the unconscious woman disappeared from their hands. Hearing the wild screams of the crazy woman some of the children who were asleep, woke up, lifted their heads from their father's shoulders and began to cry. Only one woman remained now. When people tried to hold her down, she pushed them away and stood up on her own. I recognized her immediately. She was Moolchand the jeweller's second wife. Her face was the same as I had always seen it, with a slight expression of anger on it. There was a new look on her face. In her lap was her four- or five-month-old son.'

'The Pandit shouted, "Hurry up my daughter, otherwise they'll get here", and saying this, the Pandit tried to grab her hand, she jumped to one side and screamed, "Nobody dare touch me." Her baby became agitated and began to cry.'

'She walked towards us slowly, with determined steps, a proud air about her, and asked in a clear voice, "Is it nine'o'clock yet?"

I couldn't speak because I knew why she was asking the time. Everyone knew. "It's nine already sister, hurry up," Diyaram screamed.

"Why, you don't want me to nurse my baby on time?" she said harshly, and turning her back to everyone she sat down on the ground and lifted her shirt front. The baby stopped crying. He was receiving his milk.'

'This was the first baby that had been delivered in the regional hospital. We had heard that the nurses had incised Moolchand's wife's belly to get the baby out and she had nearly died, but despite that when she returned from the hopsital after a month she loved the baby more than anything in the world. She had learned the ways of the white women, never kissing the baby's mouth but kissing his feet instead, nursing him by the clock that belonged to her father-in-law—in short, such things that the mothers in our village had never heard before, and even now she was sitting next to the pyre nursing her child on time.'

'And then what happened?' Rahmat swallowed hard in an effort to wet his dry throat.

'Then, sobbing, Moolchand tried to lift her up by the arms, but she stood up on her own and walked in the direction of the pyre. The baby was still in her arms and was now sobbing loudly because of the heat of the flames. Moolchand sprang in front of her but she quickly sidestepped his grasp and walked into the pyre and became one with the flames. Several people ran as the child's last half-finished scream was heard, but they were forced back by the fire.'

'Only daughters burn on pyres, not sons, that's why everyone started weeping loudly.'

'And then what happened?'

'There was no attack that night, and no one knows how it happened but a few military lorries arrived in the darkness of the night, and all the Hindus crammed into them and were driven to the other side.'

Chaudhry suddenly fell silent. He felt that the blood was flowing like lava in his veins. He looked back into the darkness of the night. He wanted to die bravely.

A scrawny dog had been following them and when he saw them slowing down, he let out a feeble 'wuff' and turned around dejectedly and trailed off.

Lost in conversation, they had both travelled far from Nurpur.

And in the distance, they could clearly discern the quivering flame of the lamp on the village well.

'Chaudhry, tell me one thing. Why did Moolchand's wife nurse the baby when she was going to take the baby's life herself?' Rahmat asked, struggling inside the net of a frightening enchantment.

But Chaudhry remained silent. He was thinking. And how clearly shone the flame of the lamp on the first well in their village.

11

Bargaining

In one hand I was holding the books for the Munshi Fazil (Honours in Persian), course, while clutching with the other, the front folds of my gharara to save it from the globs of spit and snot on the pavement. The bus was approaching, which would take me to the 'College That Guarantees You Will Pass the Punjab Exam.' Caught in the evening rush of traffic on Bandar Road, I was hurriedly making a dash to cross the road in order to get to the bus stop when someone pulled my dupatta from behind. Ever since I had started working on the Munshi Fazil course, my family had reluctantly given me permission to travel alone to college and back and such incidents had become commonplace. Bhaijaan, my older brother, had warned me several times that innumerable high-strung and ambitious scoundrels had arrived in Karachi in the guise of muhajirs (immigrants from UP) and the best course of action was to ignore their behaviour and continue on your way otherwise there was a chance of being kidnapped or worse, slashed with a knife. But, able now to hold forth forcefully on questions related to the freedom of women etc., memorized from women's magazines, how could I stay silent?

I turned after I felt a sharp tug at my dupatta and swore loudly. 'Idiot!' I shouted, but when I looked around glaringly I saw it wasn't a scoundrel or an idiot, it was Gulloo Mian.

'*Arrey*, hai, Gulloo Mian?' I said in surprise, and dodging a fast-moving tram and circumventing a big American-made car, we crossed the road.

Naturally, my bus had left. Gulloo Mian was staring closely at me. I felt good. I could see that my nice clothes, the dupatta draped casually over my head and my unveiled face had all impressed him. I moved the books around in my hand with an air of authority.

'You've changed completely after coming to Karachi, Banno Apa', Gulloo Mian said in a bewildered tone.

'Yes, but you haven't changed at all!' I replied with casual disdain. Actually I had been upset by his calling me 'Apa'. In Lucknow he was a young boy, just a year younger than me. Now he was a grown man. And I had put down my age as 'sixteen' only in my Munshi Fazil application form. When old aquaintances meet among new surroundings, it can sometimes be worrisome and I was acutely aware of that at this moment.

I gazed in the distance to see if there was another bus coming on Bandar Road.

'You've started going to school, Banno Apa', Gulloo Mian said naively.

'No, I go to college', I said emphasizing 'college'. Seeing another bus approach, I suddenly felt sorry for Gulloo Mian. He was inquiring after me with such interest and I hadn't even asked how he was.

'When did you come, and how is everyone?' I hurriedly asked.

'Oh? You didn't get the news from Lucknow? I brought Amma and Bajiya to Pakistan six months ago. You know that over there we've been in touch with Bhaijaan . . . ' Gulloo Mian began to go into details as the bus pulled in.

'Oh my God! The bus is here. You must come to see us Gulloo Mian, write down the address, wait I'll give it to you.' I quickly opened a book. I remembered I had an Eid card from someone that I was using as a bookmark. The envelope had our address on it.

'Here, this is our home address, you must come, all right?' I handed the card to Gulloo Mian and quickly boarded the bus.

When the bus drove off, I realized that I had given Gulloo Mian our address without first confirming if he and his family had a place to stay or not. In the past, many relatives who were survivors of *hijrat* (migration), had come to stay in our three-bedroom flat for months at a time. One of them had actually devised a scheme to have our flat alloted in their name. After this incident, Amma had ordered that no benevolence be offered to anyone. In the new country, using old values meant becoming homeless yourself. I was worried. But then I thought that Gulloo Mian had been here for six months, he must have a place to stay, he wouldn't be on the streets somewhere. But the thought of Amma began to make me uncomfortable.

When I got home, I recounted the details of my meeting with Gulloo Mian and also confessed my own foolishness.

But all our fears proved to be baseless. Gulloo Mian didn't come to our house, and I experienced a strange kind of disappointment.

Gulloo Mian was a distant cousin. I remember when his father Ayaz Khan was alive, the family lived in modest prosperity. Ayaz Khan was an ordinary government employee but the way the house was run gave the impression that they were quite well-off. When, just a few years before he died, World War II had broken out and there was a shortage of petrol, he bought an old car from somewhere at a low price. This car stood in the porch of Ayaz Khan's old, expansive ancestral home, a constant and melancholy symbol of the shortage of petrol. Ayaz Khan continued to go to work on his bicycle. However, sometimes when he visited his relatives, the car would be used and, as a result, the family members would be greatly impressed. Everyone in the family was jealous of him, but at the same time everyone wanted to meet him socially. When Ayaz Khan's oldest son Shahbaz Khan passed his BA, the extended family arranged banquets for the whole family. In fact, the truth was that were unmarried girls in every home, turning pale like mangoes rotting in the sun, and Shahbaz was a bachelor with a BA. Actually my Bhaijaan had also done his BA at the same time as Shahbaz, but no one seemed to care about him. My mother pawned her gold ring and invited Shahbaz along with his family to dinner. They sat in their car and came to our dilapidated house. I remember that my hands were red and swollen from grinding spices all day for them and then later, my hands dipped in a bowl of cold water, I sat alone in the antechamber and thought about what I was going to wear. When Shahbaz (whom we called Shaboo Mian) sat at the food-spread with his family, I peeked at him several times through a chink in the door. Shahbaz's simple features and straight hair look so strange to me.

Amma called out to me, saying, 'Don't be shy, come and eat with everyone else.' That day Amma was behaving very broad-mindedly because Shahbaz's father, Ayaz Khan, was also clearly broad-minded. That was why his daughter Zehra was in ninth class at the Muslim School, the same one who was sitting with us that day and eating pulao with a spoon, yes spoon! The spoons we had specially borrowed from our neighbour for this feast.

That night, Amma stayed awake late into the night talking to Bhaijaan. Well, just saying that Shaboo Mian for Banno, and Zehra for my Bhaijaan—nice pairs.

Although we found out later that Ayaz Khan had already arranged a match for Shaboo Mian with the daughter of a bearded officer in his department.

After all, Ayaz Khan was a man of the world. He knew what would look good where, and if there was no petrol in the car, then a two-wheeled bullock cart would suffice. A clever shopkeeper keeps his goods nicely displayed with the price cards affixed to them instead of wasting time bargaining. This is how he bejewelled his porch with his car and, in a way, displayed the price of his children's future. But when Ayaz Khan died suddenly from a heart attack, all that exuberance was burnt down by a single spark. The second day, the old car was at Ustaad Sadeeq's garage seeking a customer. The matter didn't end there. Ustaad Sadeeq arrived at the house, stood in the porch and announced within earshot of the whole family:

'Sister! Khan Sahib took with him what was in his heart. Shaboo Mian now, by God's grace, has a BA degree, but what about poor, unfortunate Gul Mian? who will support his education? He's still young, if he comes to my garage I'll teach him my trade.'

This sincere offer by Dadeeq Mian was like a blow that felled Gulloo Mian's mother's heart. A moment ago, she was sitting among the women, weeping, and in the next, she suddenly spoke at the top of her voice and said,

'I say, there's no dearth of anything in the house. May God keep my Gul, he'll not only do BA, he'll go on to MA. He'll go to England. Tell Sadeeq that Begum says just have the car sold. It reminds me of him, makes me weep. May God bless my sons with long lives, they'll buy new cars.'

Hearing this forceful speech and seeing her confidence, everyone was once again impressed. But despite this for as long as we lived in Lucknow, we saw their porch empty.

Shaboo Mian quickly became a clerk with a good word from his father-in-law and was promised quick promotions. Gulloo Mian floundered his way to metric finally. As for their sister Zehra, she had completed metric with a third division in her father's lifetime, and according to her mother was now 'at home, and by God's grace, learning housekeeping skills.'

In those days, we visited their home often because Shaboo Mian's wife was not only skilful at having children, she was also adept at revealing all the family's secrets. She always complained to anyone who visited that, 'Bad luck followed my fate.' There was always bickering going on. Gulloo Mian's mother still kept busy creating an intricate pattern of appearances, which the daughter-in-law would destroy in the blink of an eye. Zehra would huddle with her head bowed in a corner, quietly learning the art and craft of housekeeping, and Gulloo Mian would lie in bed all day, tossing and turning, or he would earnestly and seriously talk about family problems with relatives like us.

Then came the riots in Delhi and we all left for Pakistan. Bhaijaan got a lecturer's position at a college and we forgot all our past problems. I never thought of the Shaboo Mian who feasted at our house and married someone else, and whom I peeked at through a chink in the door with great hope and longing, and who I had imagined being the father of my child. Nowadays, it was odd to think of nursing babies. After all, many of the women in the neighbouring flats here looked so happy feeding their babies milk in bottles. The feeling of happiness I experienced at the thought of my present surroundings and intellectual changes was augmented by meeting old acquaintances and relatives.

And so it wasn't at all strange that I felt a little sad that Gulloo Mian didn't come to see us.

One day, Bhaijaan and I had left the house to go somewhere and we ran into Gulloo Mian walking down Bandar Road.

'*Arrey* Gulloo Mian, wah! Why didn't you come, we waited for you', I said.

'I was busy, and then I thought you must be busy too.' Gulloo Mian's expression of reproach seemed so artless.

'*Arrey*, wah! You talk as if you're a stranger', I said petulantly.

True that during our first meeting I had been detached. And perhaps Gulloo Mian had learned how to recognize these things.

Anyway, Bhaijaan asked after his mother and sister and soon won over his trust again. We discovered that they had built a cottage in the New Exhibition Grounds and everything else was all right. When Bhaijaan asked if he was working, he replied cockily, 'I'm an inspector now in the Department of Allottment.'

It was pleasant to hear him talk like this. We brought him home. Amma saw him and, as was her custom when she met someone from Lucknow, she began to weep in memory of her homeland. And Gulloo Mian hugged her so lovingly as he wept with her that I too became emotional, even though I had never missed Lucknow to the extent that I should cry like this for it.

After a cup of tea, Gulloo Mian promised that he would return the following Sunday to take us home with him. And so we went there draped as it were with our new lives and Gulloo Mian brought us to his house as if we were very special things, all of us. A large parcel of land had been enclosed by walls made of palm leaves woven together and inside, walls made of the same palm leaves along with tin scraps had been used as dividers to create two rooms, a kitchen, bathroom and toilet. Outside the dwelling, was a plaque bearing Gulloo Mian's name and position in grand letters.

His mother was weighed down by life's burdens. But despite that her clothes were clean, and everything in the house appeared neat and tidy. Gulloo's sister Zehra was thinner and paler, but she had bound her hair in two tight braids as a sign of her being educated and because of this her face looked thinner and paler. When we were all seated for tea at the crisp white tablecloth spread out on a clean dhurrie, I saw that Zehra had poured a little chutney on her pakoras and was eating them elegantly with a spoon. Their mother looked happy and satisfied and said repeatedly that some very wealthy people were living here in cottages like theirs. However, we still didn't refrain from commiserating with her—seeing her reminded us again and again of all the incidents related to the times her husband was alive. Perhaps, if she had lamented about her present circumstances we would not had this reaction. But she cleverly evaded acknowledging our sympathy. Gulloo Mian on the other hand, due to his simple nature, accepted all our sympathies without any artifice.

'Ah, what difficult times you have had to go through— one can't help remembering the Lucknow days', Amma said, sighing dolefully.

'Yes, but may God keep Gulloo Mian in His safekeeping. His superior worked under his father at one time. He's very considerate, Gulloo Mian has a special place here. And then of course, it's not just Gulloo Mian's salary, by God's grace, the money from our savings during Khan Sahib's time will take a long time to be finished.' With a mysterious smile, Gulloo Mian's mother moved her head to swing the karan phul earrings in her ears as she spoke.

'But Amma, these few pieces of jewellery are for Bajiya. I maintain that a person should depend on one's own resources—that's all. Now, just imagine. We came to Karachi with no money and no job. Shaboo Bhai said you're leaving under the illusion of success, by God you'll be back soon. But you know, the Allah who opens your mouth gives you food to eat as well. Your intentions should be honest, that's all. Not like Shaboo Bhai, who . . . ' Gulloo Mian stopped mid-sentence because his mother was glaring at him for trying to divulge family secrets.

'Zehra, you should find a job, you could teach in a private school. You should put your education to good use', Bhaijaan said without looking directly at Zehra.

Zehra turned ashen and Gulloo Mian sputtered like rapid fire from a machine gun.

'Why? Why does Bajiya have to do anything as long as I'm alive? Abba didn't send her to school with the idea that she should work.' Gulloo Mian's face darkened with rage and his lips began to quiver, as if Bhaijaan had cursed him. Bhaijaan did his best to justify his remark, saying that he personally believed in economic freedom for women, but Gulloo Mian wouldn't be pacified.

'Sir, we eat roti with chutney at the end of the month, but why should Bajiya work?'

Gulloo Mian kept ranting and his mother's face drained of colour. She stared helplessly at her son who at that moment was as separate from her and from all of us as a piece of black stone set in the middle of a glass bangle. Solid and unchangeable.

In some corner of my heart, I felt that Gulloo Mian was special and honest. He was very young when his father died and he hadn't learned how to hide his suffering from others, how to keep up appearances. When he came to understand what was going on around him, the dining table was always covered with a clean tablecloth, Zehra would change the neem tree branches in the vases every day, but Shaboo Mian's wife insisted on drying her children's diapers on the backs of chairs. Everyone would go into the kitchen, sit on the floor and eat rotis, which were numbered, by dabbing them with chutney and the daal that had just a touch of onions sauteed in ghee. Their Amma would say say angrily, especially so the daughter-in-law could overhear, '*Arrey*, why don't you eat here, there's no pulao and qorma for anyone to eat at the dining table—why soil the tablecloth for nothing?'

But when a relative arrived for a visit, even arhar khichri (rice cooked with lentils), would be served in a china platter and it would be served at the table, and the visitors would repeatedly be told that life was meaningless if one didn't have arhar khichri once a week. But this double standard had eluded Gulloo Mian. He knew that Shaboo Mian's salary was inadequate and he had a child every year, that his sister-in-law secretly wept at her fate, that his mother and sister didn't hide in the dark antechamber and weep just for fun. He had been raised with these harsh realities. His simplicity and his honesty are what appealed to me. And he always seemed so impressed by me that I began to feel as if I was becoming whole. When he came over on Sundays, he and I continued chatting even if the others got bored and left us. Amma warned repeatedly, 'Look, don't encourage Gulloo Mian, he might suddenly decide that your brother should marry his sister. No, by God's grace, your brother is a professor, he can easily get any rich girl he wants.'

Amma's viewpoint irritated me and I would start praising Gulloo Mian's family and remind her of the feast for Shaboo Mian. There was a time when she almost hit me for mentioning this. But sometimes when I thought about the matter coolly, asking myself why, indeed, did I spend so much time with Gulloo Mian instead of studying and memorizing for the Munshi Fazil exam, the answer came back to the question of feeling whole. I felt a strange kind of satisfaction after confidently discussiing various topics with Gulloo Mian and successfully convincing him of my arguments, I felt as I was someone very special, very grand. He listened to me with such devotion that I felt euphoric. Bhaijaan called me an illiterate and didn't take much notice of me. As for Amma, my arguments fell flat in her presence. But Gulloo Mian considered me to be the most accomplished and intelligent person in the world. He asked my opinion for every little thing, so much so that he even consulted me on matters that transpired in his office, the petty jealousies and quarrels, for example. This made me feel as though I was standing tall in an ocean of simplicity, like a tower of light.

But that day, I felt my lights turning off and the inferior dark, skinny Gulloo Mian whom we often referred to as just 'Gulloo' to prove he was not important, suddenly struggled on his weak legs and without warning straddled straight and upright over my feelings. All at once, the sources of my conversation dried up.

'Oh? Gulloo Mian . . . ' I leaned against the wall of the Munshi Fazil course and croaked. I blinked my eyes and stared at him. Is this Gulloo Mian or . . . But it was him. The same gray serge sherwani that Shaboo Mian used to wear once and which was now in its last stages, the same thin skinny, dark-complexioned boy whose face always reflected a yellowish hue (and which had often reminded me of a frog), very curly hair that seemed to never have had the use of hair oil. He was sitting across from my awkward table, behind the wall of the Munshi Fazil syllabus. Gulloo Mian! Very satisfied, conceited, self-confident. I felt as if a child had slipped off my lap, crossed the stairs of the flat and had gone off for a stroll. After a long awkward silence, I cleared my throat and just said,

'Really, Gulloo Mian? Hunh?'

'*Arrey* Banno Apa, do you think I would lie to you?' He lifted a finger as he continued to explain. 'You know, one should depend on the strength of one's own resources.'

I was stung by his self-confidence. I wanted to throw my books down. I realized that Gulloo Mian's devotion had merely been an act, since obviously this was going on for weeks and he should have mentioned it to me. I was silenced.

'Look Banno Apa, she was just a woman, and the greatest wealth is faith. She was very surprised by my refusal. She invited me into her drawing room, served me tea and said, "Inspector sahib, you're a very good person, you should come and see us often." I swear Banno Apa, their drawing room was so grand, you know, like the ones we see in films.' He began to go into details and I cut him off and started giving him my opinion.

'But look Gulloo Mian, this was utter foolishness. When you were getting 5,000 for a deal that was worth hundreds of thousands, why did you refuse to take it? This is how business is conducted in this world, and then your circumstances— well, you should have consulted with me.'

'Hunh! This is isn't something for which one requires any consultation. I know this. I know what is right and what is wrong. Anyway, I'll be going now, Fatima Bai has invited me for dinner.' Saying this, Gulloo Mian got up and moved towards the open door in such a way that I clearly heard the flapping of his sherwani.

I felt bad that I had been too hasty in my reaction and had lowered myself in Gulloo Mian's opinion. And I was also angry. Angry with Gulloo Mian. How could I admit that he didn't value the 5,000 rupees he was receiving for writing a legitimate report? A petty inspector like him whose older sister was still unmarried? Certainly for a dowry of 5,000 rupees even Amma would agree to make Zehra her daughter-in-law. The 5,000 rupees tinkled as they whirled before my eyes, followed in their wake by colourful saris, jewellery, and a thousand other necessities with their mouths open, and walking away from all this was Gulloo Mian. The Gulloo Mian who was given an inadequate number of chapatis to eat when he was a growing boy, and who was known to drink several glasses of water after a meal to feel full. I couldn't help feeling disappointed at Gulloo Mian's actions. If it had been someone else, they would have grabbed the money. Perhaps I would have too. No! No, I wouldn't. But Gulloo Mian should have. But he no longer needed my advice. Who did he think he was. Plato?

But when I went to sleep that night, Gulloo Mian became attached to the lights in my dream. In one dream, I saw fireflies in his thick hair, in another, I saw sparks flying around him. I woke up with a start. I only wanted to think of Gulloo Mian as just Gulloo. I couldn't manage this business of lights and illumination associated with his person.

On the first Sunday after this visit, Gulloo Mian made an appearance early in the morning. He looked terribly flustered. But he looked different. His face had been washed carefully, and his hair was neatly combed down. I was in the kitchen swallowing my last mouthful of tea. He crudely gestured to me to see him in the other room. I saw a strange kind of sliminess in his eyes that made me nauseated. Still, I got up and came to my room and after paying his respects to Amma, he followed me there.

Then he recounted the entire matter in detail, which was simply that not only was Fatima Bai impressed with his decency and honesty, her daughter Shireen was also falling for him. She wrote him a letter saying, 'I will marry only you, you don't think highly of wealth and people from my community, despite being so wealthy, want to marry me only for my money. But you . . . '

I didn't for one moment believe this slick story.

'And then you woke up', I said, irately.

'Look here now, you shouldn't . . . ' he evaded my attack. And then suddenly, his face became flushed and he quickly got up and left without waiting another minute.

Everyone was surprised that he had appeared out of the blue and left so abruptly. I felt it was necessary to tell them how after coming to Karachi this silly boy had started dreaming about getting very rich very quickly. Every laughed at him.

Bhaijaan, who was a professor of psychology, suddenly became serious and said, 'That matter about the 5,000 has also been presented to Banno to impress her. It seems that in his spare time Gulloo still reads children's magazines, which is why he's dreaming about being rewarded for being good.'

Then Bhaijaan addressed me severely,

'Banno, I think Gulloo is thinking about you. It would be best if you stop encouraging him. Why does he talk to you about such things?'

'Oh Bhaijaan, come on . . . ' I blushed. But secretly I thought, maybe—maybe, and the very thought then made me feel I had been insulted. I decided I would no longer talk to Gulloo.

But I was unable to entertain this privilege for a long time because after this incident, he didn't come to our house, and what came instead was his wedding card inscribed with gold lettering.

At first, we were all stunned into silence. Then Amma heaved a low sigh of disappointment, and said quietly, 'Allah, everything in Karachi is for sale, and may my children's fortunes fare as well.'

'Hunh!' Bhaijaan lit his cigarette as he walked away towards his room and I sat down on my trunk and started thinking about what I was going to wear at this event. After all, I was about to go to a wealthy home as the sister of the bridegroom and then, while I was grappling with the question, my eyes filled. All my clothes were ordinary.

We all went as the bridegroom's relatives. The festivities were so grand that we were sure Gulloo's father had left behind some treasure.

Gulloo's mother was beside herself with joy. She spread out her arms as soon as she saw Amma.

'Ah Sister, felicitations to you, your nephew has found such a perfect match. A curse upon those who wished us ill. Come

Sister, come, just see our gifts for the bride, you don't think
we've forgotten anything do you—you're our own blood, one
of those who would be happy to see our good fortune.' Gulloo's
mother embraced my mother and went on and on like a record,
and my poor Amma began to sheepishly shower blessings upon
the bride and groom. After that, she examined the dowry so
earnestly as requested that one would think any shortcoming
would be cause for embarrassment specially for her. Once she
had completed this task, she stood in the door of the cottage
and called out to Bhaijaan.

'My son, go to Gulloo Mian quickly, you're going to be the
shehbala (young boy from the groom's family who is like a best-
man), it's your right.'

When Amma returned she ran into Zehra, who was dressed
in shiny, glittering clothes, and feeling somewhat bewildered,
Amma rushed with, 'My dear child', and quickly embraced her.

Well, there was much to be bewildered about. The *bari*
(things the bride brings with her), was so grand, such clothes,
such jewellery—even I was dazzled by by it all. Observing our
astonishment and our remorse, Gulloo's mother chattered
endlessly about her discernment and skill, and the effective
way she had saved money. All our close and distant relatives
in Karachi had been invited, and were all mortified. Many of
the women were still wondering how they had been so stupid
as to allow Gulloo Mian to become a son-in-law to a family
from another sect. Certainly, these people had not deliberately
accepted him as a son-in-law. True, wealth bonds with wealth.

But when I sat in the groom's car along with Bhaijaan and
gazed admiringly at Gulloo Mian, I thought that he looked
quite attractive. When we were children and used to play mock
wedding games, I once pretended to be his bride.

'Why, Gulloo Mian, you invited us to the wedding at the last minute as if we were outsiders. How hard poor Mumani must have worked to arrange everything', I said, pouting.

'Oh no Banno Apa', Gulloo Mian said. 'You think Amma could have made all these arrangements? My mother-in-law sent everything. I had told her I wouldn't be able to do anything in keeping with their grand lifestyle, and she said, "We'll send all the things to your house beforehand and you just bring everything back with you when you come with the barat." I was really angry when I heard this. I said, "I don't like this arrangement, I'm poor, I'll come to wed your daughter like a poor man." But she begged me and said that already people in their family and their community were extremely opposed to this marriage, there would only be a few guests from their side and she said that she had sent the bari to me since I was going to be living in their house. "Why should you object", she said, "We're giving all this stuff to our daughter, please preserve our honour." I felt sorry for her and I agreed. It was the right thing, wasn't it?'

'Absolutely'. I looked absent-mindedly at Gulloo Mian. Loaded with flowers, he suddenly looked very dark to me.

Gulloo Mian's marriage ceremony was finally conducted in a grand bungalow, to the accompaniment of music played by a band,. One of the conditions in the nuptial agreement was that Gulloo Mian would not take the bride from her house and that he would live with her in her house. He was presented 11,000 rupees as a gift from his mother-in-law, which he declined.

Fatima Bai was a merchant's widow. Attired in her national dress, (sari worn a special way), she attended to the guests elegantly and graciously.

Shireen was a twenty-four- or twenty-five-year-old delicate, thin girl with a fat nose, a muddied complexion and large, innocent eyes. She was definitely a few years older than Gulloo Mian. Dressed in bridal clothes, she just sat there blinking her eyelashes like a doll, as if her own will and volition were not involved in the blinking of her eyelashes. I was surprised by her passivity. Included in the very elaborate dowry, were fifty pairs of shoes. I wondered if she was going to do enough walking to wear down the soles of even one pair of sandals.

'So Gul Bhaiyya, Allah opened the gates of wealth for you—you're going to have such a good time', my Bhaijaan said, running his tongue over his dry lips.

'It's Allah's blessing. But I swear by God, I told my mother-in-law that I'll continue with my job. After all there's Amma, there's Bajiya, I have to take care of them. All of this here is my wife's, I have nothing to do with it', Gulloo Mian said, cautiously eyeing his expensive suit.

And my Bhaijaan laughed as if he was looking at a donkey eating boiled rice.

'But Gul Bhaiyya, how is it possible that Zehra and Mumani won't live with you? You're the son-in-law, aren't you?' I asked apprehensively.

'They'll stay here with me, but they will live on my income. You see, I'm able to take care of them, I have a job by God's grace. I don't want my family to subsist on handouts. I've explained that to my mother-in-law clearly, and it's her business if it upsets her', Gulloo Mian boasted arrogantly and I yawned and thought it was time to go home, especially since dinner was over.

My mother ate to excess. On our way back she muttered, 'My word, this Fatima Bai must be out of her mind. Was Gulloo the only man in the world she could find for a son-in-law? He's neither good looking nor does he have any real education. I say, what good fortune. Why, Karachi is a remarkable place, a remarkable place I say.'

For many days, this wedding was the hot topic of discussion among our relatives and acquaintances. There was all kinds of gossip. But everyone agreed that because of his stupidity Gulloo Mian would remain dry as a bone despite diving into the river.

Bhaijaan, my brother, said, 'Makes no sense that the fool refused to accept the gift of money because of his feelings of inferiority? As everyone knows the gift of money is accepted by every bridegroom regardless of whether he is rich or poor. It's nothing but a gush of foolhardiness on his part. I say, can anyone find a son-in-law free like this?'

Despite this we all longed to dive into the river of foolhardiness, that is, eager to meet Gulloo Mian. We boasted to our neigbours of our relationship with Fatima Bai. Amma would say, 'I say, our boy from such a good family has been ensnared by a net cast by outsiders.' Bhaijaan embarked on a psychological analysis of Gulloo Mian's behaviour when he talked about him with his friends.

But on most evenings, we took off without much thought to Gulloo Mian's mother-in-law's house. It was a very imposing two-storey bungalow. The second floor had been set up for the daughter and the son-in-law, while Fatima Bai and some of her relatives had rooms downstairs. Receiving meagre salaries, these relatives were in the employment of Fatima Bai and didn't seem to have any special status in the household. Often one or the other would serve tea to guests like us. Among them was an elderly man with a French beard, who was in charge of household accounts but was often seen clearing up tea things. When we visited, he went out of his way to be cordial and hospitable. Actually Fatima Bai herself was no less hospitable. If we were there during teatime, she would have tea served and if we forgot the time as we chatted and it was late, she would insist we stay for dinner. Their food smelled of coconut. Gulloo Mian's mother also glowed. She would be be seated confidently on the sofa in the drawing room and on the table in front of her, a large paandaan always remained open, although the paandaan didn't always match her clothes since she would occasionally be seen in Fatima Bai's national dress.

She had said to us a few times, 'I say, what can I do, my *samdhan* (the mother-in-law of your son or daughter), is always pestering me with, wear this now, wear that—she loves me so much she won't take no for an answer.'

Fatima Bai was overjoyed when she heard this praise. And Gulloo's sister also had nothing but words of admiration for her sister-in-law. I often saw that Gulloo's sister was busy wearing out the sandals that were part of Shireen's dowry. Gulloo Mian went to work on a motorbike that Fatima Bai had bought him as a gift, and didn't travel by car because his co-workers at the office teased him if he did. I realized that Gulloo Mian often looked bewildered, as if he had mistakenly tightened the wrong nut and screw.

Speaking in her Bambaiya dialect, Shireen frequently said in our presence, 'What's this job? He should help with the business, we have our own business, he should look after it. If he gives up our car and rides around on his motorcycle, what will people say?'

Shireen's comments were always made so mechanically that they left one feeling uneasy.

'Yes, of course Gulloo Bhai', I would say hastily, offering free advice. 'You should take care of the business.'

'But what can I say, Gul Bhai doesn't regard me as one of his own', Fatima Bai would also complain and Gulloo Mian would stare at us with a surprised look like a monkey in a cage. Ignoring him, we would all agree wholeheartedly with Fatima Bai and wish in our hearts that if only we could be in his place.

Then one day, we heard that Gulloo Mian knocked his boss after receiving a reprimand for something or the other and resigned from his job, and we also heard that in accordance with Fatima Bai's request, he was now looking after the business.

We all arrived at their house one day because we didn't actually believe the news about his involvement with the business. We discovered that the news was true. Gulloo Mian's mother and sister were ecstatic. A short while later, Gulloo Mian returned home in the car and we realized he looked different, as though he was sick. But I thought whatever his illness was, it made him look romantic.

When he slowly got up and climbed the stairs with his shoulders slightly stooped his mother explained his gesture thus: 'The boy is tired, he'll go up now and take a bath.'

'No, he's upset with me', Fatima Bai said. 'See, I told him, Gul Bhai business is business, you can't make allowances. It's been a month but you haven't made any profit, I told him, and I also said, Gul Bhai don't let anyone buy anything without paying in full, no promise of pay later. Thoughtfulness and money are enemies. Business should be like a business.' Fatima Bai tried to convince us in her characteristic Urdu.

'*Arrey* Samdhan', Gulloo's mother said, shutting the lid of her paandaan. 'You're wrong to think the boy is upset. He's just kind-hearted and will slowly learn everything.'

'No Apa, business is business, otherwise everything will be finished. Ibrahim Bhai says Gul Bhai makes a lot of allowances', Fatima Bai said.

'That's right, that's right', Ibrahim said, shaking his French beard as he served us tea.

For a long time afterwards, a discussion about this domestic business-related tension ensued in which my Bhaijaan took the most active part. And Amma also kept agreeing, acting as if no one except her knew the ins and outs of business. Gulloo Mian's mother continued to be upset by this since she was trying to convince everyone that she had innate knowledge of how a business should be run, although that was a blatant lie. No one in her family had even touched a weighing scale.

Before leaving, we went up to see Gulloo Mian in his grand bedroom. He looked very restless. I lovingly taunted him about thinking less of us now that he had gone up in the world and had become important, and complained that he never visited us any more.

'*Arrey*, what are you talking about? What importance? I'm taking care of the business as if were just a job. After all, I have to do something, I'm a man, I can't just sit around doing nothing. Anyway, come, let me drop you all home in the car.'

I can't fully explain how strange Gulloo Mian looked as he drove the car. I forced him to come in but then was embarrassed at the state the house was in. Gulloo Mian was in a rush, he didn't stay.

Gulloo Mian's mother had not taken kindly to our comments so she didn't invite us to the house for a long time, and we didn't have an excuse to go either.

After a few months, we were not at all surprised to hear that Gulloo Mian had failed miserably to take care of business matters and Ibrahim Bhai with the French beard had been appointed as his superior. Now everything fell into place efficiently. Next we heard next that Gulloo Mian was seen frequenting big hotels and cinema halls. If he ever made an attempt to interfere with the business, Ibrahim Bhai would lovingly say, 'Everything is going well', offer him tea, and gently push him out the door. After hearing all these stories, I anxiously waited to see Gulloo Mian; several strategies designed to get Ibrahim Bhai out of the way were going through my head. Unfortunately, my Amma was feeling ruffled those days and every suggestion to go to Fatima Bai's house was promptly vetoed.

One day, a car horn kept screeching in front of our filthy building. I looked out from the gallery. Gulloo Mian's car was parked on the street.

'Gulloo Mian is here', I shouted to let Amma know. We rushed to get the house in order, quickly picking up clothes, dirty dishes and books that were strewn about, and dumped everything in the other room. I hastily dusted the chairs, Amma dashed off to get her dupatta, and I hurriedly removed my slippers and put on sandals. And when I opened the door, Gulloo Mian walked in looking very serious, a rose pinned to his collar, and I felt as if his face had aged by many years.

Amma greeted Gulloo Mian warmly, and then walked away to the other room on the pretext of preparing tea. I heard the sound of the rear door opening. Naturally, Amma had gone next door to get our neighbour's dowry tea set from her and also to tell her that look, my real brother-in-law's son is here, the one whose personal car is parked on the street.

'Gul, where have you been all this time, I'm not talking to you.' I felt that my tone was wrapped in a layer of dazed femininity and my heart was beating fiercely.

'I'm so busy Banno Apa, what can I do?' Gulloo Mian said, smiling with fake politeness. A smell of spirits on Gulloo Mian's breath seemed to slowly fill the room.

'*Arrey* Gul, you're not loading bricks, you're not anyone's slave', I said, feeling a little dizzy and tried to pin my gaze on Gulloo Mian. He seemed so different to me as he stood behind the wall of the Munshi Fazil course.

'I swear by God, I have no time. So many times I thought I should come and see you all, but I would forget. I don't know what's happening to my brain.' For the first time after his wedding, I saw an expression of helplessness and innocence flit across his face and I suddenly felt like reaching out to him from behind my wall of books to give him some advice. Actually, I wanted to pat him on the shoulder and console him. But he was changed in an instant.

'I swear Apa, I've become so forgetful. Only yesterday I promised someone I would go with them to Hawke's Bay, I also reserved a cottage on the beach, and then I forgot.' Gulloo Mian said haltingly, putting on a suave demeanour of sadness.

Had it been someone else saying this, I would have rushed to smack him, but at this moment it seemed that Gulloo Mian's person was slowly expanding, like Wonderland's Alice after she gulped a mouthful of the liquid from in the bottle. He appeared crammed in my small room. I started feeling suffocated. One does get upset when one's own being appears to be of no consequence. I escaped to the other room to get tea, and when I returned with Amma and an elaborate tea tray, I found him stylishly leaning against my table, a book open in his hand. And I thought, oh, this is Gulloo Mian.

Gulloo Mian gulped down the tea disinterestedly and didn't touch the samosas and sweets purchased for him, although

Amma wanted him to eat everything. As he was leaving, he invited me to come with him for a drive in his car and I readily agreed.

'Where should we go Apa?' he asked, leaning over the steering wheel.

On the way, as I was bouncing on the soft car seats, I realized that Gulloo Mian was slowly becoming very interesting to me. How disgusting are those on the streets who drink cheap alcohol and eve-tease girls, but the faint odour of alcohol in the car and the girl waiting in the cottage at Hawke's Bay had created a shiny halo around Gulloo Mian's head. Remember that I'm am educated, respectable girl. For this reason, I was reluctant to accept the truth. That day, I kept getting into a bad mood. But I would justify Gulloo Mian's behaviour by telling myself that Shireen must be cold clay and that was why poor Gulloo Mian was becoming like this. During our drive, I kept making an effort to maintain a very dignified demeanour.

The passage of time was suddenly interrupted one day, when Gulloo Mian's mother arrived at our house on a motorcycle rickshaw, all out of sorts.

'Come, please, come quickly, that fool Fatima Bai is obsessed with nikah', she said frantically.

'What?' Amma turned into a picture of astonishment and I started laughing. Did we have any control over Fatima Bai? I didn't feel much sympathy for Gulloo Mian's mother. She hadn't bothered to stay in touch with us.

'Whose nikah is she obsessed with?' Bhaijaan asked casually.

'*Arrey*, her own', Gulloo Mian's mother replied angrily.

'So let her get married', Bhaijaan said casually and Gulloo Mian's mother suddenly broke into sobs.

'Everything will fall apart if she does. What will become of us?'

When Gulloo Mian's mother began her story, she managed to convince everyone in the end. She insisted that we should go and discourage Fatima Bai from taking such a step.

Perhaps, we would not have bothered to interfere, but curiosity is a terrible thing. Amma got ready quickly. We arrived at Fatima Bai's house.

Fatima Bai looked her usual composed and graceful self. She greeted as warmly as always and offered us tea. Gulloo Mian's mother cleverly slipped in the question of the nikah, startling Fatima Bai.

'Look Samdhan, what's the need for a nikah when you have a daughter and a son-in-law', my Amma jumped in clumsily just then.

But Fatima Bai let it go. Then she explained her point of view to us in her characteristic Urdu. The crux of the matter was that if she wanted to do it for her own happiness she would have done it before her daughter was married. She herself is embarrassed to be married now, but what can she do? How will this extensive business keep going? There should be someone to take care of it. She had married her daughter off to a decent man with the idea that he would manage the business. But not everyone has the ability to run a business. She put her faith in Gulloo Mian, but he doesn't have the temperament for it, a businessman has to have a different temperament. Everything she has built up with such hard work is falling apart. This can't continue. The money the business makes will be for Gulloo Mian and his children. One can't depend on strangers and for this reason, she is forced to marry so that the business can be looked after properly.

Gulloo Mian's mother became incensed after she heard this explanation. 'What will the world say, you're getting married at this age', she shouted.

'The world already said a lot when I made Gulloo Mian my son-in-law. I don't care. Should I let my business go down the drain because of what the world says?' Fatima Bai also shouted her reply.

And fully convinced, my mother nodded. After that, as was the custom, we were served elaborate refreshments, but the person serving tea and refreshments was not Ibrahim Bhai, because he was the one who had been selected as the bridegroom for this business marriage.

It was clear that Ibrahim Bhai had played a big role in sealing the question of Gulloo Mian's ineptness in business matters. But I was comforted by the thought that Gulloo Mian would not be playing a part in any of this. As a matter of fact, he would no doubt be angered when he found out that his mother was engaged in a campaign against this business marriage, although his mother was only going through this hassle out of concern for his future. The poor woman thought it was possible Fatima Bai would have another child—she was in good shape after all—and if not this, then perhaps Ibrahim Bhai would become a partner in the business and Gulloo Mian would end up losing everything.

I thought that if Gulloo Mian was told of the schemes and plans his mother was involved in on his account, he would probably leave home. But we didn't see him. One day, I telephoned from a hotel owned by an Iranian, but he wasn't home.

Then we heard that Shireen was ill. One day, Amma and I went to inquire after her well-being. Why in the world would we ruin our relationship because of Gulloo Mian? Shireen was in her beautiful bedroom and Gulloo's mother and Zehra were sitting by her side, massaging her head. They were not happy to see us.

Fatima Bai came with in with a bottle of medicine. She looked tense.

'I say, my daughter-in-law's heart is filled with sadness, she must be missing her father. That's why she has a fever all the time.' Gulloo Mian's mother spoke sarcastically, addressing my Amma. My Amma was accustomed to agreeing with everything so without a thought she immediately agreed. Fatima Bai became livid and pushed away Gulloo Mian's mother's hand from Shireen's head.

'Hai', Gulloo Mian's mother said, 'you ensnared my gem of a boy, and now you insult me like this!' Gulloo Mian's mother used the typical female defence and began to wail.

This in turn caused Fatima Bai to fly into a rage. Right in front of us, she dragged the fever-stricken Shireen from the bed, telling her that she should go down with her and never set eyes on Gulloo again.

'You people are beggars—I know', Fatimai Bai screamed as she took Shireen with her and Gulloo Mian's mother's wails quickly turned into sniffles. Suddenly Gulloo Mian appeared in the middle of this fray. For a moment, he silently watched this spectacle and then went into the other room.

I was frightened by the expression on Gulloo Mian's face. His complexion was just like the colour of a frog's belly, his pupils fixed. Sobbing, Shireen had gone downstairs with her mother. Gulloo's mother was silent, but Gulloo Mian didn't come out of the other room.

'May God forgive us, may He never send us to the home of such rude, disrespectful people. In our families, the wealthiest parents grovel before a son-in-law, even if he is a grass cutter. Where did these brutes come from? Even if someone goes there just to spit, I won't be responsible for what I do.' Amma left the bungalow in a huff after not receiving a response to her salaam from Fatima Bai and I too told myself that we shouldn't bother with this family. We had been insulted for no reason.

Early next morning, Gulloo's mother and Zehra arrived at our house, weeping and lamenting.

'For God's sake, come quickly, take Banno as well, Banno please telephone your brother also.' Gulloo's mother fell into the chair as if she had fainted.

'*Arrey*, what's happened?' Amma calmly finished rolling the paan and put it into her mouth.

'*Arrey* what can I tell you, just go, all of you, and bring Gulloo Mian from there, he'll listen to you.' Gulloo Mian's mother grasped my hand. 'Allah saved us today, otherwise they were ready to, God forbid, finish him off.'

'Finish him off? What are you saying?' I stammered fearfully.

'Shireen's family is out for blood. It's that cursed witch's nikah tomorrow . . . last night Gul Mian was in the bathroom. It was around two o'clock when someone fired a shot . . . it struck the pillow and downstairs they raised a commotion shouting "Thief! Thief!". If Gulloo Mian had been there on the bed, what would have happened—Oh God, what would have happened!' Zehra related the story with her mouth open in distress.

And for a moment, we were all shocked into silence. Gulloo Mian's dark-complexioned face floated before my eyes, his skull shattered and gray bits of his brain splattered everywhere. I trembled with fear and hatred. Oh God, how horrifying this image was.

'Well, we had said already that it wasn't easy for this relationship to go well, why doesn't Gulloo just leave her, and everything, and get out of there?' Shaken, Amma shut the paandan quickly.

'Oh God, someone should go and get him, he doesn't want to leave, he says this is my house, I won't leave—what will happen?' Zehra started sobbing violently.

'How can we go? What can we do? And Gulloo is right, isn't he?' Amma said without meaning it. She was terrified.

Despite a great deal of pleading and coaxing by Gulloo's mother and Zehra, we didn't go with them. Naturally, when matters had advanced to this degree there seemed no reason to interfere.

When Bhaijaan returned later that evening after spending time with his friends, Amma turned on her side and said sorrowfully, 'Poor Gulloo is sitting there, playing with his life, for the sake of that consumptive Shireen. You mark my words, that girl will also take her mother's side in the end. If she didn't approve, could her mother have dared to think of marrying?'

'Hmm . . .' Bhaijaan mumbled and turned to sleep. Earlier, we had talked with him at length about this matter. He had decided that we should have nothing to do with this ridiculous problem.

And while in bed that night, I kept waiting to hear some horrible news. I was the first one to pick up the newspaper the next day. There was no mention of the horrible news I was expecting. The day after that too I woke up before everyone, and picked up the newspaper to check for the news since that was the day Fatima Bai was already Ibrahim Bhai's wife. On the third day, I woke up with the sound of the paper being dropped, and for many days after this also I waited. Finally, one day I dialled Fatima Bai's number from the Iranian's hotel.

'Hello, is Gul Bhai there?' I asked confidently.

And someone banged the phone down at the other end. But the human mind is not a telephone that can be heard when you want to or ignored when you don't. Like a child, I wanted to know the answer to 'What happened then?' My exams were approaching. I wanted to go to one of the relatives spread around in Karachi in order to get news of Gulloo Mian, but there was no time to do it because I was always studying for the exams. Again and again, I regretted not having gone with Gulloo's mother and Zehra. What would have happened? Fatima Bai wouldn't have had us hanged. I would think continuously about Gulloo Mian as I struggled with books all day. How devotedly he had gazed at these books at one time, and at me too. I've already mentioned that no one took much notice of me in my house.

One day, I said guardedly to Bhaijaan, '*Arrey* Bhaijaan, does no one ever mention Gulloo Mian?'

'Oh yes, someone was saying just yesterday that he left the house in a huff on the day of Fatima Bai's wedding', Bhaijaan yawned and said disinterestedly.

'Really? Why didn't you tell us this before?' Amma asked.

'What's there to tell? That he's a complete idiot?' Bhaijaan yawned again.

'Where are they now?' I asked cautiously.

'How would I know? And it's best we don't know. They must have no place to live now and everyone thinks we have a big flat.' Saying this, Bhaijaan started reading the paper, Amma went to the kitchen and I bent over my book.

When the worn-out hem of Gulloo Mian's old serge sherwani fluttered before my eyes I turned the page of the book—my exams were approaching, were they not!

In a few days, I was to leave for Lahore for my exams. When I came out on the last day from the 'College That Guarantees Passing the Exam from the Punjab', I stopped at the Bolton Market bus stop and decided I should go to the cloth market to buy an inexpensive but stylish dupatta. I had five rupees in my possession, which Amma had very reluctantly given me. She claimed I already had four dupattas and there was no need for another. The thought of her miserliness brought tears to my eyes. How terrible that I was going to Lahore and didn't have a chiffon dupatta. I had heard that the Lahore girls were very well-dressed. I suddenly wanted to throw away the five rupees and getting on the bus, weep without restraint.

In order to pacify my frayed nerves, I started counting the big, fancy cars driving past me that were seen in increasing numbers on the Karachi roads.

One, two . . . Oh God, what a beautiful colour . . . what if one had a sari this colour . . . three . . . look at the beautiful woman sitting in the car, her face lifted up smugly, and the colour of her sari . . . Oh God . . . *arrey* who is this bastard who just bumped me on my hip as he walked past me? Moving aside to avoid running into a wrestler-type man walking towards me, I became tearful again . . . four, five . . . many more cars passed by me. How satisfied and content were the women seated in these cars, and I was still waiting for the bus. Bus! I would have to suffer much jostling when on the bus . . . six, seven . . . what a beautiful shade of blue . . . if I buy a dupatta of this colour . . . but it was Gulloo Mian in that car.

My hand was raised involuntarily. The long, light yellow American car screeched to a halt.

'*Arrey*, it's you Gulloo Mian?' I stammered and my hand slid over the slippery surface of the car.

'Where do you have to go? Let me drop you.' Gulloo Mian removed his dark glasses, wiped them with his handkerchief and opened the door on the passenger's side for me. The car started but I had been shocked into silence. I couldn't understand Gulloo Mian's connection with this new car. Had he become a chauffeur?

'What are you doing these days Gulloo Mian?' I asked, clearing my throat.

'The same, taking care of business', Gulloo Mian said loudly and I felt anger at Bhaijaan for giving us false information.

'Thank God everything was settled in a proper manner. I telephoned once and whoever picked up hung up on hearing me mention your name. How is Shireen?'

'Oh, so you were worried about me?' Gulloo Mian looked at me strangely, and I was thrown off balance.

'You're angry with me, aren't you? You know, that day when Mumani jaan came, well, Bhaijaan . . . ' I tried to justify what had happened. I realized that his mother and sister had no doubt filled his head with resentment against us.

'Oh please, don't be silly. Why would I be angry with you?' Gulloo Mian lit a cigarette. 'Oh by the way, you must have heard the news that Zehra Bajiya is married', he said.

'Oh?' I choked with sorrow and anger. What was this if not a severing of our relationship, the fact that Zehra's marriage had been hidden from us?

The car stopped at an impressive looking shop.

'If you don't mind, I have to pick up Dulha Bhai. I have to drop him home', Gulloo Mian said, leaning over the steering wheel, the odour of alcohol making my senses reel.

Gulloo Mian walked very confidently to the stairs leading to the shop, and in a few minutes an old man with the face of a vulture came out of the shop and, supporting himself with his hands on his knees, walked down the stairs with Gulloo Mian. Gulloo Mian opened the back door of the car for him. In a few minutes the car was racing down the road. And I felt my head spinning.

'I'll drop Dulha Bhai and then I'll take you for a spin to Hawke's Bay. You'll come, won't you?' Gulloo Mian whispered secretively into my ear and a feeling of outrage flamed inside me.

'So, I . . . I . . . ' the Munshi Fazil books tumbled from my lap to the floor of the car and fell at my feet. I turned around and looked at Zehra's old, vulture-faced husband and then glanced at Gulloo Mian. I felt afraid of them both. And a muffled scream remained stuffed in my throat.

The street where I lived came into view and whizzed by.

Actually this new type of car could travel at extremely high speeds.

12

Munni at the Carnival

The quivering flame of the torch, the sounds of the drumbeat and the notes of the harmonium—the crows in the trees in the large compound were caught in the branches, and began to flutter noisily.

Chum, chum! She jangled her anklet bells and sang: *Go away, oh cruel one, I will not come with you.*

The words, once everyone heard them, caused much excitement. The drummer began to beat the drum vigorously, jumping up and down with the drum, tossing his head from side to side. The harmonium player's eyes and neck moved energetically in rhythm with his fingers, which were tapping over the keys, and as for the poor torch-bearer, his job proved to be the hardest—the dancer moved so fast within the circle of the spectators after she had finished singing, that the torch-bearer had great difficulty keeping the light focused on her face. Also, he had to make sure that proximity to the flaming torch didn't pose a threat to her. Anyway, what was this torch but a nuisance? A bottle filled with gasoline and coated with a thick layer of clay, which the torch-bearer turned upside down to soak every time the gasoline was depleted and the flame began to flicker. Munni Bibi, all bundled up in Kamal's lap, viewed the dancing, the twirling flame and the twirling woman—all through sleepy eyes. She had been dozing when Kamal suddenly picked her up from her bed and brought her out to watch this spectacle.

Munni Bibi found the sight of the twirling woman and the quivering flame in the darkness of night pleasing. But she wished she too could squat in the inner circle like the other children and the servants from the neighbourhood, and view the show with them. She wished she too could try to touch the swaying, eddying hem of the dancer's *peshwaz* (a long tunic-like shirt), and like Superintendent Sahib's servant, Maharaj Mota, make an attempt to crouch under the umbrella formed by the dancer's swirling peshwaz. But Munni Bibi knew that it would be a wasted attempt because the dancer would sing *Go away, oh cruel one, you who know nothing*, and swaying, whirling, making jangling noises with her anklets, move far away from her. And she would move with such speed that the torch-bearer would have to run very quickly in order to keep the light pinned on her. The dancer was glimmering once again. The gold and silver edging and the gilt stars of the purple dupatta covering her head and her bosom, the eddying hem of her green peshwaz and her red pyjama—all suddenly seemed ablaze. When she moved her head from side to side as she entered the circle of light, her silver earrings, her gold *jhumar* (an ornament for the forehead) and large nose ring, swayed to and fro like a swing. When her hands moved to push away 'the cruel one', the bangles with the tiny silver bells on her wrists bounced the length of her arm with a tinkling noise and were momentarily lost inside her long, baggy sleeves.

Munni Bibi was tired of handing the dancer the money that Kamal had been doling out to her. Each time, the dancer would leap towards the money, perform a gesture of appreciation and then present a reason for not going with the cruel one:

If I go with you, I will die of hunger,
My beloved has sweets—I won't go with you.

And, feeling drowsy, Munni Bibi found this entire spectacle so exhilarating that she was suddenly overcome by a wave of generosity. She felt sorry for her sisters who were stubbornly pulling and tugging at Kamal to let them personally give the money to the dancer as well, and so she handed over the paisa she had to her sister so that her sister could have her wish. After this, she turned her attention to the trees illuminated dimly in the darkness, looking for the witches Mama Bi had warned her about, but today, unlike other days, she didn't see anything in the trees. All she could see was that the trees looked even taller in the whirling light of the torch, so tall that she felt their tops had pierced the sky.

Then she dropped her head on Kamal's shoulder and overheard Kamal and Maharaj having a heated exchange, but because she was overcome by sleepiness, she couldn't understand what they were saying.

But when Abba Mian returned from the city the next day, Maharaj Mota complained to him about Kamal and the moment Abba Mian entered the house, he immediately began scolding Kamal. Kamal was not a real servant. He had been raised in Munni Bibi's house, from childhood, and despite the fact that he now earned a salary from the hospital where he was employed, he was still very scared of Abba Mian.

'How dare you send for *tawaifs* (courtesans) in our absence, you rascal, and then encourage the women and the girls in the household to watch this spectacle? You wretch! You waste your money on such wicked activities?' Twisting Kamal's ear, Abba Mian shouted.

Ammi tried her best to explain that neither she nor any of the other ladies in the compound had actually seen the dance. All they had done was take a tiny peek from the door, and since no one really thought much of the dance, the women spent the entire evening simply chatting with each other. Kamal received a box on the ears despite all this. However, he continued to insist that he had not sent for the dancer, suggesting instead that Maharaj must be the one responsible. He was blaming Maharaj because the two had had a disagreement the night before.

Munni Bibi was extremely perplexed by all this. And to make matters worse, she was feeling so sorry for Kamal that she became tearful.

Finally, as a punishment, Abba Mian placed a twenty-four-hour curfew on Kamal's movements. He said that until the scoundrel got married he was to come home directly from the hospital, and not be allowed to go anywhere else.

Munni Bibi couldn't bear to see Kamal's flushed face so she left the veranda. Her sisters and the children from the neighbourhood had assembled outside. They all told Munni Bibi that those who had given the dancer money with their own hands would suffer by having those same coins heated in the fire and stuck to their bodies, when they were in Allah Mian's house.

'Well, I only gave her one paisa—may Allah forgive me, may Allah forgive me!' Munni Bibi's sister did some counting with a sense of relief. But Munni Bibi was the one who was the most perturbed. The sadness that had been generated in her heart at Kamal's beating was now transformed into sorrow and anger at Kamal. 'Such cunning! He himself won't burn in Allah Mian's house, but he made sure I would burn.' How she regretted her foolhardiness. Her aunt from Lucknow had already warned her that singing, dancing and jumping are sins. Well-behaved children should sit quietly and read, or play games that are suitable for children.

Shortly afterwards, dragging her mother's dupatta behind her, Munni Bibi arrived in Kamal's room.

'Please help me say my prayers', she said, addressing Kamal coolly, her face turned away from him.

'Why? Is this any time for prayers?' Kamal shouted without moving from his bed.

'Everyone says that a sin has been committed in Allah Mian's house.' Munni Bibi's voice cracked.

'What sin?' Kamal sat up on the bed.

'Because you made me give money to the woman.' And Munni Bibi burst into tears.

'All right, I repent, I repent, I won't give any money now.' With a laugh Kamal pulled her towards him.

'I'll be burned in Allah Mian's house', Munni Bibi said, sobbing.

'No, no, Allah Mian won't burn my daughter. I'll say, burn me instead, all right?' And Munni Bibi wiped her tears because she knew Kamal may be a liar but he would always keep any promises he made to her.

Then, when the seasons changed, Munni Bibi became ill. After a week and a half of fever, she became so irritable and wilful that she wouldn't even listen to Kamal; as a matter of fact,

Kamal's presence served only to make her crankier. Mama Bi was the only person she tolerated, and that too sometimes. She would ask Mama Bi what Allah Mian looked like, where He lived, and if He loved children or not. And, of course, Mama Bi had the answer to every question.

Her bad humour persisted even after the fever subsided. Alone, away from the others, she would curl up on her bed as if lost in meditation. Of course, if Ammi went by she wanted to call her and have her sit next to her, but the poor woman had too many chores to attend to and had no time to spare.

One day, despite Munni Bibi's aloofness, Kamal came and sat down beside her.

'There's going to be a carnival tomorrow, Munni Bibi', he whispered.

A sullen expression covering her face, her scrawny hands held to her side and her skinny feet tucked demurely under her, Munni Bibi chose to ignore Kamal's remark.

'I would have taken you to the carnival but . . . ' Kamal began with a heavy sigh and then he started twirling the ends of his long mustache.

Unmoved, Munni Bibi maintained her lethargic stance and merely blinked her eyes.

'You poor thing, you haven't seen a carnival, have you?' Kamal said contemptuously.

'Hunh! Didn't Abba Mian take me once?' Munni Bibi thought of last year's trip.

'Hunh! Who roams around in a carnival in a tonga? Did Abba Mian allow you to get off from the tonga?'

'No, of course not—well-behaved children sit in a tonga and watch the carnival, Abba Mian said.' Munni Bibi was beginning to thaw towards Kamal.

'Hai, hai, what wonderful things there are in a carnival. A woman who is half fox and half woman, swings, the snake and mongoose show and, my dear, toys everywhere.' Kamal shut his eyes as he described one item after another.

'Well, we did sit on the swings', Munni Bibi suddenly remembered.

'And my dear, the dance show and chaat (a chickpea snack) stalls, ice cream and *murmura* (a puffed-rice snack) and *besan* (chickpea flour) sweets . . . '

Munni Bibi melted. Having been given a scanty diet during her illness, she was always feeling ravenously hungry.

At this moment, the relationship between Munni Bibi and Kamal that had been shattered, was once again mended. A promise was quietly made and Munni Bibi's sisters did not have the slightest inkling that she who sat staring into space all day could really be so clever in reality. A smile appeared on Munni Bibi's lips and she glanced furtively at her sisters who were busy celebrating a wedding between the cat and their doll. The cat repeatedly shook off the *sehra* (an ornamented or flowery veil) made of leaves from its face, and kept running away from the toy mud house.

That night, Munni Bibi was beset with dreams. Shops filled with toys. Terracotta figurines. Cloth dolls and celluloid boy dolls. And, an entire clay kitchen. Spinning wheel, oven, pots, water pitcher, goblet, rolling pin and dough board—all the things one could give as dowry to a doll. These were things the *kumharan* (female potter) also used to bring to the house to sell. But the appearance of the kumharan always annoyed Ammi because, whether it was the milkmaid with a milk pot on her head, or the washerwoman with a bundle of clothes set on her hip, the kumharan charged an anna for every toy. Not only that, the water carrier carrying the water-skin on his back and the sahib Bahadur with a hat on his head cost the same as well! And in addition, she demanded a seer of flour and half a seer of gur (caramelized chunks of unrefined sugar) as a special favour. Ammi didn't mind buying these dolls, but she would be upset for hours afterwards because she knew they were a waste of money; in no time they would break and end up as nothing more than ordinary clay. But Munni Bibi would take the milkmaid she had been given, and think, 'Why, can such a pretty milkmaid ever break?' Who could tell her that when, filled with the excitement of her doll, she runs and falls, the milkmaid will slip from her hands, land on the brick floor of the veranda and be smashed into pieces. When that happened, Munni Bibi's happiness was also shattered. And then, by God's will, Bi Bisaatan would make the rounds with *surma* (black powder for the eyes) *ubtan* (turmeric and oil mixture), hand mirrors, combs, *missi* (teeth-cleaning herbal powder) and God knows what else, and Munni Bibi would immediately ask her in. Because Bi Bisaatan's tin trunk contained dolls too. When Munni Bibi insisted on buying a doll, Ammi would say, '*Ai* hai, are these filthy dolls stuffed with smelly cotton the kind of things for you to play with? Play with your celluloid doll instead.' But Munni Bibi did not like the celluloid boy dolls at all. She liked the dolls that were dressed in colourful attire, dolls with large eyes that were the length of a finger and looked like *namak paras* (savoury crisps). She never got these dolls. True, she was promised that yes, tomorrow she should remind Ammi to make her a cloth doll. But these promises were never kept.

However, tonight Ammi and the latest Japanese toys had no power over Munni Bibi's dreams. In her dreams, Munni Bibi bought so many cloth dolls she could barely carry them all.

And Abba Mian's authority had no place in her dreams either. Without caring about germs, she ate chaat and ice cream to her heart's content. But finally, her father's tonga with its foamy-white curtains appeared, the same tonga in which her sisters, dressed in frocks, proudly made their way to the carnival. When Munni Bibi's eyes opened to a shimmering morning, she couldn't believe she had been dreaming all this time. This was the morning of the Dussehra (Hindu festival) carnival.

Intoxicated with the heavy weight of her dreams and her thoughts, Munni Bibi sat up on her cot as if she did not have the slightest care about what was going on in her house. She didn't whimper and whine the way she had been doing since her illness. She observed her sisters sitting at the ugly breakfast table. How they were all hunched over their large bowls of hot milk, greedily devouring spoonsful of bread soaked in milk, hurriedly satisfying their avid appetites. And they had no inkling that Munni Bibi was not in the least bit concerned about breakfast today. Even before today, she had wondered irately why she and her sisters received milk and bread every morning. Ammi and Abba, for example, received their breakfast set out tastefully on a tray, everything covered as if the children might cast an evil eye on the food. Why, it wasn't as if the children would have forcibly partaken of that fragrant, golden-hued tea if Mama Bi didn't cover the teapot with the tea cosy. And then those fried eggs, halva (sweet) and broth. Her brothers usually got a share of these things, but the fate of the poor girls received a reprieve only during the rainy season when some tea was poured into their bowls just to warm up the bowls. And eggs? Since Phupi's (aunt from father's side) arrival, eggs had been forbidden to the girls altogether. Without informing Abba, Phupi had decided that it was not appropriate to give the girls anything that was fatty because such things would make them develop prematurely into women. But Munni Bibi had touched an egg a thousand times and always found it to be cold. And what did she care about eggs? Anyway, whenever the girls did get eggs for breakfast, the eggs would be deposited into their plates directly from the frying pan, half-cooked and runny, and the first mouthful would make them all feel sick to their stomachs.

Mama Bi arranged the tray as usual and took it to Amma and Abba Mian's room, but Munni Bibi didn't bother to glance in her direction. Today, she wasn't thinking of such trivial things. Without waiting for anyone to speak, she got off the cot, poured the few drops of water left in the lota into her palm, applied her palm to her forehead, nose and chin all in one movement and then calmly returned to her cot.

'Munni Bibi, come here, let's see if you washed all of your face or only half', her older sister said, trying to catch her as she did every day. God knows why it made her so happy to demonstrate that Munni Bibi was a disorderly person.

'I've washed, I've even wiped my face', Munni Bibi replied, sedately.

'Don't lie, you dirty girl', the older sister said. 'I know you haven't washed your mouth and I'm sure you wiped your face with a corner of your frock.'

'And come and eat this, why are you sitting there? Do you think you'll get tea?' Her other sister pointed to the bowl filled with milk.

Munni Bibi wanted to retort with, 'Why don't you eat that, today I will . . . ' But Kamal had forbidden her to mention the carnival to anyone; everyone would want to go if the news spread. So Munni Bibi rose from her bed and taking her seat at the table, began gulping down spoonsful of milk.

Satisfied, the sisters left the table and leapt over to the enclosure in the rear of the house. Today, Master Sahib had taken a day off, which meant they could play uninterrupted for hours. Sometimes they built a house with bricks that had been discarded, sometimes a garden with leaves from the tree's branches. This enclosure was common to the six houses scattered around it, and all the children from these houses could come and play here freely on the days they didn't have school.

Munni Bibi smiled as she saw her sisters take off. She knew that Kamal was waiting for them in his room and the moment he saw them he would tell them that Bahurani who lived in the house at the far end of this neighbourhood was expecting them and all the children would make a dash for her house. Bahurani, who was childless, used to make paper flowers for every child who came to her courtyard, and the containers in her store room were always filled with ladoos, large semolina ladoos. Once there, children could not leave her courtyard for hours.

Munni Bibi was so lost in thoughts of her sisters being fooled that she finished the milk in the bowl. The horsekeeper must have fitted the carriage for Abba, Munni Bibi told herself. She could hear the sound of the horse's hooves. But she found it hard to believe that Abba Mian was off to Bhugnipur and she was going to sneak out with Kamal and roam around in a carnival all day long.

Then, when Abba Mian said goodbye to Ammi and went outside and she heard the clip-clop of the horse as the carriage departed, Munni Bibi heaved a sigh of relief. But in the very next instant she was burdened again with nervousness—were her sisters at Bahurani's house yet?

Just then Kamal came in with a joyful expression mapped on his face. He was dressed so grandly that one would think it was Eid today. A full-skirted shalwar, silk shirt, a red scarf draped round his neck and on his head, a turban made with yards of wrap looped around his head with such a rakish twist that his left ear was completely covered. Ammi lifted her eyes from the book, saw him, and smiled.

'You see Baji, if Sahib hits me now he can't hurt my ear', Kamal said, pointing to his turban.

'Yes, I see, but you are shameless! I'm telling you now, you had better be home before dark or you will receive a beating.' Ammi tried to put on a serious expression.

'I won't go, it doesn't matter. I was only thinking of Munni Bibi, the poor girl has been so sick.' Kamal's tone implied that he was doing Ammi a favour.

'Yes, yes, you poor creature', Ammi said wryly, 'You're not interested at all in the carnival. Anyway, come back early.'

And without saying another word to Ammi, Kamal dressed Munni Bibi in a red frock, and then a petite churidar pyjama, first worn at Eid and now somewhat tight, was pulled over her heels with much difficulty. Under ordinary circumstances, Munni Bibi would have yelled and screamed at having her foot twisted, but today her aunt who was sitting nearby, reciting a prayer, didn't hear even a 'seee' from her.

When Kamal was taking Munni Bibi to his room, Mama Bi reproached him, trying to make him conscious of his unfairness towards the other children, but Kamal paid no heed to her admonition. Suddenly, Munni Bibi felt her heart soften towards her sisters.

Kamal opened his small trunk and taking out a cap decorated heavily with stars and gilt edgings, set it down on Munni Bibi's head. This cap, also sporting a feather plume, was the one that Kamal had bought especially for Munni Bibi on her birthday, but he had never given it to her because Ammi had told him to put it away in his trunk for his own child.

The slanted rays of the sun were delightfully warm. Perched on Kamal's shoulder, Munni Bibi gazed at everything with a smug and happy feeling. Birds flew down from trees, spread their wings and undertook short flights into the blue sky, then alighted on the ground, pecked on the ground for a while, and soon flew off again. On the rough, stony, dusty road, the nails on the soles of Kamal's shoes rang out noisily; if Munni Bibi shut her eyes she could pretend she was on horseback. But how could she shut her eyes? Her eyes squinted, she was waiting anxiously to see from a distance the ten-headed Raavan.

Quite audible from where she was, the sounds of the carnival were like the buzzing of honeybees.

They ran into the postman, who was coming from the station with his heavy bag of mail. He recognized Munni Bibi despite her special clothes.

'Where are you going, Munni Bibi?' he asked.

'We're going to the carnival', Munni Bibi said, her voice tearful as if she were on her way to her in-laws' house. Actually, Munni Bibi was saddened by the thought that her sisters were not with her. If they were, they would see how grandly she was travelling to the carnival. The shoulder of such a well-arrayed Kamal, and her riding on it with such pomp!

Munni Bibi smelled the oil on Kamal's forehead and turned her face the other way. Her arms were wrapped around Kamal's looped turban.

The buzzing of the carnival was now growing louder. Carts filled with men in turbans and dhotis and women in lehengas (an ankle-length flowing skirt) arrived from the direction of Bhugnipir and bouncing away on the uneven road, travelled past them noisily. Bullock carts crammed with women and children squeaked as they crawled along and their female occupants, happy at the prospect of going to the carnival, sang inside their veils, their joint melody in tune with the squeaking of the cart. Munni Bibi was getting tired from turning her face constantly to see the spectacle of the bullock carts. She wanted Kamal to hurry, but God knows what kind of a mood Kamal was in. Lost in thought, he was walking slowly, at a leisurely pace. Munni Bibi was weary from being perched on his shoulder all this time.

The carnival was now very loud and noisy. She could hear the 'charakh chun' of the swings and the euphoric shrieks of women and children. Green, red and yellow dupattas flew like banners as the swings spun. Munni Bibi was able to see all this as she passed through throngs of men who, carrying coconut hookahs, laughed and chatted. Then, she glimpsed the tall black Raavan cut out from paper and cardboard, and she had to lift her head so high to see his face properly that it made her neck ache.

It seemed as if the toy and chaat carts and the makeshift stands were buried in the crowds. Looking at these people Munni felt as if all the toys in the potter woman's basket had come to life and somewhere in a clearing amongst them there was a monkey dancing, and a snake charmer playing his flute. At the entrance of a canvas tent, she saw a man inviting people to come in and see the woman who was half fox and half human. Munni Bibi wanted to stop at every step. But she was walking in Kamal's steps, while he, forgetting all his promises, was intently making his way through the crowds, interested only in pressing on.

Munni Bibi choked with anger and her eyes filled with tears. When she tried to look at the scene she had left behind through the veil of tears, she saw two of everything. And when she rested her chin on Kamal's turban in an attempt to look at Kamal's face, all she could see was his mustache extended stiffly and wide, like Raavan's many heads.

That was when Kamal stopped before an old door in a mud wall.

'Munni Bibi, are you hungry?' he asked as he lifted her off his shoulder and put her down.

About to burst with anger, Munni Bibi shook her head. She wanted Kamal to sense her anger, but Kamal seemed not to notice anything.

When the latch on the inside of the door was drawn she found herself in a courtyard plastered with a cow dung and hay.

Outside, the carnival was screaming, but in here the *kut-kut* of the black hen standing next to her coop and feeding her cottony-soft chicks little bits of grain, could be heard clearly. And how the goat tethered to the peg panted as it pecked on straw, making wisps fly in all directions—and the woman who had opened the door, how free and easy she was so that she immediately lifted in her lap Munni Bibi who, filled with anger, was at that moment like a gun ready to go off.

Laughing merrily, the woman was saying to Kamal, 'Were we lying when we said you should bring bitiya to our house?' And then she proceeded to walk with Munni Bibi set gingerly on her hip as if it wasn't Munni Bibi she was carrying, but a basket of glass bangles. Suddenly, moved by all this attention, Munni Bibi burst into tears. Was the sorrow of being separated from the carnival nothing?

The woman stared at her helplessly.

'Why? Why do you cry so child? Did we cause you some pain?' she asked, her full lips open in amazement.

'She's crying because she wants to see the carnival', Kamal said irately, taking her in his lap. Perhaps Munni Bibi would have wept with greater force after this exhibition of indifference on Kamal's part, but . . .

'Oh, so why did you bring her here first, show her the carnival first.' All at once, the woman also seemed to be as upset with Kamal as Munni Bibi.

'I thought we should let her have some kheer (rice cooked in sweetened milk) first', Kamal said with a laugh, and grabbed a corner of the woman's dupatta. But she pulled away her dupatta and, her anklets jingling melodiously, ran towards the chicken coop, grabbed a chick and ran back with it to Munni Bibi. The minute Munni Bibi held the chick in her hand she ceased whining. Now Munni Bibi carefully observed the woman against the background of the wall decorated with cow dung cakes and watched her as she poured water in a container for the goat. Like the maidservant at Munni Bibi's house, she too was wearing a churidar pyjama and kurta. Her feet were bare, her anklets jangled, and her wrists were adorned with wide bangles with bells on them; there was a nose bob in her nose, her hair was pulled back in a tight braid pleated with a ribboned braid and the kajal around her eyes was smudged. Hiding the chick in the folds of her frock, Munni Bibi tried to identify this woman. When she returned to Kamal's side, her anklets merrily tinkling, she again picked up Munni Bibi, who had been sitting calmly on a straw mat, and despite Kamal's protestations, took her in her lap. And at that time, Munni Bibi felt that the fragrance of Ammi's body was emanating from the body of the woman dressed like Mama Bi, the fragrance that always tormented Munni Bibi from afar because there were so many brothers and sisters to share it.

After a while, the three of them were sitting on the same charpoy under the tree like members of the same family. Munni Bibi gazed at the clay pots placed neatly one on top of the other on the clean, unlit stove. She looked at the guavas in the hanging basket, and the parrot in the cage hanging from the hook on the storeroom ceiling, staring at him as he chattered while happily pecking at a guava. Surrounded by all this, Munni Bibi tried to make out the clamour of the carnival, but suddenly the wretched woman dished out a bowl of kheer from a pot and Munni Bibi couldn't figure out how to eat it. Finally, at Kamal's behest, the woman ran into the storeroom as if she had made a big mistake, returned with a wide, enameled copper spoon and proceeded to feed the kheer to Munni Bibi. Munni Bibi haughtily ate her fill while Kamal, who was lying down nearby, lifted his neck repeatedly and opened his mouth for kheer, but the woman was not going to give him any and she didn't. She did, however, repeatedly glare at him, the way Ammi glared at Munni Bibi when she misbehaved in the presence of guests. Seeing Kamal treated this way made Munni Bibi laugh.

Once she was full, Munni Bibi might have been inclined to start thinking about the carnival again, but the woman would not give her an opportunity to do so. She would affectionately and profusely praise Munni Bibi's old-fashioned cap or go into raptures over her appearance. Munni Bibi was bursting with conceit.

When Munni Bibi grew tired of playing with the chick, she became wilful and petulant. She made the woman take off her bangles, slid them on her own wrist and ran around the whole house making jangling noises with them. She removed cow dung cakes from the walls, struck the goat with a stick, and then demanded that she be given a doll. She made it impossible for the woman and Kamal to concentrate on finishing their meal.

Swallowing a morsel of food, Kamal said, 'We'll buy you a doll at the carnival in a little while.' But Munni Bibi's position as a royal personage would suffer if she listened to him. And if that woman had disregarded her, surely Munni Bibi would have died. No, the woman stopped eating and went off into the storeroom. Taking off bundles of swatches from the pegs, she started putting together materials to make a doll. Standing quietly in the semi-darkness of the room, Munni Bibi played with a corner of the woman's dupatta as if she was afraid she might disappear if she let go.

A doll wasn't the kind of thing that could be ready in a few minutes. A pillow was cut open for some cotton wool, an old pyjama was ripped and the cloth measured and stretched.

Munni Bibi's eyelids grew heavy as she waited for the doll. Then, through somnolent eyes she saw Kamal seize the woman's hand.

'Don't you have any shame?' the woman shouted angrily.

'Why you—how bashful you are . . . ' Kamal hissed and then, squeezing aside her drowsiness, Munni Bibi saw that there were tears in the woman's eyes and that the doll was weeping profusely. And Kamal? Munni Bibi felt so revolted by Kamal's face, so sickened by it, that she fell over the woman's knee fearfully.

Then Munni Bibi, slumped in the woman's lap, fell asleep to the melody of a pastoral lullaby.

When Munni Bibi woke up whimpering in the woman's lap, the woman immediately handed her the doll. There were stars on the doll's forehead, under the dupatta a bosom resembling the bosoms of mothers, and she was dressed in a peshwaz decorated with gold trim and stars!

Kamal was not at home, and outside, the carnival was a deafening noise, but Munni Bibi had no care for either. Holding the doll in her hands, she happily followed the woman all over the house. The woman cleaned the floors, swept up the goat dung to one side, shut up the hen with its chicks in the coop, gave the parrot another guava, and then washed Munni Bibi's face, oiled and combed her hair, placed the hat back on her head, applied kajal to her eyes, and then lightly dabbed a dot of kajal with her finger on her forehead.

'To keep away the evil eye.' She made the gesture of warding off the evil eye with her hands and then washed her own face and sat down to comb her own hair.

That was when Kamal arrived. He had a sullen expression on his face

'Did you bring the doll's jewellery?' the woman asked gruffly, covering her head with her dupatta. And Kamal threw the packet of pewter jewellery in front of her. She immediately took the needle she had stuck on the corner of the bed and proceeded to stitch on a *chapka* (an ornament for the forehead) on the doll's forehead, the earrings on her ears. Then she placed the tiny pewter collar around her neck and also the long necklace strung with square bits. On the doll's wrists went the bracelets, the anklets on her feet.

'Come on Munni Bibi, we're late', Kamal suddenly said impatiently, pulling Munni Bibi by her hand.

'No', Munni Bibi replied.

'Wait just a while, the doll is almost ready.' The woman sounded upset

'One can find a lot of dolls at the carnival.' Kamal pulled Munni Bibi's hand again. But Munni Bibi didn't want to leave without the doll.

'You come too', Munni Bibi wouldn't let go of the woman's dupatta. Adjusting her dupatta with one hand, the woman followed Munni Bibi to the door.

'Come, I'll follow you', she said softly.

When Kamal lifted Munni Bibi up on his shoulders again, he was startled.

'You put kajal in Munni Bibi's eyes and this black dot on her forehead?' he yelled and then tried to rub out the kajal from her eyes and her forehead, but Munni Bibi wouldn't let him.

The woman said nothing. Kamal and Munni Bibi went out the door. She continued to stand in the doorway. Munni Bibi craned her neck to look at her. Suddenly, she came out of the door and ran after them. Kamal stopped walking.

'Here, take your rupee.' The woman threw a rupee before Kamal and returned to her house and, as though yanked out of her chest, Munni Bibi's heart went with her.

In the midst of that huge carnival, Munni Bibi felt alone all of a sudden. She passed through the crowds with a crestfallen look on her face.

When the sun was setting the nine-headed Raavan caught fire. The firecrackers packed in Raavan's stomach began to explode fiercely. Munni Bibi was frightened. But then she saw the procession with Ram, Lakshman and Sita and her fear was assuaged somewhat. But for some reason, Kamal was like a stranger to her.

Kamal showed Munni Bibi around everywhere in the carnival. One after another, he took her to the chaat shop, the murmare-wallah's cart and the creamy ice-wallah's stand. The shops gleamed in the light of the gas lamps, the two-headed torches and lanterns. There was a throng of children at the toy shop. But, despite all this, Munni Bibi sat passively on Kamal's shoulder. Kamal kept asking her, 'Do you want this? Do you want that?' But, as though she were a sadhu, (Hindu holy man) Munni Bibi didn't want anything. However, in spite of her indifference, Kamal bought a tiny box of kajal from the merchant's shop.

'Look Munni Bibi, don't tell anyone who put on the kajal', Kamal advised her.

'All right.'

'And listen, just say that Kamal bought the doll from a shop.'

'All right', Munni Bibi said carelessly. She was too busy looking at a woman who stood in a clearing in the middle of a huge crowd and behind whom a drummer and a harmonium player were tuning their instruments; the torch-bearer was waving the flame in front of the woman who was adjusting a corner of her dupatta . . . the light of the flame illuminated the woman, who, her face whitened with powder, kept adjusting her dupatta, the dupatta that had gold trim on one side but whose other side had gold trim missing from it . . .

Munni Bibi remembered. One night, in a moment of drowsiness, she had seen her dancing in front of her house and she had given her money and everyone had said she had committed a sin.

'Kamal . . . Kamal . . . look! That woman . . . ' Terrified, Munni Bibi tried to get Kamal's attention, but he was leaving the carnival behind.

On the way back, wrapped in Kamal's turban, Munni Bibi received a lot of advice. She kept saying 'Yes, all right', pensively and would then find herself submerged in some strange sorrow. The carnival receded after a while and Munni Bibi's heart was lost somewhere in the carnival. She began missing her little chick . . . and that woman over whom she had reigned for one day.

They reached home at night and just when Kamal had lifted off Munni Bibi from his shoulders, Abba Mian dashed out of his room and shouted.

'Where were you all day?'

'At the carnival Sahib . . . '

'Bastard! I saw you coming out of the prostitute's house myself!' Abba Mian roared and then Kamal received a thorough smacking. His turban became unravelled and he sat down on the floor with his head lowered. Abba Mian went back to his room.

Clutching her doll to her breast fearfully, Munni Bibi tiptoed to her mother's side. But seeing Kamal beaten in this fashion filled her heart with contemptuous pity for him.

'This doll—he got you a doll again, the wretch! Who knows how dirty the cotton filling is', Ammi shouted. And Munni Bibi wanted to take the doll and fly away into the heavens.

'Let go, it's a filthy thing!' Ammi snatched the doll from her hand. Then she studied the doll carefully in the light of the lantern.

'Who gave you this?' Ammi asked with a barely discernible smile.

Using the pillow story as her reference point, Munni Bibi told her the truth. She thought that now Ammi would return this immaculately clean and beautiful doll to her.

'Oh my, just look, is this a doll or a mature woman—may God forgive us! These evil women pollute even children with their tricks', Ammi muttered. Turning over the doll's dupatta, Ammi looked again at her bosom that resembled the heavy bosoms of mothers, and then threw the doll towards Mama Bi. 'There, throw it in the fire.'

And Mama Bi angrily tossed the doll into the stove. Then, when she returned from the kitchen, her heavy bulk moving from side to side, Munni Bibi thought fearfully that she might be coming to throw her into the fire as well.

'A bad woman, a bad woman!'

Munni Bibi couldn't understand who a bad woman was.

And, bewildered and confused, Munni Bibi cried so much that Abba had to come out of his room again to spank her.

13

On the Other Side of the Moon

I have occasionally passed by the Taj Mahal Hotel. Seeing the sign proclaiming 'Taj Mahal Hotel', displayed on the unsightly wooden cabin, and the cement shop selling tea spiked with crude liquor, I have also broken into a smile often. But in the last two months this hotel has assumed the role of an important bend on the new path my life has taken. It's a place where I stop, put the brake on my old cycle every day and with one foot resting on the footpath, I say casually to the old shopkeeper, 'Send over two cups of special tea.'

'In a minute Sir, it will be there before you arrive', he says diligently and the Gilgiti boy fanning the coals looks at me and smiles and, indeed, I stop my bike next to the veranda, lock it, respond to the salutations reserved for the 'king's' companions, and step into Jabbar's room and the Gilgiti boy is there with the speed of an arrow. He places before Jabbar the tray, set up nicely with a teapot of mixed tea with sugar along with two teacups in good condition, says salaam to him, and dashes off in the twinkling of an eye.

As always, like a good host, Jabbar pours tea in the cups, pushes one towards me and then proceeds to slurp noisily from the second cup, as if he's drawing tea from a smoking pipe.

Jabbar always strikes up a conversation about poetry and literature with me as though he is presenting me with cake and pastry. These moments are painful for me since I'm thinking of the desk-incharge who had warned me the first day I stepped into the office, 'Look Sir, please remember, this is not story-writing where you can sit at the desk and seek out pearls to put in your writing. Here you have to work with an eye on the clock. Do you understand?'

For this reason, when Jabbar begins a conversation about a short story I had read ages ago, I feel my head getting as heavy as a stone and I want to lift this stone with my hands and throw it at Jabbar's face. But the minute Jabbar takes the last gulp of tea, and rubs down his mustache and opens his drawer, the love I had for Jabbar in my school and college days begins to sway about in my heart.

'Okay, my friend, you take over your share of the rations now.' Jabbar utters these words very politely every day and yet as soon as I hear this sentence, my unending, meaningless smile turns into a burst of laughter. Whether this comment of Jabbar's is interesting or not, it certainly holds true.

'Look Majid, don't let anyone come in, I'm working', Jabbar orders the sentry at the door as is his custom, and opens the daily reports of the police station as if he were about to look at a wealthy man's last will and testament, and my eyes hover over the register like hungry flies.

The crimes registered in this daily report are the source of income for both of us. Jabbar has been a police officer for about six or seven years and I've been a crime reporter for two

months at a new paper. When Jabbar's father retired from the
police department, Jabbar landed a job immediately after he
received his bachelor's degree because of his father's service
in the political branch. My father was a school master and he
hoped to see me appointed as a university lecturer, at least after
a post graduate degree, so I continued with my education. But
the problem was that there is no system in place to catalogue a
school master's services. For this reason, I not only didn't get
a job at the university, I wasn't able to find employment in a
school either. Whenever I ran into Jabbar in those days, he
would say, 'My friend, when you start thinking about settling
down, having your name printed in magazines isn't going to
help. You had better look for a job, any job.' And then I got
this job, quite by accident, and Jabbar, like a good friend, was
now helping me soldify my position. Not only did he provide
me details of the crimes registered at his police station, he also
managed to get me support from other stations as well. Without
his help, an ordinary crime reporter like me would not be able
to make any money at all.

I pick up my notebook and pencil, and Jabbar begins giving
me details about all the crimes that have been reported since
yesterday evening, and shares with me the first report of a murder
case. Forgetting my master's in psychology, I immediately label
the beautiful eighteen-year-old murder victim as a woman
of loose morals and the sixty-year-old murderer as a self-
respecting, honourable husband, and have just begun writing
when we hear a commotion outside Jabbar's office which
includes obscenities yelled by policemen along with shouting
by someone who sounds like a madman, and who is screaming,
'Let me go inside! Let me go in immediately.' This is followed
by a noisy disturbance.

'Who the mother . . . is this?' Jabbar intends to swear heavily but half the expletive stays in his mouth. He's somewhat reticent now about using such language in my presence.

'Let him come, I'll keep writing', I say, scratching away with my pencil.

But I can't continue my work. It's one thing to make up news about blood and quite another to actually see real blood. There's blood flowing from the forehead of the man who comes in, covering his face in a horrifying manner and dripping over his overcoat. I hold back nausea with much difficulty.

'Sir, I was only stopping him from barging in. He dashed his head against the wall himself. This is a case of suicide, Sir.' The policeman who comes in has already classified the case.

Jabbar stares at the man closely. The case of a person openly receiving an injury within the police compound can have serious consequences.

'Give him a chair and make him stop bleeding, dip a handkerchief in cold water and press it against his wound.'

When Jabbar issues orders, everyone in the room wants to be the first to begin tending to the man. Several handkerchiefs become soaked with help from the water pot in the corner. Jabbar places his own handkerchief on the stranger's hand and presses it with his palm, I wipe his bloody face with my handkerchief and move his head back so that it is resting against the back of the chair, Majid's large handkerchief is used in vain to clean off the spots of blood from the man's overcoat.

'I'm so grateful', the stranger gently removes Jabbar's hand from his forehead and places his own hand in its place.

We all quietly watch the fearful expression on his face.

'Please write a report, Sir', the injured stranger says, trembling.

'Of what?' Jabbar asks, returning to his seat.

'Sir, why don't you listen to the whole story first', the stranger suggests and I look at Jabbar with a smile that is meant to imply, 'Yes, listen.'

'Hunh! All right, give me all the facts, no lies, do you understand?'

'That is why I've come to you, Sir. I've been forced to come, why would I lie?' A sarcastic smile crosses his thick black lips, and the hand holding the handkerchief to his forehead, shakes.

'Sir, you know that we all think our children are beautiful, but people in the family and in the neighbourhood, all thought Lalli was beautiful. Some called her a fairy, others said she was a princess, and some called her Sohni (from the legendary story of Sohni and Mahinwal, the tragic lovers of the Punjab), ' He pauses.

'Then she started flirting with someone', a policemen, irritated by the dull manner in which the story had begun, prompts. Actually, it's true that in police stations and courts, the mention of beauty is not complete without a mention of love. Such a question would compel any father sitting in the police station to hang down his head in shame, but the stranger jumps and sits up straight in his chair. The wet handkerchief falls from his forehead into his lap and droplets of blood begin to trickle down his face again.

Jabbar throws the sentry a special look and then issues an order. 'Wash his wound with cold water and look, it's best if you bandage it properly. Yes, so what is your name?'

'Taj Din.'

'Look, Taj Din, keep your head back against the chair. Understand? Don't mess up the chair.'

'Sir, such words about my Lalli . . . hunh! Sir, Sir ji, you can ask anyone about my Lalli's virtue. She didn't leave the house once she grew up, she wouldn't even stand in the doorway, she took after her mother, both in character and appearance.'

'Oh, so Lalli's mother is beautiful?'

'Not now, Sir. Yes, when she came as a bride the women in the family said, Taj Din a moon has landed in your house. As long as my mother lived, she mistreated her and I too went along with my mother's wishes. Even then Lalli's mother was never rude to my mother nor did she ever ask for anything. She remained a dutiful wife. You can go to the housing complex and ask anyone there. Has anyone ever pointed a finger at her?'

'All right, all right, what happened next?' Jabbar says harshly.

'Sir ji, she became the mother of my children. Lalli was the eighth child and when she was born . . . ' he pauses to think.

'What happened when Lalli was born?'

'Her mother gave her to me and said, here there's a new moon in your house. Sir, Lalli's mother had never placed a child like this in my lap before.'

'What did you say?' I ask impulsively. My presence was suddenly changing the atmosphere in the police station.

'What could I say, Sir. It's just that Lalli became the dearest of all the children for me. She also loved me very much. If she was in someone's lap and she saw me, she would immediately spread out her arms towards me. Sometimes, when she was sleeping with her mother, she would start crying and would only stop when she lay down on my bosom.'

'All right, all right, tell us what happened next', Jabbar says impatiently.

'Sir, I married off five daughters and brought home two daughters-in-law. But Lalli's mother never interfered with my choices. Then, when Lalli was reaching puberty, she said to me one day while she was pressing my feet, 'Lalli's father, I've never asked you for anything but now I'm asking you to find a very good-looking bridegroom for Lalli, someone who is her equal in looks, remember always.' So I made note of her request.'

After this, Taj Din's voice became hoarse, he pursed his lips together and I saw that some of the policemen in the room were beginning to feel exasperated. It seemed that if they could help it they would have thrust their fingers into his throat and pulled out the entire story at one go and place it before their superior. He talks about Lalli, then his wife in the next breath—what was this nonsense? They kept looking at Jabbar who was going at a slow pace because he saw I was taking special interest in the case.

'Hmm . . . well, then did you find an appropriate match for Lalli?'

'There were many young men, Sir, Lalli's cousins, boys in the immediate and extended family. They all asked for her hand. But Sir ji, I was looking for a handsome boy to be her bridegroom, and that's why my Lalli turned seventeen and was still unwed.'

Jabbar and I exchange looks.

'Sir, you're wise, even though a daughter is as light as a bird in a cage, people say oh how long will you bear the weight of a daughter who's as heavy as a mountain, it's time for her to go to the home of her in-laws.'

Taj Din's unwanted details are testing Jabbar's patience. 'Yes, yes, that's what people say.'

'But Sir, Lalli didn't want to go anywhere. She loved her parents so much she wouldn't even visit her married sisters. Once, when one of her sisters insisted that Lalli spend the night at her house, Lalli clung to me and broke into sobs and returned home from there with me the same day.' He seems to be talking to himself.

'So you didn't find a suitable match for Lalli . . . ' I interrupt.

'I see. So, no suitable match was found for your daughter then', Jabbar immediately resumes his duty and Taj Din looks up startled.

'We found a match, Sir. One day those people came to my door after checking around with the ration shop in your locality. They praised Afzal Hussain son of Muhammad Hussain, they said he owned his own house, had no responsibilities, is leaving for Muscat to take on a very good job, and they are in a rush to have the wedding soon. Sir, they gave us the address and said we could do all the verifying we wanted. I said, show us the boy first, and then they brought the boy over for us to meet.' Taj Din pauses and asks for a drink of water.

'What was the boy like?' Jabbar asks quickly.

'The boy was very tall, strong and a gentleman. Dressed in a flowered shirt and black trousers, he looked like a rose among flowers.' Taj Din is gazing up at the ceiling as if instead of cobwebs hanging from it, he can see roses blooming there.

'So, you immediately accepted the match?'

'No Sir, we had to verify what kind of house and family he had. I arrived at his house Sir, and asked about Afzal Hussain son of Muhammad Hussain. It was all true. His uncle's wife was there. She was very hospitable. And so, I accepted the match. Even if he hadn't been the owner of a proper house and was a common labourer like me, even then I would have agreed to the match. I had never seen Lalli's mother look so happy. To tell the truth Sir, I only found out after this what a happy woman is like.'

'Lalli was also very happy?'

'Well have you known nice, respectable girls to be happy when they're getting married? I've told you Sir, how reluctant she was to leave her home even for a day. And now her wedding party was coming from out of town and after her marriage, she was going to travel overseas. She was going to cry of course, Sir.' Taj Din choked with emotion as he said this. 'Everyone was asleep at night after the mehndi ceremony ended but she kept sobbing. I was on the veranda, still awake. I got up and went to her. Then she just clung to me and wept uncontrollably. She wasn't even thinking of the henna on her hands. She said over and over again, Baba, I'm not leaving you to go anywhere . . . then Sir, I put aside my reserve and explained to her that the boy is as handsome as a prince, he's well-off and she'll be so happy in her new home, and if she was happy then I would be happy too. So Lalli heard what I had to say and finally dozed off . . . '

'All right, I see, but then the wedding party arrived?' Jabbar is anxious to get to the heart of the story.

'Oh yes Sir, what a grand wedding party it was, decorated with flowers, the band arrived on the bus along with the boy's family and friends. The bridegroom had a sehra made of roses covering his face, a heavy garland of rupee notes was draped around his neck and he had wrapped himself in a Kashmiri shawl. It's very cold today, isn't it?'

Jabbar says to me in English, 'Looks like he's an escapee from the lunatic asylum.'

'What happened after this?' Observing his superior's helplessness, Majid asks.

'Well, what could happen Sir? When the baraat arrives, a nikah takes place. My Lalli's nikah was performed with Afzal Hussain, son of the late Muhammad Hussain. Tell me Inspector Sahib, why does a bridegroom wear a sehra over his face?' Suddenly Taj Din looks directly at Jabbar in the eyes and asks.

Those who come to the police station have to answer questions not ask them.

Before Jabbar can swear at him for this impertinence, I speak up. '*Arrey* Taj Din, the purpose of a sehra is that it should be lifted up so the guests can see the bridegroom's face.'

'Yes Sir ji, so that the guest can see the groom's face and laugh at Lalli's father, taunt him, say, "oh look Taj Din, all you could find was this hideous man for your beautiful daughter? You said you would get a perfect match for your daughter, but you were tempted by the money". Sir ji, I felt as if I was sinking into the ground in shame.' While saying all this he sobbed like a child.

'I see. You were tricked. The young man showed to you was someone else.' Majid give him a drink of water.

He gulps down a few mouthfuls of water, then wiping his mouth begins talking again.

'May God bless you, yes, you've understood what happened. I screamed in front of everyone and shouted the truth, but no one believed me. Seeing this, the bridgroom's relatives began to fight with me. I said, "I'm going to the police station to report this."'

'Oh, so you're here to lodge a complaint involving deception and trickery?' a constable asks, as though he was pulling out the tail of a mouse from a mountain that had just been dug.

'No Sir ji, the elders stopped me and said Taj Din you're a poor man, how will you manage court appearances, where will you get the money to bribe lawyers, and then these people are rich, they'll be able to procure false testimony.' Taj Din pauses.

'And then what happened?' Jabbar shifted impatiently in his chair.

'Sir ji, I said I will not allow those swindlers to take away Lalli's wedding palanquin, even if I have to sacrifice my life.' He emphasizes the last sentence.

'Hunh! What did you do next?' Jabbar asks roughly.

'I stuck to my position. First, the bridegroom's family threatened me, then they placed their caps and their turbans at my brothers' feet, touched the knees of the elders and begged my sons-in-law and my sons to make me relent, they took some of the guests aside and who knows what they whispered in their ears, and then the very same people who were taunting me and laughing at me suddenly went over to the groom's side. My brothers begged me in the name of Allah and Rasul and my sons-in-law started behaving as if the fault was all mine, and then Sir ji, the maulvi sahib stood up and said, Taj Din whatever happens is fated to happen, and there's always a reason for it. Lalli is now Afzal Hussain's wife and what came to pass, did. Get up, the food is getting cold, feed your guests. And when I didn't budge even after the maulvi sahib spoke, my brothers and my sons took up the supervision.'

'Hunh. Then tell us what you did.'

'Sir ji, what could I do? Everyone ignored me as if I were a stone by the roadside. Tell me, what fault of mine made everyone snatch my rights? And then Sir ji, they all started making arrangements to send off Lalli.' Taj Din falls silent. Everyone in the room is also quiet.

'When Lalli was brought out and she was getting ready to go with her bridegroom, Lalli's mother also appeared, her face hidden in a dupatta. When she saw me panting like a dog she said to me what she had never said before.' The pointed Adam's Apple in Taj Din's dark neck bobs up and down as he tries to swallow.

'What did Lalli's mother say?' Jabbar asks.

'She said, you don't know how beautiful girls suffer when they have to live with ugly men like you. You're letting my blossom of a girl walk into the jaws of hell. You had made a promise to me, and now you're agreeing to what the others are saying. If you're a real man, don't let her go.'

'And what did you do then?' Jabbar fidgets in his chair.

'I'm telling you the truth, I don't know how a kitchen knife lying next to the empty pot got into my hand . . . and . . . and Sir ji . . . I ran after the wedding guests who were getting on the bus. Afzal Hussain was standing at the doorway of the bus.' He picked up the glass of water with trembling hands and tried to take it to his mouth but the water spilled over his overcoat. None of us in the room asked him anything, as though we were all actually watching Taj Din attack Afzal Hussain.

'After that . . . after that, she spread out her arms and clung to me and started whispering, Baba, you should have let me go, this man is like you, how much do you love me . . . and this man will also . . . God knows what she wanted to say to me about Afzal Hussain.' Taj Din stares enquiringly at everyone, his wide nostrils, as dark as caves, begin to contract and inflate like a blacksmith's pipe and, unbuttoning his old overcoat, he rises from his chair as though he would stifle if he continues to sit on the chair a minute longer.

'So you attacked Afzal Hussain and . . . ' Jabbar says, and Taj Din quickly interrupts him.

'No Sir ji, people got in the way and saved Afzal Hussain . . .' Taj Din tries to take off his coat with trembling, unsteady hands and we all see a large bloodstain on his white shirt, the blood so fresh, so bright, as if it's trickling from his heart and being absorbed in his shirt. He wraps his arms around his bloody chest and starts weeping wildly like a madman.

'No one saved my Lalli, this is my Lalli's blood.'

'You crazy ass, you killed your innocent daughter, take him away, take him to a cell, shut up this murderer who killed his own daughter!' Jabbar roars and suddenly Taj Din's screams cease. He stares simply at Jabbar and then walks out with the guards.

Jabbar strikes a match with such force that my heart pounds like a firecracker, and I feel as if the silence in the room has been shattered like glass.

That's when the Gilgiti boy from the hotel downstairs came in to collect the empty teacups. As usual, I quietly place fifty paisas for the tea and five paisas for his tip on the tray. The boy leaves, saying salaam to Jabbar instead of me.

'*Arrey*, you've paid for the tea again. The hotel-wallah would have put it on my account', Jabbar says in the complaining tone he always adopts, but I can't smile in response to his comment as I do every day, nor can I say 'You liar' in my heart as I always do. I turn the countless pages of my notebook one by one in which I have put down Taj Din's statement in his own words, but which my pen is now required to transform into just a few lines of news.

14

The Deceased Nation

Shehni had just returned from Walton Camp.

A gauzy curtain of a light orange hue fluttered on the open window, sluggishly, clinging, like a weary female snake emerging from its old skin. Sunk into a dark orange sofa, Shehni was staring vacantly at the red gate beyond the window, outside, which became visible each time the curtain moved; the red gate, covered with a vine laden with bunches of red flowers, where Colonel Kalim had dropped her off moments ago.

'I have some things to take care of, I'll say goodbye here. Please be ready in the evening', the Colonel had said, shaking her hand.

Her own silence seemed absurd to her, but she didn't know what to say in response. She stood as if in a daze, and when the Colonel said, 'Khuda Hafiz', loudly and quickly turned the car around, she also turned and came in through the gate. In the silence of the afternoon, the car's horn could be heard screaming for a while. Exhausted, irritable, she continued to walk on the path between the flower beds bursting with colourful bushes.

The crunching of the red gravel under her white sandals seemed to create a crackling in every fibre of her being. She shuddered several times as she made her way to her room. And now, she was sitting quietly, thinking, indeed what a nice Pakistan it is that has been founded! Alas, the poor Muslims! What frightening ruin they face. The corpse of the deceased nation has been turned into mincemeat. How strange it was.

She had arrived here with her mother and younger brother, Riyaz, only four days ago. The horrifying killing rampant in Delhi and the news of the thousands of fearful, cowering people in Lal Qilla had stolen the sparkle from the eyes of many of the women who twittered in Lucknow's Chattar Manzil Club, and had snatched the restiveness from their mischievious red lips, and, for no reason, one developed a fear of the hands belonging to those who wore red bindis, to the extent that even when someone as liberal as Mr Das put his hand in his pants pocket, one thought he was going to pull out a knife.

It was obvious that Shehni and her mother were also part of this vigilant group, every day they would receive telegrams, letters, saying, we're going to Karachi, we've arrived in Karachi, we're now in Karachi. All of her relatives and family members associated with the central government had left to settle in Karachi and her mother was also now considering selling their property for a good price and going to Pakistan. Who knows what incidents in Delhi would be duplicated there. But the property didn't fetch a good price—everyone left—all the relatives have settled in Pakistan. We alone remain here. Well, perhaps we could get a little less than what we expected, but no strings moved anywhere, well, how about half the price? Shehni's mother spoke to someone at the Club. The answer she received was: Why would anyone buy what already belonged to them? It was disappointing, I felt like scratching their faces, but there was no recourse except to be patient. Finally, feeling angry and frustrated, they thought, why not stay, we'll live here, our elders have ruled this country and here we are, running away in fear. God help us, these kafirs want to erase all vestiges of the name of the God and the Prophet, but Riyaz would constantly insist, well, I will not study Hindi, I swear I won't work here. And Shehni was afraid that Rafu might fit in comfortably in Karachi, he was already quite easily swayed and then girls are always ready to set their sights on government officers, and what if Rafu starts thinking, well, what about this?

But news and rumours and the unrelenting and fierce waves of terror finally made Ammi lose her footing and eventually, on a shimmering morning, their plane zoomed through the sky that was home to pigeons and kites, and brought them here although they were to go to Karachi. A distant uncle who had settled in Lahore for the longest time demanded that they visit him first, and stay with him for two weeks at least. And his daughter Naini just wouldn't give up, and at the same time, a very good family friend, Colonel Kalim became overly attentive and insisted that it would be a gross injustice to leave without seeing their Lahore, the largest city in the Muslim world. He took on the responsibility of showing them the sights of Lahore and also made arrangements to obtain petrol from the black market.

So for three days, he had been diligently fulfilling his duty. During the first day of sightseeing, Shehni looked into Naini's brown eyes and said, 'I have to say that this Colonel of yours looks like a decent sort of man. He doesn't look at all like a Punjabi.'

And Naini put on a sullen expression on hearing the 'Colonel of yours' part. But after visiting Anarkali and Nur Jahan's mausoleums, and by the time they had arrived at Jahangir's mausoleum, she had returned to normal. She stretched out on the floor next to the actual grave and said to Shehni, '*Uff*, I wish there were a Jahangir around in this day and age, or at least that some *gir* (*jahangir*—owner of the world) descended from him were an emperor today, so that instead of learning classical dancing I would try to become a Nur Jahan. What do you think? I'm beautiful, aren't I?' Then she leaned back and closed her eyes and said in a theatrical manner, 'Ah, those royal courtyards, those ornate doors and verandas, those flowing, twirling silken curtains, the chandeliers that remind one of sad brides, those servile slavegirls and those vigilant khwaja-saras (eunuchs guarding the women's quarters in palaces), and dance performances on thick carpets, and I would be pouring wine in the goblet of some 'gir', with such style that—well, what can I say . . . it would be such fun . . . '

Then she sat up with a scream and, dusting off her clothes with the palms of her hands, she said, 'But Shehni, there's one thing. In these royal palaces there was all that to worry about, I mean there was no freedom to speak of. So let's forget all that, it's fine as it is.'

'So the Colonel is fine, isn't he?' Shehni, who had been somewhat baffled by her attractive eyes and her strange behaviour, said.

'*Unh!*' Naini's sullen expression returned.

Accompanied by Shehni's mother, the Colonel appeared from an area of the mausoleum and Shehni felt that some 'gir' had donned the Colonel's clothes—oh God, what is this nonsense . . .

And then more nonsense—Riyaz had been hiding there for who knows how long.

'Riyaz', Ammi called out and Riyaz immediately began casually examining the embellishments on the walls around them, as if implying he would wish to be struck blind if he been staring at Naini all this time. And Shehni felt herself going livid. And he thinks he's my brother, how uncouth he is . . . started shaving when he was fifteen so that the hair on his face would grow quickly and now he's in the mood for falling in love for the fifth time . . . if people see us together they'll think I'm much older than him—the wretch—some brother he is. He has no consideration for his older sister, no thought of worrying about her future. The wretch! Oh God, may Naini pound him with a shoe. Oh God please!

Shehni kept writhing on the inside and when they were all leaving, she involuntarily plunked herself into the seat next to the Colonel in the car.

'Today we've seen all the old historical buildings, what's the plan for tomorrow?' the Colonel asked, starting the car.

'Ask Naini', Shehni said on an impulse.

'Well, Naini?' the Colonel asked carelessly.

'I'm busy tomorrow', Naini snarled sullenly. And Shehni felt like killing herself rather than continuing to live in this kind of a wretched world.

During the drive, Naini remained aloof and silent. Sometimes, Riyaz looked at the blue sky and sometimes he gazed at Naini's eyes. The Colonel whistled and chatted and Shehni wondered if it was necessary for the car to take the bends with such speed, was it also essential that the passengers in the car topple over each other—and during this rumination, Shehni paid little attention to the way her poor mother had been mercilessly making comparisons between their Lucknow and Nainital bungalows and Jahangir's tomb, and how she had been lamenting her losses.

The second day was spent roaming about in Lawrence Gardens, Shalimar Gardens and Shimla Hill. In the evening, they drove down the Mall, ate dinner at the Metro and then went to the Ravi for boating.

In the sky, the nine-day-old moon looked just like a young virgin, immature but arrogant— and having melted in the waters of the Ravi, the moon had turned into a glimmering pathway fading away in the far distance. *Chap-shap, chap-shap*—the Colonel and Riyaz were rowing the boat on this pearly path and the breeze carrying the fragrance and joy of spring danced like the silken dress of a bride—and Shehni felt as if she had imbibed the soft waves of the Ravi within her. Again and again, she felt as if she were a child swinging in a with her eyes closed—or that she was a lotus flower wrapped in the incorporeal mantle of the breeze, rocked gently by the waves. She was exhausted from the constant sightseeing and travelling, the chatting and laughing, and was silent. But her mother, pulling away her netted dupatta from the wayward grip of the breeze, was continuously talking about the arrival of Punjabi refugees in Lucknow.

'*Uff!* Punjabis everywhere—or Sindhis. In the Coffee House, at Chattar Manzil, in Banarsi Bagh and on the Mall Road—there was no escaping them. *Majhas, sajhas* (derogatory reference to Punjabis) and then their extremely spoilt women, Lahore appeared like a fool in the cultivated evenings of Lucknow. I couldn't stand it. And then those Sikhs with their long beards and daggers—it was terrifying . . . ' Ammi's comments didn't cease. And Shehni was getting irritated, agonizing, wondering how she could change the subject. She was afraid the Colonel might be offended. Ammi was bent on describing the flaws of the Punjabis. Why, but how sweet the Colonel is, isn't he, so diligently showing us a good time.

And her eyes began to rove stealthily in the direction of the Colonel's muscular arms, the well-built muscles rippling under his sleeve. The poor man was listening attentively to Ammi, agreeing with interjections such as, 'Yes, yes, of course, yes.'

'When we heard that our Nainital bungalow had been occupied by Sikhs, we were devastated. Just think, the sour odour of their yogurt drinks and the presence of long unkempt hair in our bungalows, ahh, the Nainital bungalows.' Ammi talked, unchecked.

'"We will have Pakistan no matter what." You and Shehni were the ones boisterously raising this slogan all the time. One would think you were not going to rest until you had won the leadership of the Muslim League and now you have Pakistan, so?' Riyaz grumbled, irately.

And Shehni muttered to herself. Hmm, Naini isn't coming tomorrow so the man's brain is on fire, the wretch—wish I could push him into the water . . .

'Well Shehni?' the Colonel said in a warm, friendly manner, as if he was trying to make a favourite child confess to a transgression.

'Hunh', Shehni mumbled, making a face.

'What do you mean? We hadn't raised slogans so we could be destroyed. Didn't you say that when Pakistan is created, both Hindustan and Pakistan will invest jointly in trade? And you said that . . . ' Ammi embarked on another long story and, feeling distressed, Riyaz increased the speed of his paddling.

'It's all right, you know. One has to make sacrifices for one's country', the Colonel said because it was the right thing to say.

And Shehni felt as though the Colonel was a great national hero, very endearing, very grand, sweet just like Jawahar Lal Nehru, and she thought, it's a good thing after all, that Pakistan was created, otherwise we wouldn't be here and . . . and she imagined she was swirling around on the marble floor in her high heels, her mind as bashful as that of a bride entering her wedding chamber and coming to a halt at the door, unable to move.

'*Chap-shap, chap-shap* . . .' the arms propelling the oars had become heavy, Ammi was yawning and Shehni's eyes began to burn with lethargy, and it seemed the food eaten at the Metro had begun to affect the entire atmosphere.

After a short while, the boat cut through the melted moonlight and came ashore.

And today, on the third day, she had gone to see the camp at Walton.

Ammi had been saying since early in the morning, 'I won't go, my heart is already hurting like a wound after all we've been through, I won't be able to see those people and you shouldn't go either, Shehni, it will affect you, make you feel very bad.'

Riyaz came up with some other programme he had to attend. Naini had been somewhat inattentive for the last two days and when Shehni pushed her, she said, 'Look, do you know, in three days I have to take part in a show that's a fundraiser for the refugees and I haven't practised my dance at all. If I go to the camp and come back tired, who will do the practice?'

Exasperated with them all, Shehni advanced towards the Colonel's car, and when he opened the car door just for her, she forgot everything else and felt as if she was gradually shrinking, like a touch-me-not flower, stooping, overcome by shyness and with that, some moments spent in Lucknow came to mind, but she quickly shrugged them off.

An uncomfortable silence prevailed during the course of the drive, mingled occasionally with the Colonel's whistling and the hum of the car engine. Actually, the Colonel had empathized with her about the problems and difficulties she and her family had faced regarding the bungalows in Nainital and out of nowhere, she found herself thinking of Rafu, imagining herself on the top of a mountain, bathed in virgin sunshine, while he is scrambling about in the ravine below among rocks and bushes. Alas . . . the poor fellow . . . but unh! Was she ever the object of Rafu's desire? So why should she be waiting patiently for him now? There was a time when she had thought she would go to America and have plastic surgery done on her somewhat flat nose and return with a beautiful nose, but not any more. Rafu had made fun of her nose for no reason, it's a nice nose—and, Lahore is also a nice city. Her eyes fixed on the road before her that glistened like a black cobra, she was overcome by a joyous cascade of thoughts, but the Colonel returned again to expressing his concern at the problems she and her family were facing because of their exile. And wearied by her thoughts, she allowed her mind to start roaming around the Colonel's concern in the hope that somewhere, she might spot a tiny hole through which she could peep into the Colonel's heart.

The car stopped before a barrack in Walton and, as he opened the car door for her, the Colonel again said a few words of consolation about her difficulties.

'Yes, but one has to make sacrifices for one's country', she said, dispiritedly.

'But I can't bear to see your sadness', the Colonel said, shutting the car door with a bang. And Shehni found the hole she was looking for and, in her great joy, she forgot how she and her family were going to survive on a few thousand rupees in Pakistan.

'Come, let's first meet my friend Dr Zaidi and take him along with us', the Colonel said as he walked alongside her.

And she, who was looking anxiously at the grimy human beings in the barracks and the moving bundles of rags and tatters in the open space, was taken aback and said, 'All right.'

Once introductions were out of the way, the doctor began saying after a short pause, in his nasal voice echoing through his unusually long nose, 'First, please rest a little, I'm ready for any kind of service, I'll take you on a tour of the whole place. It will take some time, so you should have a snack, I too have to have breakfast. Last night I drank a little more than one or two pegs and for that reason, was still in bed. By God's grace and with your good wishes, we have a suitable food service.'

And they had to go to the dining table.

The doctor continued his conversation. 'It's very sad that you had to leave your country and take refuge here . . . I'm very sensitive, that's why I feel so very distressed.' The doctor extended a plate of sandwiches towards her and, for a moment, the images of the bundles of rags and tatters swam before her eyes.

'What kind of arrangements are there to feed the refugees?' the Colonel asked, biting into a sandwich.

'By God's grace and with your good wishes, the government is very worried about them, but what can one do? Because of an increase in population there is a scarcity of food in our provinces', the doctor replied, moving the carrot halwa around with a spoon. 'And that's the reason the refugees can only be given cracked rice, an inferior quality of flour, and chana and masoor dal.' His voice was filled with sadness. 'By God's grace and with your good wishes, I'm aware of both the government's limitations and the health of the refugees, and for this reason, I'm constantly involved in research about the nutritional components in foods.'

'No, no, Doctor', the Colonel said passionately waving his spoon, 'I think the government has the resources to give the refugees one sandwich each, but it doesn't, it doesn't, I say, Sir.'

Shehni sipped the last mouthful of tea with a great deal of enjoyment and satisfaction. How honest the Colonel is and how sympathetic—ah, so endearing!

The Colonel's car was moving at a slow pace past the barracks. Half-naked, inadequately-dressed, lethargic, grimy men and filthy women—inside the barracks and outside—they all gave the impression that a garbage pail had been overstuffed and the overflowing rubbish had gathered in piles around it. Strong waves of stench attacked Shehni's nose repeatedly. On the ground, groups of refugees sat around with their belongings in the open as if they were enjoying moonlight. And at some distance, one could see women, children and men sitting without reserve on their haunches, getting rid of the dal and rice they had gulped down. A few of the women hid their faces with their dupattas when in this state, but the men and children were completely unconcerned about their condition. Poor Shehni could neither open her eyes completely nor could she keep them completely shut.

'By God's grace and with your good wishes, we have now built many toilets, but in the past one's nose was affected with this "fragrance" from five miles away.' And saying this, the doctor laughed as if he had just told a joke.

'Then why don't these people now go to the toilets?' Shehni asked.

'With your good wishes, people have become lazy from sitting around all day, doing nothing, so walking to the toilets is a chore for them', the doctor replied.

'True, they don't have to do anything to obtain their food and they've become so lazy', Shehni thought. 'They should feel ashamed, at least they should be aware that other people come to see the camps.'

The car picked up speed as it went past the barracks. On every side, one could see the same scenes, the same filthy people, like writhing worms, inside and outside the baracks, some children and women openly bathing under water pumps, and men casually walking around nearby, the thick rotis being cooked on makeshift brick fires, unruly, ravenous children with swollen bellies, people sitting in the open with water-pots—the same scenes. Shehni felt a headache coming on. She was tired of all this. And the Colonel and the doctor were arguing about the legal ban on drinking alcohol in public.

'Having a drink in a hotel is an altogether different experience', the Colonel said, with a slight movement of his stiff neck. 'As you know, people go for their honeymoon to some nice place, don't they, although their purpose can be served at the family home.'

And Shehni suddenly wondered that if one wanted to get away for a honeymoon in Pakistan, where would one go? They weren't even able to lay their hands on a good hill station, all they have is 'Murree.' And that's like having one pomegranate to share among a hundred sick individuals. What a deficit our nation has had to endure, and all at once, she recalled her Nainital bungalow.

'You must be tired from sitting in the car for such a long time. Why don't you get down and see the camp on foot', the doctor suggested.

The car stopped in front of another filthy ground, which had two barracks on one side and piles of recent and not so recent refuse spread all over on the other.

'By God's grace and with your good wishes, these two barracks have been reserved for old men and women who have no relatives', the doctor informed them.

Skinny, asthmatic, bald, blind old men with white beards and women were lying about on soiled and grimy mattresses. It seemed that throbbing in their muddied eyes, their thick-veined trembling hands, and their winded breath were the remains of their life, the residue of a life drowned in the darkness of horrifying experiences—well-fed flies hovering lazily over spit and sputum.

'They're filthy, these people, they can't get up and go out, they just lie here and spit next to the mattresses', the doctor muttered irately, trying to shoo the flies off himself.

And overwhelmed by the attack of the flies, Shehni began walking towards the car. And the residue of life kept trying to grasp at her, its hands stretched out.

An older man was recounting his story to the Colonel in a loud voice.

'The tyrants took out my son's intestines and strung them around my neck, and tore off my daughter's clothes and then forced her down on the ground naked, right in front of me.'

When the car started, Shehni's limp body fell against the Colonel's arm and to her horror the thought crossed her mind— what if someone tears her clothes off and—God help her!

The car stopped and Shehni wished she could fall out and roll in the hot earth and punish herself for this abhorrent thought.

'This is the labour room, there are many other labour rooms as well. By God's grace and with your best wishes, we have now obtained cots. Before this, both mother and infant had to lie down on the floor. It's very painful, I'm very sensitive, by your good wishes.'

Waving about hands and feet as red as pieces of meat, crying naked babies, babies covered in filth and flies, babies squeezing their mother's breasts—new mothers moaning in pain, ugly, frail and naked, soiled clothes, soiled bed linen and women feeling embarrassed—Shehni's head began to swim. She quickly came out into the veranda. These empty, innocent and bewildered looks of life, the new gasps, seemed to be wrapping themselves around her, she felt a strange kind of stirring and tickling and she felt that a baby, unlike all these babies, a baby as beautiful as a boy doll, was clutching at her breast, she wanted to cast off this tiny burden from her chest and think, think of something, that is, Pakistan's new generation, ill-fated generation, alas, freedom, what sorrow, Partition—but who cares!

'Will you see our Surgical Ward?' the doctor interrupted her thoughts.

'No, no, that's enough, it will make her feel uncomfortable', the Colonel interjected, and got into the driver's seat.

The bouncing of the car brought Shehni back to her senses.

'These mounds of earth that you see over there, do you know what they are?' the doctor asked and then answered his own question. 'These are the graves of refugees.'

'So many graves, they're all over.' Shehni was surprised.

'These refugees don't know how to maintain sanitary conditions and for this reason, we have a lot of disease in these camps.' The doctor's voice seemed to be drowning. 'The result is that the population in the graveyard is increasing. Colonel Sahib is my friend so I'm saying this, otherwise I'm a very cautious man.'

'How true. These poor people had no idea that they could die even when they had arrived in Pakistan.' The Colonel drew a long sigh. 'They must have thought that death could not come in any other way except through the daggers of Hindus and Sikhs.'

'A pity, what a pity . . . ' the three of them continued to heave sighs of sorrow until a cloud of dust suddenly blocked their noses and Shehni wondered how many germs had wrapped themselves around her.

'That's the Walton Railway Station', the doctor pointed with his finger.

'A train has just arrived with refugees and by God's grace and with your good wishes, it got through safely.'

Shehni cast a look at the crowds. Somewhat satisfied expressions, smiles on their lips, as if they're saying, 'We've come to Pakistan, we've arrived.' Carrying big bundles on their heads, women were running around like camels, picking up their belongings and the men were mostly busy with smoking hookah or beedis, and the children were romping around on the warm earth.

'Why are they all gathered here in the sun?' Shehni asked sadly. 'Why don't they go to the barracks?'

'They'll first receive cholera shots', the doctor said, as if if was giving an interview. 'And then they will be kept in the Hospitality Camp, so that if someone develops cholera, it happens here.'

'These are suitable arrangements', the Colonel said, just to say something.

'Hospitality Camp!' Images of her bungalows in Lucknow and Nainital swam before her eyes.

'Yes, Hospitality Camp, look, over there', the doctor replied seriously.

Shehni saw that two or three tin sheets had been put together and under them was nothing but dust. 'Oh no, how hot their shade must be', Shehni realized for the first time, and she felt as though the smiles of the newcomers were turning into dust under this shelter. She longed to dance at some fundraiser with such passion that her clothes would become tattered, her body is exhausted and she is gasping until her chest seems ready to explode and Naini's dance practice fails, and the . . . her thoughts paused—Lahore is a very nice city and Rafu is a fool, and suddenly, she wanted to press the car horn with her palm and keep pressing it—and she felt as if she was standing at some great height and looking down below at a stormy ocean with a fearful hatred and she said, apprehensively, 'Let's go home now.'

'I think you're very sensitive', the doctor said sadly. 'By God's grace and with your good wishes, my condition is the same as yours. Last night, I became so absorbed in thinking about the refugees that I drank too much. Anyway, try not to feel so bad.' And touching the Colonel's shoulder he said, 'Please drop me right here, I have to meet Dr Razia.'

And when the doctor got off, being alone with the Colonel once again made her feel that the waves of the River Ravi had been absorbed into her body.

'You were very upset', the Colonel said, leaning towards her and Shehni felt as though she was in the lap of a whirlpool, slowly sinking in.

The car screeched to a halt. Carrying bundles of shisham leaves and sticks on their heads, the refugee women walking across the road barely escaped with their lives.

'By God's grace and with your good wishes, they were saved', the Colonel said bursting into laughter, and Shehni broke into a laugh as well.

The car left Walton and came out on the main road leading to the city.

'Let's go to the Gymkhana Club in the evening', the Colonel said. 'It will help you get rid of this moroseness you're feeling.'

Shehni remained silent. But the Colonel started talking and continued chatting non-stop. Details about Miss Daniyal, Mrs Nath and Prem Kaur—the colour of Miss Daniyal's eyes and the blinking of her curved lashes—And Mrs Nath!

'Oh my, Miss Shehni, what can I tell you? There was only one woman in the club worth looking at. Honey-coloured complexion, large dreamy eyes. And her sari-draping style was such that not a curve of her body was hidden, she looked just like a statue from the Ajanta caves—and that Prem Kaur! May God forgive me! What a Partition this has been, it destroyed the Gymkhana Club, you know.'

And sitting next to him, she didn't know how many stories she listened to about eyes, saris and bodies, and the speed of the car accelerated. She wasn't sure if the Colonel had his foot on the accelerator or her heart—Shehni felt she was a doll stuffed with rags, a silly doll into whose heart a tiny ember had descended and the rags inside were slowly smouldering . . . burning . . . and from somewhere appeared that wretch Naini's face, her cheeks resting on the windscreen, her brown eyes blinking dramatically . . . ahh that Mughal palace and the ornate courtyard and veranda . . . the chandeliers as sad as a bride . . . and then the refugee camp . . . my son's intestines . . . my daughter's clothes . . . my fields—everything became fused together and turned into, was distorted, as something she couldn't fathom . . . maybe Jahangir's mausoleum or Ajanta's caves . . . and she felt the waves of the River Ravi washing over her, and Shehni murmured, 'The poor, unfortunate Muslims.'

'You're very sensitive', the Colonel said in a worried tone as the car pulled up to her house.

And since then she had been sitting on the sofa, lost in her thoughts, agonizing over the ruination of the Muslims. The orange-coloured silken curtains were swaying and twirling and she was staring at the gate laden with bright red flowers, and she was thinking, alas, all of us refugees are in a terrible state, some stuffed into barracks like refuse, some left in the company of crude and coarse Punjabis.

And in the evening, when she entered her uncle's grand drawing room, everyone, from her mother to Naini, was surprised to see the downcast expression on her face.

'Get ready to go to the Club', the Colonel said enthusiastically.

'I'm not going', she said and walking over to the window, she stared outside.

'Why?' her mother asked in a startled tone.

And she turned around and said with stately solemnity, 'Today I have seen Walton Camp.'

1948

15

Drizzle

That too had been a winter evening. During the day, a drizzle
had come down the smoky clouds softly. It fell noiselessly over
the roof and in the courtyard of the old, abandoned bungalow,
and was continuously absorbed. But when this same drizzle fell
on the moss-laden parapets and borders of the walls around
the old-fashioned, long, red veranda, it diminished, turned into
drops of moisture and then dribbled into the tiny puddles below.
Farkhanda Khanam, sitting on a chair, apparently reviewing a
sample MA psychology paper, felt as if her entire being was
being bathed in moisture. She thought that a cool breeze in the
winter cleared one's mind, and as long as her mind could be
made to deal with psychological complexities, she didn't care
that her body, wrapped in an old coat, shivered from the cold.

'*Tip, tip.*'

To Farkhanda Khanam, the drops of water sounded like
the ticking of a clock, making her conscious of the passage of
time. Just then, dragging his feet in a pair of rubber slippers,
a stranger appeared from a room at the far end of the long

veranda. Farkhanda Khanam observed him through her lowered gaze. His hair was carefully combed and behind his glasses, his vigilant gaze seemed to be pinned on some point in the distance. At this moment, on this wet evening, Farkhanda Khanam found this man to be extremely attractive. But she continued with her work. She knew how to curb her feelings.

The stranger was Abdul Rahman, a mathematics lecturer who taught in a faraway college in the district. In his hand, was a book on mathematics that he was tired of reading. He had come here to get advice from the professors at the University regarding a possible Doctorate. Like a very cautious neighbour, he glanced across the row of flower plots neatly arranged in a straight line, his gaze wandering to the spot where Farkhanda Khanam sat unravelling the psychology paper. When Abdul Rahman's young nephew brought him a cup of tea, he thought it wouldn't hurt to ask this 'poor female student' if she would like some tea as well.

For Abdul Rahman, every boy or girl bent over a book assumed the guise of a student. From the corner of her eye, Farkhanda Khanam saw him walking towards the flowerpots with a resolute, fearless step.

'Have you had tea?' Abdul Rahman asked in a serious, solicitous tone.

'Not yet.' Farkhanda Khanam raised her head slowly and looked first at Abdul Rahman's extended hand offering her the teacup, then at his face on which there was an expression of a strange kind of simplicity and beauty.

'Then drink this', Abdul Rahman said.

As if indeed she had a right to this tea, Farkhanda Khanam stretched out her hand and took the teacup from him. Their fingers touched. Farkhanda Khanam lowered her eyes and began drinking her tea. But Farkhanda Khanam knew that her big eyes didn't look too bad on her light brown complexion, but once lowered they could not possibly create an impression because her lashes were sparse and drooping. She immediately lifted her eyes.

'It's very boring to study after one has passed exams', Abdul Rahman said, as if speaking to himself.

'No, it's not that boring, really. In my opinion, the decision to accomplish a goal becomes interesting in itself', Farkhanda Khanam said, with a certain degree of confidence and then, lowering her gaze, she began gulping down the tea.

The subject of their conversation had been exhausted. They were not looking at each other. Drops of water dribbled with a regular beat from the moss-ridden forehead of the veranda, but Farkhanda Khanam could discern all the musical rhythms in that sound. A tonga rode past them on the road with a '*cham-cham*', and Farkhanda Khanam felt as though a girl with bells on her ankles was dancing somewhere. A crow flapped its wings in the tree in front of her and disappeared among the leaves. Farkhanda Khanam found the rustling of the leaves very pleasing.

Then, in the distance, near the stream, the blue smoke arising from the burning, dry leaves in Jano Mai's oven under the shed, tore through the light blanket of mist and began climbing upward like a minaret, and Farkhanda Khanam felt as if encased in this blue smoke, she too was being lifted up.

Farkhanda Khanam finished drinking her tea and, holding the empty teacup in her hand, she wondered what to do next. Then, she extended the empty teacup towards Abdul Rahman.

The brief story begun on this rainy, winter evening reached its conclusion the very next day when Abdul Rahman's aunt leaped over the boundary created by the flower pots and, entering Farkhanda Khanam's house with a disgruntled expression on her face, offered a proposal for her to her family. When Farkhanda Khanam heard of this, she felt as if a lightning bolt had struck her head. Such a weighty issue and it took only a few moments to resolve it. Her composure regained, Farkhanda Khanam stood in front of the dusty, blurred mirror in her room for a long time. She suddenly realized that all those young men who were with her at the university simply stayed away from her because they were disconcerted by her beauty.

Before the exams were over, Farkhanda Khanam became Begum Abdul Rahman. All this happened so quickly and simply that like her only best friend, Farkhanda Khanam too couldn't believe that she was indeed getting married. Although Abdul Rahman had insisted that the wedding be simple, everyone missed the festivity and revelry that such an occasion entails.

On her wedding night, Farkhanda Khanam's entire being was in listening mode. She wanted to hear, 'You're very beautiful, I lost my heart to you at the first glance, I could have given my life to win you.'

Finally, Abdul Rahman began to speak.

'We'll be living here for three or four days only. Please excuse Mumani Jaan if she upsets you in any way.'

'Why?' Farkhand Khanam asked, lifting her eyelashes.

'She must be angry with both of us because I ignored her daughter and married you instead.' Abdul Rahman spoke softly.

Farkhada Khanam felt that her heart, which had been pounding in her chest, had suddenly stopped. She stared at her husband and then all at once it seemed that her whole body had been transformed into a burning ear.

'Why?' How this word escaped from Farkhanda Khanam's inflamed throat, she didn't know. All of her body was about to burst with the heat of bashfulness and joy.

Now he will say, 'The minute I saw you I lost my heart.' Hai, what an impudent thing to say. But Abdul Rahman was saying slowly, 'I ignored Shamsa because she was immature in her thinking. I look at the relationship between a man and a woman from a rational point of view. It is natural that a man and a woman should need each other. Why is it necessary to recite poems and deliver a dialogue about flowers and the moon? How can a sensible woman be happy with such irrational things? Isn't that right?'

Abdul Rahman fell silent, as if he had uttered the last word.

'Then why . . . why me . . . why . . . ' Farkhanda Khanam wanted to ask this question but words failed her.

'The confidence and simplicity you expressed impressed me greatly', Abdul Rahman said with a smile, and Farkhanda Khanam thought how the eyes and the face lie.

'Who you were and what you were didn't concern me. Nor am I interested in what you will become. You were pleasing to me in that one moment, and that's what's important for me, Farkhanda Khanam.'

Farkhanda Khanun felt as if Abdul Rahman had broken her being in two and one half had dropped into the horizon like a falling star and she had been reborn in the form of the incomplete other half.

'What if I hadn't accepted you?' Farkhanda Khanam tried to look for the broken star.

'I would have been somewhat disappointed, but it would have made me happy to know that you have the courage of your convictions. I would have remembered you with great respect all my life.' Gazing into the space before him, Abdul Rahman spoke in a very loving manner.

'Yes . . . yes . . . ' Farkhanda Khanam voiced these words as if she were accepting him as her sovereign.

She was a student of psychology, and psychology transforms all the innocence of love, all its delicacy, into a ball of tangled yarn. But it is odd that even after having read every book, a woman never turns away from the book that dictates her nature, and which is lies on a shelf in the safest part of her heart. But Farkhanda Khanam strongly assured herself that she was, in reality, the person Abdul Rahman had discovered and, in a short while, the two of them departed to set up housekeeping in his aunt's home.

But what was strange was that although Farkhanda Khanam managed the house all day, she still had the feeling that she would be leaving soon to go somewhere else. Since Abdul Rahman was the kind of man who considered a woman to be his equal and regarded the economic freedom of women to be the first step on the ladder of progress, she would have got a job after she completed her master's. But she was pregnant. Abdul Rahman didn't even ask her to sew on a button for him nor did he ever ask her to bring him a glass of water.

In the second place, Farkhanada Khanuum turned out to such be a perfect housewife that even when she and Abdul Rahman were having a conversation about some weighty literary subject, she would suddenly remember that she had forgotten to dust the bookshelves. What if someone paid them a surprise visit?

When, dressed in nice, neat clothes, Abdul Rahman left for college, a wave of inferiority would invade Farkhanda Khanam's body and to escape from its grip, she would immediately tighten her pallu around her waist and start dusting everything. At the same time, she would begin scolding the young servant in such a way that it made her somewhat ordinary looks appear even less attractive. But as soon as Abdul Rahman returned from college, she would wash up and look presentable. When she applied pink lipstick, she would shape her lower lip carefully, and she would circle her big eyes with kajal; she had also learnt how to lift her drooping lashes with the aid of mascara.

'Anything new?' she would ask Adbul Rahman with a smile, when she greeted him at the door.

'I'm here', Abdul Rahman would say with a laugh. He always had the same answer for her. And in no time, his entire personality would pervade every part of the house. Farkhanda Begum would shrink in the shadow of this personality.

At night, after both of them had had their fill of reading their books, Abdul Rahman would begin a conversation in a very interesting way. He would talk about his college staff, his students, and Farkhanda Begum would listen to him with such interest, and carry on a discussion in a way that would make one think she had personally experienced all of the incidents and happenings.

Abdul Rahman was going through some problems as well. For example, his promotion was being delayed since he didn't curry favour with the principal.

'Why, just resign and then we'll see how easily they get another mathematics professor', Farkhanda Begum would proudly say, and Abdul Rahman would feel as if his problems had suddenly diminished.

Sometimes, Abdul Rahman recounted stories of his childhood days.

'When I was young, I went on the roof one day to cut off a kite string.' Abdul Rahman would begin speaking and Farkhanda Khanam would follow him in her imagination.

'Oh my God! You climbed up on the roof when you were a boy? What if, God forbid, you had fallen off?' Farkhanda Begum would convey her anxiety in an agitated voice.

'And when I was playing hockey one day, I hurt my ankle.'

'Oh my! It doesn't still hurt, does it? These sports are really bad.' Farkhanda Begum would feel the pain of his injury in her heart and, drawing a long breath of satisfaction, smiling, swimming against the current, bobbing up and down in the pond of his past, he reached for the water lilies. Sometimes Farkhanda Begum wondered why Abdul Rahman loved to talk about his own past with such interest. Then, she would surmise that their life together was so full and so perfect that it did not merit discussion.

In this way, Farkhanda Begum became so familiar with Abdul Rahman's past life that she began to feel as if she been with him since childhood, as if she were older than him and had always protected him. Her sense of being older than him became so strong that now when he left for work she would warn, 'Look, ride your bike on the side of the road, and don't argue with the principal.'

At night, in the small courtyard, in the dim light of the stars, Farkhanda Khanam would bend over the sleeping form of Abdul Rahman. She would gently touch his soft, thick hair, and if she found his hand pressed in an uncomfortable position, she would gently straighten it, and she would watch him for a long time. When, still asleep, Abdul Rahman turned on his side, her delicate heart would be buried under a heavy weight of loneliness.

The barking of the dogs in the middle of the night made Farkhanda Khanam shiver with a sense of foreboding. It seemed to her that there were robbers trying to climb over the small walls encircling the house. And when the life in her belly stirred, she trembled fearfully. She was terrified at the thought of giving birth. Farkhanda Khanam wanted to share all these thoughts and fears with Abdul Rahman, but she desisted from telling him anything because she was afraid that he might begin to see her as an ordinary woman, a thought that filled her with shame. If only she too could talk to him about her childhood, the childhood in which her fears were rooted. But Abdul Rahman had broken her into two the very first day and she couldn't forget that.

One day, Farkhanda Khanam had a headache and was in bed, feeling and looking miserable.

'Can I put some lipstick on your lips?' Abdul Rahman suddenly asked her.

'Why?'

Abdul Rahman didn't give an answer to her 'why' and busied himself with looking for Aspro. A sense of ugliness began to snarl like a viper in Farkhanda Khanam's heart, and sorrow began to drip inside her head.

'What did I think of when I was unmarried—so many thoughts there were like soft, clean cotton balls', Farkhanda Khanam started saying and then, her eyes gazing into space, she waited for Abdul Rahman's question, 'What did you think about?' She didn't volunteer any information about her thoughts and he didn't ask. Perhaps they both knew that a man's mind becomes clouded when faced with the flight of a woman's imagination.

Then, 'munna' came into their lives. Munna's cooing became part of their conversation. Farkhanda Khanam no longer had the time to examine herself in the mirror. Within a year of her marriage, she was beginning to feel so old and wise that the burden of this knowledge began to tire her out. Every day felt the same, every night the same. Then, this sameness coated Farkhanda Khanam's cheeks like layers of ice, kept falling, every passing day was buried in its depths, was hidden. Suddenly, Farkhanda Khanam remembered her incomplete master's and she busied herself with studying.

When she went to bed late at night after her studies, she would see Abdul Rahman sleeping soundly. She would look at him pityingly. For some reason, she felt that there existed something between her and Abdul Rahman that shouldn't be there.

Moved by sympathy, she would reach out to touch Abdul Rahman and then she would fall asleep with the thought that she should spend more time taking care of him.

The December holidays brought them back to the same bungalow where their story had begun and ended quickly as well. So, what was left now after the ending of the story that had permeated every fibre of Farkhanda Khanam's being?

Just recently, she had told her best friend that she was the luckiest woman in the world. Her friend had narrated her own sob story, explaining that her husband not only rules over her, but he also doesn't trust her. As usual, Farkhanda Khanam sat in the veranda with a book on psychology. The line of flower pots constituted the boundary between her parents' home and the home of her in-laws. She was sitting on a chair that had been brought from her parents' house. It was a strange coincidence that it had been raining heavily that day as well. There were clouds in the sky and a light drizzle was now falling, and being absorbed into the soft moist earth.

Flapping his slippers, Abdul Rahman came out of the room that used to belong to Mumani. Farkhanda Khanam didn't lift her gaze. The teacup in one hand, Abdul Rahman tried to grasp her finger, but Farkhanda Begum felt nauseated.

A tonga jangled down the road. The crows kept making a din as they tried to descend on the tree for the night, and when Mai Janu began heating up her oven, as was her custom, the smoke from the the burning of dry leaves rose like a swirl in the air. But Farkhanda Begum didn't move from her chair. '*Tip, tip, tip.*' Drops of water dripped from the moss-covered parapets into the ditches below. Just then, a scooter came in through the gate. Farkhanda Begum didn't see who it was.

The scooter came to a halt in the shadow of the wall.

Farkhanda Khanam sat quietly without moving.

Then, a man in a raincoat came and handed her an invitation card. It was an invitation to a child's birthday.

'Who is this person?' Farkhanda Khanam said after reading the name on the invitation.

'He knows you, he lived in your neighbourhood in Bareilly, he's here with me. Shall I ask him to come in?'

And Farkhanda Khanam remembered who this man was. Flinging off the burden that weighed her down, she jumped over the border created by the flower pots and ran towards the section belonging to her in-laws. She bumped into Abdul Rahman who had come out after hearing the sound of the scooter.

'I don't know who he is. Just say, maybe we'll come, just say anything.' Her lips quivering, Farkhanda Begum uttered these words with great difficulty and fell on her bed.

When Abdul Rahman returned, he saw Farkhanda sitting on the bed, her gaze pinned to the fire in the fireplace.

'What has frightened you, what's the matter?' Abdul Rahman touched her hand, and Farkhanda Khanam collapsed on the bed like a wall of sand and broke into violent sobs.

Abdul Rahman quickly covered her body with a blanket and she began to shiver uncontrollably.

'Is it a sin if someone washes the feet of an eleven-year-old?' Farkhanda Khanam asked in a quivering, hysterical voice.

'No', Abdul Rahman replied, tearfully.

'I used to like roaming about in my bare feet in those days. One day he said, come you dirty girl, let me wash your feet, and I felt very ticklish and grabbed his hair. Was this a sin?' Farkhanda Khanam murmured as if speaking to herself.

'And then?' Abdul Rahman asked in a heavy voice.

'And then when I was older, he sent a proposal of marriage, my mother refused', Farkhanda Begum said, trembling.

'Did you want to say yes?' Abdul Rahman asked, managing the words with difficulty.

'I don't know, but why is he following me, why has he come? I'm scared of him, he hasn't forgotten me.' Farkhanda spoke in an unsteady voice and broke into sobs.

'Oh Farro, can anyone forget you? Look what happened after I saw you just once.' Looking into her wide, staring eyes, Abdul Rahman said tearfully, and Farkhanda Khanam felt a languor taking hold of her.

'Who knows where the poor fellow has been looking for you? Why are you frightened? No one can take you away from me, no one.' Abdul Rahman spread his arms over Farkhanda Khanam's body.

And for the first time in her life, Farkhanda Khanam felt safe from every danger in the world. For the first time, sobbing, buried under the weight of these arms like a stubborn little girl, she sank into a pleasant dream that was as soft as pods of cotton. It was as if she had been in a state of insomnia for the last twenty-five years just so she could hear these few words from Abdul Rahman. She felt as though Abdul Rahman's arms were becoming longer, very long, until they held the whole world within their embrace.

16

The Slap

Najma Apa had finally arrived at her husband's house after the wedding. She was exhausted from sitting with her head lowered all day, surrounded by the female guests. Now, alone at last, she drew a sigh of relief and, lifting her veil, she surveyed her surroundings. Then, to relieve the stiffness in her legs, she drew together her wedding dress and getting off from the soft bed, she stood straight and stretched her tired body. Suddenly, her gaze fell upon the full-length mirror in front of her, in which she could see her adorned and ornamented beauty reflected. For a minute, she was stunned at the sight of her beguiling appearance. She was beautiful to begin with, and then to top it, the wedding adornments. She went up close to the mirror and stared joyfully at every single piece of jewellery, and excitedly caressed her silken dress with her pink fingers. These clothes, this jewellery—she had not seen these even in her dreams because she was a girl from a poor family. A diamond among rags. Those who saw her noticed that her eyes always had a dreamy look, and a permanent glow seemed to light her face from within.

Najma gazed at her beautiful reflection again and again, and lowered her eyes bashfully. At this moment, she thought that if her Zia Bhai saw her now he would probably not be able to tear his gaze away. He was mesmerized even when he saw her in her shabby clothes. How strange he is. He would come to the house and stay for hours but two days before the wedding he just disappeared, despite Amma's insistence that he come, as if he had forgotten the way to the house. The day she was clositered for the *mayun* (a celebration on the day before the wedding), was the only day she saw him. For some reason, he was very quiet that day. And his eyes were so red, one would think he had been weeping soundlessly.

The bedroom door opened noisily and Najma's eyes returned to the mirror ardently. This time, along with her reflection, a black image that looked like a small mass of slimy clay dredged from a pond had spread over the mirror. Eyes shining like that of a snake's and lips dangling like those of a camel. This was the beautiful Najma's rich husband. Najma's innocent heart was suddenly stilled and her white, velvety lids covered her astonished gaze. The sounds of sobbing began to echo in the decorated, bedecked room.

'Please come down for lunch', the maidservant said to her the next morning.

'I'm not hungry', Najma said, turning away, as though she didn't want anyone to see her face. A sad smile appeared on the maidservant's face and she left with a nod.

After she had gone, Najma got up and began to pace about the room like a demented person. She was filled with hatred and horror for everything around her. She wanted to run away from here. But where could she run to? Who in the world was hers now? Her mother and father had fulfilled their 'duty'.

They had let out the animal only after ensuring that the pasture was filled with green grass, and anyway, what meaning does a girl's preference have? Zia! He too had said nothing. Now, Najma felt he had wronged her. He was a distant cousin, and he was fond of her but he was never able to make a show of his feelings to her or to anyone else. Perhaps, because he was an unemployed man with a bachelor's degree. Najma liked him too. But neither of them expressed their emotions. Bashfulness and shyness had placed a lock upon Najma's lips, and perhaps Zia was afraid that having been raised in an old-fashioned family Najma might view his love as a sin and reject him, and then he would be deprived even of seeing her sweet, innocent face. In any case, love and the struggle to be prudent turned their emotions into embers hidden deep in the ashes.

Najma was thinking, now that all her paths are blocked, where will she go. What should she do? Should she, in accoradance with custom and tradition, give up forever her pristine and beautiful youth to this ugly and terrifying man? Should she be courageous and show the world that just as a man can't be attracted to an ugly woman, in the same way a beautiful woman can't spend her life with an ugly, loathsome man? What will the world say to her? All kinds of thoughts were racing through her mind. Finally, she lay down and tears from her eyes fell and were absorbed into the pillow. She wanted to drown the weight of her failure by weeping at her condition. A helpless woman can only cry. Only this can provide her with peace and tranquility for a short while. She didn't know how long she stayed like this, weeping at her lot. At last, evening fell and she went home in keeping with the custom of *chauthi*.

* * *

'Amma', she said, and broke into sobs.

'My daughter! What has happened?' her mother embraced her and asked. She could understand a great deal, but what could she do? Helpless at the hands of her poverty, she had happily buried her daughter in a pile of gold and silver.

'Amma, I won't go back.' Najma was shaping her thoughts into words.

'Where, my daughter?' Her mother pretended not to understand.

'Back, Amma!'

'No, no daughter, don't say such things. For a woman, her husband's home is her entire world.' The mother was bound in the cruel grip of custom and tradition.

'But Amma, I'm terrified of him. For God's sake don't send me back. I beg you!'

'Heaven forbid, child! This is a sin that Allah will never forgive. Have you ever heard a Muslim women denigrating her husband? My child! In our religion, the husband holds a very high status.' The mother had absolute faith in her own religious education and training. Mercy. What better tactic than religion to suppress the rebellious thoughts of a girl whose education has been limited to the study of Raah-e-nijaat (the path to salvation) and Mirat-ul-uruus (the mirror of the bride)?

Then, suddenly, Najma appeared to come to her senses. She got up quickly and rushed to the other room. In her head echoed, 'Have you ever heard a Muslim woman denigrating her husband? My child, in our religion the husband holds a very high status . . . Heaven forbid, child, this is a terrible sin that Allah will never forgive.' She felt her strength ebbing and she began to weep.

'Najma!' She heard the sound of a quivering voice. Zia was standing before her. She wiped her tears and pulled herself together.

'You're crying, Najma.' Zia came up to her.

'Yes.'

'Why?'

'Because I hate my husband.'

'So, do you want to love that animal?'

'Yes.'

'Why?' Zia asked.

'He's my husband. God will be angered by my hatred for him, He will put me in hell.'

'So in your opinion, closeness to this animal is heaven?'

'But this was my fate. I couldn't change it, nor could you.'

'Who is the master of our fate?'

'God!' Najma's tone was steely.

'Oh! Then it's really strange that God handed you this fate when you had been worshipping Him so passionately.'

'Only He knows what these mysteries mean.'

'How pathetic is this belief of yours. Deliberately turning your life into hell is called fate.' He broke into a laugh.

Najma was sitting on the bed, her legs dangling. The skin on her face seemed to have darkened.

'You're laughing Zia?' she asked dejectedly.

'Yes.'

'Why?'

'Feeling sorry at your fate. He disregarded your strong faith and destined a two-legged bull for you.'

'Don't say that. Aren't you afraid of God?'

'What has He given me for being afraid of Him until now? He snatched you from me and handed you over to a depraved man so you could adorn his bed.'

This was the first time Najma had heard from Zia an expression of his love for her, but this was a moment when she was finding herself caught in the jaws of fate's horrifying demon.

'Don't talk like this in front of me now. You'll be committing a sin.'

'Sin? I want to commit an even greater sin. I want to snatch you from the dangerous clutches of this animal and run off somwhere.'

'For God's sake, Zia, don't stand in my way now. If only you had mustered courage before all this happened. Now, to love me means you let me continue on my path.'

'You can deceive your tongue, but not your heart.' Zia's voice was thick with emotion. He lowered his eyes and a few drops of tears fell on Najma's gold shoes. Najma was stunned. Zia got up and left the room and she followed him with her gaze even though she didn't want to. Then a prolonged, heaving moan echoed in the bedroom.

* * *

That night Najma was leaving for her husband's house. Before she climbed into the palanquin, her mother said, 'Daughter, think of your husband's home as your own, respect him, and love him.' The mother was paraphrasing a famous verse, 'Hand over poison and then follow with instructions that you drink it.'

Najma's eyes were dry but her heart was weeping. She gazed at the palanquin waiting with its mouth open to take her into its embrace like a dark grave.

'All right', was all she could say.

When she arrived at the house, she got off the palanquin. Her head was swimming. If her husband hadn't caught her she would have collapsed and fallen. But the moment her husband's hand touched her body she recoiled, as if she had been bitten by a snake. Her yearning eyes turned to her pink arm, which was in the grip of two black, unsightly hands and, for a moment, Najma felt that God had ignored her devoutness.

'Najma!' One day her repulsive-looking husband called out as he stepped into the house and Najma lowered her head fearfully as always.

'Look! What an exquisite necklace I've brought to put around your beautiful neck.'

Najma thought he had described her neck as hideous. Words coming out of an ugly person's mouth sound hideous even if they are in praise of beauty. Her husband put the necklace around her neck and Najma felt as if a snake had been wrapped around her throat, and impelled by fear she began to feel that her neck was about to snap. She quickly took off the necklace and put it on the dressing table.

'Why did you take it off?' he asked imperiously.

'No reason', Najma whispered.

'Don't you have any regard for my happiness?'

She remained silent. Her eyes were on the shiny pearls in the necklace and in one pearl she could see Zia's tearful gaze as in her ears echoed the words, 'Najma, you can deceive your tongue but you can't deceive your heart.'

'Put it on', he grabbed her lovingly and said.

'All right.' She began to laugh. Her laugh was like the sound made by a pick plucking broken strings.

'Come on, put it on, put it on.' He was squeezing her hard as he laughed.

'All right, all right!' She did not stop laughing.

They were both laughing. His large belly shook as if an earthquake was erupting inside, in her bosom was a tomb of emotions.

* * *

Six months had passed since they were married, but she felt as if she had been burning in this fire for six years. In keeping with the demands of society, she tried to love her husband but she failed. The moment she saw him she would become paralyzed, just like a tiny bird that felt the power ebb from its arms on finding itself face-to-face with a cat. Her childlike thoughts and her sprightly body was tied up in the tight grip of fate, religion and the vague notion of her husband's rights. But her rebel heart? That continued to beat. Hiding in its depths a beautiful and delightful world, her heart wanted to take her to the colourful valleys of youth and beauty. But her beliefs repeatedly pulled her back into the burning oven of uncertainty. Finally, a day came when these worries made her ill and confined her to her bed. Her husband was observing her failing health in the hope of a child, but Najma was thinking instead about something special for a special time.

* * *

A mysterious silence hung about the house. Najma was lying unconscious in her room, surrounded by the lady doctor and nurses, and outside, her husband, mother, father and other close relatives were standing around in a state of anxiety, their ears pinned to the murmuring voices on the other side of the door. Every moment of waiting seemed like a year. Every now and then, the tinkle of instruments coming from the room accelerated their heartbeats, and then again, silence would fall.

The mother had her ears pinned to the door. The lady doctor's high heels clicked as she approached the door. The mother moved back quickly.

The door opened and the lady doctor's face, made up with powder and lipstick, appeared, and suddenly it was as if everyone's heartbeats slowed down from fatigue.

'She's had the baby, but the baby was dead.'

No one uttered a word.

'And my daughter!' The mother spread out her arms.

'She's still unconscious.' The door was closed again.

Everyone was still standing, worried and agitated, as if they wanted to hear something else.

'If you want to see the mother, you can.' The lady doctor re-appeared an hour later. There was a look of extreme sadness in her eyes.

They all entered the room as if they were murderers walking into a courtroom. Najma lay on a bed in the middle of the room, listless, her eyes shut. Her frail and thin body was covered with a white bedsheet. At the foot of the bed, on a tray, was the body of the dead infant.

'Najma.' Tears rolled down her husband's puffy cheeks.

Najma opened her dark, sunken eyes with great difficulty.

'Will you see the baby?'

'Yes', she whispered.

The nurse brought her the dead baby.

Najma's lips moved. 'The . . . baby is very beautiful . . . the beautiful child of its beautiful father. If only he could also see it.' Najma's bluish lips parted and blood rushed to her ashen face. She was feeling happy as she lay dying.

Everyone looked at each other, as if asking,

Is this true? But they already knew the answer.

The husband's narrow forehead shrunk with rage and his wide nostrils began to heave like a blacksmith's bellows.

Najma saw his condition and, on her face, her eyes began to twinkle like stars. She was happy that before dying she had left a resounding slap on society's face. She gazed at everyone one by one to make sure that they had all suffered a blow. Then, quietly, her shining eyes closed, and it was as if a cloud had wafted over twinkling stars.

17

Kaneez

Weary from lumbering for a mile and a half on the widest and the most beautiful road in the Civil Lines, Kaneez and her grandmother were now dragging their feet as they approached the bungalow. Daadi's chaddar fluttered in the hot gusting breeze and Kaneez's old black burka kept slipping from her head. Impeding their progress were Nammi and Chammi! Nammi was holding her mother's hand but Chammi didn't have that kind of energy. Daadi's frail and stooped body and Chammi on her hip—she had turned copper-red from the heat.

'Thank you God, we have been patient, but please you should not be patient', Daadi would moan intermittently. But Kaneez couldn't stop wishing they had accepted the tonga fare from the Begum. 'If only we had taken it', she thought, 'we wouldn't be frying ourselves in this heat. What's so dishonourable about borrowing money? Daadi would have paid it off eventually just to avoid the dishonour, even though she's stingy with other things.' But despite all these ruminations, the road seemed to be getting longer and longer. With every bungalow that came along, she wished it was the one they were going to so that they could go in and take refuge from the blistering road. But the minute she blinked her eyes in the sun and looked carefully she would see that their destination was still far away . . . on the other side of the canal was their little bungalow, nestled in the thick shade of tall shisham, eucalyptus, mango, jamun and gular trees. Here, the sun took a beating and hot gusts came with a whimper instead of a roar.

Anyway, it's best to keep moving. They were finally at the bungalow. Everyone dashed inside to seek refuge in their corner of safety. The door hadn't been shut yet, chaddar and burka had not yet been removed when suddenly Kaneez was attacked by a surge of emotions brought on by her misfortune.

'Well, so is it all over?' Suddenly, overcome, in deep anguish, she slapped her thighs and began to weep.

'*Arrey* Ishrat Mian, you deceived me, I ask you, who was the one who sank the boat, the answer is it was Khwaja Khizr who did it', Kaneez lamented wildly and slapped her forehead. Daadi took off her chaddar with trembling hands, the corners of her lips, red with paan, quivered, her chin convulsed, every single line on her face trembled, and tears began to fall through the grooves of her wrinkles and spread over face. When she put Chammi down, the child started crying loudly. 'Daadi, Daadi', she whimpered in a monotone to get her attention. But Daadi was not in her senses after seeing Kaneez in this condition. Nammi was thirsty. Not willing to be left behind, she began crying out for water.

'*Arrey*, you separated my child from me, Ishrat, may you be separated from your mother, may you die, Ishrat.'

Recalling the scene in the court when she had to hand over Mumtaz to Ishrat, Kaneez beat her chest and then fell to the floor in a faint. At this point Chammi and Nammi and Daadi made such a commotion that those in the main bungalow were also roused. Bari Begum woke up with a terrible start and when she scrambled out of bed the bunch of keys struck her shin bone like a hammer. She was immobilized for a moment as she grabbed her foot in pain, but then she came out of her room quickly. Salma Bi yawned sleepily and muttering, 'The case seems to have been settled', turned on her side.

'Kaneez, ai Kaneez, come here—what's the matter?'

'Hai, where is Kaneez? Kaneez has passed away', Daadi's rasping voice echoed and Bari Begum ran towards them in her bare feet. Carefully handling her satin petticoat, Salma Bi also emerged.

'Passed away? This is dreadful. What should we do now?' This was heartbreaking.

But Kaneez was right there and she hadn't died. She was breathing normally.

'Ai Asghari Begum, you gave us such a scare. What happened?' Bari Begum was still feeling as if she had stepped on cinders.

'What could it be, my daughter? What was written came to pass. Never has something like this happened in our family. This Pakistan has brought us to ruination.'

'Stop the moaning and weeping Bua, it's good that the girl is rid of that blackguard. What was decided about the *mehr*? He must have got the boy. You should have thrown the girls into his face as well—rotten broth from rotten bones.'

'*Arrey* daughter, how can one give up one's offspring. I was left without a home in my love for those I had raised, these are her own flesh and blood. She's unconscious from the shock of losing her son.' Daadi wept as she spoke.

Bari Begum sprinkled water on Kaneez's face. She immediately opened her eyes. Then she drank a bowlful of water and holding her head between her hands, she heaved long sighs. Bari Begum put her arm around her and gave her a hug.

Her eyes filling with tears, she said, 'Kaneez you're like my own daughter, why are you worried? Be thankful that you're rid of that wretch. You're still young and you wait and see, I'll arrange a match for you that will make you so happy you'll even forget me. Just day before yesterday there was an enquiry. The boy earns 500 a month. I said the case hasn't been decided yet, and I also didn't care much for the boy's looks. Ai Asghari Bua, the boy should be as good looking as our Kaneez, a proper match.'

Salma Bi had returned to her room. She had left all such matters to her mother. She was only interested in doing her own work . . . Daadi glared at Salma Bi as she walked away towards her room. She didn't like the girl one bit. She was friendly with Kaneez but she didn't bother to greet Daadi properly, as though Daadi was a servant. Why, does respect die when one is faced with poverty? There was no need for Daadi to suck up to anyone. Her own 'Bare Mian' had a nice house in Muradabad. He wrote frequently, asking her to come back, complaining that she had abandoned him for the sake of her nephew's children. But the poor woman was childless. She had raised her late nephew's baby daughter just like her own and arranged her marriage when she grew up, but it was fate that brought her niece's husband to Pakistan and like an idiot, she followed without thinking. The intensity of feeling for those one raises is greater than that for those one gives birth to. But what do the girls these days know? It was Bari Begum's kindness that made her ignore Salma Bi's ill will. And so Bari

Begum drew together all of them as if they were members of her own family and took them to her room.

There were only two beds in her room. Salma Bi was lying in a torpor on one. How could so many people sit on Bari Begum's bed? So it was on the floor that the paandaan was finally opened, memories of happy and sad days were revived to the fullest extent. Daadi wept and when Kaneez placed a corner of her dupatta on her face and sobbed, Bari Begum voice became hoarse with emotion. Salma Bi murmured 'hunh, hunh' several times during Bari Begum's demonstration of sincere goodwill. Finally, Bari Begum's back began to hurt from sitting on the floor for so long and on Daadi's inistence she lay down on her bed, but she couldn't be too far from Kaneez at this time so she said, 'Kaneez, daughter, come and sit next to me, arri what is this love that one feels, how unhappy I will be when you're married.'

On hearing this, Daadi lifted her hands towards the Qibla in gratitude. Allah sends angels to help those who are helpless; Daadi's eyes filled with tears again and Kaneez felt her burning wounds get some relief. She sat down shyly at the foot of Begum's bed. In that moment her respect and attachment for Bari Begum grew greater than her feelings for saints and holy men. Begum leaned forward and patted her head but in the next instant she felt a twinge of pain in her joints and started rubbing her calves.

'Amma Begum, go to sleep', Kaneez said and leaned forward to massage her legs. Bari Begum didn't protest. Daadi was disturbed by Kaneez's devotion and gave her a disapproving look. But she ignored it. She thought, 'What's wrong with massaging your mother's feet . . . she's like my own mother, isn't she, what does she have to gain from us, who in this country cares for anyone else . . . she was one of us, we were lucky to find her because Amma Begum was not wrong when she said the country is full of Punjabis, who even make fun of our respectul modes of greeting . . . but why would Ishrat have to think of any of this. With a few words on the divorce paper, he threw me out of his tiny room saying you have to be in purdah from me now, he didn't think that if he'd done this in Muradabad it wouldn't have been so bad, unfortunate creature that I am, I had Mian's house there, who thought of me as more than a grand-daughter and raised me with such care—Daada would have been ready to help even though he's so old . . .

     But in this Pakistan, poor Daadi's company was of no help at all either . . . there was no way even a penny from Daada could get across . . . there was nothing to sustain them here and they would not be able to afford a return. Those whom they once knew had become strangers. *Arrey*, this lifelong companion, he's turned his gaze away as well, even a parrot, known for disloyalty, would not do this . . . no mehr, nor any childcare allowance, and if I had made a claim that it was my fault, he says he would have agreed to give me allowance, but now he's riled and won't budge . . . *arrey* if this is what you had planned why did you ask us to come to Pakistan, we had been separated for so long, you should have thought, she's dead, I'm rid of her . . . and then after getting us out there why did you abandon us in this quagmire? The lawyer said it would be difficult to go back to Muradabad, it would take a month or more to get a travel permit . . . Daadi could return to live there because of Daada, but it wouldn't be possible for me . . . hai, we're homeless because of you now, *arrey* Ishrat may your loved ones weep for you . . .'

And Kaneez burst into violent sobs. Bari Begum had fallen asleep. Exhausted, Daadi had also dozed off, everyone was resigned now, but how could Kaneez exercise restraint? The son she had raised for seven years had been snatched from her. Who knows what was to become of Nammi and Chammi. Daadi wasn't going to live forever, and she herself would never find a job somewhere and be able to live on her own. As Bari Begum had said, she was twenty-four, twenty-five maybe, as nice-looking as a photograph, and despite this, Ishrat the ill-fated man, had let his heart get tangled up somewhere else. He had left Muradabad for Pakistan with their savings rolled up in a belt on his waist. The wife and children were left behind with the promise that he would soon set up a factory to make pots and pans, and then send for them. Daadi was well aware of Ishrat's real character but at the same time Kaneez's sharp temperament was also not hidden from her . . .

When, pretending to be serious, Ishrat sent for Kaneez, Daadi immediately began making preparations to accompany her. How could she send her off alone? Would the world not say that she had deliberately sent the girl to a strange country and stayed back so she could be with her old husband? She thought that once the girl was settled she would come back, but when they arrived here they found out that the factory had gone under and Ishrat Mian was working at some shop for seventy or sixty rupees a month, and was living in the servants' quarters attached to some bungalow, paying five rupees in rent. Daadi was devastated.

However, they could have all managed to go on like this if it weren't for Ishrat's roving eye and Kaneez's foul temper. Daadi did her best to rein in Kaneez, but she was out of control and one day, Ishrat handed her a divorce paper, faulting her with bad language and overspending, grabbed the boy's hand, forced Kaneez out of the quarter and put a lock on the door. While Kaneez was roaming about, weeping and lamenting as she looked for a servants' quarter in some bungalow, she ran into Bari Begum. At first Bari Begum was very unsympathetic, but after hearing her tale of woe she melted. She not only gave Kaneez a quarter for free, she also referred to her as 'daughter'. It's all about the good fortune of the one who asks—ask for fire and get a prophethood.[1]

And Bari Begum, who had now become Kaneez's Amma Begum, had been rid of her arthritis pain and was now sound asleep, her mouth open. Kaneez, sitting next to her feet, had become weary from weeping silently. Even if someone close to you dies you do have to show fortitude after a period of mourning . . . gradually you begin to feel better.

In a few days Kaneez not only felt better, she felt light as a flower. Ishrat was now just like some incomplete story she may have heard from Daadi as a young girl, one that Daadi fell asleep narrating, and after which she too, after a few 'hunh, hunhs', following Daadi's snoring, would have fallen asleep . . . and when you woke up the next morning you didn't have the time to remember the story when there was a bowful of milk, stale bread, and rag dolls with eyes as large as namakparas (savoury pastry) to contend with? You need to have free time to think of someone and Kaneez didn't have any free time now that she was in Amma Begum's bungalow. When Daadi reviled Ishrat, Kaneez would make a face and say, 'Ai Daadi, don't you have anything to do except mention his name all day? I only remember my child when he is mentioned, may God give him

---

[1]   Reference to the Prophet Moses.

enough sense to come and see his mother one day, he will spit
on his father's face when he leaves him.'

And saying this, Kaneez, tears strung on her lashes, would
rush off to take care of a chore. Like lightning, she tore all over
the bungalow and a new sorrow would descend on Daadi and
spread like the approaching darkness of evening. Daadi shivered
at the manner in which Kaneez showed a glimpse of herself
and then disappeared. She wanted to sit in front of Kaneez
and lament her misfortune so that she would never forget
that Daadi had deep maternal feelings for her. She waited to
see Kaneez all day, she would scurry after her but her legs no
longer had any stamina left to carry her. She would arrive in
the kicthen in pursuit of her only to hear Kaneez talking in
Salma Bi's room. Coughing and moaning, she would cross the
veranda and reach Salma Bi's room but Kaneez would now be
in the lawn, rearranging chairs. Unable to take this any more,
Daadi would start shouting:

'Arri Kaneez, you've turned into a shameless creature, here
one minute, gone the next like a restless spirit! You wretch,
during *iddat* (a period of waiting after divorce) respectable girls
don't even step out of their room . . . arri if you had shown this
kind of ordered behaviour in your own home, Ishrat wouldn't
have spat you out and we wouldn't be wandering from place to
place now.'

This announcement would ring through the entire
household and Bari Begum would suffer a fit of extreme
distresss, and Salma Bi's frowning would make her acne-filled
face assume a poisonous look. Bari Begum would appear from
somewhere, thrust the bunch of keys in her waistband and
embracing Kaneez she would say tearfully, 'Go daughter, go
to your grandmother . . . regardless of how we treat you, we'll

always be regarded as outsiders . . . even a little bit of work you do upsets your grandmother. Oh Hameedo, where have you gone to, come and make my bed.'

And Kaneez would feel that her blood had been squeezed out of her body. Daadi was like a rope binding her feet. *She's stingy with her emotions, Amma Begum lavishes so much love on me and all Daadi can do is resent every little thing I do for Amma Begum. What do we have left now to use to repay anyone's favours?*

Kaneez was tired of explaining things to Daadi. But Daadi understood nothing. She did the opposite of what she should do. Chammi was in her lap night and day. 'Get down, you wretched creature or else I'll throw you down, oh God, my back is broken', Daadi would shake the whole bungalow with her screaming. Salma Bi objected to her own mother raising her voice, after all there were some manners that you had to observe if you were living in this house. But she would practice restraint when she saw Kaneez's face.

Wearing Salma Bi's green *kamdani* (sequinned) dupatta, Kaneez went to Daadi and said in an embarrassed tone, 'Daadi, please control yourself, people will think we're not from a respectable family.' Saying this she waved her dupatta about and covered her head with it. 'Hand me my daughter, you resent my children . . . one has been snatched from me already.' And she grabbed Chammi from her, plunked her on her hip, and then she muttered, 'How filthy she is, she'll mess up my new dupatta.'

'New dupatta? Why, you've lost your eyesight, there are two big holes in it, you're giving yourself airs with this dirty, soiled dupatta', Daadi growled.

'Wah', Kaneez said in an embarrassed tone, 'only yesterday Salma Bi wore it to college. It must have got caught in the bicycle wheel. Ai Daadi, you have such a mean temperament.'

Daadi lost her temper. '*Arrey*, the one for whom you shave your head is the one who asks why are you here with a shaved head! Now you can see only the flaws in me, I gave up my country for you, I sell everything I have in order to provide for you and the girls, and that woman is the one who becomes Amma . . . '

Kaneez would place a hand over Daadi's mouth and then weep and taunt Daadi by saying yes she fed her and but then made a show of it, yes, her luck has run out and that is why Daadi has also turned her back on her. But when Kaneez's eyes were swollen from excessive crying, Daadi would try to appease her and the two would make up. Chammi would climb into Daadi's lap again and taking Nammi's hand in hers, Daadi would leave for the bazaar to make arrangements for supper and Kaneez would turn into a restless spirit again, in the kitchen, then off to the living room and in Salmi Bi's room from there.

Sometimes she made playful demands. 'Ai Salma Bi, this shirt is going to be mine.'

'Oh no, no, I just had it made', Salma Bi would respond brusquely.

Bari Begum would interrupt. 'It wasn't easy for my daughter to ask. She's so proud, she never looks at anything. Come, give it to her.'

'Well, then have another one made for me, I have so few shirts', Salma Bibi would say petulantly.

'Why, where is it going to come from? Your father didn't leave behind a fortune for me . . . I don't even know how Altaf Mian's educational expenses and your constant demands are being met. There's not much left in the bank . . . I don't even know how we're making ends meet . . . your eyes are covered with a bandage.' Bari Begum sighed heavily.

Well, it's all about making ends meet. What to do when one doesn't have enough? Kaneez's burka and purdah weren't going to last long. She was spending more and more time with Salma Bi now. If Kaneez wasn't busy and Salma Bi's cycle had a puncture, then the two would be off for a jaunt on the big, wide road. The minute Kaneez made a plan to go out, Daadi would appear with the burka that was the colour of a dead mouse's skin and insist she put it on. One day she went too far. Bari Begum was right there and Daadi said to Kaneez, 'No girl, it disturbs me very much when I see a woman without a burka.'

Bari Begum always tried to be courteous to Daadi and addressed her as Asghari Bua. But this time, she lost her cool. 'Ai Bua, stop showing off. You can't compete with the kind of purdah that was observed in our family. My daughter wouldn't even dare to peep out of the window. But now we've lost our country, we've lost our traditions. What is so special about Kaneez now? She'll be married soon to someone with whom she'll go out for a walk . . . but anyway, we don't have any right, do we? We do everything for your comfort while you . . . '

Daadi held her tongue but that day, Kaneez washed her old burka and stitched frocks on the sewing machine with it for Nammi and Chammi. For sure, the poor things had been roaming around in threadbare clothes. This way, at least these clothes would be good for a month or two. 'After that . . . after that . . . *arrey* doesn't Allah put compassion into the hearts of stepfathers?' Kaneez thought and she felt at peace.

But how were they going to get by? Their bodies were covered to an extent, but their bellies began to remain empty. The moment Daadi set eyes on Kaneez, she would begin to whine, 'Where can I bring it from, I swear I don't have anything left.' Every day, it was the same story. Chammi and Nammi abandoned Daadi and followed Kaneez day and night, crying, 'Ammi give us roti, Ammi we're hungry.' Bari Begum was so generous she immediately handed over whatever was lying in front of her and, feeling embarrased, Kaneez would gather her children as if they were her rags and tatters . . . that was when she felt she should die of shame.

'Ai daughter, there's no need to feel embarrassed, I won't be able to swallow a morsel if I see the girls are hungry. You feel for them as a mother, and I too feel for them, but I say my child, you're not going to live in my house forever. May Allah bless you with that day when you'll have your own house, with your husband. You know, men don't have any patience with stepchildren, here's what I say, my daughter, and give them both to that wretch Ishrat, the rascal will at least know it's not child's play to divorce someone.' Bari Begum placed a hand on Kaneez's back and showered her with this advice.

Kaneez finally accepted the idea but Daadi was not willing to take this step. Kaneez would sob and moan and say, 'Daadi, why will you let the girls suffer along with me? Where will you get the money to feed them?' But Daadi would cover her ears with her hands and shut out Kaneez's laments.

But then one day, when Daadi couldn't open her suitcase and there was no fire in the stove the whole day, Kaneez could no longer control herself. 'Ai Daadi, come on now, get the money out, why are you killing the girls by torturing them with hunger.'

'Scratch my bones and see—what do I have left? Why don't you ask your "bungalow mother" for help?' Daadi responded sharply.

'Don't say that! Why are you bringing up Amma Begum's name? Where should she get money from? If she had any she would readily help my children. What will she do? Wah, wah, this is like saying a porcupine is hiding in a snake's hole.' Kaneez's eyes became red hot.

'All right, let's go back to our own Muradabad, surely we can get a permit for a month or two', Daadi used her last tactic and Kaneez felt life ebbing from her.

'All right, arrange for the money for tickets and have a permit made', Kaneez said and then lay down on the cot and covered her face with her dupatta. Daadi's outburst subsided. Let's say somehow, four plane tickets can be bought, let's assume the permit will also be obtained, but then remember what the lawyer said about having to return after the permit expires . . . what will happen then?

That night, Kaneez wept uncontrollably while saying goodbye to Nammi and Chammi as they left with Daadi. With the sobbing, shivering Chammi in her lap and Nammi's hand grasped in hers, Daadi managed somehow to reach Ishrat's quarter. He immediately picked up Nammi and hugged and kissed her and didn't once look in the direction of Chammi.

'How can I go about with this weak, scrawny creature. Keep one girl with you. Have you no maternal feelings left?'

Daadi felt herself smouldering. When she tried to force Chammi out of her lap she was devastated by Chammi's screams. Without saying a word, she returned with Chammi, and Begum was shaken to the core when she saw Kaneez running towards Chammi with outstretched arms, sobbing. Daadi shook her already throbbing head and said, 'It's true, motherly feelings cannot die.'

But in a few days the frail, weak and sickly Chammi began to seek Daadi's constant attention, especially when she missed Nammi, and overwhelmed by her clingy behaviour, Daadi's thoughts about maternal feelings underwent a revolutionary change.

'May God put you out of your misery, the poor creature has no one she can call her own, neither mother, nor father . . .' Daadi's loud cries echoed in every corner of the bungalow, and listening to these constant lamentations, these moans, Bari Begum felt her heart breaking. A grown-up daughter in the house, a handsome, strong son studying abroad for five years, and in a corner of the house, an old, infirm father-in-law who was listless from opium use—the only man in the house, and on top of this, the additional strain of exile . . . and in these circumstances, Daadi's repeated laments that echoed in the bungalow with no regard to what time of day it was or whether the azan was being called in the background . . . instead, she was constantly railing about the transience of this world, and whether anyone listened or not, she continued to bemoan her calamitous misfortunes. To counteract all this abomination, Begum would begin to talk loudly about Salma and Altaf's wedding, and would turn to Salma to consult her on the matter of dowry for Kaneez.

'Ai girl, we have to think about Kaneez as well, we owe her. If we start now, only then we'll have something nice ready in two or three years, something that a man with a salary of 500 to 1,000 will be happy with . . . Salma, how about that suit with the beads for Kaneez . . . she'll look like a princess in a film. Believe me, she looks so youthful that if she doesn't reveal she has children she could easily pass for an unmarried girl.'

Chammi had developed diarrhoea from the qalmi (a variety of mangoes) mangoes Bari Begum had been feeding her. Kaneez was too busy with her errands to notice. When she did get some time, she went and stood in front of Salma Bi's dressing table, a black kamdani dupatta hanging from her shoulders, and started to comb her hair. She might have just continued her little game with the mirror and her hair had Daadi's hoarse voice not get through to her.

'Arri Kaneez, you wretch, come and see, the girl's eyes are turning up.' Grabbing the front of her gharara, Kaneez ran only to find that that yes, Chammi's neck was lolling.

'Hai Daadi, what is this poisonous thing you've fed my child? Hai, I have already lost everyone and now you can't abide this girl—if she dies you won't see me either, Daadi.'

That night, Chammi died quietly in the hospital. Kaneez tried her best to die too. She bashed her head, she tore up the yellow kamdani dupatta with her teeth, but Daadi was always at her side, stumbling as she tried to keep up with her, and never gave her the chance to kill herself. Daadi was so fiercely attached to the one she had raised, it is no secret how someone who had actually carried a child in her belly for nine months feels.

For a long time, Kaneez wouldn't even look at food. Her eyes were so puffed up from crying perpetually that she couldn't move her lids. Unable to see her in this condition, Bari Begum wept with her dupatta over her eyes . . . Salma Bi also hugged Kaneez and wept, and then, her eyes covered with her hand, dashed off to her room sobbing. But who weeps forever? Even the rising rivers, when they find an outlet, fall. And then, of course, there were all those efforts by Bari Begum to distract Kaneez. She kept her by her side and discouraged long silences. Salma Bi too began to take very good care of her.

'Come Kaneez, let's stitch the sequins on to this dupatta.' She would sit down with her dupatta and like a puppet the sorrowing Kaneez would comply and carefully tack each shiny star-shaped sequin to the dupatta, as though she was positioning the wounds in her heart for display.

'Come, my daughter Kaneez, let's sew Dada Mian's pyjamas.' Bari Begum would spread out the roll of white cotton and Kaneez would become involved with this new task. In short, Bari Begum and Salma Bi did everything in their power to make Kaneez forget her sorrow. Often, Bari Begum would accompany the two girls to the cinema to make Kaneez happy. Salma Bi invited her to take any clothes she wanted from her almirah. Bari Begum took off the silver band from her little finger and slipped it on her finger and leaning towards her, whispered gently, 'Our Kaneez's bridegroom will put a ring on her finger just like this . . .'

And that was the day, when for the first time after Chammi's death, Kaneez felt overcome by shyness and self-consciously ran out of the room. After this, she gradually became as spirited and active as before as she dashed about in that small, mysterious bungalow huddled among the shisham, eucalyptus and gular trees. In Salma Bi's room this moment, in the kitchen cooking sevaiyyan-zarda (dessert with milk and vermicelli), the next, disappearing in Bari Begum's bathroom in the flash of an eye, and in the next instant, dressed in Bari Begum's churidar (tight pyjamas) and Salma Bi's dupatta, she is mopping the smooth floor of the veranda with a wet cloth. Does it make sense to be engaging in such unsuitable activity after washing and dressing up? Bari Begum keeps saying 'Kaneez, who is asking you to do this, why do we have the sweeper woman?' But Kaneez turns a deaf ear to all her protestations. When Bari Begum gets very upset, Kaneez drops everything, goes to the tap to wash her hands and, taking the bottle of oil, arrives in Bari Begum's room, insistent on massaging her hair. Love flows from Bari

Begum's eyes like waves of light. Heaving a long sigh, she says, 'Kaneez you will light up the house where you're wed. That idiot Ishrat, he didn't know your worth.'

'Ai, then find a husband for Kaneez who is good enough for her, my husband is writing, telling me to come back so I can be with him when he dies. How long will I stay here to keep watch over a young girl? If not, then I'll take her with me, there are many boys in the family still not married.' Daadi's demands never ceased.

'Oh Asghari Bua, don't mention your relatives. You didn't leave any stone unturned to destroy her life. Don't force me to speak the truth. She's not that old. She's probably just two or three years older than our Salma, and as for rushing to get her married, I'll investigate exactly the way I would for Salma. Now when she departs from our bungalow, it will be with someone who is our equal—don't complain about proposals, I've asked many matchmakers to stay alert, we're constantly getting enquiries. I can't keep telling you about every single one . . . ' Bari Begum muttered for hours.

And the very next week, a man arrived on a motorbike. Bari Begum took this as an excuse to send for Daadi.

'Well, he's nice, let's go ahead then', Daadi said joyfully.

'What are you saying? Go ahead? I investigated and found out he drinks. I won't agree to the match even if he comes every day and begs', Bari Begum said haughtily.

'I say, go ahead, this will brighten Kaneez's fate.' Daadi was in a hurry. She thought the man looked all right, didn't have the appearance of a swindler. And when had she seen such a 'sahib' come to the door before this? She thought that anyone remotely resembling a man, one who was willing to take a divorced woman off her hands, would be acceptable.

'Well, why don't you talk to the boy himself then, I won't interfere, it will be your responsibility, don't complain later.' Bari Begum moved to one side, away from the door.

Daadi felt miserable. She couldn't believe that her Kaneez had become such a desirable match. Bari Begum frequently pointed to people walking past, saying, '*Arrey* look Asghari Bua, that boy's mother said to me that she would take either Salma or Kaneez. I won't bother with that one, Bua, he's dark as coal.'

Everyone had some flaw or the other. Making clothes for the dowry went into full swing, pots and pans and tableware began to be bought and Daadi began to feel comforted by the thought that indeed those who are not related by blood can also have some value. She wrote to her husband: 'Be patient Mian, once I've taken care of the girl, I'll be there in a flash . . . after that, we can even come here and spend our last days in Pakistan. There's no doubt we'll get a small room in the girl's house.'

But one day, all of Daadi's dreams were swept away. Daadi was livid that day at Kaneez's indifference. After Chammi's death, Begum had insisted that Daadi not maintain a separate kitchen and so she now ate from the kitchen in Sharma Hazoori's kitchen. Hameedo had run away and Bari Begum insisted he had made off with her gold earrings. Who was going to bother with the police etc., but she avowed never to hire a male servant again to work in the bungalow. If anything had to be purchased from nearby, Daadi would somehow do the job, but she couldn't handle travelling far to the bazaar. Kaneez had learned how to ride Salma Bi's cycle. One day she said, 'Here Daadi, let me get the provisions we need, it will take only two minutes if I take the cycle.' Now, who in Daadi's family would allow young women to indulge in such boldness. She became livid.

'Ai girl, are you out of your mind? Why are you bent on dragging your parents' name into the dirt! I'll dig your grave and bury you in it without the slightest hesitation!'

This was a declaration of war against Bari Begum's training and Salma Bi's behaviour. There's a limit to how patient one can be. If someone else had said this in Bari Begum's presence, she would have picked up a shoe and rubbed it into that person's face. She didn't pick up a shoe but she gave her hell. 'Aren't you ashamed? Don't you realize how old you are? If you're going to live in bungalows, you can't scream and shout like butchers and stupid low-class women. Why, you're giving us a bad name, those who can hear your ranting will think we're just the same as you.'

'Ai Daadi, you're not going to let me be, unfortunate creature that I am . . . she's not going to rest until she kills me, Oh Allah rid me of her somehow.' Kaneez couldn't take it any longer either. After all, she had been observing with her own eyes Daadi's rude and cruel manner for a long time. Allah, this world doesn't even refrain from finding fault with angels. Daadi couldn't endure this attack from Kaneez, she fought viciously with her, enumerated one by one all the favours she had done for her, and left the house in a huff to apply for a travel permit to go to Hindustan.

Despite Kaneez's taunts, Daadi had her permit made. The jewellery she had hidden away came in handy now. If she had sold these last pieces to feed Kaneez and her family, she wouldn't even have been able to beg for the money. Kaneez had turned away from her just because she hadn't paid to feed and sustain her. Daadi believed that he who had money would have many to mourn him when he died.

A clerk at the office where she got her permit arranged a flight for her without delay, and so, grabbing her small bundle,

Daadi got ready to leave, broken-hearted, ready to die with her husband by her side.

Just before she got into the tonga, Daadi became very emotional. 'Kaneez, you'll realize my worth, nothing is lost yet . . . sell your earrings and come to Muradabad—in a month or two we'll make some arrangements . . . '

'Stop this Daadi . . . you killed my Chammi, made me lose my Nammi. Because you said you had nothing left . . . where did the money for the fare come from? Ah, mother, why did you give me birth?' Kaneez turned away her face and Daadi felt a bitter taste in her mouth.

When the tonga drove off, Kaneez was glued to the screen weeping so wildly that all the scabs from her wounds came off, drops of blood began to trickle. Ishrat, Mumtaz, Nammi, Chammi, and Daadi leaped over her wounded heart and disappeared. Bari Begum clasped her to her breast. Salma Bi consoled her and went so far as to kiss her face. Even Salma Bi's grandfather patted her head and Kaneez's tears dried on her lashes.

But she remained lost for many days afterwards. She would stop without reason as she went from one room of the bungalow to the other, she would stare out at the road and then quickly lower her eyes . . . as if the sticks on the cage were broken and she had been flung out into the open and now this new atmosphere was frightening her . . . she picked up a splintered stick, kissed it, held it close to her bosom, and then she would put it back . . . she felt a stranger to herself after breaking all her bonds.

The cold winter wind blew in gusts, the dry, yellowed leaves of the mango, gular and peepul trees crunched under foot, a strange silence reigned everywhere, a thoughtful desolation.

Bari Begum was generally on the bedstead she had set up in the lawn and spent most of her time getting oil massages on her calves and her back. Even though the sun shone brightly right above her, the chill seeped into her joints and caused aches and pains . . . a doctor had started coming to the house to check on her. One day, Bari Begum asked a tired, worn-out Kaneez, 'What do you think of Doctor Sahib?'

Kaneez was taken aback. Since Daadi's departure, this had been the first time she broke into a smile like a young, unwed girl and blushing, she quickly got up and left. For the first time in many days, her hands suddenly seemed to be filled with a strange current . . . she cleaned the kitchen thoroughly, vigorously scrubbed the pots and pans with dry ash until they shone like new silver jewellery . . . then she took the jharu and cleaned the house so diligently that not a single cobweb remained, not a single speck of dirt could be seen anywhere.

'Ai Salma, Ai Salma, give your sister a hand . . . why are you sitting there and just looking on . . . I'll see which house you end up in where you won't have to do a lick of work', Bari Begum would call out in a loud voice. Salma continued to apply pink nail polish to her nails. Kaneez thought, 'A lazy lump of meat like Salma Bi loses all respect even in her own parent's eyes. It is a person's service that earns him respect, not his looks.'

Preparing clothes for the dowry was also part of that service. Kaneez would be busy with the sewing machine even at night. *Lachka, gota*, sequins and mirrors were being tacked on dupattas and garments. Begum would stretch her legs languidly, yawn and say, 'Let's see which of my two daughters fate favours first.' And in Kaneez's mind, the race for the favours had begun.

Doctor Sahib would arrive with his stethoscope, the medicine bag swinging from his hand. After looking in on

Bari Begum, he would be seated in the sitting room. Her face plastered with makeup, Salma Bi would sit down on the old sofa with her face raised at a particular angle and Kaneez would appear in the background with the tea tray, her eyes lowered, her legs encased in churidar pyjamas, body covered in Salma Bi's frock tight around the waist. At this moment, Salma Bi regarded herself as a queen in a palace. Everything in her opinion, from the old sofa all the way to Kaneez, added to her beauty and finery. And as Kaneez disappeared shyly behind the curtains, she thought, 'Ai what kind of looks does Salma Bi have—irregular features, on top of that pimples all over her face—she thinks she's a fairy from Koh Kaaf.'

A month later, Salmi Bi was engaged and then one chilly night, she became a bride and left with her bridegroom. As Bari Begum had said, it was all about fate's favours. It was Salma Bi who was favoured first. Also, at the same time, the large trunks and the spacious cupboards that were connected to bygone assets were flung open. The old dressing table was polished to a shine and it left as well. The old sofas were reupholstered and they too departed leaving the sitting room looking bleak and forsaken. Like the bungalow, the empty, deserted trunks and cupboards reverberated with desolation. The condition of Kaneez's heart's was worse than these trunks and cupboards. Ever since the night of the wedding, a strange kind of chill permeated the atmosphere. Everything was cold and wet. The next morning, her eyes burning after a sleepless night, Kaneez left her bed to make tea for Bari Begum who was moaning from the pain in her joints, and observed the sadness of the trees in the dim light of the fog.

It broke Bari Begum's heart to see Kaneez look so weary and downtrodden. After Salmi Bi's wedding, she herself felt bereft. No one came to the bungalow any more so how was Kaneez ever going to receive a proposal . . . she would call out for Kaneez, talk to her and embrace her. 'Kaneez', she would say, 'One day you too will go to your own house, and then I will be left alone to suffer at the hands of fate . . . if only time would pass quickly, if only Altaf would return . . . I want to see him don the flowers of a bridegroom before I die . . . ' Bari Begum's eyes would well with tears. Hearing her talk like this, Kaneez would feel a spark of energy but it was shortlived. She didn't want to do anything. She wanted to just sit quietly or weep like Bari Begum. Dust collected in the rooms, there were webs in every corner, the pots and pans in the kitchen turned black. Bari Begum's father-in-law no longer smoked the hookah and dozed all day long; he was taking so much opium now that he was barely awake even to cough. A stagnation seemed to have settled over everything, as if time had paused to think.

Salmi Bi's husband had been transferred. After a long time, she came with her husband for a two-day visit. She was shocked to see the condition the house was in and was worried about the impression it would create on her husband. She mentioned her concern to her mother. Bari Begum was upset by her complaints. How was she to bear the burden of life alone? What was left now with which she could hire servants to clean the house for her complaining daughter? Salma Bi was embarassed. On the third day, she left for Murree with her husband for the summer. Before she left, she met Kaneez in her old room and said, 'I've already bought such beautiful fabric for a suit to give you at your wedding, you'll be stunned when you see it.' But after Salmi Bi left, Kaneez couldn't imagine the fabric fully in her mind's eye. Her heart was in some other place. She would try to remember Ishrat but when his memory didn't materialize, then all she wanted to do was to lie down with her eyes closed. It was also very hot.

'Amma, whose letter is this?' Kaneez saw a large overseas envelope and asked dully. For some reason, she had been waiting for a letter from Daadi. Begum opened the envelope and took out a big photograph. It was the picture of a good-looking man. Bari Begum eagerly kissed the photo.

'Who is this Amma?' Kaneez asked casually.

'*Arrey*, don't you know? This is my Altaf. I had asked him to send me a new picture. Can you imagine, he's shaved his mustache, a man's face doesn't look nice without a mustache.' Bari Begum's eyes filled with love for her son.

The unframed picture was set down on a table in the sitting room right away. Kaneez had seen a small photograph in Salma Bi's album that was not very clear. But now, every feature was distinct. In all the time Salma Bi was here, Altaf was not much of a subject for conversation. But now that she was alone, Bari Begum could talk and think of nothing else. Like birds, daughters live in their parents' homes and then they fly off to their own nests. A son is a son, whether he is abroad or whether he is here. He will live in his parent's house and now, only three more years remained before Altaf would finish his education and return home. But Begum counted the days.

'Ai daughter, dear daughter Kaneez, where are you? Come here.' Bari Begum would call out for Kaneez. Wiping her hands with her dupatta, Kaneez would come in to her room.

'What do you think, my child, which room should we clean up for Altaf? We should do it now otherwise when he's here I'll be too excited to manage anything.' Bari Begum spoke animatedly, as if Altaf was about to arrive by the night train.

'The same one, Salma Bi's', Kaneez would say aloud what was in Bari Begum's heart.

'All right, then tomorrow you and I will clean the room together', Begum would say determinedly, but Kaneez would forget this 'tomorrow' as she busied herself with chores in the house. Not only that, Kaneez forgot to comb her hair for days. For a long time now, she had forgotten to look at herself in the small mirror lying in Bari Begum's small wooden box. She didn't even think of Ishrat any more, nor Mumtaz, or Nammi or Daadi . . . and as for Chammi, it was as if she had never given her birth. There were moments when she forgot where she was sitting, and couldn't tell if Bari Begum, whom she loved dearly, was like a mother to her or a dried leaf. When Altaf's letter arrived every month, Bari Begum would forget the pain in her joints and dance about joyfully in the house as if it was Eid.

So that was one of those days. The rainy season had ended, but there was humidity in the air. At least that's what Kaneez felt. Her thin nose and the area on her upper lip always remained covered in perspiration. And she had no desire for food. She had barely finished swallowing, with difficulty, half a roti when Bari Begum startled her with her sudden entry, dancing in with her keys jangling, and saying, 'Ai Kaneez, my daughter, listen to this.' Kaneez was taken aback as if she had been caught stealing. Her heart beat violently in her chest. These days, even the slightest noise startled her like this.

'Altaf Mian has written, if you give me permission Amma, I'll bring a daughter-in-law for you, a daughter-in-law who doesn't look English at all—dear girl, the fates have decided to be unkind to me.' Bari Begum's voice broke. Kaneez sat still, detached, as if she was watching the road from the kitchen window.

'God forgive us! A daughter-in-law in this house who eats pork, such a one will not even lift a hand to help in the house, all of her husband's salary will be wasted on servants and cooks . . . we spent all our savings on our son and daughter and will now be left staring at their faces helplessly—no no girl . . . why would I give him permission? I'll write to him and say I won't forgive you even on my deathbed, I'll poison myself, then do what you want after I'm gone . . . I'm dead for this son—I had hoped that a daughter-in-law will come and bring me some comfort.' And with this, Bari Begum burst into tears and began to weep noisily.

'Amma, then why didn't you get him married before you sent him abroad?' Kaneez said as if she were complaining.

'Ai, I searched and searched. One can find many fashiobale, well-educated girls like our own Salma Bi, but there has to be the ability to take care of the house also, a pretty face doesn't last long, don't you understand?' Bari Begum seemed to gazing into space as if looking for something. 'I wonder how much Daadi had paid for the ticket to Muradabad', Kaneez was thinking. And then suddenly, Bari Begum spoke in a dreamy voice, 'Well, you know . . . I was looking for someone . . . like you . . . yes', Bari Begum stammered.

And Kaneez felt she had been struck by lightning. For a long time she was still, as if paralyzed and then, she got up and launched into all the chores that had been ignored with the speed of a machine. That day, Altaf Mian's room was ready. After that, his room was always the one that was cleaned early in the morning. Begum's body was massaged and pressed so much that her joint pain would disappear somewhere. So many bottles of oil were emptied to massage her hair that it would be no surprise if her hair turned black again, or if she passed the

BA exam one day without moving from her bed. Bari Begum's mouth ached from showering blessings on Kaneez. But Kaneez did not show any signs of fatigue. She became so obsessed with reducing the spending in the house that there were days she ate leftover food or nothing at all despite Begum's protestations. She also let the washerman go. 'Wah, he's charging two annas apiece for the smallest garments . . . who wants to waste money?' Begum protested, but Kaneez didn't relent. However, the next day, when she wore the clothes Kaneez had washed herself she couldn't hold back a 'wah!'

Despite all the hard work, when Kaneez sat down to rest for a while, a smile broke out in every fibre of her being and spread on her thin, pale face like a shower and when she smiled from the emotion bubbling in her blood from all this attention, she would feel her head swim, a cold sweat would break out on her forehead. And then a day came when she couldn't tolerate the weight of this state she was in and she fell in a heap on the kitchen floor.

The doctor said that her blood was drying up. Many seasons of spring arrived and passed. Changes in the weather came about turbulently and then died. But Kaneez clung to her grind like a machine. Begum would see her and exclaim fearfully, 'Girl, have you no care to your health? Sit next to me for a while and rest, you silly girl, if you don't eat properly you'll start having fainting spells every day.' Begum's tearful gaze followed Kaneez, who restlessly roamed about like a stubborn soul in the small bungalow nestled among the eucalyptus, gular, shisham and jamun trees.

Time passed quickly, as if it was travelling on a train. When Salmi Bi came recently, she was the mother of two children and was expecting a third. The effects of the weather could

be seen in the form of lichen on the parapets of the clean and
tidy bungalow. The mango seed Chammi had planted was now
about as tall as Chammi might have been had she lived. But
her slender feet went past this tree with such speed that the tree
quivered in the breeze created artificially for a minute, but this
speed, this swiftness, had become Kaneez's life.

Then, one morning in summer, Altaf Mian returned from
England. Such a monumental happening, such intense joy, all
occurred in one day. Begum's tears appeared in her eyes and were
stilled on her eyelashes. Unable to contain her joyful excitement,
Salmi Bi was speaking in louder tones than Daadi and her
children were bawling as they sought their mother's attention.
Salma Bi's husband listened excitedly to the stories Altaf Mian
had to recount about life in England and as for Kaneez, she
would repeatedly wash her hands and go from the kitchen to
stand behind the door and view all the festivities. Once, as her
eyes met Altaf Mian's, she almost became dizzy and fell. 'Hai,
how he looks at me', Kaneez thought when she was alone and
then, returning to the kitchen, she would start washing her face.

'Mai, can you give me some water', Altaf Mian called out.
His mouth was dry from talking non-stop about England.

'Oh my child, don't call her that', Bari Begum got upset. 'Ai,
she's so careful, and has had a sad life. You know, because of
her the monthly household expenditure is less than fifty rupees,
and we're safe from thieves. How do you think I was able to
send you 200- and 400-rupee installments? She knows how to
do things competently, she's organized, I can't say enough good
things about her.' Begum launched into a lengthy description
of Kaneez's talents.

'And Khan Bahadar Waseem's daughter is just as competent
and talented. I am thinking . . . ' and the daughter-in-law's

palanquin passed over this bridge as well, but the water didn't turn up.

'Amma, where's the water . . . ' Altaf Mian grumbled.

'*Arrey*, where's the water? Oh Kaneez, did you pour oil in your ears, girl?' Bari Begum got up muttering.

There was no water . . . Kaneez had used it all to wash her face. She wasn't thinking at all about her lack of good training . . . now in the shade of the trees, as she was stepping on the dry, yellowed autumn leaves, she was thinking . . . these trees are useless . . . how many times have I swept up these leaves, there are still leaves everywhere in the garden . . .

She left the bungalow and came out on the widest road in the Civil Lines. How cool it had been in the kitchen. She could feel the pain of arthritis in her bones, her dupatta fluttered in the fiery heat, but she kept walking, on and on, and fatigue overtook her. She sat down to rest with her back against a gate belonging to one of the bungalows lining the road. Her throat was parched but she didn't think of drinking water from a tap right next to the gate. She just sat there, feeling the steel bars of the gate with her hand. All around her, the dried-out yellow leaves kept rattling, and the scorching heat kept roaring.

A new car drove out from the bungalow and stopped. A fresh young begum, doused in perfume got out from the car and approached Kaneez.

'*Arrey*, you're Kaneez, aren't you? You were working at Salma Bi's house?' the young begum asked excitedly.

Kaneez remained silent.

'Did she throw you out?' the begum said, her eyes dancing.

Kaneez did not respond. The begum turned to go back to her car. Then, as if remembering something, she returned. 'Come and stay at my house. Food and clothing will be my responsibility . . . I will treat you like my mother', the begum said, and Kaneez was stunned.

'Mother! The mother of this youthful begum. Ai, what are people saying? Suddenly their vision has become blurred. My real age is only thirty-and-five.'

Kaneez picked up a yellow leaf and crushed it in her fist. She had aged in five years. She couldn't believe it.

A few tears fell from her eyes and were absorbed into the fine crevices on her face and a lock of hair speckled with gray dangled on her forehead. In the space of a minute, she scrunched up dry leaves to form a pile in front of her.

18

The Flame of the Oil Lamp

Everything in front of her was slowly becoming indistinct in the increasing gloom of the evening. She turned her gaze around to look at the unplastered walls made of Lakhori bricks, which were becoming more and more frightening as they sank into the murkiness, looking as though they were submerged in black dye! Darkness and solitude! She started feeling agitated and quickly sat up. She was waiting for her father, who had gone somewhere else instead of coming home after finishing work.

'God knows where he is, doesn't he know I feel anxious when I'm alone in the house like this?' she kept telling herself, irately. She wanted to start weeping loudly. But it was as if the supply of tears had got stuck in her throat. She couldn't even bring herself to cry.

Feeling restless, she looked into the space in front of her and suddenly, it seemed to her that there were skeletons clothed in white garments emerging from the small, dark room before her and moving around in the whole house. The clattering sound of the bones of these skeletons and the soft rustling of their new, white clothes flooded her thoughts until she was forced to squeeze her eyes shut and fall back on her charpoy. Devoid of feeling, immobile, as if she was dead. The clattering sound of the bones of skeletons clad in white clothing was just her imagination, just an illusion. For some time now, her mind had become as enfeebled as her body. Not only did she have these hallucinations at night, she saw such images during the day as well. Wherever she pinned her gaze, she saw figures clad in white advancing towards her, wearing exactly the same kind of apparel that her mother had been attired in when she died.

The door creaked in a familiar way and then she heard it being shut. She trembled as she opened her eyes. When she didn't see anyone, she asked in a stifled voice, 'Who is it?'

'It's me, Acchan.' This was her father's voice.

'Where were you Abba? My heart was sinking with anxiety', she complained and once again the cache of tears seemed to stick in her throat and her eyes began to burn.

'*Arrey*, I had some work to take care of. Why didn't you light the oil lamp?' Her father snapped when he bumped into the charpoy. He sat down.

'There were no matches.'

'Here are the matches.' He took out matches from his pocket and when he lit a cigarette, his face looked frightening in the light of the match. An untidy, peppery beard, a mustache falling over his lips, forehead full of lines, and red-shot eyes. The match burned and the flame moved and curved like a fine red arrow and the crackling beedi's smoke spread in the tiny courtyard.

Coughing, she supported herself with her hands on the wooden frame of the charpoy and sat up. The smoke of the beedi was making her feel sick.

'How are you feeling Acchan?' the father asked, drawing heavily on the beedi and in the dim red light his red-shot eyes lit up.

'Don't smoke the beedi, Abba! The smoke makes me feel nauseated.' And bending her fever-ridden head over her shoulders, she began to cough wearily.

The father got upset. He had lit the beedi after a long time. Ever since the price of a bunch of beedis had gone up to six paisas, he smoked only four beedis all day. The craving for a beedi made him sleepy, but he curbed his urge. And now his daughter had ordered that he not smoke.

'Everything makes you nauseated. Have you gone mad?' The father said sharply and without replying, Acchan took the matches, got up and slowly walked away to the outer chamber.

The sound of the match being struck echoed in the desolate gloom of the house and a tiny flame sputtered as it shone dimly in the oil lamp on the shelf. When the shadow of the pillar in the decaying veranda travelled across the small passage and climbed the wall in front of her, she tightened her grip on the box of matches in her hand, rested her head against the shelf, and turned her eyes up towards the quivering flame of the oil lamp.

The father stubbed out the beedi on the wooden frame of the charpoy and with the intention of smoking it again later, he stuck the butt behind his ear, and looking up, he saw Acchan. He was shocked by her appearance. She looked frightening standing like this in the light seeking refuge in the darkness— the black skin stretched over bones, hair tangled, unkempt, mouth open, and her pupils raised upward—it seemed as if she had died while standing against the wall.

It had only been two years ago that the father had discovered Acchan's mother on the bed in this very same condition. Mouth open and pupils turned up. Instead of weeping and grieving, he got busy with the task of acquiring yards of new fabric. The body of an impoverished woman lying on a heap of rags and tattered quilts; custom dictated an immediate shroud for that body, yards of new fabric taken off from a roll, even though in life, Acchan's mother had yearned unsuccessfully for a long time for a flared pyjama made from fancy clippings. But what difference does that make? The poor get only one chance to be equal to the wealthy in this world and that is in the matter of the shroud. Aha! As a matter of fact, the poor come into the world just so they can be equal to the rich after death. So, a shroud was required for Acchan's mother. And Acchan's father was sick with worry. He was thinking that if Acchan's mother had roamed around in life dressed in rags, it didn't mean that she should be consigned to her grave unclothed, naked. This was the place where angels come to interrogate and cross-examine. Can these angels remain in the grave of a naked, unclothed woman? And this was the reason he knocked on the doors of his acquaintances, ran around trying to obtain money from somewhere, but he failed to arrange enough funds to buy a shroud. How could he make any arrangements anyway? His acquaintances were barely able to eke out a living. Finally, after he had run out of options, he went to the owner of the shop, his employer for whom he recorded accounts from morning till night for ten rupees a month.

His tangled, unkempt beard wet with tears, he pressed his hands together and pleaded, 'Master, there's a body without a shroud in my house, if you could loan me . . .' The shop owner interrupted him gently.

'Munshi Ji, this is God's work, no need for a loan, here's the money, you don't have to return it.'

The shop owner took out twenty-five rupees and, making sure all the workers saw the money, handed it to Acchan's father. He was doing this in the hope that in the next world he would be rewarded for his act of kindness. Trade in God's world. It was only two days earlier that Acchan's father had asked for a two-rupee advance on his pay to buy medicine from the hakim sahib for his suffering wife, and the master had scolded him harshly, saying he was not obligated to keep people alive. And now, twenty-five rupees in the name of death. *Uffoh!* How generous he was in providing a shroud to the poor, and what a good rule it was to give generously for a shroud but refuse to help with buying medicine—because medicine is consumed in this life and the shroud remains a proof of generosity until Judgement Day.

Acchan's mother, pining for food, yearning for clothes, in desperate need of medicine from hakim sahib, suddenly had twenty-five rupees disbursed in her name, after which she went to hide in the ground.

'And now . . . now it's Acchan . . . ' the father thought as he scrutinized Acchan apprehensively. She was still staring at the dim light of the oil lamp, her body immobile, her head propped against the wall, her pupils turned up.

Something had started happening to her after her mother's death. It seemed she was slowly fading away. The same hoarse cough as her mother's, a slight fever, lying down here, lying down there. The father knew what was wrong, but he could do nothing to provide treatment. At best, they had access to the medicines from the Charity Hopsital, which were being diluted with water after the war. As for the medicines from the government hospital, these were known to do more harm than good. When he hadn't been able to help Acchan's mother, how was he going to bring in a doctor for Acchan?

Yes, the rupee had decreased further in value. Flour used to be four seers for a rupee, but now you would be lucky if you could get two-and-a-half seers for a rupee. Affordability was no longer within reach. But the shop's accountant was as cheap as he was twenty years ago. As he watched, the products stocked in the shop that had been bought for two paisas immediately increased in price the moment the war began, until finally the merchandise that initially cost two paisas made an eight to ten times profit. In other words, the older something was the more expensive it became.

But the value of this old accountant's ten rupees fell in the marketplace. What did it matter if there was money raining in the shop and in the bank, mountains of gold and silver were being erected in the owner's name? It was like this dialogue between a mistress and her servant girl: 'Bibi, it's Eid', the servant girl asks in the hope of a bonus. The mistress snaps, 'Begone silly girl, you should be thinking only of your small roti.'

It was as if he had been left to rot in the shadow of his ten rupees, where the noose of the price of life's necessities was slowly tightening. He heard that mill workers were getting a stipend because of the higher cost of living, the farmers were also seeing a change in their earnings, workers in ordinary shops were getting pay raises, and that was not all—even the coolies had increased their rates. He too wanted to ask the shop owner to increase his salary. But perhaps his employer guessed that he was planning to demand a raise so he began to drop hints like, 'Munshi ji, you've become senile in your old age, you should retire and stay home now, look you've made errors adding up these amounts . . . I have no dearth of accountants, I'm just being sympathetic because you've been with me for such a long time, do you understand?' Hearing him talk like this made Acchan's father very nervous because he was afraid he might lose even the ten rupees he was getting. He cursed the day he thought of asking for a pay raise.

Acchan was getting weaker. He was very worried about her. His acquantances said, 'Munshi ji if you can't afford her medicines and food, then the best thing to do is to marry her off to someone well-to-do, she'll improve when her lifestyle improves.' But these advisors didn't take into account the fact that a poor man's daughter could only marry a poor man. What will the wife of a man who earns ten or twelve rupees a month eat and wear? After all, Acchan's mother also had a husband, but what did she gain from being married?

Seeing Acchan standing next to the wall in this manner proved disconcerting. Her father's anxiety and concern were growing. Suddenly, he thought she might be upset because he was smoking a beedi.

'Acchan, why are you standing like this? Look, I'm not going to smoke the beedi any more.'

'It's nothing, Abba.' She moved her head away from the wall and gazed at her father. 'I was thinking I should raise the wick on the oil lamp.' Her tone was filled with pleading and longing.

But the father was overcome with relief when he heard this. This was the only reason she had been standing like this? He thought, surely Acchan has gone mad.

The thought of transforming darkness into light was in his opinion, madness. But why?

He said, 'Do you know how difficult it is to buy even two paisas' worth of kerosene, and then the crowds these days are enough to crush your feet, rip your clothes. Haven't I been saying that kerosene is regulated, and you just keep asking to raise the wick on the oil lamp.'

'Then what's the use of this light? The shopkeepers should not sell even this much. Darkness is better than this, at least one doesn't have to say the lamp is burning.' The tiny lights of longing sparkling in her eyes were suddenly extinguished.

'I don't know whether there is any use or not', the father retorted sharply as though angered by this idea. 'We'll get just enough oil to keep the lamp burning.'

'Whether it gives us any light or not?' Her lips quivered.

'Yes.' The father's reply further deepened the desolate half-darkness of the house.

'This kind of light makes me feel anxious', she said listlessly.

But her father didn't respond, as though upset by his daughter's continuous mention of the word 'anxious'.

Disappointed, she stumbled out of the outer chamber and sat down on her charpoy with her legs dangling on the edge of the bed. She was angry with her father. Why was he satisfied with just this much light when in the beautiful, two-storey house at the corner of the street, large lanterns burned all night? But her anxiety-ridden brain couldn't figure out that if kerosene did become readily available where would the money for it come from, when after working extremely hard he got just enough money not to actually live but to crudely immitate the act of living, exactly like the lamp in the darkened niche whose dim light was being overtaken by a growing darkness.

Acchan rolled back on her bed. She was feeling anxious again and the crackling sound of new, white fabric could be heard everywhere. She wanted to weep loudly and shout out her father's apathy. But she couldn't even weep. Her tears seemed to be trapped in her throat.

Bibliography

Masroor, Hajra. *Sab Afsanay Meray*. Lahore: Maqbool Academy, 1991.